"Do you know how incredibly perfect you are?"

Zane's hands wrapped around Jess's waist, and thrilling warmth heated her skin. "I'm not."

"You are. You can't let what those two did to you change who you are. That guy was the stupidest man on earth. You have every right to feel hurt, Jess. But don't let what he did change the person that you are."

"You think that's what I'm doing?"

"Isn't it? You changed your hair, your eyes. You dress differently now. Don't get me wrong, you look beautiful, sweetheart. But you were beautiful before."

She shrugged. She found it hard to believe.

"I needed the change." Tears misted in her eyes.

"I get that." Zane took her into his arms and hugged her, as a friend now. "But promise me one thing?"

"What?"

"Don't try to find what you need with another man. It makes me crazy."

* * *

Her Forbidden Cowboy
is part of the Moonlight Beach Bachelors series—
Three men living ...   re.

NEV

D1322384

HER FORBIDDEN
COWBOY

BY
CHARLENE SANDS

MILLS
BOON

All rights reserved including the right of reproduction in whole or in part in any form. This edition is published by arrangement with Harlequin Books S.A.

This is a work of fiction. Names, characters, places, locations and incidents are purely fictional and bear no relationship to any real life individuals, living or dead, or to any actual places, business establishments, locations, events or incidents. Any resemblance is entirely coincidental.

This book is sold subject to the condition that it shall not, by way of trade or otherwise, be lent, resold, hired out or otherwise circulated without the prior consent of the publisher in any form of binding or cover other than that in which it is published and without a similar condition including this condition being imposed on the subsequent purchaser.

® and ™ are trademarks owned and used by the trademark owner and/or its licensee. Trademarks marked with ® are registered with the United Kingdom Patent Office and/or the Office for Harmonisation in the Internal Market and in other countries.

Published in Great Britain 2015
by Mills & Boon, an imprint of Harlequin (UK) Limited,
Eton House, 18-24 Paradise Road, Richmond, Surrey, TW9 1SR

© 2015 Charlene Swink

ISBN: 978-0-263-25250-7

51-0215

Harlequin (UK) Limited's policy is to use papers that are natural, renewable and recyclable products and made from wood grown in sustainable forests. The logging and manufacturing processes conform to the legal environmental regulations of the country of origin.

Printed and bound in Spain
by CPI, Barcelona

Charlene Sands is a *USA TODAY* bestselling author of more than thirty-five romance novels, writing sensual contemporary romances and stories of the Old West. Her books have been honored with a National Readers' Choice Award, a CataRomance Reviewers' Choice Award, and she's a double recipient of the Booksellers' Best Award. She belongs to the Orange County chapter and the Los Angeles chapter of RWA.

Charlene writes "hunky heroes with heart." She knows a little something about true romance—she married her high school sweetheart! When not writing, Charlene enjoys sunny Pacific beaches, great coffee, reading books from her favorite authors and spending time with her family. You can find her on Facebook and Twitter. Charlene loves to hear from her readers! You can write her at PO Box 4883, West Hills, CA 91308, USA, or sign up for her newsletter for fun blogs and ongoing contests at charlenesands.com.

To our own Zane William (Pettis), the bright little light
in our family. And to his mommy, Angi,
and daddy, Kent, with love to all!

One

The heels of Jessica's boots beat against the redwood of Zane Williams's sun-drenched deck overlooking the Pacific Ocean. Shielded by the shade of an overhang, he didn't miss a move his new houseguest made as he leaned forward on his chaise longue. His sister-in-law had officially arrived.

Was he still allowed to call her that?

Gusty breezes lifted her caramel hair, loosening the knot at the back of her head. A few wayward tendrils whipped across her eyes and, as she followed behind his assistant Mariah, her hand came up to brush them away. Late afternoon winds were strong on Moonlight Beach, swirling up from the shore as the sun lowered on the horizon. It was the time most sunbathers packed up their gear and went home and the locals came out. Shirt-billowing weather and one of the few things he'd come to like about California beach living.

He removed his sunglasses to get a better look at her. She wore a snowdrift-white blouse tucked into washed-to-the-millionth-degree jeans and a wide brown belt. Tortoiseshell-rimmed eyeglasses delicately in place didn't hide the pain and distress in her eyes.

Sweet Jess. Seeing her brought back so many memories, and the frigidness in his heart thawed a bit.

She looked like...*home*.

It hurt to think about Beckon, Texas. About his ranch

and the life he'd had there once. It hurt to think about how he'd met Jessica's sister, Janie, and the way their small-town lives had entwined. In one respect, the tragedy that occurred more than two years ago might've been a lifetime ago. In another, it seemed as if time was standing still. Either way, his wife, Janie, and their unborn child were gone. They were never coming back. His mouth began to twitch. An ache in the pit of his stomach spread like wildfire and scorched him from the inside out.

He focused on Jessica. She carried a large tapestry suitcase woven in muted tones of gray and mauve and peach. He'd given Janie and Jessica matching luggage three years ago on their birthdays. It had been a fluke that both girls, the only two offspring of Mae and Harold Holcomb, were born on the same day, seven years apart.

Grabbing at the crutches propped beside his lounge chair, Zane slowly lifted himself up, careful not to fall and break his other foot. Mariah would have his head if he got hurt again. His casted wrist ached like the devil, but he refused to have his assistant come running every damn time he wanted to get up. It was bad enough she'd taken on the extra role of nursemaid. He reminded himself to have his business manager give Mariah a big fat bonus.

She halted midway on the deck, her disapproving gaze dropping to his busted wrist and crutches before she shot him a silent warning. "Here he is, Jessica." Mariah's peach-pie voice was sweet as ever for his houseguest. "I'll leave you two alone now."

"Thanks, Mariah," he said.

Her mouth pursed tight, she about-faced and marched off, none too pleased with him.

Jessica came forward. "Still such a gentleman, Zane," she said. "Even on crutches."

He'd forgotten how much she sounded like Janie. Hearing her sultry tone stirred him up inside. But that's about all Janie and Jessica had in common. The two sisters were different in most other ways. Jess wasn't as tall as her sister. Her eyes were a light shade of green instead of the deep emerald that had sparkled from Janie's eyes. Jess was brunette, Janie blonde. And their personalities were miles apart. Janie had been a risk-taker, a strong woman who could hold her own against Zane's country-star fame, which might've intimidated a less confident woman. From what he remembered about Jess, she was quieter, more subtle, a schoolteacher who loved her profession, a real sweetheart.

"Sorry about your accident."

Zane nodded. "Wasn't much of an accident. More like stupidity. I lost focus and fell off the stage. Broke my foot in three places." He'd been at the Los Angeles Amphitheater, singing a silly tune about chasing ducks on the farm, all the while thinking about Janie. A video of his fall went viral on the internet. Everyone in country music and then some had witnessed his loss of concentration. "My tour's postponed for the duration. Can't strum a guitar with a broken wrist."

"Don't suppose you can."

She put down her luggage and gazed over the railing to the shore below. Sunlight glossed over deep steely-blue water as whitecaps foamed over wet sand, the tide rising. "I suppose Mama must've strong-armed you into doing this."

"Your mama couldn't strong-arm a puppy."

She whipped around to face him, her eyes sharp. "You know what I mean."

He did. Fact was, he wouldn't refuse Mae Holcomb anything. And she'd asked him this favor. *It's huge*, she'd said to him. *My Jess is hurtin' and needs to clear her head. I'm asking you to let her stay with you a week, maybe two. Please, Zane, watch out for her.*

He'd given his word. He'd take care of Jess and make sure she had time to heal. Mae was counting on him, and there wasn't anything he wouldn't do for Janie's mother. She deserved that much from him.

"You can stay as long as you like, Jess. You've got to know that."

Her mouth began to tremble. "Th-thanks. You heard what happened?"

"I did."

"I—I couldn't stay in town. I had to get out of Texas. The farther, the better."

"Well, Jess, you're as far west as you could possibly go." Five miles north of Malibu by way of the Pacific Coast Highway.

Her shoulders slumped. "I feel like such a fool."

Reaching out, he cupped her chin, forcing her eyes to his, the darn crutch under his arm falling to rest on the railing. "Don't."

"I won't be very good company," she whispered, dang near breathless.

His body swayed, not allowing him another unassisted moment. He released her and grabbed for his crutch just in time. He tucked it under his arm and righted his position. "That makes two of us."

Her soft laughter carried on the breeze. Probably the first bit of amusement she'd felt in days.

He smiled.

"I just need a week, Zane."

"Like I said, take as long as you need."

"Thanks." She blinked, and her eyes drifted down to his injuries. "Uh, are you in a lot of pain?"

"More like, I'm being a pain. Mariah's getting the brunt of my sour mood."

"Now I can share it with her." Her eyes twinkled for a second.

He'd forgotten what it was like having Jess around. She was ten years younger than him, and he'd always called her his little sis. He hadn't seen much of her since Janie's death. Cursed by guilt and anguish, he'd deliberately removed himself from the Holcombs' lives. He'd done enough damage to them.

"Hand up your luggage to me," he told her. With his good hand, he tucked his crutches under his armpits and propped himself, then wiggled his fingers. If he could get a grip on the bag...

Jessica rolled her eyes and hoisted her valise. "I appreciate it, Zane. But I've got this. Really, it's not heavy. I packed light. You know, summer-at-the-beach kind of clothes."

She let him off the hook. He would've tried, but fooling with her luggage wouldn't have been pretty. The doggone crutches made him clumsy as a drunken sailor, and he wasn't supposed to put any weight on his foot yet. "Fine, then. Why don't you settle in and rest up a bit? I'm bunking on this level. You've got an entire wing of rooms to yourself upstairs. Take your pick and spread out."

He followed behind as she made her way inside the wide set of light oak French doors leading to the living room. "Feel free to look around. I can have Mariah give you a tour."

"No, that's not necessary." She scanned over what she could see of the house, taking in the expanse—vaulted ceilings, textured walls, art deco interior and sleek contemporary furniture. He caught her vibe, sensing her confusion. What was Zane Williams, a country-western artist and a born and bred Texan, doing living on a California beach? When he'd leased this place with the option to buy, he told himself it was because he wanted a change. He was building Zane's on the Beach, his second restaurant in as many years, and he'd been offered roles in several Hollywood movies. He didn't know if he was cut out for acting, so the pending offers were still on the table.

She sent him an over-the-shoulder glance. "It's...a beautiful house, Zane."

His crutches supporting him, he sidled up next to her, seeing the house from her perspective. "But not *me*?"

"I guess I don't know what that is anymore."

"It's just a house. A place to hang my hat."

She gave his hatless head a glance. "It's a palace on the sea."

He chuckled. So much for his attempt at humble. The house was a masterpiece. One of three designed by the architect who lived next door. "Okay, you got me there. Mariah found the house and leased it on the spot. She said it would shake the cobwebs from my head. Had it awhile, but this is my first summer here." He leaned back, darting a glance around. "At least the humidity is bearable and it never seems to rain, so no threat of thunderstorms. The neighbors are nice."

"A good place to rest up."

"I suppose, if that's what I'm doing."

"Isn't it?"

He shrugged, fearing he'd opened up a can of worms. Why was he revealing his innermost thoughts to her? They weren't close anymore. He hardly knew Jessica as an adult, and yet they shared a deeply powerful connection. "Sure it is. Are you hungry? I can have my housekeeper make you—"

"Oh, uh…no. I'm not hungry right now. Just a bit tired from the trip. I'd better go upstairs before I collapse right here on your floor. Thanks for having a limo pick me up. And, well, thanks for everything, Zane."

She rose on her tiptoes, and the soft brush of her lips on his cheek squeezed something tight in his chest. Her hair smelled of summer strawberries, and the fresh scent lingered in his nose as she backed away.

"Welcome." The crutches dug into his armpits as they supported his weight. He hated the damn things. Couldn't wait to be free of them. "Just a suggestion, but the room to the right of the stairs and farthest down the hall has the best view of the ocean. Sunsets here are pretty glorious."

"I'll keep that in mind." Her quick smile was probably

meant to fake him out. She could pretend she wasn't hurting all that badly if she wanted to, but dark circles under her eyes and the pallor of her skin told the real story. He understood. He'd been there. He knew how pain could strangle a person until all the breath was sucked out. Hell, he'd lived it. Was still living it. And he knew something about Holcomb family pride, too.

What kind of jerk would leave any Holcomb woman standing at the altar?

Only a damn fool.

Jessica took Zane's advice and chose the guest room at the end of the hallway. Not for the amazing sunsets as Zane had suggested, but to keep out of his hair. Privacy was a precious commodity. He valued it, and so did she now. A powerful urge summoned her to slump down on the bed and cry her eyes out, but she managed to fight through the sensation. She was done with self-pity. She wasn't the first woman to be dumped at the altar. She'd been duped by a man she'd loved and trusted. She'd been so sure and missed all of the telling signs. Now she saw them through crystal clear eyes.

She busied herself unpacking her one suitcase, layering her clothes into a long, stylish light wood dresser. Carefully she set her jeans, shorts, swimsuits and undies into two of the nine drawers. She plucked out a few sleeveless sundresses and walked over the closet. With a slight tug, the double doors opened in a whoosh. The scents of cedar and freshness filled her nostrils as she gazed into a girl cave almost the size of her first-grade classroom back in Beckon. Cedar drawers, shoe racks and silken hangers were a far cry from the tiny drywalled closet in her one-bedroom apartment.

Deftly she scooped the delicate hangers under the straps of her dresses and hung them up. Next she laid her tennis shoes, flip-flops and two pairs of boots, one flat, one high-heeled, onto the floor just under her clothes. Her meager collection barely made a dent in the closet space. She closed the double doors and leaned against them. Then she took her first real glimpse at the view from her second-story bedroom.

"Wow." Breath tunneled from her chest.

Aqua seas and the sun-glazed sky made for a spectacular vista from the wide windows facing the horizon. She swallowed in a gulp of awe. Then suddenly, a strange bone-rattling feeling of loss hit her. She shivered as if assailed by a winter storm.

Why now? Why wasn't she reveling in the beauty surrounding her?

Nothing's beautiful. You lost your sister, her unborn baby and your fiancé.

"Would you like to go out onto the balcony?"

She whirled around, surprised to find Mariah, Zane's fortyish blonde assistant standing in the doorway. She'd worked for him since before he had married Janie. Jessica and Mariah's paths had crossed a few times since then. "Oh, hi." She glanced at the narrow glass door at the far end of the wall that led to the balcony. It was obviously situated there to keep from detracting from the room's sweeping view of the Pacific. "Thanks, but maybe later."

"Sure, you must be tired from the flight. Is there anything I can do for you?"

"I don't think so. I've unpacked. A shower and a nap and I'll be good to go."

Mariah smiled. "I'll be leaving for the day. Mrs. Lopez, Zane's housekeeper, is here. If you need anything, just ask her."

"Thank you… I'll be fine."

"Zane will want to have dinner with you. He eats dinner just before sunset. But he'd make an exception if you're hungry earlier."

"Sunset is fine."

Mariah studied her, her eyes unflinching and kind. "You look a little like Janie."

"I doubt that. Janie was beautiful."

"I see a resemblance. If you don't mind me saying, you have the same soulful eyes and lovely complexion."

She was pale as a ghost, and ten freckles dotted her nose. Yep, she'd counted them. Though, she'd never had acne or even a full-fledged zit to speak of in her teens. She supposed her complexion wasn't half-bad. "Thank you. I, uh, don't want to cause Zane or you any trouble. I'm basically here because it would've been harder to convince my mother otherwise, and I didn't want her to worry about me off in some deserted location to search my soul. Mama's had enough on her plate. She doesn't need to fret over me."

"I get it. Actually, you might be exactly what Zane needs to get his head out of the sand."

That was an odd statement. She narrowed her eyes, trying to make sense of it.

"He's not been himself for a while now," Mariah explained without spelling it out. Jessica gave her credit for the delicate way she put it.

"I figured. He lost his family. We all did," Jess said. She missed Janie something awful. Sometimes life was cruel.

Mariah nodded. "But having family around might be good for both of you."

She doubted that. She'd be a thorn in Zane's side. A kink in his plans. She would bide her time here, soak up some fresh sea air and then return home to face the music. Humiliation and desperate hurt had made her flee Texas. But she'd have to go back eventually. Her face pulled tight. She didn't want to think about that right now.

"Maybe," she said to Mariah.

"Well, have a good evening."

"Thanks. You, too."

After Mariah left, Jessica plucked up her shampoo and entered the bathroom. Oh, boy, and she'd thought the closet was something. The guest bathroom came equipped with a television, a huge oval Jacuzzi tub and an intricately tiled spacious shower that was digitized for each of the three shower heads looming above. She peered closer to read the monitor. She could program the time, temperature and force of the shower and heaven knew what else.

After she punched in a few commands, the shower spurted to life, and water rained down. Jess smiled. A new toy. Peeling off her clothes, she opened the clear glass door and stepped inside. Steamy spray hit her from three sides, with two heads spewing softly and one pulsing like the pumping of her heart. She turned around and around, using the fragrant liquid soap from a dispenser in the wall. She lingered there, lost in the mist and jet stream as pent-up tension seeped out of her bones, her limbs loose and free. Eventually, she got down to business and worked shampoo into her hair. Much too early, the shower turned off automatically. As she stepped out, the steam followed her. She dried herself with a cushy white towel. How nice.

She dressed in a pair of tan midthigh shorts and a cocoa-brown tank top. She hoped dinner with Zane wasn't a formal thing. She hadn't brought anything remotely fashionable.

After blow-drying her hair, she lifted the long strands up in a ponytail, leaving bangs to rest on her forehead. A little nap had sounded wonderful minutes ago, but now she was too keyed up to sleep. The time change would probably hit her like a ton of bricks later, but right now, the sandy wind-blown beach below beckoned her. She slipped her feet into flip-flops and headed downstairs.

Lured by the scent of spices and sauce wafting to her nose, she headed in that direction. Inside a magnificent granite-and-stone kitchen, she came face to face with an older woman, a little hefty in the hips, wearing an apron and humming to herself.

The woman turned around. "*Hola*, Miss Holcomb?"

"Yes, I'm Jessica."

"*Hola*, Jessica." She nodded. "I'm Mrs. Lopez. Do you like enchiladas?"

She was Texan. She loved everything Mexican. "Yes. Smells yummy."

Mrs. Lopez lowered the oven door, and a stainless-steel rack automatically pushed forward.

"They will be ready in half an hour. Can I get you a drink? Or a snack?"

"No, thank you. I'll wait for Zane. Well, it's nice to meet you," she said, retreating from the kitchen. "I'll be back in—"

A boom sounded. "Double damn you!" Zane's loud curse echoed throughout the house.

Jessica froze in place.

Mrs. Lopez grinned and shook her head. "He cannot dress himself too well. He will not let anyone help him. He is not such a good patient."

They shared a smile. "I see." But when she'd first arrived, he was wearing jeans and a casual cotton shirt. Was he dressing up now? "Do I need to change my clothes for dinner?"

"No, no. Mr. Zane spilled iced tea on his shirt. You are dressed nice."

"Thank you." Okay, great. She felt better now. When she'd packed her clothes, she hadn't given much thought to her wardrobe. All she hoped for was to clear her head a little while here. "I thought I'd go for a walk on the beach. I'll be back in plenty of time for dinner. See you later."

Mrs. Lopez nodded and focused on the stove. Jess's stomach grumbled as she left the spicy smells of the kitchen and walked out the double doors to the deck. From there, she climbed a few more stairs down, until warm sand crept onto her flip-flops.

There were no lakes or rivers back home that compared with the balmy breezes whipping at her hair, the briny taste on her lips or the glistening golden hues reflecting off the ocean. Her steps fell lightly, making a slight impression in the packed wet sand until the next wave inched up the shore and carried her footprints out to sea. Even with the sun low over the water's edge, her skin warmed as she walked along the beach. To her right, beachfront mansions overlooking the sea filled her line of vision, each one different in design and structure. She was so intent on gauging the houses, she didn't notice a jogger approaching until he'd stopped right in front of her.

"Hi," he said, his breaths heaving.

"Hello." A swift glance at his face made her gasp silently. He was stunning and tanned and one of the most famous movie stars in the world. Dylan McKay.

He hunched over, hands on knees, catching his breath. "Give me a sec."

For what? She wanted to ask, yet she stood there, feet implanted in the sand, waiting. He was easy on the eyes, and she tried not to stare at his bare chest and the dip of his jogging shorts below a trim waist.

He righted his posture, and blood drained from her body as he aimed a heart-melting smile her way. "Thank you."

Puzzled, she stared at him. "For?"

"Being here. For giving me an excuse to stop running." He chuckled, and white teeth flashed. Was the sun-gleaming twinkle from his smile real? Could've been. Dylan McKay was every red-blooded woman's idea of the perfect man.

Except hers. She knew there was no such thing.

"Okay. But…you could've just stopped on your own, couldn't you?"

He shook his head. "No, I'm supposed to run ten miles a day. It's a work thing. I'm preparing for a role as a Navy SEAL."

No kidding? She wasn't going to pretend she didn't know who he was. Or that his bronzed body wasn't already honed and ripped. "Gotcha. How many did you do?"

His lips twisted with self-loathing. "Eight."

"That's not bad." Judging by the pained look on his face, he was a man who expected perfection of himself. "There aren't too many people who can run eight miles."

His expression lightened and he seemed to appreciate her encouragement. "I'm Dylan, by the way." He put out his hand.

"Jessica." It was a one-pump handshake.

"Are we neighbors?" he asked, his brows gathering. "I live over there." He pointed to a trilevel mansion looming close by.

She shook her head. "Not really. I'm staying with Zane Williams for a short time."

When his brows lifted ever so slightly and his eyes flashed, she read his mind. "He's…he's *family*."

He nodded. "I know Zane. Good guy."

"He is. My sister…well, he was married to Janie."

A moment passed as he put two and two together. "I'm sorry about what happened."

"Thank you."

"Well, I think I've gotten my second wind. Thanks to you. Only two miles to go. Nice meeting you, Jessica. Say hi to Zane for me."

He about-faced, trotted down the beach in the opposite direction and soon picked up his pace to a full-out jog.

She headed back to the house, a smile on her lips, a song humming in her heart. Maybe coming here wasn't such a bad idea after all.

She spotted Zane braced against the patio railing and waved. Had he been watching her? She was hit with a surge of self-consciousness. She wasn't a beach babe. Her curvy figure didn't allow two-piece bathing suits, and her pale skin tone could be compared only with the bark of a birch tree or the peel of a honeydew melon.

As she climbed the stairs, her gaze hit upon his shirt, a Hawaiian print with repeating palm trees. She'd never seen

Zane look more casual and yet appear so ill at ease in his surroundings.

"Nice walk?" he asked, removing his sunglasses.

"It beats a stroll to Beckon's Cinema Palace."

Zane laughed, a knowing glint in his eyes. "You got that right. I haven't thought about the Palace in a long time." His voice sounded gruff as if he'd go back to those days in a heartbeat.

There wasn't a whole lot to do in Beckon, Texas, so on Saturday night the parking lot at the Palace swarmed with kids from the high school. Hanging out and hooking up. It's where Jessica had had her first awkward kiss. With Miles Bernardy. Gosh, he was such a geek. But then, so was she.

It was also where Janie and Zane had fallen in love.

"I met one of your neighbors."

"Judging by the glow on your face, must've been Dylan. He runs this time of day."

"My face is not glowing." She blinked.

"Nothing to worry over. Happens all the time with women."

"I'm not a wom—I mean, I am not gawking over a movie star, for heaven's sake."

He should talk. Former brother-in-law or not, Zane Williams was a country superstar hunk. Dark-haired, six foot two, a chiseled-jawed Grammy winner, Zane wasn't hard on the eyes, either. The tabloids painted him as an eligible widower who needed love in his life. So far, they'd been kind to him, a rare thing for a superstar.

He picked up his crutches and lifted one to gesture to a table. "This okay with you?"

Two adjacent places were set along a rectangular glass table large enough for ten. Votive candles and a spray of flowers accented the place settings facing the sunset. "It's nice, Zane. I hope you didn't go to too much trouble. I don't expect you to entertain me."

"Not going to any trouble, Jess. Fact is, I eat out here

most days. I hate being cooped up inside the house. Just another week and I'll be out of these dang confinements." He raised his wrapped wrist.

"That's good news. Then what will you do?"

Inclining his head, he considered her question. "Some rehab, I'm told. And continue working out details on the restaurant." He frowned, and the light dimmed in his eyes. "My tour's not due to pick up until September sometime. *Maybe.*"

She wouldn't pry about the maybe. He hobbled to the table. Leaning a crutch against the table's edge, he managed to pull out her chair—such chivalry—and she took her seat. Then he scooted his butt into his own chair. Plop. Poor Zane. His injuries put him completely out of his element.

Mrs. Lopez appeared with platters of food. She set them on the table with efficient haste and nodded to him. "I made a pitcher of margaritas to go with the enchiladas and rice. Or maybe some iced tea or soda?"

"Jessica?" he asked.

"A margarita sounds like heaven."

He glanced at the housekeeper. "Bring the pitcher, please."

She nodded. Within a minute, a pitcher appeared along with two bottle-green wide-rimmed margarita glasses. "Thanks," he said. Zane leaned forward and gripped the pitcher with his wrapped hand. His face pinched tight as he struggled to upend the weighty pitcher. He sighed, and she sensed his frustration over not being able to perform the simple task of pouring a drink with his right hand.

"Let me help," she said softly.

She slipped her hand under the pitcher and helped guide the slushy concoction into the glasses. She gave him credit for clamping his mouth shut and not complaining about his limitations.

"Thanks," he said. He reached out, and the slide of his rough fingers over hers sent warm tingles to her heart. They were still connected through Janie, and she valued his friendship now. She'd made the right decision in coming here.

The food was delicious. She inhaled the meal, emptying her plate within minutes. "I guess I didn't know how hungry I was. Or thirsty."

She reached for her second margarita and took a long sip. Tart icy goodness slid down her throat. "Mmm."

The sun had set with a parfait of swirling color, and now half the moon lit the night. The beach was quiet and calm. The roar of the waves had given way to an occasional lulling swish.

Zane sipped his third margarita. She remembered that about him. He could hold his liquor.

"So what are your plans now, Jess?" he asked.

"Hit the beach, work on my tan and stay out of your way. Shouldn't be too hard. The place is huge."

Tiny lines crinkled around his eyes, and he chuckled. "You don't need to stay out of my way. But feel free to do whatever you want. There are two cars parked in the garage, fueled and ready to go. I can't drive them."

"So how do you get around?"

"Mariah, usually. When I'm needed at the restaurant site or somewhere, she's drives me or I hire a car. She's been a trouper, going above and beyond since my accident."

Mrs. Lopez picked up the empty dishes, leaving the margarita pitcher. A smart woman.

"Thank you, Mrs. Lopez. Have a good night," Zane said. "See you tomorrow."

"Good night," she said to both of them.

"Thanks for the delicious enchiladas."

On a humble nod and smile, she exited the patio.

Zane pointed to her half-empty glass. "How many of those can you handle, darlin'?"

"Oh, uh...I don't know. Why?"

"'Cause if you fall flat on your face, I won't be able to pick you up and carry you to your room."

He winked, and a sudden vision of Zane carrying her to the bedroom burst into her mind. It wasn't as weird a notion as she might've thought. She felt safe with Zane. She truly liked him and didn't buy into his guilt over Janie's death. He wasn't to blame. He couldn't have known about faulty wiring in the house or the fire that would claim her life. Janie had loved Zane for the man that he was, had always been. She wouldn't want Zane's guilt to follow him into old age.

"Well, then, we're even. If you got pie-eyed, I wouldn't be able to pick you up, either." She took another long sip of her drink. Darn, but it tasted good. Her spirits lifted. Let the healing begin.

Zane cocked a crooked smile. "I like your style, *Miss Holcomb*."

"Ugh. To think I would've been Mrs. Monahan by now. Thank God I'm not."

"The guy's an ass."

"Thanks for saying that. He sure had me fooled. Up until the minute I was having my bridal veil pinned in my hair, I thought I knew what the future had in store for me. I saw myself married to a man I had a common bond with. He was a high school principal. I was a grade-school teacher. We both loved education. But I was too blind to see that Steven had commitment phobia. He'd had one broken relationship after another before we started dating. I invested three years of my life in the guy, and I thought surely he'd gotten over it. I thought I was the one. But he was fooling himself as well as me." A pent-up breath whooshed out of her. A little bit of tequila loosened her tongue, and out poured her heart. The unburdening was liberating. "My friend Sally said Steven looked up his old girlfriend seeking sympathy after the wedding that never happened. Can you imagine?"

Zane stared at her. "No. He should be on his knees begging you for forgiveness. He did one thing right. He didn't marry you and make your life miserable. I hate to say it, darlin', but you're better off without him. The man doesn't deserve you. But you're hurt right now, and I get that. You probably still love him."

"I don't," she said, hoisting her glass and swallowing a big gulp. "I pretty much hate him."

Zane leaned back in his seat, his gaze soft on her. "Okay. You hate him. He's out of your life."

She braced folded elbows on the table and rested her chin on her hands. The sea was black as pitch now, the sky lit only with a few stars and clouded moonlight. "I just wanted…I wanted what you and Janie had. I wanted that kind of love."

Her fuzzy brain cleared. Oh, no. She hadn't just said that? She whipped her head around. Zane's expression of sympathy didn't change. He didn't flinch. He simply stared out to sea. "We had something pretty special."

"You did. I'm sorry for bringing it up."

"Don't be." His tone held no malice. "You're Janie's sister. You have as much right to talk about her as I do."

Tears misted in her eyes. "I miss her."

"I miss her, too."

She sighed. She didn't mean to put such a somber mood on the evening. Zane was gracious enough to allow her to stay here. She didn't want to bring him down. It was definitely time to call it a night. She put on a cheery face. "Well, this has been nice."

She rose, and her head immediately clouded up. The table, the railing, the ocean blurred before her. She batted her eyes over and over, trying to focus. Two Zanes popped into her line of vision. She reached for the tabletop, struggling to remain upright on her own steam. She swayed back and forth, unable to keep her body still. "Zane?"

"It just hit you, didn't it?"

"Oh, yeah. I think so." She giggled.

"Don't move for a second."

"I'll…try." A tornado swirled in her head. "Why?"

He rose and hobbled over to her. Using one crutch, he

Two

Jessica gazed at the digital clock on the nightstand. Eight-thirty! She flashed back to last night and drinking those two giant margaritas, then slowly looked around. She was in an unfamiliar bed.

She'd finally let go and given herself permission to have a good time, and where had that gotten her? She'd made a fool of herself. Zane had hobbled her inside the house and slept heaven only knew where. Was there another bedroom on this floor? Maybe a servant's quarters? She'd seen an office, a screening room and a game room. No beds, just couches. "Oh, man," she mumbled.

She scanned the stark but stylish bedroom where she'd slept. A flat-screen TV, a dresser and a low fabric sofa were the only other furniture in the room. If it wasn't for a shelf that housed Zane's five Grammys, as well as a couple of CMA and ACM awards, she wouldn't have guessed it was his master suite. There was nothing personal, warm and cozy about the space.

Hitching her body forward, she waited for signs of pain, but there was nothing. Thank goodness—no hangover. She grabbed her glasses from the nightstand, tossed off the covers and rose. Seeing she was still dressed in her shorts and tank top, she emitted a low groan from her throat as she slipped her feet into her flip-flops. How reckless of her. She'd abused Zane's hospitality already.

She entered the bathroom, another ode to magnificence, and glanced at herself in the mirror. Smudged mascara and rumpled hair reflected back at her. She washed her face and finger-combed her long wayward tresses. She'd take care of the rest once she reached her own room.

Exiting Zane's room, she made her way down a short hallway. Voices coming from the kitchen perked up her ears.

Mrs. Lopez spotted her and waved her inside. "Just in time for breakfast."

Mariah and Zane sat at the kitchen table, coffee mugs piping hot in front of them. Upon the housekeeper's announcement, both heads lifted her way. Blood rushed up her neck, and her face flamed.

"Morning," Zane said, peering into her eyes and not at her wrinkled mess of clothes. "You ready for some breakfast?"

"Good morning, Jessica," Mariah said. They'd obviously been deep in concentration, poring over a stack of papers.

"Yes, yes. Sit down," Mrs. Lopez insisted.

"Oh, uh…good morning. I don't want to intrude. You look busy."

"Just same old, same old," Mariah said. "We're going over plans for Zane's new restaurant. We could use your input."

She'd given Zane her input last night. God. She'd kissed him. Remembering that kiss sent a warm rash of heat through her body. She'd missed his cheek and gotten hold of his lips. Was it the alcohol, or had her heart strummed from that kiss? The alcohol. Had to be. He must have known it was a genuine miscalculation on her part. She hadn't meant to kiss him that way.

"Yes, have a seat, Jess," he said casually. "You need to eat. And we sure need a fresh perspective."

Before her shower? Luckily Zane hadn't mentioned anything about her lack of discretion last night or her state of dress today. She'd overslept, that much was a given. Back home, she rose before six every morning. She loved to go through the morning newspaper, take a walk in the backwoods and then eat a light breakfast before heading to her classroom.

There were a platter of bagels with cream cheese, a scrambled egg jalapeno dish and cereal boxes on the table. The eggs smelled heavenly, and her stomach grumbled. Seeing no other option, she sat down and reached for the eggs as Mrs. Lopez provided her with a bowl and a cup of coffee.

"Bien." She gave a satisfied nod.

Jessica smiled at her.

As Zane and his assistant finished up their breakfast, she ate, too, complimenting Mrs. Lopez on the food she'd prepared.

Zane told Mariah, "Janie and Jessica worked at their folks' café in Beckon. They served the best fried chicken in all of Texas."

"That's what most folks said," she agreed. She couldn't claim modesty. Her parents *did* make the best fried chicken in the state. "My parents opened Holcomb House when I was young. They worked hard to make a go of it. It wasn't anything as grand as what you're probably planning, but in Beckon, the Holcomb House was known for good eats and a friendly atmosphere. When Dad died five years ago, my mom couldn't make a go of it by herself. I think she lost the will, so she sold the restaurant. I'm no expert, but if I can help in any way, I'll give it a try."

"Great," Mariah said.

"Appreciate it," Zane added. "This restaurant will be a little different than the one in Reno, in cuisine and atmosphere. The beach is a big draw for tourists, and we want it to be a great experience."

Zane probably had half a dozen financial advisors, but if he needed her help in any way, she'd oblige. How could she not? She cringed thinking that Zane slept on a sofa last night. A quick glance at his less than crisp clothes, the same clothes he'd worn last night, meant that he probably hadn't got to shower this morning, either. Because of her.

Once the dishes were cleared, Mariah pushed a few papers over to her. "If you don't mind, could you tell us what you think of the menu? Are the prices fair? Do the titles of the dishes make sense? We're working with a few chefs and want to get it just right. These are renderings of what Zane's on the Beach will look like once all done, exterior and interior."

For the next hour, Jessica worked with the two of them, giving her opinion, voicing her concerns when they probed and offering praise honestly if not sparingly. Zane's on the Beach had everything a restaurant could offer. Outside, patio tables facing the beach included a sand bar for summer nights of drinking under the moonlight. Inside, window tables were premium, with the next row of tables raised to gain a view of the ocean, as well. It wasn't posh, but it wasn't family dining, either. "I like that you've made it accessible to a younger crowd. The prices are fair. Have you thought about putting a little stage in the bar? Invite in local entertainment to perform?"

Mariah shot a look at Zane. "We discussed it. I think it's a great idea. Zane isn't so sure."

Zane scrubbed his chin, deep in thought. "I've got to get a handle on what I want from this restaurant. My name and reputation are at stake. Do I want ocean views and great food or a hot spot for a younger crowd?"

"Why can't you have both?" Jessica asked. "Quality is quality. Diners will come for the cuisine and ambiance. After hours, the place can transform into a nightspot for the millennials."

Amused, Zane's dark eyes sparked. "Millennials? Are you one?"

"I guess so."

His head tilted, and his mouth quirked up. "Why do I suddenly feel old?"

"Because you are," Mariah jabbed. "You're cranking toward forty."

"Thirty-five is a far shot from forty, and that's all I'm saying."

"You're wise to stop there," Mariah said playfully, yet with a note of warning. Jessica could tell that Mariah Jacobellis wasn't a woman who put up with age jokes. Although Mariah was physically lovely, she seemed to take no prisoners when it came to business or her personal life. Jessica admired that about her. Maybe she could take a lesson from her rule book.

Zane leaned way back in his seat. "You got that right."

Mariah stacked the papers on the table and rose, hugging them to her chest. "Well, I'm off to make some phone calls. Zane, think about when you want to resume your tour. I've got to let the event coordinators know. They're on my back about it. Oh, and be sure to read through that contract that Bernie sent over the other day."

Zane's lips pursed. "I'll do my best."

"Jessica, have a nice morning. And if you're around Zane today, please give him a hand. He may look like a superhero, but he's really not Superman."

Could've fooled her. Last night, he'd been super *heroic*.

Mariah pivoted on her heels and strode out the door.

Zane chuckled.

"What?"

"The look on your face."

"I'm mortified about last night. Where on earth did you sleep, and does Mariah know what happened?"

"First off, don't be upset. It's our little secret. Mariah doesn't know that you're a margarita lightweight." He smiled. "That woman's been babying me for weeks. Doesn't do a man a bit of good being so dang useless. For the first time in a month of Sundays, I was able to help out and do something useful with this banged-up body."

"I took your bed."

"Glad to give it up."

"Where did you sleep?"

"The office sofa is the most comfortable place in the whole house."

"Oh, boy. I'm sorry. The first night I'm here, I give you trouble."

He smiled again, a stunning heart-melter. "If livening up my life some is trouble, then bring it on. Fact is, I'm glad you're here. You bring a bit of home with you. I miss that."

She needed to believe him. She'd been afraid coming here would remind him of Janie and all that he'd lost. To have him say he was glad she'd come made a big difference. "Okay."

He put his palms on her cheeks and leaned forward. Her heart stopped. Was he going to kiss her? His touch sent tingles parading up and down her chest. Oh, wow. It wasn't alcohol this time. Probably wasn't the alcohol last night, either. She'd been dumped by a scoundrel, and now a man she had no right responding to made her feel giddy inside. How screwed up was that?

She gazed into his eyes. He was looking somewhere above her eyeglasses. Then he lowered his mouth—she stilled—and he brushed a brotherly kiss across her forehead. Breath eased from her chest, and her foolish heart tumbled. Of course, Zane wasn't going to kiss her *that* way.

"And thanks for the input about the restaurant," he said. "I respect your honesty and what you have to offer."

She swallowed hard. Tamping down her silly emotions, she offered a quick smile. "Anytime."

Beaming sunshine simmered over Jessica's body, the invading heat soaking into her bones. Salty air, a cushion of sand beneath her and the soothing sounds of waves crashing upon the shore gave her good reason to forget her disastrous relationship with Steven Monahan. He didn't deserve any more of her time. But the sting of his rejection stayed with her, leaving her hollowed out inside, afraid to trust, questioning her intuition. She feared she'd never fully recover the innocence of her first love. Good thing she didn't have to make any decisions here on Moonlight Beach. She could just be.

Drenched in sunscreen, she lay on a beach blanket in a modest one-piece bathing suit, a folded towel under her head. Slight breezes just outside Zane's beachfront home deposited flecks of sand onto her arms and legs. Children's giggles and adult conversations drifted to her ears. For the first time in days, her nerves were completely calm.

She promised herself to keep out of Zane's hair, and she had for the most part these past three days. He spent hours inside his office working with Mariah, and occasionally they would ask for her input on the restaurant. She figured it was just a way for him to keep her entertained and make her feel welcome. Each morning, under an overcast sky that would burn off before noon, she walked a three-mile stretch of beach, loosening up her limbs and clearing her head. At night, she'd dine with Zane on the patio facing the ocean, and except for having an occasional glass of white wine or a cold beer, she kept her alcohol consumption to a bare minimum. The Pacific Ocean and fresh air were her balm. She didn't need to rely on anything else.

She wiggled her tush into the sand, carving out a more comfy spot on her blanket, and closed her eyes. The flapping of wings and piercing squawk of a seagull overhead made her smile.

"Glad to see you've taken to Moonlight Beach."

Blocking rays of sunlight with a hand salute, she opened her eyes. The handsome face of Dylan McKay came into view.

"Hi, Jessica." He stared at her with his million-dollar smile. "Don't let me disturb you."

Gosh, he remembered her name.

Wearing plaid board shorts and a muscle-hugging white

T-shirt, and fitting into beach society with the casualness of a megastar, he sort of did disturb her. Yet he did so in such a friendly way, she didn't mind the intrusion. As she sat up on her elbows, his gaze dipped to her chest. To his credit, his eyes didn't linger on her breasts, and that was more than she could say about most men.

"Hello, and I am enjoying the beach. When in Rome, as they say." She chuckled at the cliché. It was Mama's favorite saying, and she'd used it a zillion times over the years. The most recent was last night when they'd talked on the phone. Did others in her generation get that phrase?

Her eyes fell on a black portfolio tucked under his arm. It looked odd there, as if he should be wearing a three-piece suit while carrying that austere leather case. Instead of moving on, he squatted down beside her, his tanned knees nearly in her face. Obviously, he wanted to chat.

"I see you sometimes in the morning, walking along the beach."

"You've inspired me," she said. "Of course, I only do three miles. How are your runs going?"

"Killing me, but I'm getting in the ten miles."

His legs were taut, like those of a natural runner, and the rest of his body, well…it would be hard not to notice his muscles and the way his T-shirt nearly split at the seams around his shoulders and upper arms. "Good for you."

"So, how's it going?" he asked. "Other than sunbathing and taking long walks, are you having a good time?"

"Yes. It's nice here. I'm working on some new lesson plans for my class. I teach first grade back home."

"Ah…a teacher. Such an honorable profession."

She waggled her brows. Was he poking fun at her? Or was he being genuine?

"My mother taught school for thirty-five years," he added, his smile wistful, pride filling his voice. "She was loved by her students, but she wasn't a pushover. It wasn't easy pulling my antics on her. She was too savvy. She knew when kids were up to no good."

"I bet you gave her a run for her money."

He laughed, the gleam of his lake-blue eyes touching her. "I did."

"What grade did she teach?"

"All grades, but she preferred fourth and fifth. Then, later on, she became dean of a middle school, and eventually, the principal of the high school."

She nodded. She didn't have much else to add to the conversation. Not that Dylan McKay wasn't easy to talk to. He was. And she loved talking about education to anyone who would listen. It was just that he was fabulous, famous Dylan McKay. And he kept smiling at her.

"Hey, I'm having a party on Saturday night. If you're still here, I'd love for you to come. Maybe you can get Zane to get out and have a little fun."

"Oh, thanks." He'd caught her off guard. Wasn't that what she needed right now, to be a wallflower at an A-list party? "I'm…uh, I'm not the partying type. Especially now."

"Now?"

She shrugged. "I'm going through something and need a little R and R."

"Ah…a breakup?"

She nodded. Her pride aside, she opened up a little to make her point. "Broken engagement as the wedding guests were taking their seats in church."

"Ah…gotcha. I've been there once, a long time ago, when I was too young to know better. It turned out for the best, so believe me, I understand. Listen, I promise you, the party is low-key. Just a few friends and neighbors for a barbecue on the beach. I'd love to see you there."

"Thanks."

He smiled, and she smiled back. Then he pointed to her upper thigh, on the right side, closest to him. "Uh-oh. Looks like you missed a spot. You're starting to burn."

Grabbing the sunscreen tube from the blanket, his long fingers brushed the soft underside of her hand as he set the sunscreen into her palm. "Better lather up and—"

"Stop corrupting my little sis, McKay."

Jessica whipped her head around. Zane stood on the sundeck railing, staring at Dylan. His voice was a far cry from menacing, but the cool look he shot Dylan made her wonder what was up.

Dylan winked at her. "Maybe she wants to be corrupted."

"And maybe you want to turn tail and go home. I don't have to read that script, you know."

"Whoops," he said, flashing a charming smile. "He's got me there. Maybe you can help me convince him to take this role. Wanna try? Since you're about to turn into a fried tomato out here."

Under normal circumstances, she was probably the least starstruck person in Beckon, Texas, but how could she not take Dylan up on his offer to go over a movie script? The notion got her juices flowing, and excitement buzzed around her like a busy little bee.

She glanced down at her legs. Oh, wow. Dylan was right. There were more than a few splotchy patches on her body. Time to get out of the sun. "Sure, why not?"

"Great." He swiveled his head in Zane's direction. "We're coming up right now."

Gallantly, he offered her his hand. She couldn't very well refuse the gesture. She slipped one hand into his and simultaneously clutched her cover-up with the other as they rose together. He was too close for comfort, his eyes smiling on her, their hands entwined. Gently she pulled away, making herself busy zipping herself into a white cotton cover up and ignoring his rapt attention. He was a charmer, but thankfully his touch hadn't elicited a jolt of any kind. She glanced at Zane, leaning by the railing, his sharp gaze fixed on her.

Something hot and unruly sizzled in the pit of her belly.

She ignored it and pushed on, climbing the steps with Dylan McKay following behind.

"Did he ask you out?" Zane probed the minute Dylan McKay exited the house. Looming over her, Zane was a bit foreboding, as if he was her white knight protecting her from the wicked prince of darkness. Geesh.

"Wh-what?"

"The guy couldn't take his eyes off you down on the beach."

She shrugged and picked up three empty glasses, reminiscent of her waitress days at Holcomb House.

After coming back into the house she'd left the two men to take a quick shower and slip on a sundress. She'd listened to Dylan's script proposal to Zane with keen interest in a spacious light oak–paneled office on the main level of the house. The meeting took almost an hour. Then they'd had drinks in the cool shade of the patio. Iced tea for her. The men were content to knock back whiskey and soda.

Dylan was a charming lady's man to the millionth degree, and she knew enough to steer clear. The idea that he'd be interested in a little ol' school teacher from Beckon, Texas, was ridiculous. She had no illusions of anything else going on between them, and Zane should know that.

Her mama's image flashed before her eyes. That was it. She bet her mother put Zane up to watching out for her, making sure her tender heart didn't get broken again. Well, heck. She'd let him off the hook, but not without giving him some grief. Her chin up, she said, "He invited me to his beach party Saturday night. It was just a friendly invitation."

Zane's mouth tightened into a snarl and he snorted. "Doubtful."

"I told him I probably wouldn't go."

"Good." Zane nodded, satisfied. "You don't need to get involved with him. He's—"

"Out of my league?"

His eyes widened. "Hell, no."

"Well, he is. And I know it all too well. Heck, my life is messy enough right now. There's no room for romance, though it's absurd to think of Dylan McKay actually being into me."

Zane immediately reached out to grab her arm. Surprised, she jerked from his touch, and the glasses she held nearly slipped from her hand. "Don't put yourself down, Jess."

A jolt sprang to life, spiraling out of control where the strong fingers of his bandaged hand pressed into her skin. Sharpness left Zane's dark eyes, and he gave her a bone-melting look. "I was going to say, he would never appreciate you. You're special, Jess. You always have been."

Because she was Janie's sister.

Zane held dear her sister's memory, closing his heart around it and not allowing anyone else into his life. He was a sought-after hunky bachelor, but he'd been true to Janie's love even now, years later. Jessica understood she was only here because Zane was too nice a guy to refuse her mama a favor. "Thank you."

He nodded and released her to go lean against the railing.

Free of his touch, she marched the glasses into the kitchen, handing them to Mrs. Lopez one at a time. She had to do something to quell her pounding heart. What the heck was wrong with her?

"*Dios*, you do not do the work around here. That's my job, no?"

"Yes. But I like to help."

It was the same conversation she'd had with Mrs. Lopez since she'd arrived here. Jessica saw nothing wrong with putting clothes in the washer and turning the thing on, or clearing the dishes, or helping slice potatoes for a meal. Today, especially, she needed to do something with her hands.

"*Sí*, okay." A relenting sigh echoed in the kitchen.

She picked up dirty dishes on the counter, loaded them in the dishwasher and put things back in the refrigerator. A few chores later, after scanning the clean kitchen they'd both worked on, she gave Mrs. Lopez a bright smile. The woman was shaking her head, but with a twinkle in her eyes. Progress.

Jessica strode out the kitchen door and was immediately knocked against the doorjamb. Pain shot to her shoulder. The jarring bump brought Mariah's face into view. "Oh, sorry."

Mariah was equally shocked from the collision. "I didn't see you."

"My fault. I should learn how to slow down."

She chuckled. "I'm the same way. I've got to get where I'm going fast, no matter if it's just to sip coffee and read the newspaper." Mariah, always impeccably dressed, rubbed her shoulder through her cognac-colored silk blouse. "Guess we're alike in that regard. Where were you going in such a hurry?"

"Nowhere. Just outside. I left Zane hanging and I wanted to go back to talk to him."

"Good luck with that. I just left him, and he's a bear right now."

"Oh, really? Why?" It couldn't be the Dylan McKay thing, could it?

"I don't know exactly what set him off other than he hates being confined. He feels like a caged animal. Though he doesn't make an effort to go anywhere, other than for business."

"I can see how that would make him restless."

Mariah smiled. "That's the perfect way to describe it. He's restless. But I'm afraid that came on well before his fall. I think a change of pace is good for him. I've helped him make the decision to open this second restaurant, and now he's thinking about movie roles. It might be just what he needs."

Or maybe he was running away from his past, the same way she was. Zane loved music. He loved writing lyrics and composing songs. He was meant to entertain. His sexy, deep baritone voice made his fans swoon. That's the only Zane she'd known.

"Dylan invited you in to hear his pitch, I understand. What did you think of the movie?"

"Me? Well, I, uh…to be honest, I think the idea of Zane and Dylan being estranged brothers coming home after the death of their father might work. If Zane can act, he'd be great in the role. The only issue I see is the love triangle about the girl back home. I saw Zane's reaction to Dylan's description of the romantic scenes he'd have to do. Zane instantly shut down. I'm not sure if Zane's up to that."

"That's exactly what I think, too. Zane's not going to do something he's not comfortable with. Believe me, I know. I've had plenty of discussions with him about his recent decisions. He bounces things off me. He asks me a question, and I tell him the truth."

"Which is?"

"I will say this. Zane can act. He's been doing so for over two years now. His public persona is far different than the real Zane." Mariah was ready to say more and then clamped shut. Her eyes downcast, she shook her head. "Forgive me. I keep forgetting who you are."

Jessica drew her brows together. "It's because of Janie. He's still hurting."

Mariah nodded. "I'm afraid so."

Mariah's eyes fell on her softly, her genuine warmth shining through. "Please forget I said anything. It's none of my business."

The idea that after two years, Zane was still making decisions based on the love he had for Janie, nestled deep into her heart. It was beautiful in a way, but also incredibly sad. "You're Zane's personal assistant. You spend a lot of time together. I can see that you care about him as a friend, too, so maybe it's more your business than mine."

"Zane thinks of you as family. He's said so a dozen times since you've come here."

"I'm the little sis he never had." Wasn't that the term he'd used this afternoon with Dylan McKay?

Stop corrupting my little sis.

Zane's loyalty to her family was very sweet. She didn't take it lightly, but she also didn't want him to think of her as a pity case. From the moment her shocked guests walked out of the church on her wedding day, weeks ago now, something harsh and cold seeped into her soul. Trust would be a long time coming, if ever again. So Zane didn't have to worry over her. She wasn't a woman looking for love. She wasn't on the rebound. He could sleep well at night.

"So, what are you up to today?" she asked Mariah. She was learning the ins and outs of Zane's superstardom. Mariah sifted through a dozen offers a day for special appearances, television interviews and charity events on Zane's behalf. She'd learned that Zane was a generous contributor to children and military charities, but lately, he'd declined any personal appearances. Mariah worked with his fan club president on occasion and took care of any personal business, such as setting up medical appointments or shopping trips. It was a different world, one that her sister, Janie, had resigned herself to because she'd been with Zane from the launch of his career. They'd grown into this life together.

"More restaurant business to do today. We've got a decorator working on the interior design, but Zane's not sure about the motif." Mariah's cell phone rang, and she excused herself.

Jessica walked over to the French door leading out to the deck. Zane was sprawled out on a lounge chair, shaded from the sun, his booted foot elevated, reading the script Dylan had brought over. Keen on the subject matter, he seemed deep in thought. As her gaze lingered, she watched him close the binder and stare out to sea, his expression incredibly wistful.

She followed the direction of his gaze and honed in on the vast view of the ocean. The sounds of the sea lulled her into a soothing state of mind. It was a place to find infinite peace, if there ever was such a thing. Her nerves no longer throbbed against her skin. These past few days, she'd been much calmer. Were time and distance all she'd needed to get over Steven Monahan? Geesh, Jessica felt at one with nature and started to believe. A chuckle rose from her throat at the notion. She was beginning to sound like a true Californian.

"Crap! Damn things."

Out of the corner of her eye, she witnessed Zane's crutches fall to the ground. The slap echoed against the wood deck. Zane was off the chair, bending to pick them up and trying to keep weight off his bad foot. It looked like a yoga move gone bad. She moved quickly, her legs eating up the length of the deck to get to him.

"Zane, hang on."

He stumbled and fell over, landing on his bad hand. "Ow!"

By the time she reached him, he was on his butt, cursing like the devil, shaking out his wrist. She kneeled beside him. "Are you okay?" she asked softly.

He tilted his head toward her. "You mean other than my pride?"

She smiled. "Yes, we'll deal with that later. How's the hand?"

"I managed to catch the fall on the tips of my fingers, so the wrist should be fine."

He moved his fingers one by one as if he was playing keys on a piano. So much for keeping his hand immobilized. "Maybe your doctor would be a better judge of that."

"Now you sound like Mariah."

"I knew an old goat like you once," she said, putting his right arm over her shoulder. "Let me help you up."

"I knew the same goat," he bounced back. "Smart critter."

"Pleeeze. Okay, are you ready? On three." She swung her arm around his waist. "One. Two. Three."

His weight drew her toward him, the side of her face against his chest, her hair brushing his shirt. He smelled like soap and lime shaving lotion. His heart pounded in her ear as she strained to help lift him.

Zane did most of the work, his brawny strength a blessing. Together, they managed to stand steady, Zane keeping weight off his foot by using her as his right crutch. Once again, just like the other night, she was wrapped tight in his arms. Ridiculous warmth flowed through her body. She couldn't explain it except she felt safe with him, which was silly because this time she'd done the rescuing. "There," she said, satisfied she'd gotten him upright. "Now, we're even."

His arm over her shoulder, he turned to her with eyes flickering. "Is that so?"

Well, maybe not. She was getting drunk on him, minus the alcohol. "Yes, that's so."

"I could've gotten up on my own, you know."

"It wouldn't have been pretty."

He laughed. "True."

"So, I'm glad I was here to help. Show a little gratitude."

He wasn't a man who liked taking help. That was part of the problem. His gaze roamed over the deck where he'd spent most of his day, and she sensed his frustration.

"Wanna get out of here?" he asked.

"Sure. Where would you like to go?" Mariah said he didn't like to go out, so she couldn't let this opportunity pass by. If he needed some breathing room, away from his gorgeous house and his familiar surroundings, who was she to deny him?

"Anywhere. I don't care. Are you up to driving my car?"

"I can manage that. I'm going to get your crutches now, okay?" She didn't wait for an answer.

She released him and he stood there, balancing himself for the two seconds it took her to pick up both of his crutches and hand them over. Tucking one under each arm, he pointed a crutch toward the door. "After you."

Three

To her surprise, Zane picked his silver convertible sports car for her to drive over the black SUV sitting in his three-car garage. The other car, a little blue sedan, had to be Mariah's car. Jessica helped him get into his seat, taking his crutches and setting them into the narrow backseat before closing his door.

As soon as she climbed behind the steering wheel, she understood why Zane didn't venture out much. Sitting in the passenger seat, he was encumbered by his foot, broken in three places, which required him to be extremely careful. He also put on a disguise. Well, a Dodgers baseball cap instead of his signature Stetson and sunglasses wasn't much of a disguise, but she knew where he was coming from. He couldn't afford to be recognized and surrounded by fans or paparazzi. In his condition, he couldn't make a fast getaway. "Why am I driving this car?"

"More fun for you."

"You mean more scary, don't you? How much is this car worth, just in case I wreck it, or—heaven forbid—put a scratch on it?"

He smiled. "Don't worry. It's insured."

Stalling for time, she fidgeted with her glasses and took several deep breaths before she turned to Zane. He was still smiling at her. At the moment, she didn't enjoy being his source of amusement.

"Here goes." With the press of a button, the engine purred to life. Zane showed her how to adjust her seat and mirrors using the control buttons. Once set, she supposed she was as ready as she would ever be. She pumped the gas pedal and gripped the steering wheel. She'd never driven anything but a sedan, a boring four-door family car with no bells and whistles. This car had it all. A thrill shimmied up her legs…all that power under her control.

She backed the car out of the garage and made the turn into a long driveway that reached the front gate. Upon Zane's voice command, the gate slid open, and she pulled forward and onto the highway. She drove along the shoreline, keeping her eyes trained on the road and her speed under thirty miles per hour.

His back was angled against the passenger door and his seat. She sensed him watching her. He'd opted to keep the top up on the convertible, for anonymity, she supposed. Even though he'd not had a hint of scandal to his name, every time Zane went out, he risked being photographed. Putting the top down on his car in the light of day would be like asking for trouble.

She didn't dare shoot him a glance, keeping her focus on the road.

"What?" she asked finally. "Your grandmother drives faster than me?"

"I didn't say a word." His Texas drawl seeped into her bones. "But now that you mention it, I think my great-grandmother drove her horse and buggy a mite faster than you."

"Ha. Ha. Very funny. Maybe I'd drive faster if I knew where I was going."

He sighed. "I've learned that sometimes, it's better not to know where you're going. Sometimes, planning isn't all it's cracked up to be. Some roads are better not mapped out."

After that cryptic statement, she did look his way and found him resting his head against the window. His sunglasses hid his eyes and his true expression. The mood in the car grew heavy, and she didn't know how to answer him, so she buttoned her lips and continued to drive.

After five minutes of silence, Zane shifted in his seat. "Wanna see the site of the restaurant? The framework is up."

"I'd love to."

He directed her down a side road that wound around a cove. Then the beach opened up again to a street that faced the ocean. Unique shops and a few other small restaurants sparsely dotted the shoreline before she came upon the skeletal frame of a building.

"There it is. You can park along the side of the road here." He gestured to a space, and she swung the car into the spot.

"This is a great location."

"I think so, too. On a clear day, there's visibility for miles going in either direction."

The beach was wide where the restaurant would sit, far enough from the water to avoid high tides. A rock embankment jutted out to the left, where pelicans rested, scoping out their next meal. Above them and across the road, far up on the cliffs sat zillion-dollar homes overlooking the coastline.

"Do you want to get out?" she asked.

"Yep."

"Hold on," she said, killing the engine and climbing out. She reached into the backseat and grabbed his crutches, then strolled to his side of the car. He was lifting himself out of his seat by the time she got there. "Here you go."

"Thanks."

She waited for him to get his bearings, and they moved through the sand until they reached the beach side of the restaurant. "So this is Zane's on the Beach."

"Yep. Gonna be."

"I suppose it's good that you're branching out. You've become a regular entrepreneur."

"Can't sing forever."

Why not? Willie Nelson, George Strait and Dolly Parton weren't having career problems. And neither was Zane. "Why do I get the feeling you're not eager to go back to doing what you love to do?"

It was a personal question. Maybe too personal, given that Zane didn't react to it at all. He simply stared at the ocean, thinking.

"I'm sorry. It's none of my business."

"Don't apologize, Jess," he rasped with a note of irritation. "You can ask me anything you want."

Okay, she'd take him up on that. "So, then, why are you searching for something else when you've established yourself as a superstar and you have fans all over the world waiting for your return?"

He closed his eyes briefly. "I don't know. Maybe I'm tired of being in my own skin."

It was the most honest answer he could've given her. Zane was hurting. Still. And he didn't know how to deal with it. "I get that. After my disastrous breakup with Steven, I felt totally out of options. I didn't know who to trust, what to believe. I couldn't make a decision to save my life. That's why when I had to get out of Dodge, I let my mother take over and make arrangements. After she did, I didn't have the gumption to argue with her. No offense, but visiting you wasn't even on my radar."

He chuckled. "Should I be insulted?"

She softened her voice. "You made a point of keeping away from the entire family after Janie…"

He winced at her honesty. Maybe she shouldn't have been so blunt. "It's not for the reasons you think."

"I know why you did it, Zane."

He put his head down. "I was having a hard time."

"I know." He'd been swallowed up with guilt. Janie was five months pregnant when she lost her life. Zane was touring in London, and Janie wanted desperately to travel with him. Zane had given her a flat-out no. He didn't want her away from her doctors, on a whirlwind schedule that would sap her energy. They'd argued until Zane had gotten his way. He'd loved Janie so much, trying to protect her and keep her safe. It was a tragic irony that she'd died in her own home on the night Zane had performed for Prince Charles and the royal family. Momentary grief swept over his features. He'd probably feel the guilt of his decision until his dying day. But there was no one to blame. No one could've known that Janie would've been safer in London than resting in her own sprawling, comfortable ranch house while Zane was gone. Her mother had recognized that. Jessica recognized that, but Zane wouldn't let himself off the hook.

Braced by the crutches under his arms, Zane let go of one handle and took her right hand. Lacing their fingers, he applied slight pressure there, squeezing her hand as they stared at the ocean. "I'm glad you're here, Jess."

Peace and pain mingled together, a bittersweet and odd combination of emotions that she was certain Zane was experiencing, too. They'd both lost so much and shared a profound connection.

Afternoon winds blew her hair onto her cheek and Zane touched her face, removing the wayward strands, tucking them behind her ear. "It's good to have someone who understands," he whispered.

She nodded.

"You can trust me," he said.

"I do." Strangely, she did trust Zane. He wasn't a threat to her, not the way every other man in the universe might be. She had learned some harsh lessons about men and about herself. She'd never overlook the obvious the way she had with Steven. She'd never allow herself to be fooled into believing a relationship would work when there were three strikes against it from the get-go.

"This is nice," she murmured.

"Mmm," he replied.

Zane released her hand, and they fell into comfortable silence, watching wave upon wave hit the shore. After a minute, he turned her way. "Do you want to see the inside of the restaurant?"

Her gaze was drawn to the framed, unroofed, sandy-floored structure behind her. "I sure do!"

He laughed. "Follow me, if you can keep up." He hobbled ahead of her. "I'll give you the grand tour."

Zane folded his arms and leaned back in the booth of Amigos del Sol—friends of the sun—watching Jess pore over the menu items of his favorite off-the-beaten-path Mexican restaurant. It was a small hacienda-style place known for making the most delicious, fresh guacamole right at the table. "Everything is great here, but the tamales are out of this world."

And the guacamole was on its way.

Jessica's head was down, and her glasses dropped to the tip of her nose. With her index finger, she pushed them up to the bridge of her nose. He grinned. It was a habit of hers that he found adorable.

"Tamales it is. I will bow to your vast culinary taste. But I'm even more impressed at how you managed to sneak us in the back way and get this corner booth."

"I shouldn't give away my secrets, but while you were navigating turns and learning how to gun the engine on my car, I texted Mariah to call the owner and let him know we needed a quiet spot and we'd appreciate coming in through the back door."

"Ah…Mariah. Your secret weapon."

"She makes things happen."

"I've noticed. She anticipates your every move and watches out for you."

"Yeah, like a mother hen," he said. "Not that I'm ungrateful. She's like my second right arm." He lifted his broken wrist. "And in my condition, that's important."

A uniformed waiter pushed a food cart to their table. Zane practically salivated. He'd been craving the homemade guacamole since earlier in the day. The waiter set out a *molcajete* and *tejolote*, a mortar and pestle carved from volcanic rock, to begin preparations. Squeezing lime juice into the bowl first, he added cilantro, bits of tomato, garlic and other spices. Next he used the pestle to grind all the flavors together and scooped out three perfectly ripe avocados. The aroma of the blended spices and avocados flavored the air. Once done, the guacamole and warm tortilla chips were placed on the table.

After the waiter took their dinner order, he walked off with his cart. Zane grabbed a tortilla chip and dipped it into the fresh green mixture, offering it to Jess first. "Taste this and tell me it's not heaven."

She leaned in close enough for him to place the chip into her mouth. As she chewed, a beautiful smile emerged, and her eyes closed. She sighed. "Oh, this is so good."

Drawn to the sublime expression on her face, he forgot about his craving for a few seconds. Eyeing her reaction distracted him in ways that might've been worrisome, if it hadn't been Jess. As soon as she finished chewing, she snapped her eyes open. "You didn't have one yet?"

"No…it was too much fun watching you."

"I seem to be a source of your amusement lately."

That much was true. Jess being here brightened up his solemn mood. That wasn't a bad thing, was it? He dipped a chip in and came up with a large chunk of guacamole. He shoved it into his mouth and chewed. On a swallow, he said. "Oh, man. That's good."

Jess's eyes darted past him, focusing on something happening behind his back.

"Uh…oh. Don't turn around, Zane," she whispered.

As soon as her words were out, two twentysomething girls approached the table, giddy and bumping shoulders with each other. "Hello. Excuse me," one of them said. "But we're big fans of yours."

"Thank you," he said.

"Would you mind signing a napkin for us?"

He glanced at Jessica and she nodded.

"Sure will."

They produced two white napkins and a pen, which made things a little less awkward. Zane hated waiting around while fans scrambled for something for him to autograph. They gave him their names, and he signed the napkins and handed them back.

"Thank you. Thank you. You're our favorite country singer. I just can't believe we've met you. Your last ballad was amazing. You have the best voice. I saw you in concert five years ago, when I was living in Abilene with my folks."

Zane kept a smile on his face. The girls were clueless that they were interrupting his meal with Jessica. "Well, that's nice to hear."

They stared at him, hovering close.

Jessica stood up then. Bracing her hands on the table, she smiled at the girls. "Hello. I'm Jessica, Zane's sister-in-law." The girls seemed baffled when she shook both of their hands. "We were having a little family talk, and we're limited on time. Otherwise I'm sure Zane would love to speak to you. If you give me your names and addresses, I'll see that you get a signed CD of his latest album. And please be discreet when you leave here," she whispered. "Zane loves meeting his fans, but we really need a few private moments during our meal tonight."

"Oh, okay. Sure," one of them said congenially.

The other girl wrote their addresses on the napkin Jessica provided before she wished them well. Giggling quietly, the two women walked away.

Zane stared at Jessica. "I'm impressed."

"I've been listening to how Mariah deals with your fan club members. I hope it's okay that I offered them a CD."

"It's fine. Happens all the time. I wish I'd have thought of it myself."

"They were persistent."

Zane shook his head. "I could tell you stories." But he wouldn't. Some of the things that had happened to him while touring on the road weren't worth repeating. "Actually, these two were a little subtle compared with some of the people who approach me."

"You mean, compared with the *women* who approach you."

He scrubbed his chin, his fingers brushing over prickly stubble. "I suppose."

Jessica snorted. "You don't have to be modest on my account. I know you're in demand."

He tossed his head back and laughed. "In demand? What are you getting at?"

"You're single, available, successful and handsome. Those two women who left here would probably describe you as a hottie, a hunk, a heartthrob and a hero. You're in the 4-H club of men."

His smile broadened. "The 4-H club of men? You just made that up."

"Maybe," she said, taking a big scoop of guacamole and downing the chip in one big swallow. "Maybe not."

"You constantly surprise me," he said, sipping water. He could use something stronger. "I like that about you."

"And I like that you're decent to folks who admire you."

Their eyes met, and something warm zipped through his gut. Jessica's compliments meant more to him than ten thousand wide-eyed, giddy fans. He admired her, too. "Ah, shucks, ma'am. Now you're gonna make me blush."

Another unladylike snort escaped through her mouth. Zane grinned and leaned way back in his seat just as his cell phone rang. Dang, he didn't want to speak to anyone now, but only a few close friends and family knew his number. He fished the phone out of his pocket. "It's Mariah," he said to Jessica. He turned his wrist to glance at his watch. It was after eight. "That's odd. She usually texts me if she needs me for something after hours. Excuse me a second."

"Hi," he said. "What's up?"

"Zane, s-something terrible's h-happened." Sobs came through the phone, Mariah's voice frantic and unsteady. Zane froze, those words instilling fear and flashing a bad memory. "My mother had a stroke. It's pretty b-bad."

"Oh, man. Sorry to hear that, Mariah."

"I have to fly home right away. Th-they don't know... oh, Zane...she's so young. Only sixty-four. She never had health problems before. Oh, God."

"Mariah, you just do what you have to do. Don't worry about a thing." Her voice broke down, her sobs growing louder. "Where are you?"

"At Patty's h-house in Santa Monica." She shared a place temporarily with an old college roommate. The situation was perfect while he was staying on Moonlight Beach. She was close by without living under his roof.

"Pack up a few things and try to stay calm. Do you have a flight?"

"Patty got me on a midnight flight to Miami."

"Okay...I'll send a car for you in an hour. Hang in there, Mariah."

"It's okay, Zane. I a-appreciate it, but Patty offered to d-drive me. I'll be fine." A deep, sorrowful sigh whispered through the phone. "Are you going to be all right? I don't know how long I'll be gone."

"Don't worry about me." He stared at Jessica. Her eyes were softly sympathetic and kind. "Take all the time you need. And call if there's any way I can help, okay?"

"Okay. Thanks. Goodbye, Zane."

Zane hung up the phone. "Man, that's rough. Mariah's mother had a stroke. She's on her way to Florida now."

"Gosh, I'm sorry to hear that. Is it serious?"

"Seems that way." He ran a hand down his face, pulling the skin taut. "I've never heard her so unraveled before. She may be gone a long time."

"I would think so. Will you find a replacement for her?"

Zane wasn't thinking along those lines. Not yet. He kept hearing the disbelief and pain in Mariah's voice and understood it all too well.

Your wife didn't make it, Zane.

Didn't make what? he'd asked the doctor over and over, screaming into the phone. Then, all the way home from London, he kept thinking, hoping, praying it had been a mistake. A horrible, sick mistake. It wasn't until he saw the desolate ruins of his once proud home in Beckon that it finally sank in Janie was gone. Forever.

The meal was served, and as his gaze landed on the plate of saucy cheese-topped tamales, blood drained from his face, and his gut rebelled. For Jessica's sake, he pushed his haunting memories aside. He didn't want to ruin her meal.

Jessica reached for him across the table, her fingertips feathering over his good hand gently, comforting him with the slightest touch. When he lifted his lids, he gazed into her knowing, sensitive eyes, and she smiled. "Let's have them pack up this food. We'll eat it later on."

"Do you mind?" he asked.

"Not at all. I'm ready to go anytime you are."

He felt at peace suddenly, a glowing warmth usurping the dread inside his gut.

And then it hit him. Sweet Jess. She was good for him. She understood him, perhaps better than anyone else on this earth. She was a true friend, an authentic reminder of home, and he needed her here.

"You asked me before if I'd find a replacement for Mariah."

"Yes, I did. Hard shoes to fill, I would imagine."

"Yeah, I agree." He looked her squarely in the eyes. "Except I've already found someone, and I'm looking straight at her."

Four

Jessica woke to a glorious sunrise, the stream of light cutting through early morning haze and clouds in a host of color. Every morning brought something new from the view outside her bedroom window, and she was beginning to enjoy the variance from fog to haze to brilliance that took place before her eyes.

She stretched her arms above her head, working out the kinks, not so much in her shoulders and neck, but the ones baffling her brain. Last night, Zane told her to keep an open mind and sleep on his suggestion of replacing Mariah as his personal assistant. Her mouth had dropped open, and she thought him insane for a few seconds, but then he pointed out that he wasn't working, he had no gigs lined up, and he wasn't doing interviews right now. Most of what she had to do was hold off the press and postpone anything pending to future dates.

She wouldn't go into it cold. Mariah would be in touch to give her the guidance she needed to get her through anything remotely difficult.

"You're an intelligent woman, Jess. I'm convinced you'd have no problem, and I'm right here to help you," he'd said.

Zane's assurances last night gave her the push over the edge she'd needed this morning. Her head was clear now, and she valued the challenge and even looked forward to it. She wasn't ready to return to Texas anyway. Zane wanted freedom from his agent and manager's constant urging to get back on the horse. Zane wasn't ready yet and she could understand that. He needed more time, just as she did.

The new, bronzer Jessica no longer had freckles on her nose, thanks to a wonderful suntan that had connected those freckly dots and browned up her light skin. How many more hours could she feasibly sunbathe her day away? Staying on for a few weeks and helping Zane out would give her a new sense of purpose.

Jessica showered and dressed quickly. Putting on a pair of khaki shorts and a loose mocha-brown blouse, she slipped her feet into flip-flops and strode toward the kitchen. There were no wickedly delicious aromas drifting from the kitchen this morning. Mrs. Lopez had yet to arrive.

"Sonofabitch!"

A string of Zane's profanities carried to her ears. She grinned. Poor guy. He hated being confined.

She ventured into his bedroom. "Zane?"

"In here!"

She followed the sound of his cursing. He was standing over the bathroom sink, and their eyes met in the mirror. A scowl marred his handsome face, and three blood dots covered with bits of tissue spotted his cheeks and chin. Remnants of lime-scented shaving cream covered the rest of his face. "Damn hand. It's impossible to get a good shave."

"Whoops." With her index finger, she caught a drop of blood dripping from his chin before it landed on his white ribbed tank. "Got it."

He peered at her in the mirror and handed her a tissue. "Thanks."

"Thank me later, after I shave you. We'll see if I can't do a better job."

"You?"

"I used to lather up my dad and shave him when I was a kid." She hoisted herself up onto the marble counter to face him and picked up his razor. "It used to be a game, but darn it, I did an excellent job. Dad was surprised. Seems I'm pretty good with one of these."

Doubtful eyes peered at the razor in her hand.

"What? You don't trust me? It's a guarantee I'd do a better job than what I see on your face now. Or, I can drive you to the local barbershop. Since I'm going to be your new personal assistant and all."

The scowl left his face immediately, and her heart warmed at seeing approval in his eyes. "You've decided, then?"

"Yes, I'm on the clock now. So what will it be? A shave by your PA or a drive to the barber?"

"Try not to cut me," he said.

"You've already done a good job of that." She handed him a towel. "Wipe your face clean. We'll start from scratch."

Zane's eyes widened.

She chuckled at her bad choice of words. "You know what I mean." Pressing down on the canister, she released a mound of shave cream in her hand and leaned forward to rub it over his cheeks, chin and throat.

Zane leaned a little closer, his body braced by the counter. Her heart did a little dance in her chest. His nearness, the refreshing heady lime scent, her position sitting on the counter, *touching him*—suddenly she was all too aware of the intimate act she was performing on her brother-in-law.

What on earth was she doing?

Zane needed help and she'd rushed to his aid. But she hadn't thought this through.

He still towered over her, but only by a few inches now. She lifted her eyes and found him, waiting and watching her through the mirror.

Her hand wasn't so steady anymore.

She couldn't fall down on her first official act as Zane's personal assistant, intimate as it was.

"Okay, are you ready?"

He kept perfectly still. "Hmm."

Her legs were near his hip, and she angled her body to get closer to his face. Bracing her left hand on his shoulder to steady herself, she was taken by the strong rock-hard feel of him under her fingertips. She stroked his face, and the razor met with stubble and gently scraped it away. Carefully she proceeded, gliding the razor over his skin in the smoothest strokes she could manage.

His breath drifted her way as heat from his body radiated out, surrounding her. Cocooned in Zane's warmth, she fought an unwelcome attraction to him by thinking of Steven, the man who'd shattered her faith. And that reminder worked. Thoughts of Steven could destroy any thrilling moment in her life. She dipped the razor into the sink and shook it off. Zane's gaze left the mirror, and as she lifted her eyes to his, there in that moment, a sudden surprising sizzle passed between them.

One, two, three seconds went by.

And then he focused his attention back on the mirror, keeping a silent vigil on her reflection.

"How are you holding up?" she asked, breaking the quiet tension.

"Am I bleeding?"

Her lips hitched at his intense tone. "No."

"Then, I'm good."

Yes. Yes, he was.

"Okay, now for your throat. Chin up, please."

He obeyed without quarrel. Gosh, he really did trust her. Something warm slid into her belly, and the feeling clung to her as she finished up his shave.

"All done," she said after another minute. "Not a nick on you, I might add." At least one of them had come out of this unscathed.

"I think I hear Mrs. Lopez tinkering in the kitchen now." She handed him his razor and jumped down from the counter. "Do you want breakfast? Coffee?"

She was partway out the door when Zane caught her arm

just above the elbow. He looked gorgeous in his white ribbed tank, his face and throat shaved clean but for the last traces of shave cream. "Just a sec. I haven't thanked you. And you don't have to worry about breakfast for me."

"I don't?"

"No. That's not part of your job description."

Well, duh. She knew that. Mariah hadn't served him his meals, but Jessica couldn't very well tell him she'd run her mouth in order to get away from him as quickly as possible.

"We'll go over what I expect of you as my assistant this morning. Thanks for the shave." He slid his hands down his smooth face, and his eyes filled with admiration. "Feels great. You're pretty good."

She swallowed. Did this mean she'd have to shave him every day?

Gosh, she really didn't think this through thoroughly enough.

"Thanks. Well, I'll see you at breakfast."

"Oh, and Jess?"

"Yeah?"

He released her arm. "I'm glad you'll be staying on. I do need your help. And I think you'll enjoy it, but whenever you're ready to head home, I'll…understand."

"Thanks, Zane. I'll do my best."

Four hours later, Jessica sat behind the desk in Zane's office, satisfied she had things under control. It had been a little scary at first. What did she really know about Zane's celebrity life? But Mariah had been acutely efficient, keeping good records and documenting things, which made it easier for Jess to slide into the role of personal assistant. She seemed to live by a detailed calendar, and Zane's appointments, events and meetings were clearly labeled. *Thank you, Mariah, for not being a slouch.* In the day planner she came to regard as The Book, Mariah had jotted down phone numbers next to names and brief reminders of what needed to be said or done.

No to the *People* magazine interview.

Yes to donating twenty thousand dollars to the Children's Hospital charity. Zane would make an appearance in the future.

No to an appearance on *The Ellen DeGeneres Show*.

And so on.

With a little help from Zane earlier this morning, she was able to field a few phone calls and make the necessary arrangements for him. It was clear Zane was in a state of celebrity hibernation. Other than opening a new restaurant, Zane was pretty much in a deep freeze. Maybe he needed the break away from the limelight, or maybe he wasn't through running away from his demons.

In a sense, she was doing the same thing by being here, afraid to go home, afraid to face the pitfalls in her own life. She, too, was hiding out, so she had no right to judge him or try to fix the situation. It wasn't any of her business. That was for sure.

"How're you doing?" he asked.

She glanced up from The Book to find him standing at the office threshold, leaning on his crutches. She flashed back to shaving him this morning and the baffling emotions that followed her into breakfast. Her heart tumbled a little.

"Good, I think."

He smiled. "Anything I can help you with?"

"No, not at the moment."

He didn't leave. He didn't enter the room.

"Is there anything I can do for you?" she asked.

"Sort of." His lips twisted back and forth. "You see, Dylan's bugging me about this script. Fact is, I don't know if acting is right for me. I never had an acting lesson in my life. So I want to say no to him. But…"

She braced her elbows on the desk and leaned forward. "But, just maybe it's something you want to do?"

He stared at her. "Hell, I don't know, Jess. I guess I need a reason to say no."

"And how can I help you with that?"

"Dylan's got this idea that if I had someone run lines with me, I'd feel better about accepting the role. Or not. I didn't ask Mariah, well…because she works for me and I'm not sure she would be—"

"Honest?"

"Objective. She tends to encourage me to try new things, so she might not be the person to ask."

"So you're saying I'd have no problem telling you 'you suck'?"

He chuckled. "Would you?"

"No, no problem at all."

His brows gathered. "I'm not sure how to take that."

"I'd have only your best interests at heart. But honestly, Zane, what do I know about acting? What if my instincts aren't dead-on? What if I get it wrong?"

"Bad acting is bad acting. You can tell if someone sings off-key, can't you?"

"Sometimes, but my ear for music isn't as good as yours."

"But you're *real*, Jess. You would know when something is authentic. That's all I'm asking you to do."

His faith in her was a heady thing. She couldn't deny she was flattered. And as his personal assistant, she couldn't really tell him she didn't want to do it.

"Okay. What did you have in mind?"

"We read through some scenes. See if I can grasp the character."

"Where?"

He pointed to the long beige leather sofa—the most comfortable place to sleep in Zane's world. "Right here." He hobbled into the room on his crutches and sank down, resting the crutches on the floor. "The script is behind you on the bookcase. If you could get it and bring it over…"

"Sure." She turned and found it quickly. *"Wildflower?"*

"That's the one. You know most of the story."

She did. She was there when Dylan explained the premise of the romantic mystery to both of them the other day. It was about a man who comes home to his family's ranch after a long estrangement and finds his brother romantically involved with the woman he'd left behind. There's a mystery surrounding their father's death and a whole cast of characters who are implicated, including both brothers. "I think it's a good story, Zane."

"Well, let's see if I can do it justice."

"Sure."

She walked over to the couch and took a seat one cushion away from him.

"I don't think that's going to work," Zane said. "You have to sit next to me." He waved the script in the air. "There's only one of these."

"Right." As she scooted closer to him, Zane's eyes flicked over her legs and lingered for half a second. Oh, boy. The back of her neck prickled with heat. In a subtle move, she adjusted her position and lowered the shorts riding up her legs to midthigh. Zane didn't seem to notice. He'd focused back on the script and was busy flipping through story pages.

"Okay, here's a scene we can do together. It's where Josh and Bridget meet for the first time since his return."

She peered at the pages and read the lines silently. It was easy enough to follow. There were one or two sentences of description to set up the scene and action taking place. The rest was dialogue, and each character's part was designated by a name printed in bold letters.

"You start first," he said, pointing to the top of the page. "Where Josh speaks to Bridget in front of her house."

"Okay, here goes." She glanced at him and smiled.

He didn't smile back. He was taking this very seriously. She cleared her throat and concentrated on the lines before her. "Josh? You're home? When did you get back? I…I didn't know you'd come."

"My father is dead. You thought I wouldn't return for his burial?"

"No. I mean…it's just that you've been gone so long."

"So you wrote me off?"

A note of anger came through in Zane's voice. It was perfect.

"That's not how it happened. You left me, remember? You said you couldn't take living here anymore."

"I gave you a choice, Bridget. You didn't choose me."

"That wasn't a choice. You asked me to leave everything behind. My family, my friends, my job and a town I love. I don't hate the way you do."

"You think I hate this place?"

"Don't you?"

"Once, I loved everything about this place. Including you."

Jessica stared at him. The way he dropped his voice to a gravelly tone and spoke his lines was so real, so genuine, it impressed the hell out of her.

"But you've moved on." Now Zane's voice turned cold. He had a definite knack for dialogue. "With my brother."

They read the next three pages, bantering back and forth, learning the characters and living them. The scene was intense, and Zane held his own. He had a lot of angst inside him and found his release using the screenwriter's words on the page.

The scene was almost finished. Just a few more lines to go.

"Don't come back here, Josh," she said, meeting Zane's eyes. "I don't want to see you again."

Zane was really into the character now. "That's too bad, Bridget." The depth of his emotion had her believing. "I'm back to stay."

"I'm going to marry your brother."

"Like hell you are," Zane said fiercely, leaning toward Jessica, his face inches from hers.

"Don't…Josh…don't mess with my life again."

"This is where he grabs her and kisses her," Zane whispered. His breath swept over her mouth, and she found herself wanting to be kissed. By Zane. Heat crept up her throat and burned her cheeks.

Zane glanced at her mouth. Was he thinking the same thing? Did he want to kiss her?

He was a man she trusted. He was a man she truly liked. "Do you want to, uh, bypass the kiss?"

He shook his head, his gaze dropping to her mouth. "No," he rasped. "I don't."

Her pulse pounded as he took her head in his hands and caressed the sides of her overheated cheeks with his long, slender fingers. Her head was tilted slightly to the left, and then his mouth lowered to hers. He touched her lips gently, and she felt the beautiful connection from the depths of her soul. Was she supposed to stay in character? How would she accomplish that? Everything inside her was spinning like crazy.

The script called for a brutal, crushing kiss, but this kiss was nothing like that. His lips were firm and giving and generous…pure heaven.

"I'm not through messing with your life, Bridget." The gravel in his voice convinced her. He did *harsh* perfectly. "I might never be through."

As Zane backed away, his gaze remained on her. He blinked a few times, as if coming to his senses, and then cleared his throat.

The air sizzled around her. Was Zane feeling it, too? She didn't know where to look, what to say.

"It's your line," Zane whispered.

Oh! She glanced at the page and read her last line. "I—I can't do this again, Josh."

Zane paused for a second, glaring at her for a beat. "I'm not gonna give you a choice this time."

There. They'd made it through the entire scene. Zane flipped the script closed, and as he braced his elbows on his knees, he leaned forward.

Her heart was zipping along. She needed space, a few inches of separation from Zane. She flopped back against the sofa and silently sighed.

"Thank you," Zane said quietly.

"Hmm."

"Now for the hard part. I respect your opinion. No hard feelings either way, so lay it on me."

He'd convinced her he could act. Aside from the kiss that still had her reeling, she was completely enthralled with his character. He'd stepped into Josh's shoes without a bit of awkwardness. "I'm no expert, but I know when something's good. I'd say you were a natural, Zane."

He leaned back and looked into her eyes. Oh, God. She didn't want him to notice how nervous she was. "You really think so?"

"I do. You dove into that character and had me believing."

He stroked his jaw and sighed.

"I'm sorry if you wanted to hear you stink at acting. But I don't think so."

A crooked smile lifted the corner of his mouth. "I admit, I was hoping that was the case. Makes my decision harder now."

"Sorry?" she squeaked.

He released a noisy breath. "Don't be. I asked for your opinion. I appreciate you, Jess," he said. "I trust your judgment. I, uh…sort of got caught up in the scene. Hope you didn't mind about the little kiss I gave you."

Little kiss? If that was his little kiss, what would a real, genuine, from-the-heart kiss feel like from her one time brother-in-law? He didn't know the kiss had sent her senses soaring, and it would have to stay that way.

She'd never admit she'd wanted to kiss him. He was her brother-in-law, for heaven's sake. He was her employer now. And he was a good, decent man who'd never take advantage of her situation. She knew all that about Zane.

Of course he'd wanted to stay true to the script. He'd delved so deeply into character that he didn't want to lose the momentum of the scene. But, oh…for that brief moment when he'd looked into her eyes and her heartbeat soared, she believed he, Zane Williams, really wanted to kiss her.

And it had been a wow moment. "No, I didn't mind at all."

Her cell phone on the desk rang and she jumped up to answer it. "Oh, uh, excuse me, Zane. It's Mama."

"Sure."

He began to rise, and she put up her hand. She wasn't going to have him leave his own office. "No, don't get up. I'll take it in my room." Her mother's timing couldn't have been better. She needed to get away from Zane and the silly notions entering her head.

She walked out of the office and climbed the stairs. "Hi, Mama."

"Hi, honey. How're you doing this afternoon? Oh, I guess it's still morning there."

"Yes, it's just before noon. I'm doing fine." Her heartbeat had finally slinked down to normal since Zane's kiss a few minutes ago.

"Really?"

"Yes, I'm fine." It was weird how distance and the new surroundings made her see things differently. She wasn't thrilled with the way her life was turning out—she'd invested a lot of time on Steven Monahan—but she didn't need to worry her mother over it. Right now, she was taking it one day at a time. "Actually, I'm glad you called this morning. I have news. Zane's personal assistant, Mariah, had to take a leave of absence. Her mother's very ill and, well, since I'm here and Zane needs help, he's asked me to take over the position. It's temporary, but I won't be coming home this week or the next, probably. I might be here longer than that."

"Oh, that's good, honey."

"It is?" There was something in her mother's too-cheerful tone that raised her suspicions. She entered her bedroom wondering what was up? "What I mean to say is, I'm sorry Mariah's mother is ill. Bless her heart. I'll be sure to say a prayer for her. But you staying there for a little longer might be best for you, after all."

Really? Her overprotective mother—the woman who had set her alarm at 3 a.m. every night to get up and check on her two sleeping little girls when they were young, the woman who'd worried and fretted during their teen years, and the woman who, after Jessica's disastrous nonwedding, arranged for her to move into Zane's house just so he could keep an eye on her—*that mother* was actually glad that she wasn't coming home anytime soon?

Now she knew something was going on.

She lowered herself onto the bed. "Why, Mom? What's happened?"

"I hate to tell you this, honey. But better it come from me than you hear about it another way."

Her heart nearly stopped. Was her mother ill? Was it something severe? She flashed back to Janie's death. How the news had seemed unreal. She'd gotten physically sick, acid drenching her stomach and her breaths coming in short, uneven bursts. Now she held her breath. "Please, just tell me."

"Okay, honey. I'm sorry…but I just found out that your Steven eloped with Judy McGinnis. They just up and left town two nights ago. Went to Vegas, I hear. The whole town's crackling about it."

"W-with Judy?"

"I'm afraid so. I never expected that from Judy. Honey, are you okay?"

She might never be okay again. She'd just learned that the man she'd banked on for three full years, the man who had sworn up and down in her dressing room on their wedding day that he wasn't ready for marriage and that it wasn't anything she'd done, had just gotten married. The fault was all his for not recognizing his problem sooner, he'd told her. She'd believed he had commitment issues. But now she knew the truth. He wasn't ready for marriage to *her*. Instead, he chose one of her bridesmaids to speak vows with.

Judy had been her friend since grade school. Oh, God. She'd accepted losing Steven and any future they might've had together, but losing Judy's friendship, too? That was a double blow to her self-esteem. They'd both betrayed her. Made a fool out of her. She hadn't seen the signs. How long had Judy and Steven been hooking up behind her back?

Her eyes burned with unshed tears.

Being here and having a new sense of purpose in helping Zane, she was beginning to feel better and gain control of her emotions. But now, fresh new pain seared her from the inside out. What an idiot she'd been. That was the worst part of all, this hopeless sense of loss of *herself*. Her heart ached in a way it never had before. She felt herself slipping away.

She couldn't give in to it. If she did, she'd be totally lost. She couldn't dwell. She wouldn't let their betrayal dictate her life. She wouldn't curl into a pitiful ball and let the world spin without her.

"Jessica?"

"I'm going to be fine, Mama. I just need some time to digest this."

"I'm here if you need me, honey. I'm so, so sorry."

"I know. I love you. I'll call you tonight. Bye for now."

Jessica pushed End on her cell phone and faced the mirror. Her mousy-brown-haired reflection stared back at her through tortoiseshell-rimmed glasses. "What's happened to you, Jess?" she muttered.

She was tired of feeling like crap. Being a victim didn't suit her. She wasn't going to put up with it another second. The old Jessica had to go.

It was time for her to take hold of her life.

Afternoon breezes whispered through Zane's hair as he sat on his deck, gazing out to sea. Dylan McKay sat beside him, sipping a glass of iced tea. He didn't mind Dylan's company as long as he wasn't pressuring him about taking on an acting role.

"How soon before you're all healed up and ready to start living again?" Dylan asked.

Not soon enough for him. The confinement was getting to him. The only good thing about being temporarily disabled was that he didn't have to make any decisions right away. And he was milking that for all it was worth.

"The blasted boot comes off on Monday."

"And how's the wrist doing?"

His wrist? He flashed to trying to shave himself this morning. He'd been hopeless. Mariah usually took him to the barber twice a week. He hated being so damn helpless, and Jess had rescued him. She'd given him a clean, smooth shave and for a second there, as she leaned in close to him, her honeyed breath mingled with his and his body zinged to life. Electricity stifled his breathing for those few moments.

Jess?

He'd written it off as nothing and gone about his business.

Then he'd asked Jess to read lines with him. He'd gotten so caught up in the scene that when it came time to kiss her…he didn't want to deny himself the opportunity. Had it been only because the scene demanded a kiss? Or had it been something more?

A tick worked his jaw. It damn well couldn't be something more.

Though kissing her soft giving mouth packed a wallop. He'd forgotten what it felt like to have a sweet woman respond to him. He'd backed off immediately and didn't dare take it any further. The complication was the last thing either of them needed.

"My wrist should be healed soon, too…with any luck." He wiggled the tips of his fingers unencumbered by the cast. "I can't do a damn thing left-handed. You have no idea how uncoordinated you really are until you lose the use of your right hand."

"I hear you. How long will Mariah be gone?"

"Not sure. I spoke with her this morning. Her mom might have some permanent paralysis. Mariah's pretty torn up about it."

"So it's just you and Jessica now, living in this itty-bitty ole house?"

Zane rolled his eyes. The house was enormous, much more than he needed. He was hardly bumping into her in the hallway in the middle of the night.

Now, there was a thought. He struck that from his mind.

"She's taken on Mariah's duties here."

"You hired her?"

Zane nodded. Dylan didn't need to know that having Jessica around made him feel closer to Janie. She, above everyone else, understood the loss he felt. They shared that horrific pain together. Jess was *home* to him, without him having to return to Beckon. He liked that about her. So maybe it was selfish of him to ask her to stay on, but he hadn't pressured her. Much. He'd like to think she wanted to stay.

"I did. I didn't have a backup for Mariah. You know as well as I do it's hard to find a replacement for a trusted employee. I trust Jess. She'll do her best."

Dylan eyed him carefully. "You sure sing her praises."

"She's bright and learns quickly." He shrugged. "She's family."

"You keep saying that."

"It's true. Why wouldn't I say it?"

Dylan flashed a wry smile and then shook his head. "No real reason, I guess. Any chance I can convince you to be my costar before you head back on tour?"

"I haven't made up my mind yet, McKay. I told you I'm not making you any promises."

"Yeah, yeah. So I've heard. Remember what they say about people who drag their feet."

"No, what the hell do they say?"

"They risk getting them cut off at the ankles."

He laughed. "I should be flattered you're so persistent. Honestly, if I lose the role to someone else, so be it. I'm not sure." About anything, he wanted to add.

"Buddy, you're not going to lose the role to someone else. I'm the executive producer, and I see you doing this character."

"You want my fan base."

"That, too. I'd be a fool not to want to reel in your fans. I know they'd turn out for you. But I have no doubt in my mind you'd be—"

"Zane?" A sultry voice carried to the deck. His heart stopped for a second. Sometimes, when he was least expecting it, Jess would call out his name and he'd swear it was Janie asking for him.

"Out here," he called to her.

Jessica popped her head out the doorway. "Oh, sorry. I didn't realize you had a guest."

"Hi," Dylan said. "How're you doing, Jess?" Dylan sent her a brilliant smile. The guy could charm a billy goat out of a field of alfalfa.

"Hi, Dylan."

"Come on out here, Jess." Zane hadn't seen much of her since they'd run lines and *kissed* earlier in the day. He'd heard her working in the office, but she hadn't asked for his help, and he'd let her be. "Have a cool drink with us?"

"Uh, no thanks," she said, taking a few steps toward them. She wore a loose-fitting flowery sundress. Her hair was up in a ponytail, and a straw satchel hung from her shoulder. "Actually, I finished up what I could this afternoon. I was hoping to go shopping now. I wanted to see if you needed anything while I was out."

"Oh, yeah? What are you shopping for?" Was he so dang bored that he had to nose into Jessica's private business?

"I, uh, didn't bring enough clothes with me. I thought I'd pick up a few things."

"Hey, I know a great little boutique in the canyon," Dylan said. "I'd be happy to drive you there."

Zane swiveled his head toward Dylan. Was he kidding?

Jessica chuckled. "Thanks, that's a kind offer, but I'm good. I'm anxious to explore and see what I can find."

"Gotcha," Dylan said. "A little me time. I hope Zane hasn't been working you too hard."

"Not at all. I'm enjoying the work." With her finger, she pushed her sunglasses up her nose. She did that when she was nervous, and obviously, Dylan McKay made her nervous. Zane wasn't sure that was a good thing. He inhaled deep into his chest. Jessica was vulnerable right now, and she didn't need Dylan hitting on her.

"But you're both coming to the party tomorrow night, right?" Another charming smile creased his neighbor's face.

"Nope, sorry," Zane said. "We're not available."

Jessica faced him a second and blinked, then shifted her focus to Dylan. "Actually, I've changed my mind. I'd love to come. What time?"

Dylan's grin seemed to spread wider than the ocean view. "Six o'clock."

"I'll be there."

"You will?" Zane asked. They'd both decided on not going.

She nodded. "Sure, why not? Sounds like fun."

Zane couldn't argue the point. If she wanted to go to Dylan's little party, he had no right to stop her. "Well, then… I guess we're coming."

"We?" Jessica asked. A genuine spark of delight lit her expression. "You're going now? That's great, Zane."

He shrugged it off but couldn't stop his chest from puffing out. Why did it make him so doggone happy that Jessica wanted him around?

"Well, I'd better be off. Zane, is it still okay that I take one of your cars?"

"Yep. You know where the keys are in the office."

"Okay, thanks. I'll take the SUV. Bye for now," she said. She pivoted and walked back into the house.

"She's nice," Dylan said.

"Very nice. "

"Too nice for me? Are you warning me off?"

"Damn straight I am." Zane eyed him. "You know darn well Jessica isn't your type. So stay away. I'm serious. She's had it rough lately."

The patio chair creaked as Dylan leaned over the arm and focused on him. "You like her?"

"Of course I like her. She's like my…" But this time Zane couldn't finish his thought. He couldn't say she was like a sister to him. An image of taking her mouth in a daring kiss burst through his mind again. In that moment, he'd forgotten she was Janie's sister. All that filled his mind was how sweet and soft her lips were. How much he wanted to go on kissing her. He'd felt at peace with Jess, yet electrified at the same time.

He'd had women in the past to satisfy his physical needs. He hadn't been a total saint after Janie died, but he hadn't had a real relationship, either, and he sure as hell wasn't going in headfirst with Jessica. So why in hell was the memory of kissing her earlier torturing him?

"I meant you want her for yourself."

Zane snorted. "Are you not hearing what I'm saying? She's off-limits. To everyone. She has a lot of healing to do. Until then, no one gets near her." He'd promised her mother he'd protect her and make sure she didn't get hurt again.

"Okay, okay. I get it, Papa Bear. Now, let's get back to the script. I think Josh's character is perfect for you, like it was written with you in mind."

For once, Zane was grateful the subject changed to his possible acting career.

Five

Thank goodness for credit cards. They gave Jessica the freedom to spend, spend, spend at the boutique Mariah had once raved about. She scoured the golden wardrobe racks at Misty Blue, and every time something struck her as daring and unlike her small-town schoolmarm image, she handed it to Misty Blue's *attire concierge* to put aside for her to try on. Sybil, the thirtysomething saleswoman, was dogging her, making suggestions and flattering her at every turn.

"Oh, you must have that," and "you'll never find a better fit," and "you'll be the envy of every woman on Moonlight Beach," were her mantras.

Jessica ate up her compliments. Why not? She needed them as much as she needed to buy a whole new wardrobe. The old Jessica was put to rest the minute she'd heard about her so-called good friend eloping with her fiancé. So be it. Jessica would return to Beckon a new woman.

Her clothes would be stylish. Her attitude would brook no pity. And she'd have a few thousand dollars less in her very tidy bankroll.

Saving money wasn't everything.

"I'll just put these items in your dressing room," Sybil announced. "Take your time looking around. When you're ready, you'll be in the Waves room."

Jessica blinked. Even the dressing rooms had names. "Okay, thank you."

She moved around the boutique slowly, taking her time perusing the shelves and racks. She picked out a two-piece bathing suit, a few hip-hugging dresses, two pairs of designer slim-cut jeans, and four blouses in varying colors and styles.

Sybil came racing forward. "Let me take those off your hands, too. I'll put them in the dressing room."

She transferred the clothes into Sybil's outstretched arms. "Thanks."

"Would you like to keep shopping?"

Jessica eyed several pairs of shoes on top of a lovely glass display case. "Yes, I'll need some shoes, too."

"I'll have Carmine, our shoe attendant, help you with that."

Thirty minutes later, Jessica glanced around the Waves dressing room. Clothes hung on every pretty golden hook, and shoes dotted the floor around her feet. She'd gone a bit hog-wild in her choices and needed guidance from someone who knew her well. She punched the speed dial on her cell phone and was relieved when her best friend, Sally, answered.

"Help me, Sally. I need your honest opinion," she whispered. "I texted you pictures of five of the dresses I've tried on. Did you get them?"

"Sure did. I'm looking at them now."

"Good." The inventor of cell phone technology was a genius. It made shopping a whole lot easier. "Which ones do you like?"

"Gosh, none of them look bad on you. You have a great figure," Sally said, almost in disbelief. "You've been hiding it."

"I guess I have." She'd never been comfortable with her busty appearance and had always chosen clothes to hide rather than highlight her figure. Now, all bets were off.

"Did you like the red one?"

"Definitely the red. That's a given," Sally said. "Whose eyeballs are you trying to ruin?"

"What do you mean?"

"That dress is an eye-popper."

She pictured Zane. Why had he come to mind so easily? It was ridiculous and yet, something had hummed in her heart when he'd kissed her today. He'd been caught up in the scene. She shouldn't make a darn thing out of it. But she was having a hard time forgetting the feel of his lips claiming hers. As short as the kiss was, it had been potent enough to shoot endorphins through her body. That wasn't necessarily a good thing.

"Do you think maybe I shouldn't be doing this?" she asked Sally, her bravado fading.

"Doing what? Pampering yourself? Spending some of your hard-earned money on yourself? Indulging a little? I'm only sorry I'm not there to help you with your TLC gone wild. Believe me, if I could swing it, I'd hop on a plane today."

She chuckled. "TLC gone wild? That's a new one, Sal."

"I'm clever. What can I say? Buy the clothes, Jess. I'll let you decide on the shoes, but those red stiletto heels will kick some major butt. Oh, and while you're at it, lose the eyeglasses. You brought your contacts, didn't you?"

"Yes, I have them."

"Well, use them. If you're going to do it, do it right."

Of course, Sally was dead-on. If she was going to invest in these clothes, she had to go all the way. She'd already decided to ditch her tortoiseshell glasses. Her hair could use some highlights, and her California tan was coming along nicely. Already she felt better about herself.

"And Sal, I wish you could come out here. It's really... nice."

"I bet. Zane's place sounds like heaven. Right on the beach. I bet you don't even have any swamp heat and humidity."

"Nope, not like home."

"Tell me you haven't met any big movie stars and I swear I won't be jealous."

"I, uh, well," her voice squeaked.

"Who? Tell me or I'll haunt you into forever."

"Would you believe Dylan McKay lives two doors down?" Jessica squeezed her eyes shut, anticipating the bombardment. No one was a bigger fan of the Hollywood heartthrob than her bestie Sally.

"You've met him?"

"Yes, I sort of ran into him on the beach." Or rather, the other way around—he'd run into her. "He's a friend of Zane's."

"No way! I can't believe it. Tell me everything."

A knock on the dressing-room door startled her, and she jumped. She'd forgotten where she was.

"Miss Holcomb, can I help you with anything?" Sybil asked.

"Whoops, gotta go," she said in a low voice. "I've got to get dressed. I'll call you later."

"You better!"

Jessica smiled as she ended the call and answered the saleswoman. "No thanks. I'm doing great.

"I'll be out in one minute."

"You sound happy. Find anything to your liking?"

"Just about everything," she answered.

She imagined the attire concierge who worked on commission smiling on the other side of the door.

Her purchases today would make both of them happy.

Zane had received a text message from Jessica half an hour ago telling him not to wait for her to have his meal. She was going to be late. But he didn't feel much like eating without her. It had taken Jessica living here for him to realize he'd eaten too many meals alone.

She must've gotten carried away on her little shopping spree.

When Jessica finally pulled through the gates, driving toward the garage, Zane made his way to the living room and, with the grace of an ox, plunked down onto the sofa.

A minute later the door opened into the back foyer, and he heard the crunch of bags and footsteps approaching. He picked up a magazine and flipped through the pages.

"Hi, Zane," Jessica said. Her voice sounded breezy and carefree. "Sorry I'm so late."

When he lifted his head, he found her loaded down with shopping bags. "Did you buy out the store?"

She chuckled from a warm and deep place in her throat. "Let's just say the store manager couldn't do enough for me. They offered me a vanilla latte and a chocolate mini croissant, and the shoe salesman almost gave me a foot massage."

His brows gathered. "A foot massage?"

"I told him no. I didn't have time. Is that done here?"

"I don't know if it's done *anywhere*," Zane said. For heaven's sake, she was buying shoes, not asking for a damn foot rub. His nerves started to sizzle. He studied the assortment of shiny teal-blue bags she held. "Where did you go?"

"Misty Blue. Mariah recommended the shop to me. It's just up the coast."

"Leave it to Mariah," Zane muttered. She had impeccable taste, but she could be indulgent at times.

"Speaking of Mariah, have you heard from her today?"

"Yes, we spoke earlier this morning. Do you need to talk to her about anything in particular?"

She shook her head and lowered her packages to the floor, releasing the handles. "I'm managing for right now." She walked over to lean her elbows on the back of his angular sofa. From his spot on the couch, he had a clear view of her face. "How is her mother doing?"

Zane shook his head. "Not great." He was lucky his mother and father were in their seventies and still quite active living in a retirement community in Arizona. He saw them several times a year. And when something like this happened, he thought about spending more time with them. "Mariah said her mom might have some permanent damage from the stroke, but it's too soon to tell. She spends most of her day at the hospital or meeting with doctors."

"I'm sorry to hear that."

"Yeah, me, too. And with all that, she asked about you. She made me promise to have you call her with any questions."

Jessica sent him a rigid look. "Unless it's an emergency, I'm not going to call her, Zane. You and I both know what it's like having to deal with a family crisis."

A lump formed in his throat. "Yeah. I agree, and I told her as much. There's nothing so important that it can't wait. Between the two of us, we'll figure out what needs figuring from this end."

"Right. Hey, I almost forgot. I bought you a present."

His heavy heart lightened. "You did?"

She bent to forage in one of the bags and came up holding a long, shiny black box. It wasn't a gift from Misty Blue, that was for sure. She stretched as far as her arms could reach, eyeing the box carefully one last time, before handing it over. "I, uh, hope this doesn't upset you, but I know how much you loved the one Janie got you, and, well…this one is from me."

Her fingers gently brushed over his hand, and her caring touch seized his heart for a moment. With his good hand, he managed to lift the lid and gaze at his gift. He found himself momentarily speechless. It was an almost identical replica of a bolo tie with a turquoise stone set on a stamped silver backing that Janie had given him on the anniversary of their first date. It had been lost in the fire, and he'd never replaced it. It wouldn't have had the same sentimental meaning. But the fact that Jessica gave it to him meant something. He lifted the rope tie out of the box and shifted his gaze to her. "It's a thoughtful gift, Jess."

"I know you treasured the first one. I helped Janie pick it out, so I remember exactly what it looked like."

"You didn't have to do this." But he was glad she had.

"You're putting a roof over my head and feeding me, but more importantly, being here is helping me heal. It's the least I could do for you. And I wanted it to be…something special."

"It is. Very special."

He rose from the sofa, found his footing and, using his crutches, shuffled over to her. He gazed through the lenses of her glasses to dewy, softly speckled green eyes. They were warm and friendly and genuine. He bent to kiss her forehead the way a brother would a sister, but then awareness flickered in her eyes, and he felt it, too. He lowered his mouth, heady in his need to taste the giving warmth of her lips again. When he touched his mouth to hers, he savored her sweetness and assigned this moment to memory for safekeeping. He backed away just in time to keep the kiss to one of thanks. "Thank you."

"You're welcome." Her deep, sultry voice thrilled him and churned his stomach at the same time. She sounded so much like Janie.

"I haven't had dinner yet. I waited for you. Mrs. Lopez put our meal in the oven to keep warm. Are you hungry?"

"Starving," she said. "Shopping is tough. I worked up an appetite."

He laughed. The women he knew loved to shop and spend endlessly. He'd never heard one remark about hard work.

"I'll put the bags away in my room. Meet you in the kitchen?"

He nodded. He hated that he couldn't offer to help her. He watched her climb the stairway holding three maxed-out shopping bags in one hand and two in the other. The next time she wanted to shop, he'd be damn ready to take the packages off her hands and carry them upstairs for her.

Zane made his way into the kitchen. Mrs. Lopez had left chicken and dumplings warming in the oven. Zane lifted a periwinkle-striped kitchen towel tucked over a basket and eyed cheesy biscuits, still warm. He dipped into the basket and sank his teeth into a biscuit. Warmth spread throughout his mouth and reminded him he was ready for a hearty meal.

"Wow, smells good in here." Jessica entered the kitchen.

"Mrs. Lopez made one of my favorites tonight."

"In that case, I'm surprised you waited for me."

"I figured a Southern girl like you would appreciate sharing chicken and dumplings. It's my mother's recipe."

"You figured right. Well, then. Have a seat." She gestured to the table. "I'll dish it up. Unless you want to eat outside?"

He shook his head. The sun had already set, and winds howled over the shoreline, spraying sand everywhere. "Here is just fine."

Before he knew it, the table was set, plates were dished up and he had the company of one of his favorite people sitting across from him.

The chicken was tender, the dumplings melted in his mouth and Zane spent the next few minutes quietly diving into his meal. He liked that he could sit in silence with Jess without feeling as though he had to entertain her. She was as comfortable with the quiet as he was.

"Mmm, this was so good." Jess took a last bite of food, and as she wiped her mouth, his gaze drifted down to where the napkin touched her lips. "I'll have to steal the recipe from Mrs. Lopez and make it for my mother when I get home."

"No problem." He shouldn't be noticing the things he was noticing about Jess. Like the cute way she pushed her glasses up her nose, or the way she smelled right after a shower, or how her light skin had burnished to a golden tone from days of sunbathing. The sound of her voice dug deep into his gut. Janie and Jess were the only two women he knew that had a low, raspy yet very feminine voice. Janie had been sultry, sexy, alluring, but…Jess?

"Zane?"

He lifted his gaze to her meadow-green eyes.

"You went someplace just now."

"I'm sorry."

"No need to be sorry. Are you okay?"

He nodded and cleared his throat. "So, did you have fun shopping today?"

"Fun?" Her head tilted as a slow, easy smile spread across her face. "I had an attire concierge help me. That was weirdly entertaining. She dogged my every step but was nice as can be. Actually my best friend, Sally, helped me make the right choices. Sally was my maid of honor in the wedding that never was."

"Is your friend in town?"

She laughed and shook her head. "No, not at all. I texted her pictures of the clothes I tried on, and she helped me decide. I'm *so* not a shopper."

"Ah, the power of technology."

"Yeah, ain't it great?"

It beat having Dylan McKay help her shop. Zane wasn't about to allow that to happen.

A heartbreaking ladies' man was the last thing sweet Jess needed in her life right now.

"Actually, it is pretty great. I'm glad you had a good day."

"I plan to have a lot of good days from now on." A glint of something resolute beamed in her eyes, her face an open expression of hope.

Jess was healing, and that was a good thing. He liked seeing her feeling better. That was the whole point of her coming here. But it seemed too soon. And she seemed a little too happy for a woman who'd been betrayed and heartbroken. Right now, Jessica Holcomb looked ready to conquer the world, or at least Moonlight Beach. Instincts that rarely failed him told him something else was going on with Jess.

And he didn't know if he was going to like it.

"Hi, Zane." Jessica stepped into the living room, dressed and ready for Dylan's party.

Zane turned from the window… His hair was combed back, shiny and straight, the stubble on his face a reflection of not having a shave in two days. He looked gorgeous in a white billowy shirt and light khaki trousers. When his gaze fell on the *new* her, his lips parted and his eyes popped as he took in her appearance from the top of her head to her sandaled toes. Pain entered his eyes, and he blinked several times as if trying to make it go away. Relying on the two crutches under his arms, he straightened to his full height and sighed heavily.

"Zane?" Her lips began to quiver. What was wrong with him? "Are you all right?"

He stared at her, his expression unreadable. "I'm fine."

"Are you? Have I done something? Don't you like the dress?" Her mind rushed back to the clothes she'd laid out on the bed. She'd chosen the cornflower-blue sundress that accented her slender waist in a scoop-neck design that, granted, revealed more cleavage that she was comfortable with, but wasn't indecent by any means.

His mouth opened partly, but no words tumbled forth, and then he gulped as if swallowing his words.

"What is it?" she pressed.

"You look like Janie," he rushed out, as though once pressured, he couldn't stop himself from saying it.

"I…do?"

How could she possibly look like Janie? Janie was stunning. She had natural beauty, a perfectly symmetrical face. She wore stylish clothes, had the prettiest long, silken hair, and oh…now she understood. Of course she and Janie resembled each other—they were sisters—but Jessica had always stood in Janie's shadow where beauty was concerned. Her blonde-from-a-bottle hair color had turned out a little less dark honey and much more sweet wheat, similar to Janie's hair color. Jessica didn't usually wear her contacts, but she imagined her eyes looked more vibrant green than ever before. Like Janie's brilliant gemstone eyes. Did Zane think he was seeing a ghost of his former wife? She didn't believe she looked enough like Janie for that and never thought about how it might appear. "I, um, wasn't trying to, but I take that as a compliment." She shrugged, compelled to explain. "I guess I needed a change."

An awkward moment passed between them, which was weird. They didn't do awkward. Usually they were completely at peace with each other.

"You didn't need to change a thing," he said firmly.

Was he trying to make her feel better? Even she had to admit, after looking at herself in the mirror today, that her new look made her appear revitalized and well, better than she had in years. Zane had no idea what she was really going through right now, the pain, rejection, anger. He didn't know, because she hadn't told him. He wasn't her shrink, her sounding board. And call it pride, but she wasn't ready to talk about Steven's quick marriage to her once-friend/bridesmaid to anyone, much less him. "I'm sorry if I upset you. Obviously you don't approve. I don't have to go tonight."

The last thing she wanted to do was cause Zane any upheaval in his life. He was still in love with Janie. She got that. No one knew what a special person her sister was better than she did.

She was staying here thanks to Zane's generosity. He was her employer now, too, and she had to remember that, yet underlying hurt simmered inside her. He had no idea how hard this was for her. She'd come into this room hoping for some sort of approval. She'd made a change in her appearance, but it was more than that. She looked upon this makeover as a fresh start, a way to say "screw you" to all the Stevens in the world. She'd come into this room with newfound confidence, and Zane's dismal attitude had caused her heart to plummet. Why did it matter so much to her what Zane thought?

She pivoted on her heels, taking a step toward the staircase, and Zane's voice boomed across the room. "Damn it, Jess. Don't leave."

She whirled around and stared at him. A dark storm raged in his eyes.

Was he angry with her? Maybe she should be angry with him. Maybe she'd had enough of men dictating what they wanted from her. "Is that an order from the boss?"

"Hell, no." His head thumped against the window behind him once, twice, and then he lowered his voice. "It wasn't an order."

"Then what was it?"

Zane's gaze scoured over her body again, and as he took in her appearance, approval, desire and *heat* entered his eyes. Her bones could have just about melted from that look. Then, with a quick shake of his head, he said, "Nothing, I guess. Jess, you don't need my approval for anything. Fact is, you look beautiful tonight. You surprised me and, well…I don't like surprises."

She didn't move. She was torn with indecision.

From the depth of his eyes, his sincerity came through. "I'm a jerk."

Her lips almost lifted. She fought it tooth and nail, but Zane could be charming when he had to be.

"Blond hair looks great on you."

She drew breath into her lungs.

"The dress is killer. You're a real knockout in it."

His compliments went straight to her head. He'd finally gotten to her. "Okay, Zane. Enough said." She'd been touchy with him, maybe because she'd hoped to impress him a little. Maybe because, in the back of her mind, she'd wanted to please Zane or at least win his approval. "Let's forget about this." She didn't like confrontation, not one bit.

"You'll go to the party?"

She nodded. "Yes. I'm ready."

They'd had their first real argument. Granted, it wasn't much of one. A few minutes of tension was all. But she'd stood her ground, and she could feel good about that. One thing that loving Steven had taught her was never to turn a blind eye. From now on, she wanted to deal in absolute truth.

"You mind driving?" he asked.

"I should make you trudge through the sand all the way to Dylan's place."

"I'd do it if it would put a smile back on your face."

"It's tempting. But I'm not that cruel."

Amused, Zane's mouth lifted, and they seemed back on even footing again.

Whatever that was.

Six

Zane stood outside in the shadows, his shoulder braced against the wall of Dylan's home. The setting sun cast pastel colors across the cobalt sky, and waves pounded the shoreline. The Pacific breezes had died down and no longer lifted Jessica's blond locks into a flowing silky sheet in the wind. She stood in front of a circular fire pit on the deck. Her flowery summer dress had been a victim of the wind, too, and hell if he hadn't noticed her hem billow up, *every single time*. And every single time, something powerful zinged inside him.

He couldn't figure why Jessica had made such a drastic turnabout in her appearance. He wouldn't have called her an ugly duckling before—she'd been perfect in her own natural way—but tonight, she'd bloomed into a beautiful swan and he feared he was in deep trouble.

He liked her. A lot. And he knew damn well she was as off-limits to him as any woman would ever be. The old Jess he could deal with. She was like his kid sister. But now, as he watched the predusk light filter through her hair and heard the sound of her sultry laughter carry to him as she spoke with Dylan and his friends, she seemed like a different woman.

Sweet Jess was a knockout, and every man here had noticed.

Dylan popped his head up from the group and gestured to him. "Come on over and join the party."

Well, damn. He couldn't very well stay in the shadows the entire night. He'd have to shelve his confused thoughts about Jessica and join them. He pushed off from the wall using his crutches for balance and made his way over to the fire pit.

"I thought Adam was the only recluse on the beach," Dylan said.

"There's a difference between savoring one's privacy as opposed to hiding out from the world," Adam said.

Adam Chase was his next-door neighbor, the architect of many of the homes on the beachfront and a man who didn't give much away about himself. He'd been featured in *Architectural Digest* and agreed to a rare magazine interview, but mostly the man's astonishing work spoke for itself. The one thing he'd learned about Adam in the time he'd known him was that he shied away from attention.

"He's got you there, Dylan. Being someone who craves attention, you wouldn't understand." Zane zinged him because he knew Dylan was a good sport and could handle the teasing.

Dylan took Jess's hand, entwining their fingers. "They're ganging up on me, Jess. I need someone in my corner."

Jess's giggles swept over Zane, and he eyed the half-empty blended mojito she held in her other hand. She freed her hand and inched away from Dylan. It was hardly a noticeable move, except maybe to Zane, who was eyeballing her every step. "You boys are on your own. I'm staying out of this."

Dylan slammed his hand to his chest. "Oh, you're breaking my heart, Jess."

Adam's eyes flickered over Jess and touched on the valley between her breasts in the revealing sundress she wore. She was dazzling tonight, and Zane had a hard time keeping

his eyes off her, too. He shouldn't fault the guys for flirting, yet every inappropriate glance at her boiled his blood.

"You're a smart woman, Jessica," Adam said.

"The smartest," Zane added. "She's going home with
me tonight."

All eyes turned his way. Ah, hell. He'd shocked them,
but no more than he'd shocked himself. He spared Dylan a
glance, and the guy's smug grin was bright enough to light
the night sky. Adam's face was unreadable, and the four
others around the fire pit became awkwardly silent. "She's
my houseguest and she's…"

"I think what Zane meant," Jess chimed in, "was that I've
had a tough time lately. I'm getting over a broken engagement and, well, he's sweet enough to want to protect me."
Her eyes scanned the seven people sitting around the fire
pit. "Not that I'd need protecting from anyone here. You've
all been so nice and welcoming."

They had. And now Zane felt like an ass for staking his
claim when he had no right and for putting her in an awkward position.

"But I do make my own decisions. And I'd love to get to
know each of you better."

"You *are* a smart woman." Dylan turned to Zane with
genuine understanding. He and Dylan had had this conversation before. "And we all knew what Zane was getting at."

Zane clamped his mouth shut for the moment. He'd said
enough, and he had a feeling that Jessica wasn't too thrilled
with him right now. His big brother act had probably started
to wear thin on her. He didn't say boo when she walked
down to the water deep in conversation with Adam Chase
for a few minutes. He didn't register an inkling of irritation
when Dylan offered to give her a tour of his house. But darn
if he wasn't keenly relieved when Jessica made friends with
three of the women at the party. She'd spent a good deal of
time with them. He recognized one woman as an actress

recently cast in a film about a Southern girl. She'd gobbled up a good deal of time asking Jess questions about Texas.

"You look like you could use a beer." Adam handed him one of the two longnecks he clasped between his fingers.

"You read my mind. That sounds good." Adam's mouth twitched. The man didn't often smile, but obviously Zane had amused him. "Right. How's the restaurant coming?"

Zane had asked Adam for a recommendation of someone whose specialty was designing shoreline commercial establishments since Adam didn't work with small restaurants. "We've broken ground. The framework is up, and we should open our doors in a few months. I'm hoping for Labor Day."

"Glad things are going smoothly."

He nodded. Last year, he'd opened a restaurant in Reno, and his friend and CEO of Sentinel Construction had overseen the building. But Casey's business didn't reach the west coast, and Adam had connections all over the world. He wound up hiring a builder Adam said was top-notch. "They seem to be."

Adam sipped his beer. "Jessica seems like a nice girl. She said she's indirectly related to you."

Indirectly? Though those were true words, it still stung hearing them coming from her mouth secondhand that way. There was something painful in the truth, and if he was being gut-honest with himself, it was liberating, as well. "Uh, yeah. She was my wife's little sis. She's staying in Moonlight Beach for a while."

"With you. Yes, you made that clear earlier." Adam's mouth hitched again. It was more animation than Zane had seen in the guy practically since he'd met him. "I'm going out on a limb here, but either you're hooked on her, or you've got a bad case of Big Brother syndrome."

Zane peered over Adam's shoulder and caught a glimpse of Jessica speaking with a man who looked enough like Dylan to be his twin. "Who the hell is that?"

Adam swiveled his head and gave the guy a once-over.

"Dylan introduced him to me before you arrived. That's Roy. He's Dylan's stunt double."

Roy and Jessica stood in the sand under the light of a tiki torch and away from the crowd of people beginning to swarm the barbecue pit, where a chef prepared food on the grill. Zane didn't like it, but he couldn't very well pull her away from every guy who approached her.

"So, which is it?" Adam asked.

"Which is what?" He watched Jessica laugh at something Roy said.

"Are you playing big brother? Cause if you're not, I think you have to amp up your game, neighbor. Or you're going to lose something special, before you know what hit you."

Zane stared at Adam. The guy had no clue what he was talking about. Adam had no idea how hard he'd loved Janie. He had no idea how he couldn't get past what happened. He'd tried over and over to put his emotions to lyrics, to gain some sort of closure in a song meant to honor his love for Janie, but the words wouldn't come. "I've already lost—"

Adam began shaking his head. "I'm not talking about the past, Zane. I'm talking about the future."

"Spoken by a man who rarely steps foot out of his house."

Now Adam did laugh. "I'm here now, aren't I?"

"Yeah, that surprises me. Why are you?"

He shrugged. "I've got a temperamental artist painting a wall in my gallery. It's going to be fantastic when he's through, and he insists on complete privacy. I'm staying at Dylan's for a few days."

"Well, damn. You're sorta here by default, then."

"It's not so bad. At least I got to meet Jessica and all her Southern charm."

"Why, that's very nice of you to say, Adam."

A sweet strawberry scent wafted to his nostrils, announcing Jessica's presence even before she'd uttered a word.

He'd come to recognize her scent, and every time she approached, a little bitty buzz would rush through his belly. She took a place by his side, and he refrained from puffing out his chest.

"Just speaking the truth," Adam said.

"Hey, Jess," Zane said.

"Hey, yourself," she said to him. He wasn't sure if she'd been deliberately avoiding him since his dopey remark earlier, or if she was flitting around like a butterfly to make new friends. Either way, he was glad she'd come over to him.

"Having fun?"

"Sure am. I'm meeting some great people here. It was sweet of Dylan to invite me. Sorry if I abandoned you."

He raised his beer bottle to his lips. "No problem. I spent my time keeping Adam amused."

Jessica shot a questioning glance at Adam.

"He's quite a party animal these days," Adam explained, tucking his free hand into his trouser pockets.

Zane gulped the rest of his beer. He wouldn't be here if Jessica hadn't changed her mind about coming. "C'mon Jess. Looks like the meal's being served. I've got me a hankering for some barbecue chicken."

"Adam, will you join us?" she asked.

Adam shook his head. "I'll see you over at the table later. I'm going to have another drink first."

Zane began moving, and Jessica kept by his side as he headed for a table occupying the far corner of the massive patio. "Chances are we won't see much of Adam tonight. He keeps to himself pretty much."

"Does he?" she asked. "Why?"

"I don't really know. We got friendly when I leased the house from him. And we had some business dealings, but I sensed he's a loner. It's probably why he was standing with me, over against the wall."

"Well, he was cordial to me."

"Yeah, I know." Zane dipped his gaze to the swell of her breasts teasing the top of her frilly sundress. Her skin looked creamy soft and—Lord help him—inviting. With that blond hair flowing down her back and her eyes as green as a grassy meadow, she made his heart ache. "I saw the two of you walking out to the water."

"All I did was ask him about his designs. Architecture has always fascinated me."

"Yeah, that's probably why he spent time with you. He loves talking shop." Lucky for him, Jess didn't notice the sarcasm in his voice. He managed to pull a chair out for her, crutches and all.

Man, he'd be glad to rid himself of them.

It couldn't happen soon enough.

They'd stayed at the party a little too long. Zane was smashed, going over his liquor limit an hour ago, and now she struggled to get him out of the car. He obviously didn't take his own advice. Hadn't he warned her of not drinking too much, because in his handicapped state, he wouldn't be able to help her? Well…now the shoe was on the other foot. "Hang on to me," she said, reaching inside the car.

"Glad to, darlin'."

He slung his arm around her shoulder, nearly pulling her onto his lap.

"Zane!"

An earthy laugh rumbled from his throat.

"Not cute."

"Neither are y-you," he said.

After a few seconds of maneuvering, she managed to get him upright.

"You're b-beautiful."

Oh, boy. She rolled her eyes and ignored his comment.

He swayed to the left. Sure-footed he was not. She leaned him up against the car. "Here." She shoved a crutch under his arm, tucking it carefully but none too gently. "Please, please, try to concentrate."

Maybe she should've taken Dylan up on his offer to drive Zane home. But Zane wouldn't have any of it, insisting he could manage.

Men and their egos.

Now she had two hundred pounds of sheer brawn and muscle to contend with. "Lean against me, Zane. Try not to topple. Ready?"

He nodded forcefully, and his whole body coasted away from her. "Whoa!" She gripped him around the waist and tugged with all of her might to bring him close. Letting him go right now would be a disaster. "Don't make sudden moves like that."

"Mmm."

He sounded happy about something. She was glad someone was enjoying this. When he seemed secure in his stance, she took a step and then another. With his body pressed to hers and one shoulder supporting his arm, she managed to get him through the garage and inside the house. By the time she made it to his bed, her strength was almost sapped. "Here we go. I'm going to let go of you now."

"Don't," he said.

"Why? Are you feeling dizzy?"

He shook his head, and his arm tightened around her shoulder. She was trapped in his warmth, his heat. And as she gazed up into his eyes, they cleared. Just like that. The haze that seemed to keep him in a woozy state was gone. "No. I'm feeling pretty damn good. Because you're here with me. Because I can't get you out of my head."

As if his own weight was too much to bear, he sat down, taking her with him. She plopped on the bed, and the mattress sighed. Streaming moonlight filtered into the room, and their reflection in the window bounced back at her. Two souls, searching for something that they'd lost. Was that what the attraction was?

"Are you drunk?" she asked.

"Not too much anymore." He pushed aside her hair at her nape, his touch as gentle as a Texas breeze. He nipped her there, his teeth scraping around to the top of her throat and the sensation claimed all the breath in her lungs.

"You sobered up fast," she whispered, barely able to form a coherent thought. Having his delicious mouth taking liberties on her neck was pure heaven.

"I know when I want something."

His nips were heady, and she tilted her head to the side, offering him more of her throat. "Wh-what do you want?"

With his good hand under her chin, he turned her head, and then his lips were on hers, pressing firm against her softness, igniting fireworks that started with her brain and rushed all the way down to her belly. She turned to him, roping her arm around his neck, kissing him back. He smelled like pure male animal, his scent mingling with whiskey and heat. Her breasts perked up, and her nipples pebbled against the silky material of her dress.

"I want to kiss you again and again," he rasped over her lips. "I want to touch your body and have you touch mine. I need you, too. So badly, sweetheart."

Oh, wow. Oh, wow. Oh, wow. A fierce physical attraction pulled at her like a giant magnet. She couldn't fight the force or the combustible chemistry between them. And Zane didn't give her time to refuse. With his left hand, he began unbuttoning his shirt and did a lousy job of slipping the buttons free until she came to his rescue.

"Let me." She shoved his hand away and quickly finished for him. With his shirt open now, his chest was a work of art, muscled and bronzed. She itched to touch him, to put her hands exactly where he wanted her to. She inhaled, and as she released a breath, she spread her palms over his hot, moist skin. From the contours of his waist up his torso to where crisp chest hairs tickled the underside of her fingers, she savored each inch of him.

A guttural groan exploded in the room, and she wasn't sure if she'd made that sound, but one look into Zane's eyes darkened by desire and she knew it wasn't her.

He was on fire. His skin sizzled hot and steamy, his breathing hitched and all of that combined was enough to blanket her body with burning heat. "We can't," she said softly.

She had to say it. Because of Janie. Because of Steven. She and Zane were both trying to heal, but none of that resonated right now. None of it seemed powerful enough to derail the sensations whipping them into a frenzied state.

Maybe this was what both of them needed.

One night.

His mouth claimed her again as he lay down on the bed, tugging her along with him. She fell beside him. Promptly he snaked his arm under her waist and flipped her on top of him.

She had his answer. Yes, they could.

His good hand cupped her cheek, and his eyes bored into her. "Don't question this, Jess. Not if it's what you want right now."

That was Zane. The man who didn't plan for the future anymore, the man who'd said it was better sometimes not to know where you were going. And Jessica certainly didn't have a clue what her future held or where the heck she was going from here.

But she knew what she wanted tonight.

How could she not? Her breasts were crushed against Zane's chest, her body trembling and so ready for whatever would come next. Zane was a good, decent man who also happened to be sexy as sin but he had also been her sis— She stopped thinking. Enough. She might talk herself out of this. "It's what I want."

He gave her a serious smile and kissed her again, his lips soft and tender, taking his time with her, making her come apart in small doses.

In the moment, Jessica gave herself permission to let go completely. He pushed the straps down on her dress and her breasts popped free of restraint. Zane caressed her, running his hand over her sensitive skin, lightly touching one wanton crest that seemed made for his touch.

A deep moan rose from her throat. She closed her eyes and enjoyed every second of his tender ministrations. "You have a beautiful body, sweetheart," he said, then rose up to place his mouth over one breast, his tongue flicking the nub, wetting it in a flurry of sweeps. He moved to the other side and did the same, a little more frenzied, faster, rougher. She squealed, the exquisite pain sending shock waves down past her belly.

Zane reacted with a jerk of his hips. "Get naked for me, Jess."

She pulled her dress over her shoulders, and he helped as much as he could to lift it the rest of the way off. She gave it a gentle toss to the floor and straddled him, bare but for her panties, and looking into eyes that seemed distant for a moment. "Are you sure about this?" he rasped, his brows gathering.

He was giving her a way out, but she was in too deep now. Her body hummed from his touch and the promise of the pulsing manhood beneath her. She wanted more…she wanted it all.

She was the *new* Jess.

"I'm sure, Zane."

He nodded and blew out a breath in apparent relief, but there was something else. A part of him seemed undecided. It was only a feeling she had, a vibe that worried her in some small part of her consciousness. Don't think. Don't think. Don't think.

The new Jess wasn't a thinker. She was a doer.

She bent to his mouth, her sensitized nipples reaching his chest first. He bucked under her. "Oh, man, babe." She smiled at him and opened her mouth, coaxing his tongue to play with hers. His strokes made her dizzy, and her desire for him soared. She was almost ready. She reached for his zipper.

"No," he said. He gently rolled her to her side and leaned over her. "There might be something I'm good at with my left hand."

A smile broke out on her face, but Zane wiped the smile away the second his fingers probed inside her panties. He cupped her there, and a melodic sigh escaped her throat. He kissed her, swallowing the rest of her sounds as he stroked her with deft fingers. Her body moved, arched, reached as he became more and more merciless. "Zane," she cried.

She climbed over the top immediately, her limbs shaking, her breathing quickened and labored. A drawn-out, piercing scream rang from her throat. She was cocooned in heat. Zane held her patiently while her tingles ebbed and she came down to earth.

"Reach over to the bed stand, sweetheart," he said as she caught her breath. "Dig deep in the drawer." He nuzzled her ear and said softly, "It's been a while."

Seconds later, with a little of her help, he was sheathed. She reeled from the passion she witnessed in his eyes. It wasn't lust, but something more. Something she could feel good about when she remembered this night. They were connected, always had been, and right now all things powerful in the universe were pulling her toward this man.

"Ready?" he asked.

As she nodded, boldly she lifted her leg over his waist to straddle him. Both of his hands came around her back, encouraging her to lean down. She did, and he pressed a dozen molten kisses to her mouth before he set her onto him.

Instinctively she rose up, and he helped guide her down. The tip of his shaft teased her entrance, and she closed her eyes.

"So beautiful," she heard him say softly as he filled her body.

They moved together as one, his thrusts setting the pace. Her heart beat rapid-fire; she was in the Zane zone now and offered to him everything he wanted to take.

He was all she could ever hope for in a lover. His kiss drove her crazy, and he was more adept with one good hand than the men she'd known in the past who'd had the use of both. He explored her body with tender kisses and bold touches, with harmonious rhythm and unexpected caresses. He was wild and tender, sweet and wicked. And when he pressed her for finality that he seemingly couldn't hold back another second, her release astonished and satisfied her. "Wow," she whimpered, her body still buzzing. She lay sated and spent on the bed.

"Yeah, babe. Wow." Zane sighed heavily, an uncomplicated sound telling her how much pleasure she'd brought him. She wasn't sorry. She had no regrets. But then, she hadn't let her mind wander since she'd entered Zane's bedroom. She didn't want to think. Not now.

Zane wrapped his arm around her, tucking her into him, and soon the sound of his quiet breaths steadied. With all that he'd consumed tonight, there was no reason to hope that he would wake soon.

She closed her eyes, savoring the safety and serenity the night brought to her.

Zane's eyes snapped open to the ceiling above. It was funny how the crater-like texture seemed odd to him this morning. He'd never noticed it before. Back home, solid wood beams supported the house. The rich smell of pines and oaks and cedar lent warmth and gave him a true sense of belonging. He missed home, longed for it actually, but how in hell could he complain? He lived in a rich man's paradise, on a sandy windswept beach with dazzling pastel sunsets and beautiful people surrounding him.

He didn't have to look over to know Jess wasn't beside him on the bed. He'd heard her exit the room in the wee hours of the morning. He should've stopped her. He should've reached out and tugged her back to bed. If he had, she'd be here with him now, and he would nestle into her warmth again.

Sweet Jess. *Sexy Jess.*

Oxygen pushed out of his lungs. He was still feeling the effects of last night. The alcohol, the soft woman—the entire night played back in his mind. He was in deep now.

He hinged his body up and swiveled his feet over the bed to meet with the floor. He made a grab for his crutches that lay against the wall and luckily hung on to them. Rising, still wearing the pants he'd worn last night, he ambled from the bedroom to the living room. From there, he spotted Jess pressed against the deck railing in a pair of sexy shorts and a ruffled blouse, gazing out to sea. It was just after dawn, and the beach was empty but for a few seagulls milling about. Low curling waves splashed against the shore almost silently. It was a beautiful time of day.

Made even more beautiful by his golden-haired houseguest.

As quietly as a man on crutches could, he made his way out the double French doors and headed toward her. Her concentration was intense, and she didn't hear him approach until he was behind her. He put his crutches near the wall and braced his arms on the railing, trapping her in his embrace.

She stood with her back to his chest. Her hair whipped in the breeze and tickled his cheeks as he nibbled on her nape. She tasted like a woman who'd had a delicious night of sex. She smelled like a woman who'd been sated and well loved. He breathed her in. "Mornin', Jess."

"Hmm."

"Wish you hadn't left my bed. Wish you were still in there with me."

As she nodded, she leaned her head against his shoulder. "I don't know what we're doing," she said softly.

"Helping each other heal, maybe." He nipped the soft skin under her ear. "All I know is, I haven't felt this alive in a long time. And that's because of you."

"It's only because I remind you of—"

"Home." He wouldn't allow her to think for a second she was a replacement for his dead wife. He wasn't certain in his own mind that wasn't the case—her transformation last night had knocked the vinegar out of him, she'd looked so much like Janie—but he didn't want Jess believing it. What kind of a scoundrel would that make him? "But it's more than that. You remind me of the good things in my life."

"You're romanticizing about Beckon. It's really not all that."

In a way, they were both in the same situation. She'd had her heart broken. Of course she wouldn't look upon home with fond memories now. He couldn't go home because it wouldn't be the same. He blamed himself for Janie's death, and the guilt wracked him ten ways to Sunday, each and every day. "Maybe you're right, sweetheart."

Memories being what they were, he couldn't deny he held Beckon close to his heart. But he didn't need to win this round with Jessica today.

"I don't have a single regret about last night. Well, except that I had the damn boot and cast still on."

She turned away from the ocean and captured his attention with her pretty fresh-meadow eyes. "Not one, Zane? Not one regret?"

He blinked at the intensity of her question. This was important to her. "No."

What he had were doubts. He wasn't ready for anything heavy, with her or anyone else. The thought of entering into a relationship gave him hives. He might never be ready. He'd removed himself from any thoughts of the future and lived in the present. He'd shut himself off for two years. It was safe. His haven of sanity.

"Are you regretting what happened last night?" He wasn't sure he wanted to hear her answer.

Her chin lifted as she thought about it for an eternity of seconds. "*Regret* isn't the right word. I think you're right. We both needed each other."

"We don't have to attach any labels to last night," Zane said. "It just happened." He wanted it to happen again. But it wasn't his decision. He was smart enough to know that.

"But where do we go from here?"

Breezes blew her hair off her shoulders, the golden strands dancing in the morning light. Her face was clean of makeup, glowing with a fresh-washed look. All of Zane's impulses heightened.

"First," he said, dipping his head to her mouth, "I give you a good morning kiss." He pressed his lips to hers and kissed her soundly. She made a tiny noise in the back of her throat that made him smile inside. He could kiss her until the sun set and wouldn't tire of it. He inched away from her face as her eyes opened, glowing with warmth. God, she was sweet. "If you're inclined to do some cooking this morning, we have breakfast. Mrs. Lopez doesn't work on Sunday. And then we do whatever comes natural. No pressure, Jess."

He'd had sex with Janie's younger sister. He should be beating himself up about that now, but oddly he wasn't. He couldn't figure the why of it. Why was being with Jess making him feel better about himself instead of worse? He had nothing to offer her but strong arms to hold her and a warm body to comfort her, if she needed them. He couldn't pursue her. It wouldn't be fair to her, but that didn't stop him from wanting her.

A soft, relieved breath blew from her lips. "That sounds good to me, Zane." She gave him a sweet smile and handed him his crutches. "Meet me in the kitchen in half an hour."

His gaze landed on the curvy form of her backside as she strode inside the house. He hung his head. Oh, man. He was in deep.

Life at 211 Moonlight Drive wasn't going to get any easier.

Seven

Two and a half months after his accidental fall off a Los Angeles stage, Zane had gotten a good report from his doctor. His foot had healed nicely and was now out of the cast. His wrist had taken longer than expected to heal, but that, too, was in great shape and cast-free. Jessica was almost as relieved as he was, hearing the news today after driving him to his appointment. Zane had never gotten used to the crutches and now, with a little physical therapy, he'd be back to normal, good as new. And her duties wouldn't be so up close and personal with him any longer. She could concentrate on work and try to forget about making love with him two nights ago.

The new Jess would've let it go by now.

But traces of the old Jess were resurfacing, and she wanted to kick her to the curb. Falling in love with Zane would be a bonehead stupid move. He was still in love with Janie, and nothing much could persuade her otherwise. How could she be sure that the night they'd had sex wasn't more about her resemblance to her sister than any intense affection Zane had for her?

"I feel like celebrating," Zane said as she drove toward the gates of his home.

"I bet you do. But you can't go dancing just yet. You have to get through physical therapy."

From out of the corner of her eye, she spied Zane flexing his hand. "I'm fine. Just dandy. Even wearing my own boots for a change."

She took her eyes off the road for a split second to gaze at his expensive boots. Snakeskin. Gorgeous. Studded black leather. They made her mouth water. "You do know you live on the beach. Sandals are expected. Even admired."

A belly laugh rolled out of his mouth. "I could say the same about you. Lately, you've been wearing those high-falutin heels."

"Me?" Yes, it was true. The new Jess wore pricey heels when she wasn't in her morning walk tennis shoes.

"Yeah, you. Admit it. You're happier in a pair of soft leather boots with flat heels than those skyscrapers you've taken to wearing. Not that I mind. You look hot in those heels."

The compliment lit her up inside, but she couldn't let him see how it affected her. She lowered her sunglasses and gave him a deadpan look.

He grinned.

The man was in a great mood today, happier than she'd seen him in days. It was certainly better than putting up with his sourpuss, like on Sunday afternoon when he'd balked at her going to Dylan's house for the screening of *Time of Her Life*. She'd thought he'd be okay with it. After all, he'd said to do what came natural, and she had promised Dylan she'd be there. When she'd walked in past nine, missing dinner with him, he'd been sullen and distant, none too pleased with her.

Yes, they'd had sex the night before, and it had been amazing. Surely Zane had to know that Dylan McKay, handsome as he was, didn't strike her fancy. She'd gone because she'd promised and because she needed time away from Zane to clear her head, yet that entire afternoon and evening, she'd wondered if she'd made a mistake by going to Dylan's.

"You know what I feel like doing?" Zane asked, breaking into her thoughts.

"I'm afraid to ask."

"I feel like taking a dip."

"In your Jacuzzi? That's a good idea. I bet the warm water—"

"In the ocean, Jess. Tonight, after dinner."

She pulled through the gates and drove along the winding road to his house. "I don't know if that's wise, Zane. You shouldn't push it. You only just—"

"I'm going, Jess." He set his face stubbornly, and she couldn't think of anything to say to change his mind. "I've been confined long enough."

Pulling into the garage, she cut the engine. "I get that, but I won't be—"

Oh, shoot. He wasn't going to like this.

"Won't be what?"

"Home after dinner."

"Another shopping trip?"

A lie could fall from her lips very easily. But she wasn't going to lie to Zane. "No. I'm invited over to your neighbor's house."

Zane's lips thinned. "Dylan again?"

"Adam Chase."

Zane's eyes sharpened on her. "You're going over to Adam's tonight?"

"I kind of didn't give him a choice the other night. He was telling me about his new artwork, and I hinted at wanting to see it. I guess he was just being nice by inviting me over." She'd been a little stunned and humbled when he'd asked her since, according to Zane, invitations from Adam were rare.

Zane closed his eyes briefly. "That's Adam. Mr. Nice Guy."

"You don't think he is?"

Zane snorted. "I think he's a genius. But I don't know much about his personal life."

"I don't want to know about his personal life, either. This isn't anything, Zane." If only she could melt the disapproval off his face with an explanation. "It's just me, being curious. The teacher in me loves learning."

They'd been carefully dancing around what had happened between them. It seemed neither wanted to bring the subject up. So how could she admit that she'd rather be home with him? That after making love with him, it was better that they spend time apart. Too much alone time with him could prove disastrous. One disaster per decade was her limit. One disaster in her entire life would be preferable.

She cared deeply for Zane, thought he was gorgeous and more appealing than any man she'd ever met, but she couldn't be dumb again. And that meant not reading too much into having sex with him, wonderful as it was. She rationalized it was all about healing. Isn't that how Zane passed it off?

"I'm sure Adam wouldn't mind if you joined me."

He reached for the door handle. "I've seen his house, Jess. You go on. Have a nice time," he said through tight lips.

She didn't buy his comment for a second, but she clamped her mouth shut, and as he opened the car door, she rushed around the front end to meet him. Putting his good foot down, he braced his hands on the sides of the car and brought himself up and out.

"Lean on me," she said. "I'm here if you need me."

"I'll make it just fine."

She moved out of his way, and he walked slowly but on his own power, his boots scraping the garage floor as he made his way into the house.

Her shoulders fell, and black emptiness seemed to swallow her up. She wanted Zane to need her.

Or maybe, she just plain wanted Zane. Either way

wasn't an option. She couldn't very well count the days until Mariah returned. Nobody knew when that would be.

But for the first time, she hoped it would be soon.

Zane leaned his elbows over his deck banister, grateful to be on his own two feet now. His gaze focused on Jess as she made her way down the deck steps to the beach. "Bye, Zane. I won't be long."

Her sultry voice hammered inside his brain. It was unique, and he was beginning to hear the slight nuances that differed from her sister's. There was more sugary rasp and a lightness in her tone that made him think of only good things.

She held the straps of her heeled sandals up by two fingers and waved at him once her bare feet hit the sand. In her other hand, she held a flashlight to guide her way over to Adam's house. It wasn't too far, just about one hundred yards from back door to back door, but the half moon's light wasn't enough illumination on the darkened beach, so the flashlight was a good idea.

Her blond hair touched the top of a nipped-at-the-waist snowy white dress that flared out to just above her knees. She looked ethereal in a delicate way that would turn any man's head.

"Bye" he heard himself growl, and lifted his hand up, a semiwave back, watching her trudge through the sand and out of his line of vision.

She was determined to go, yet he'd noted a flicker in her eyes earlier, a moment of doubt as if she waited for him to tell her to stay. He wanted her, and his newly healed body was in a state of arousal around her most of the time now, but he held back. He let her go off to another man's house tonight instead of giving in to his lust.

Was he an idiot or being smart, for her sake?

His cell phone rang, and he plucked it from his pocket. It was probably Mariah. She'd been a saint, checking in and worrying about him when she was the one who needed the support. He'd had Jess send her flowers this morning to cheer her up.

He answered the ring. "Hello?"

"Hello, Zane. This is Mae."

His brows rose. It wasn't Mariah after all, but Jessica's mother. "Hi, Mae. This is a nice surprise."

"I hope so. Zane, how are you feeling these days?"

"Better. I'm out of my cast and healing up real good. And how are you, Mae?"

"I could be better. You know I'm an eternal worrier. And I'm worried about my Jess. I haven't heard from her in three days."

"Is that unusual?"

"Yes, very. She usually checks in with me every day or every other day. We've been playing phone tag over the weekend, and I can't seem to reach her. She didn't answer my call today. I wondered if something was wrong with her phone. Thought it'd be best to check in with you."

"Well...I can assure you, she's doing fine."

"Really?"

"Yes, ma'am."

"That's a relief. I thought after I gave her the news, she'd be crushed. My dear girl has been through a lot this past month. She can't be happy about Steven."

Steven? Just hearing the guy's name made his hand ball into a fist. "What news is that, Mae?"

"I couldn't hide it from my sweet girl. She didn't need to hear it from anyone else but her mama."

"Yes, I think you were right." Zane hadn't a clue what she was getting at, but he knew Mae. She'd eventually get around to telling him what was going on.

"Can you imagine her bridesmaid, Judy, running off with Steven to get married? Why, she'd been like a member of our family when the girls were younger. And Steven? I thought I knew that boy. I'd like to wallop both of them for the hurt they put my daughter through."

His face tightened and he squeezed his eyes shut, wishing like hell he could give that jerk a piece of his mind. And to add to the insult, he'd run away with one of Jess's good friends. A woman who'd vowed to stand up for her at her wedding.

Something clicked in his head. "Wait a minute, Mae. When did you tell Jess about this?"

"Oh, let me see. It must have been on Thursday. Yes, that's right. I remember, because I was getting my hair done at the salon and, well, it was the talk of the entire beauty shop. I felt so bad when I heard, I walked out after my cut with a wet head, didn't bother having my hair styled. All I kept thinking about was my Jess and how she would take the news. But you know, when I told her, I was surprised at her reaction. She seemed calm. I think she was in shock. Have you noticed anything different about her, lately?"

Had he? Hell, yeah. Now he understood her transformation. She'd dyed her hair blond, gotten rid of her eyeglasses, starting wearing provocative clothes. Was it rebellion? Or worse yet, had Jess decided to throw caution to the wind and... No, he wouldn't let his mind go there. She wasn't promiscuous. She was a woman who'd been betrayed by people she trusted. He could only imagine what hearing that news did to her.

And what had he done? She'd come into the room the night of party and he'd shot her down, doing the unthinkable by telling her she looked like Janie in a voice that held nothing but disapproval. He'd been selfish, thinking only about how much it hurt to look at her that way. If he was damn honest with himself, seeing that daring side of Jess had excited him. He hadn't known how to handle his initial reaction to her. She almost didn't go to the party because he'd given her a hard time about the way she looked, gorgeous as she was.

And he'd been jealous because he couldn't have her, and yet he didn't want any other man going after her, either. Wow. What a revelation.

"Zane, I asked if Jessica has been acting differently lately?"

Uh, yeah. But in this case, he saw no reason not to bend the truth a little. "She's been keeping busy, Mae. She tells me she likes the work. And she's made a few friends here, too. She seems to fit in real nice. In fact, she's visiting my neighbor now. When she comes in, I'll be sure to tell her you called."

"I'm happy about that, Zane. I knew coming to stay with you would be good for her."

Zane scrunched his face up. He'd taken Mae's daughter to bed, and if he had his way, he would do so again. His mind muddied up, and he didn't understand any of it other than that Jess was under his roof and getting under his skin. He felt for her and the hurt she'd gone through. Nothing about liking her seemed wrong, even though he could count the bullet points in his mind why he shouldn't.

"I can't thank you enough. You know how much I love my girls."

Her comment dug deep into his heart. Mae would never stop loving Janie. She always spoke of her as if she were still with them. Zane loved that about her. "Yep, I know, Mae."

"So tell me what you've been doing. That's if you have the time."

"I have the time. Let's see, the restaurant is coming along as scheduled and…"

Thirty minutes later, after he'd hung up with Mae, he sat down with his guitar and strummed lightly to reacquaint himself to the feel of the instrument in his hands and the resiliency of the strings. He had words in his head struggling to get out, lyrics that were just beginning to flow, and he jotted them down as he struck chord after chord. The pick in his hand felt awkward at first, but he pressed on.

Thoughts of Jess distracted him. He couldn't stop thinking about her and what Mae had revealed. He wanted to protect her. Yet he desired her. Her heartache scored his heart. He felt sorry for her, but not enough to keep his distance. He was *conflicted*, as Dylan would say. He needed some release.

Only a dunk in the ocean would help clear his mind and cool his body.

And minutes later, dressed in his swim trunks, he made his way to the shoreline and dived straight in, propelling his arms and legs past the shallow waters, pushing his body to the limit.

After enjoying a pleasant visit with Adam and declining his offer to walk her home, she trudged across the beach alone. Cool sand squished between her toes as she made her way to the shoreline, where the moist grains under her feet became smoother, making it much easier to move. She knew this beach; she'd walked it in the mornings many times.

As she entered Zane's home, silence surrounded her. It was too quiet for this time of the evening. Zane never turned in before ten. "Zane? Are you here?"

Nothing.

"Zane?" She stepped into the office, then the kitchen, and peeked into his bedroom.

There was no sign of him.

She sighed wearily and shook her head. He must have gone for a swim in the ocean. Half a dozen worries entered her head about his night swim. Geesh, he'd just gotten his cast off. What was the doggone rush?

Hurrying to her room, she flung off her clothes and put on her bathing suit. In her haste to rid herself of the old Jess, she'd tossed out her one-piece swimsuits she'd brought from Texas, which left her with the daring bikini she'd bought the other day. She slipped into it and then wiggled a T-shirt over her head. Without wasting a second, she strode down the stairs, grabbed her flashlight and ventured out the sliding door.

If she were lucky, she'd find Zane walking toward the house, whistling a happy tune.

Who was she kidding? Luck wasn't with her lately. Zane's towel was on the beach, which meant he was out there somewhere. The crashing waves that usually lulled her to sleep made her wary now. Her flashlight pointed out to sea illuminated only a narrow strip of water at a time. She squinted, trying to make out shapes, searching corridors of ocean, back and forth. "Zane! Zane!"

She couldn't find him. Nibbling her lip, she paced the beach, aiming her flashlight onto the water over and over. She'd never swum in the ocean before coming to California, but she'd quickly learned how the currents could take you away, making you drift in one direction or another. She'd start out in front of Zane's house and wind up hundreds of feet away when it was time to come in. Those currents had to be stronger at night, more powerful and…

She spotted something. A head bobbing in the water? She pointed the flashlight and struggled to focus. Yep, someone was out there. But then the form dropped down as if being swallowed up by the sea. She ran into the surf, targeting that bit of water with the flashlight. "Zane!" she shouted, but her voice was muted by the crash of the waves.

He couldn't hear her. He was out past the shallows. She waited several long seconds for him to reappear. She prayed that he would. She couldn't see much, only what the moonlight and stars and her flashlight allowed, but she'd always had a good sense of direction. She knew the exact spot where she'd seen him go down.

"Oh, God. Zane!"

With no time to waste, she dived in, her arms pumping, her feet kicking, fighting against the tide. She swam as fast as she ever had in her life, her eyes trying to focus on the spot she'd seen him. She was almost there, a little farther, just another few strokes.

A thunderous sound boomed in her ears. She looked up. Oh, no. A monstrous wave was coming toward her like a coiling snake. It was too late to get out of its path. The pounding surf reached her in midstroke. The force slammed her back. She flew in the air and belly-flopped facedown against a sheet of ocean as hard as a slab of granite.

Waves buried her, and she sputtered for breath.

Seconds later, she felt herself being lifted, her head popping above the water. She gasped.

"Jess."

Zane. He'd come for her. How did he get here? As she struggled to catch her breath, he half dragged, half swam her to the shallows by floating on his back and keeping her head above water. Once he got his footing, he stopped and stood upright in the water, then scooped her into his arms, carrying her to the beach.

He laid her down carefully away from high tide. The sand granules scratched at her back, but she was never happier to be on dry land. And Zane was safe. That mattered just as much.

He fell to his knees beside her. Huffing breaths, he shook his head. "You gave me a scare."

He bent to her, pushing aside the locks of hair hiding her face, and his magnificent eyes were soft and concerned. "Are you okay?"

She nodded. "I'm okay. Got the wind knocked out of me."

"You almost drowned, sweetheart. What on earth were you doing?"

She filled her lungs with oxygen, this time without gulping water along with it. "Saving you," she said quietly. "I thought I saw you out there, going under."

Zane's eyes were warm on her face, the heat enough to keep the cool drops on her body from freezing. His hands were working wonders, too, caressing her cheeks and stroking her chin, heating her up in ways no other man ever had. He rasped softly, "You mean you thought I was drowning, and you risked your life to save me?"

She nodded.

"That wasn't me, sweetheart."

"It wasn't? I saw someone go under. I thought for sure you were out there."

"I was. I lasted only ten minutes before I came in. What you saw was probably a school of sea lions. They frequent the shallower waters here at night. I've seen one of them pop a head up and then go under and, yeah...I guess in the dark, it might look like a swimmer out there."

"Then how...how did you find me?"

"After my swim, I took a long walk. Thankfully, I returned just in time to hear you calling my name. Took me only a second to figure out where you were."

He began to rub her arms and legs. She was cold, but that didn't stop her from reacting to his touch. As warmth spread through her body, her gentle cooing seemed to draw Zane's attention to her lips. "That feels good," she said.

"Tell me about it." The corner of his mouth crooked up.

His palms heated her through and through, her skin highly sensitized to his touch. She was overwhelmed with relief that he hadn't drowned and grateful that he'd saved her, but there was more...so much more that she was feeling right now. "Thank you, Zane."

She touched his shoulder and felt his cool skin under her fingertips. His eyes gleamed with a fiery invitation to do more. Bravely, she wound her arms around his neck. It didn't take an ounce of effort to pull him close. His mouth hovered near hers.

It was crazy. They were on the beach under the moonlight and dripping wet after the rescue, and nothing seemed amiss in her world. She wouldn't trade places with another living soul right now.

"I'd give you what-for," he said, "but that will have to wait."

"It will?"

"Yep. Cause I think you're about to kiss me."

"Smart man."

She ran her fingers through his thick wet hair and lowered his head down to her lips. Oh…he tasted warm and inviting and salty. His kiss made her tremble in a good way, and she opened her mouth for him.

He plunged inside and swept her up in one burning kiss after another. What was left of her body when he finished kissing her was a pulsing bundle of need. "Zane," she whispered over his lips.

"I need to get you inside the house…"

He didn't have to finish. She knew. They'd get arrested if they acted on their impulses right here on the beach.

"Can you walk?" he asked.

"Yes, with your help."

"Okay, sweetheart. Seems one of us is always leaning on the other."

She smiled. How true.

He bounded up and then entwined their hands. Gently he helped her to her feet. The world didn't go dizzy on her—well, except for the hot looks Zane was giving her. "I actually feel pretty good."

"Glad to hear it." He kissed her earlobe. "Ready?"

"Ready."

Side by side, bracing each other, they walked through the sand and up the steps that led into the house.

As soon as they entered the house, Zane did an about-face and walked her backward until she was pressed against the living room wall. He trapped her there, his body pulsing near hers, his gaze generating enough heat to burn the building down.

"Are you about to give me what-for?"

A low rumble of laughter rose from his throat. Her senses heightened. He was one sexy man. "You know it, Jess." He glanced down at her dripping wet T-shirt plastered to her body and sighed as if he was in pain. "Do you know how incredibly perfect you are?"

His hands wrapped around her waist, and thrilling warmth penetrated through her shirt to heat her skin. "I'm not."

His mouth grazed her throat. "You are. You can't let what those two did to you change who you are. That guy was about the stupidest man on earth."

She stilled. "What do you mean, 'those two'?"

Zane's lips were doing amazing things to her throat. And his body pressing against hers made it hard to think. Her breasts were ready for his touch. Her nipples pebbled hard and beckoned him through the flimsy T-shirt and bikini.

She had to ignore her body. She needed to know what he meant. "Zane?"

He stopped kissing her and inched away enough to gaze into her eyes. "Oh, uh. Your mama called while you were out. She was worried about you, and well…she told me about Steven running off with a friend of yours."

She'd told him about Judy?

All the wind left her lungs, and a different kind of burn seared through her stomach. She wished Mama hadn't revealed to Zane her latest humiliation. She felt so exposed, so vulnerable. Did she have an ounce of pride left?

"You have every right to feel hurt, Jess. But don't let what he did change the person that you are."

"You think that's what I'm doing?"

"Isn't it? You changed your hair, wear your contacts all the time. You dress differently now. Don't get me wrong. You look beautiful, sweetheart. But you were beautiful before."

She shrugged. She found it hard to believe. It was a platitude, a cliché, a way to make her feel better about herself.

"I need the change." Tears misted in her eyes. She really did. She needed to look at herself in the mirror and see a strong, independent woman who had style and confidence. She needed to see that transformation, more than anything else.

"I get that." Zane took her into his arms and hugged her, as a friend now. She felt safe again, protected. And just being with him made her problems seem trivial. "But promise me one thing?"

"What?"

"Don't try to find what you need with another man. Makes me crazy."

Makes me crazy. Oh, wow. There was no mistaking what he meant. Not from the genuine pain she found in his eyes, or the intensity in his voice. "You mean like Dylan or Adam? I told you, they're not—"

He shushed her with a kiss, right smack on the lips. Her body instantly reacted, and goose bumps rose on her arms.

"*You* make me crazy, too," he rasped and began rolling the hem of her T-shirt up. With his coaxing, she raised her arms as he brought the wet garment over her head and her breasts jiggled back into place. Zane's hot gaze touched her there and lingered, then traveled over the rest her body clad in a skimpy New Jess bikini. He made a loud noise from sucking oxygen into his lungs. "From now on, sweet Jess, I want to be the man you go to when you need something."

"You mean, like my rebound guy?"

"Call it whatever you want, honey."

Jess didn't have to think twice. Zane just abolished all deprecating thoughts she'd had about herself and totally wiped out any pain she'd felt about Steven. Even her pride was restored somewhat. The Steven ship had sailed, and she wasn't going to waste another second thinking of him. Not when she had Zane offering her the moon.

He was a real man.

If she had any doubts before about her feelings for him,

they were banished the second she'd thought he was drowning. She'd rushed in to save him, praying that God wouldn't take him from her. And she wasn't going to feel bad about it or apologize to anyone. Forbidden or not, she wanted him.

"I promise."

He hooked his fingers with hers. "Your room or mine?"

"Neither," she said. Her confidence soaring and her heart melting, she let go of every inhibition she'd ever had. "I think we need a hot, steamy shower to warm up, don't you?"

"As long as I get to peel this bikini off you, you've got yourself a deal."

Eight

The peeling was blissful torture. Jessica lay her head against cool slate, her arms behind her. Steam rose up as the customized shower streams poured down, warming her bones. It was like being tucked inside a large waterfall, cascading water all around her. Zane came to her naked, his sculpted, bronzed beach body equal to that of an ancient god. There was enough room for twelve people in the master shower, but she knew Zane would make good use of the space for the two of them.

"You're beautiful, Jess."

His mouth covered hers as both of his hands came under her bikini top. Weighing her full breasts, he groaned deep in his throat, and his appreciation of her body flowed to her ears. She roped her arms around his neck and continued to kiss him even as he unhooked the back of the bathing suit, releasing her breasts. Warm spray moistened them and he worked magic on her, gliding his hands over her bare, wet skin and arousing her in tortuous increments. His thumb caressed her already pebbled nipples until she muted a cry.

He was amazingly gentle, but brutal in his determination to make it good for her. As he removed the bottom half of her bikini, his hands shaking with need, she'd never felt more desirable and powerful.

Drizzling kisses along her throat, his hands came to the small of her back, and she bowed her body for him. He took one jutted breast in his mouth and suckled her, his tongue swirling and flicking. She screamed then, but the pleasured sounds were drowned out by the thunderous showerheads. He gave the other breast equal treatment, and it was almost too much.

"Are you warm yet?" he asked, nuzzling her throat.

"Just getting there."

"Let me help you with that."

He picked up a bar of soap and lathered her from head to toe, bathing her in a soft and subtle flowery scent that reminded her of a spring afternoon. He didn't miss one inch of her, paying special attention to the crux of her womanhood, stroking, washing, cupping her, making her moan. "Oh, oh, oh."

Jess thought every woman should experience a shower this way, just once.

She smiled, gritted her teeth and savored the pleasure he brought her.

His hands moved to her backside and slid over the rounded halves of her derriere, molding her form, spreading his fingers wide as if savoring the feel of her. His manhood pressed her belly, rock-hard and pulsing. She shuddered, unable to hold back another second. Her body released gently, in beautifully timid waves that nudged her forever toward him. His mouth covered hers, and she enjoyed the sweetly erotic taste of his passion.

Wow.

She'd never had an orgasm like that before.

She clung to him and let the full force of her feelings consume her.

"Did you like that, sweetheart?"

"So much."

She sensed his smile, and it made her heart nearly burst.

She moved down on him, letting her mouth and breasts caress the middle of his chest, his belly, and then she touched his full-fledged erection.

"Oh, man," he uttered. "Jess."

He fisted a handful of her hair and helped move her along the length of him. Water pounded her back, the showerhead pulsing now. It was deliciously sexy, and when she was through, she rose to meet him. The hungry look on his face, teeth gritted, eyes gleaming like a wolf about to devour his prey, would have been almost frightening if it wasn't Zane.

He lifted her, and on instinct she wrapped her legs around his waist. He held her tight and murmured, "Hang on."

She clung to him, and his manhood nudged into her, filling her with gentle force. He was patient and oh, so ready. She moved on him, letting him know she was okay with whatever he wanted to do. The beat, beat, beat of the raining drops set the pace of his thrusts. He arched and drove deeper.

"Oh." She sighed. "So good."

He kissed her throat, her breasts, and continued to thrust into her, hard, harder.

It was pure heaven. She'd never made love like this before. Her heart pounded in her chest, and her body soared. Spasms of tight, sweet pain released, and she cried out softly "Oh, Zane."

His eyes were on her, burning hot. He waited for her to come down off the clouds, and then he began to thrust into her again. He set a fast rhythm, and she gave back equally. She wanted to make it good for him, too.

Guttural groans rose up his throat, and she knew he was close. He impaled her one last, amazing time, his reach touching the very core of her womanhood. And waves of his orgasm struck her, one after the other, until he was spent, sated.

He took her with him as he sat down on the stone shower bench, raining kisses all over her face, cheeks, chin, throat. He pushed her hair away from her face. "Are you okay, sweetheart?"

How could she not be? She was overjoyed. "It was beautiful, Zane."

"It was," he said, leaning way back.

She stroked his face, running her hand over his stubbly cheek. He grabbed her wrist and planted a kiss on her palm.

The shower turned off. Perfect timing. It was a perfect night. Well, except for those few minutes she thought Zane was drowning. He'd taxed his body tonight. "You must be tired," she said.

His eyes darkened, and he hiked a brow. "I'm ready to be in bed with you."

"Sounds good."

She didn't want the night to end. She no longer worried about what tomorrow would bring. She was living in the moment, and these moments had been pretty darn spectacular.

Zane lifted her off him and grabbed two giant towels. He took his time drying her off, sneaking kisses on parts of her body, arousing her. She did the same to him, teasing him with her mouth.

They entered his bedroom clean, dry and exhausted.

She took a few steps toward his door, and his arm snaked around her. "Where do you think you're going?"

"To my room. I need to get my nightie."

"No, you don't. Come to bed. I promise to keep you warm."

"Part of your duties as my rebound guy?"

"You know it, honey. Now get in."

Spooning with Zane in his big, comfortable bed, Jessica's eyes eased open. It was slightly after dawn, and the usual early morning cloud cover allowed a smidgen of struggling sunshine into the room. Zane stroked her hip, lightly, possessively, his touch becoming familiar to her, and she purred like a kitten given a big bowl of cream.

"I'm giving you the day off," he murmured, his breath whispering over her hair.

"Mmm." A lovely thought. "I have work to do today."

"It'll keep, Jess. I want to spend the day with you."

"You already do."

He nipped her earlobe, then planted tiny kisses along her nape. His hand traveled deliciously to her waist, just under her belly. "Not the way I want to."

They'd made love twice last night. It was incredible and frightening at the same time. Every so often, thoughts of her future would break through her steely resolve to live in the moment. She'd shudder, and sudden panic would set in. What was she doing? Where was all this leading? They hadn't used protection in the shower last night, but Jess was on birth control, sort of. She'd skipped a few days during the height of her wedding fiasco, but she'd resumed when she'd arrived here to keep her hormones from getting out of whack.

She turned to Zane, roping her arms around his neck. "What did you have in mind?"

He kissed her quickly and then tugged her closer. "A day of play. We can get out of here. Have fun."

A lock of his thick hair fell to his forehead. In many ways, he looked like a little boy, eager to play hooky. He lived in this dream house on the beach and spoke of getting away, as if he'd been in living in the slums all this time. The irony made her smile, and she toyed with that wayward lock of hair, curling it around her finger, mesmerized by the man she shared a bed with.

"You're the boss," she whispered.

"I'm not your boss," he said softly. "Not when it comes to this."

He began kissing her shoulder, her throat, her chin. And then he stopped suddenly and inched away. He shot her a solid, earnest look. "Would you like to spend the day with me?"

Oh, wow. Like a date? "Yes." She yanked the lock of hair. "Of course, silly."

He gave her backside a gentle squeeze. "Then we'd better get up and get showered. You first. If we share another shower, we'll never make it out of here this morning." He waggled his brows. "On second thought, maybe…"

She laughed and jumped out of bed. "I'm going in first."

Less than an hour later, Zane was sitting behind the wheel of his SUV and pulling out of the gates of his home. "Feels good to be driving again. I hated feeling helpless, having to rely on someone to take me places."

A few days of stubble on his face had led to a short, sexy beard. The new look turned her on. Everything about him seemed to do that. All she had to do was think about making love with him last night and tingles fluttered inside her belly.

He wore a baseball cap instead of his Stetson. The beard and sunglasses also helped disguise him. He'd healed so well, she would've never guessed he'd broken his foot, except for his slight limp as he tried not to put too much pressure on it. She already knew she'd be arguing with him about going to his rehab appointments.

He'd told her to wear her boots, dress in jeans and not question where they were going. He wanted to surprise her. She sat in her comfortable clothes, watching the stunning landscape go by as they left the blue waters behind and drove up a mountain road. The scenery lent itself to light conversation and soft music. Zane sang along with the tune on the radio, his voice deep and rich, her own personal concert. She couldn't help but grin.

Thirty minutes later, they were atop the mountain at a sprawling ranch-style home overlooking the city to the south and the valley to the north. The air was clean up here, the smog of the day blown away by ocean breezes. "Where are we?" she asked.

"My friend Chuck Bowen owns this place with his mother. It's called Ruby Ranch."

She glanced around and spotted white-fenced corrals, vineyards off in the distance and acres and acres of hilly, tree-dotted land. The sound of horses whinnying and snorting reached her ears.

"C'mon."

Zane exited the car and walked around to help her out. He took her hand. That little boy excitement once again lit his expression. "We're going riding."

"Riding?" She hadn't been on a horse since she was a teenager. She'd go riding every weekend with her good friend Jolie Burns when she wasn't working at Holcomb House. Jolie lived on a cattle ranch ten miles outside of Beckon. Jessica had the use of a pretty palomino named Sparkle, and she'd learned how to wash down and groom a horse back then, too. It was expected. If you exercised a horse, got him lathered up, then it was your responsibility to see to his needs after the ride. Jessica had fallen in love with Sparkle. She never minded the hard work that came with him.

She rubbed her hands together. This could be fun. "Oh, boy!"

Zane chuckled and kissed the tip of nose. "That's what I thought."

A fiftysomething woman with hair the color of deep, rich red wine walked out of the house. She was flawless in her appearance, neat and tidy, and her pretty face must have stopped men in their tracks when she was younger. Even now, she was stunning and dressed in Western clothes that looked as if they'd just come off a fashion runway.

"Hi, Ruby," Zane said.

"Zane. It's good to see you again."

Zane took Jessica's hand as he moved toward the house. Ruby tried not to react, but her eyes dipped to their interlocked hands for a second before she gave them both a smile. "Ruby, I'd like you to meet Jessica Holcomb. Jess, this is Ruby Bowen. She and Chuck own this amazing land."

They came to a stop on her veranda. "Hello," Jessica said. "The place is lovely. You have vineyards?"

"Thank you. Yes, we grow grapes and raise horses. It's a rare mix, but it works for Chuck and me. We don't bottle the wine here—we're too small for that—but we do have our own label. It's fun, hectic and keeps us plenty busy."

"I bet," Jessica said.

"I met Ruby and Chuck at a charity auction six months ago," Zane said. "Being original Texans, they've been gracious enough to offer their stables for whenever I wanted to ride."

"Absolutely. We've got over a thousand acres and plenty of horses that need exercising. We figured Zane was like a fish out of water, living at the beach these days. We're happy he took us up on the offer. Chuck's out of town and due back later. He'll be sorry he missed you. But please, make use of the grounds. The stables are just down the hill a ways. Our wrangler, Stewie, is waiting for you. He'll find a good fit for both of you."

"Thanks, Ruby. Would've been by sooner, but it's hard to ride with a broken foot and wrist. Just recently got the dang cast off."

"Well, you're here now, and that's all that matters. Have a good time. Be sure to stop by afterward. Chuck may be home by then."

"Will do, and thanks again," Zane said.

Just minutes later, Jessica rode atop a sweet bay mare named Adobe, and Zane sat a few hands taller on a black gelding named Triumph. In her hometown of Beckon, the terrain was flat as the tires in Jeb's Junkyard. But here at Ruby Ranch, set in the Santa Monica Mountains, the powder-blue sky seemed nearly touchable. They ambled along a path that led away from the house into land that rose high and dipped gently alongside a creek.

"No rain lately," Zane offered. "I bet this creek was a rushing stream at one time."

"It's still pretty awesome up here."

"It is. You miss riding?"

She nodded, holding on to the silver-gray felt hat Ruby's wrangler had offered her. Zane kept his ball cap on his head, but there was no doubt he was a cowboy, through and through. He may have great wealth and live in a contemporary beach house, but you couldn't take Texas out of a Texan. And that was fact. "I do. I love horses."

Zane gave a nod of agreement. "Yeah, me, too."

It was a sore subject and one Jess didn't want to press at the moment. Zane had abandoned his home after the fire that took Janie and their unborn baby's life. The place still stood as it was. Acres and acres of land gated off, going to waste. He hadn't had the heart to demolish what was left of his house or improve upon the land. He'd had an agent sell off the livestock, and that was that.

Heartbroken, Zane had picked up roots, leaving memories he couldn't deal with behind. Losing him had taken a big chunk out the hearts of the fine people of Beckon. Zane was their golden boy, a singer whose talent brought him great fame. The townsfolk were darn proud of their hometown hero. He'd had no more loyal fans in the world.

"I'm glad you brought me up here, Zane."

He eyed her, studying her face as if trying to puzzle something out. "I'd have never come without you. Fact is, Chuck's been after me to ride for months, and I never took him up on it." His voice seemed sort of strange, and then he took a giant swallow. "I didn't want to, until now."

She shouldn't read too much into it, but her heart jumped in her chest anyway. Hope could be just as drastic as despair to her right now. She shoved it away and took a different approach. "You were confined a long time. I bet getting up on a horse and riding is just what you needed. It's freeing."

"Maybe," he said. His index finger pushed at the corner of his mouth, contemplating. He gave his head a shake. "Maybe it's something else. Having to do with you."

Oh, God. Out in the open air, in these beautiful surroundings, anything seemed possible. *Don't hope. Don't hope.* "Me?"

He slowed his horse to a stop.

She did the same.

His dark eyes grazed her face. "Yeah, you," he said, his voice husky.

Her cheeks burned, and she hoped her new suntan along with the brim of her hat hid her emotions. Zane didn't need another groupie. They'd already established he was her rebound guy, whatever that really meant. She was his bed partner, for sure. But after that…she had no clue where she stood with him.

Maybe her crazy heart didn't want to know. Maybe she couldn't survive another disappointment. It was better not knowing, not thinking at all.

She clicked the heels of her boots and took off. "Race you to that plateau up ahead. First one to the oak tree wins!" She was already three lengths ahead of him when she heard his laughter.

"You're on!"

Westerly winds blew cool air at her face, her hair a riotous mess, as she leaned low on her mare and pressed the animal faster. The path was wide enough here for two horses, but branches hung low, and she expertly navigated through a thick patch of trees to reach the innermost edge of the clearing. Another fifty yards to go.

From behind, resounding hooves beat the ground, and she sensed Zane catching up.

"C'mon girl!" The mare was shorter, her legs not quite as long as Triumph's, and of course, Jessica was rusty as a rider.

It was a valiant effort, even if she'd cheated at the starting line, but Zane caught her. His gelding made the pass just five yards out, and yet Adobe wrestled to move faster. Her mare didn't like to lose, it seemed. They reached the oak tree, Triumph just nosing Adobe out.

Jess reined her mare in and circled around to the base of the oak tree. Zane sat atop his horse, grinning wide. His joy seared her heart. He was so dang happy. How could she not join in?

He dismounted and sauntered over to her, his confident strides stealing her breath. His recovery looked damn good on him, the smile on his face, the gleam in his eyes, the breadth of his shoulders…

"I win, Jess."

"Just barely." She gave a good fight.

"Still, a win is a win."

He reached up and helped her off, his large hands handling her with ease as she slid down the length of him. Tucked close, she didn't mind being in his trap. The exhilaration of the race and the handsomest darn face she'd ever seen brought on palpitations. Her heart pounded like crazy.

"So what do I win?" he asked.

"Is this a trick question?"

"Not even close."

"What do you want?"

A soap-opera villain couldn't have produced a more wicked grin. "A kiss, for starters."

"For starters?" Her gaze darted to his beautiful mouth, and a delicious craving began to develop. She didn't think she could play coy. She wanted him to kiss her, more than anything.

He nodded and bent his head. The second his yummy lips met hers, her mind rewound to last night and how his mouth had trailed pleasure all over her body. He'd tasted every inch of her. "Oh," she squeaked.

She sensed his smile from her noisy outburst as he continued to kiss her. Then he plucked the hat from her head and angled his mouth over hers again and again.

Backing up an inch, she gulped air to catch her breath and gazed into his mischievous eyes.

"You cheated in the race, sweetheart. You're gonna have to pay for that."

A dozen illicit notions popped into her head regarding how he'd make her pay, and a hot thrill spread like wildfire in her belly.

He tugged on her hand, and she followed as he led her behind the solid base of the sprawling oak tree. Hidden by drooping branches and fully shaded by overlapping leaves, he sat down, his back to the tree, and spread his legs. "Sit." He gestured to the place between his legs. "Relax."

Hardly a position that would have her relaxing, but she sat down, facing out, and rested her head on his chest. His arms wrapped around her, and he whispered in her ear, "Comfortable?"

She snuggled in deeper, her butt grazing his groin. A groan rose from his throat, and she chuckled. "Very."

His hands splayed across her ribcage. "Close your eyes."

She did.

"Now for your punishment."

He began to kiss the back of her neck, but it was what his hands were doing that made her dizzy. Deftly the tips of his fingers glided just under her breasts. Through the rough plaid material of her shirt, her nipples puckered in anticipation of his next move.

The snaps of her blouse popped open, his doing, and a startled gasp exploded from her lungs. "Zane!"

He brought his head around and kissed the corner of her mouth. "Shh. I'm pretty sure we're alone out here, but just in case, keep your shrieks to a minimum."

"You mean there's going to be more?"

He laughed quietly. Dipping into her bra, he flicked the pads of his thumbs over her responsive nipples. Her mouth opened, and he immediately stymied her next shriek with another kiss. "You are a loud one."

"You didn't mind last night," she breathed. He was doing amazing things to her with his hands.

"I don't mind now, but we're not on my turf anymore."

Damn it. She was his turf. It was becoming clearer and clearer to her. "So, maybe we should stop before someone sees us?"

"No one's out here, Jess. But I'll stop if you want me to. And that would be *my punishment*. I didn't think I could go all day without touching you again."

With a confession like that, how in the world could she tell him to stop? "You won, fair and square, Zane. I'm a big girl. I can take whatever you dish out."

Nine

"I like playing hooky with you," Zane said to Jessica over dinner at an exclusive, out-of-the-way nightspot overlooking the beach. He'd heard about this place from his neighbors, who commended the food, the privacy and the music. He sat beside her in a booth, listening to smooth jazz from a sax player with a powerful set of lungs.

Every time his gaze landed on Jessica tonight, he was reminded of the way she fell apart in his arms under that oak tree this morning. He hadn't planned on taking it as far as he did, but there was something about Jess that made him do wild things.

Maybe it was the sweet, squeaky sounds she sighed when he kissed her.

Or maybe it was the forbidden lust that came over him when she entered a room.

Or maybe it was her vulnerability and her honesty that drew him to her the most.

Those sexy shaves she'd given him didn't hurt, either.

"I like playing hooky with you, too." Her deep, sultry tone fit the atmosphere in the nightclub, reminding him every second he needed to finish what he'd started up on that plateau today.

She wore red tonight, a daring dress with a scoop neckline, the hem hiking up inches above her knees. The dress fit each sumptuous curve of her form to perfection. There were times when he forgot who she was, that he'd been married to Jessica's sister and that she wasn't ready for another relationship. He was her go-to guy, and he'd wanted it that way, but where it led from here, he didn't know. He didn't think past the present these days. He couldn't hope, didn't want to hope for more. He'd been sliced up pretty badly when Janie and his child died. The guilt ate at him every day.

He raised his wineglass and sipped, turning his gaze to the scant number of people dancing. He hadn't disguised himself tonight. He'd relied on the dimly lit surroundings and the back booth to keep his privacy. Sometimes his fame came at too high a price, and tonight he wanted to show Jess a good time. He wanted to hold her again. He roped his arm around her shoulder and spoke into her ear. "Dance with me?"

Her gaze moved to the dance floor and the amber hues focusing on couples sharing the spotlight. Yearning entered her eyes, and he'd be damned not to deliver her this little bit of pleasure.

"Are you sure?"

"Positive."

He rose and grabbed her hand, leading her to the center of the room. As soon as he stepped foot on the wood floor, he turned and tugged her to his chest. She fit him, her curves finding his angles, and they moved as if they were born to dance together.

"How's your foot?" she asked.

"It's floating on air right now. Fact is, both feet aren't touching the ground."

She chuckled. "Sweet, but I'm serious. You rode today, and now you're dancing."

"Thank you for your concern." He kissed her temple. "But I'm fine. Feels darn good doing some normal things again. And with the most beautiful woman in the room."

"How do you know? Have you checked all the other women out?"

"I, uh…not going to answer that one."

"Smart man."

He laughed, wrapping his arms tighter around her slim waist. Her breasts touched his chest, and he imagined her nipples pebbling for him, hardening through the delicate lace of her dress. Her hand wove through his hair, her fingertips playing with the strands as her arm lay on his shoulder, and it was the most intimate thing she'd done to him this entire day. His groin tightened instantly, and he backed away from her, fearing they'd get thrown out for an X-rated dance. Her gaze lifted, and pools of soft pasture green questioned him.

He shrugged, helpless.

She smiled then, and nodded.

He and Jess were on the same wavelength lately. They *got* each other, and everything felt right when he held her in his arms. He wasn't ready to let that feeling go. Luckily, he didn't have to think about that now.

Two dances later, they noticed their meals were being delivered to their table.

"Ready for dinner?"

Jessica nodded. "I think I've worked up an appetite."

"For food?"

"Among other things."

Jessica scooted into the booth, and he took his seat beside her as the waiter set down plates of pasta and petite loaves of garlic bread. Jess had chosen penne with sweet pesto sauce, and he'd ordered linguine with meat sauce. Steam rose up, the air around them flavored with spicy goodness.

"Looks heavenly," Jess said, picking up her fork.

"Yep," he said, staring at her. "Sure does."

He didn't think Jess would blush over such an easy compliment, but color rose to her cheeks, and she blinked and wiggled in her seat. He liked flustering her.

"Hey, you two." A familiar voice sounded from the shadows, and Dylan McKay's smug face came into view. "I hope you don't mind me coming over to say hello. Saw the two of you dancing a minute ago. Didn't have the balls to cut in, Zane. Excuse my language, Jessica, but the two of you looked hot and heavy out there. And Zane, it's good to see you without those crutches."

"Hi, Dylan," she said with enough damn cheerfulness for both of them.

"Hey, you," he said, giving Jess a wink.

Zane kept a smile plastered on his face. He liked Dylan, but damn his keen perception and his untimely interruption. "Dylan."

"So, how do you like this place?" the actor asked.

"Very much," Jess said.

"We were just about to dive into our meal." Zane picked up his fork.

"Yeah, the food's pretty good here. And you can't beat…"

Lights flashed, and cameras snapped, one, two, three clicks a second. Zane caught sight of a trio of paparazzi, kneeling down, angling cameras and snapping pictures of Dylan. Damn it.

Dylan turned, giving them a charming smile as Zane wrangled Jess into his arms, turning away from the cameras. Shielding Jess, his first instinct was to protect her from the intrusive photographers. He hated paparazzi ambushes. But Dylan didn't seem fazed. He posed for a few shots, and then the manager rushed over, shooing the photographers away from his customers.

"So sorry, Mr. McKay. This usually doesn't happen."

"I know, Jeffrey. It's okay. It must be a slow news day. I'm here with some buddies. No hot chicks on my arm tonight."

The manager didn't smile at Dylan's attempt at humor. He took his job seriously. "I apologize to you as well, Mr. Williams," he said.

"No harm done." He had to be gracious. The manager couldn't have prevented this from happening. It happened all the time in every place imaginable, especially to Dylan.

The guy was a walking magnet for the tabloids. He seemed to love the attention.

After the manager walked off, Dylan shrugged. "What can I say? I'm sorry. This place used to be off their radar."

"It's not your fault," Jess was quick to say. "Like Zane said, no harm done."

Dylan stared at Jess for a moment, his eyes smiling, and then focused on Zane. "It's good to see you two together like this."

Like what? Zane was tempted to ask. Instead, he sent him his best mind-your-business look.

"O…kay," Dylan said. "Well, I'll be getting back to my friends now. Have a nice evening. Oh, and Jess, I'll see you on the beach."

Jess smiled.

"Bye, Dylan," Zane said, and the guy walked off. If only Dylan's flirty relationship with Jessica didn't grate so much on his nerves.

She touched his arm. "Are you angry?"

Dylan pissed him off, but that's not what she meant. "No. But I don't like having our time together interrupted like that. You don't need to be exposed to my real world. It's bad enough I have to deal with it."

"It's okay." Her face went gooey soft. "It wasn't so bad."

They'd never set boundaries or labeled what was happening between them, except to say she was on the rebound and he was the guy enjoying the privilege. But he wanted to spend every minute with her while she was here. She would go home soon. And he'd have to deal with it. She was forbidden fruit, and at times, his conscience warred with his desire for her. She was vulnerable right now and had come to live with him to heal her wounds. The last thing he wanted was to add to her pain. He'd never knowingly take advantage of her, but was he leading her on or helping her heal? He had to think it was healing for them to be together.

Right now, things were simple, but when the time came for her to return home, he'd have to let her go.

Her palm caressed his cheek. The touch was gentle, caring, and her eyes simmered with enough warmth to light a fire. When she leaned in and kissed him, something snapped in his heart. He wouldn't name it, didn't want to think about it. The sensations roiling in his gut scared the stuffing out of him. The mistake he'd made had cost his wife her life, and he wasn't going back there again. Falling in love was already checked off his bucket list.

Leaning back in his seat, he gave her a smile. "Our food's getting cold, sweetheart."

She blinked, and the heat in her eyes evaporated.

He hated disappointing her, but he had nothing else to say on the subject.

Jessica loved working for Zane. It gave her a sense of purpose, and she enjoyed gaining a new perspective on life. As a grade-school teacher, her world revolved around children, shaping and molding them into good students and eager learners. But this work had its own rewards. This morning she'd already spoken to Zane's fan club president, made a list of devotees she needed to send autographed photos to, and spoken with Mrs. Elise Woolery, a senior citizen who wrote to Zane every month. Yes, at the age of eighty-four, the woman was a Zane Zealot. She was his Super Fan. Mariah had made a special point to make sure Zane read and answered this woman's letters. Jessica would do no less.

Sitting at the office desk, she was reading her heartwarming letter when her cell phone rang. She glanced at the screen and smiled before answering. "Hi, Mama."

"Hi, honey."

"Is something wrong? Your voice…"

"Honey, I'm fine. It's not that, but how are you?"

She was flying high, happy as a clam, strolling on Moonlight Beach shores and spending time with Zane. Last night had been incredible. Except for the crazy camera goons coming out of the woodwork and some odd moments afterward, it had been a picture-perfect day and night. Riding at Ruby Ranch, dinner, dancing and making love with Zane afterward was up there on her Top Ten List of Best Days. What more could a girl ask for?

A lot, a voice in her head screamed.

She ignored it.

"I'm fine, Mom. What is it? Did Steven make another stupid move? Is Judy pregnant or something? I'm telling you right now I'm over it, whatever it is."

"No, honey. I haven't heard anything more about Steven. It's just that…well, have you read the *Daily Inquiry* this morning?"

"Mama, you know I don't read that stuff. And neither do you. What's this all about?"

"I mean, I was sort of used to it with Janie. Zane protected her mostly, and the press loved them. But you, honey. Well, there's a picture of you and Zane, and it's quite shocking."

"There's a picture of me and Zane?"

"On the front page. My neighbor Esther showed it to me this morning. And after that, my phone hasn't stopped ringing."

"It hasn't?" It was noon in Texas. Damn those photographers. She'd thought they were only after Dylan. She should've known better, not that she had any way of stopping the invasion of privacy. "Mama, it's nothing, really. You know the life Zane leads. We were dining out and were ambushed by the Hollywood nut jobs. That's all."

"You changed your hair. You're blonde now. And the dress you were wearing…well, it was quite revealing. Zane had you in his arms, baby girl, and it looked to me as if—"

"He was protecting me from the cameras, that's all."

"Is that *all*, honey?"

She nibbled her lip. What could she say to her mother?

That she'd been sleeping with Zane and they'd been helping each other come to terms with their own personal demons? Could she honestly tell her mother that? No. Her mother would worry like crazy. She didn't know that the new and improved Jessica could handle anything that came her way. God, she only hoped she wasn't wrong about that.

"Jessica, that picture of you…well, do you know how much you look like Janie now?"

Something powerful stung her heart. The subtle implication wasn't anything she hadn't already thought of a hundred times in her head. Was that the attraction Zane had to her? She looked enough like Janie for him to gravitate her way.

"I don't want you to get hurt again."

"I know, Mama. I don't plan to."

Swinging her chair toward the computer, she keyed into the *Daily Inquiry* site on the internet. The front-page picture came up, and there she was, her neckline plunging and Zane's arms around her shoulders possessively, his body half covering hers in a proprietary way. But the headline was what grabbed her the most. "Zane Williams Dating Wife Look-alike." The subtitle wasn't much better. "Who Is His Mystery Love?"

"Holy moly, Mama. I just looked it up." Good thing the paparazzi didn't do much investigating. She could only imagine the headline if they knew she was Janie's younger sister.

"See what I mean?"

"I do. But this will pass. Tomorrow someone else will be their fodder."

"I know that. I'm not worried about the picture or the headline. I'm only worried about you and what you're feeling right now."

"Mama, just know I'm happy. Zane has been incredible, and I'm making friends, enjoying the work I'm doing here."

"Is Zane there now?"

"No, he's having physical therapy." She gasped as a

thought struck her. "Mama, you're not going to call him about this, are you?"

Her mother paused long enough to worry her. "Mother?"

"No, not if you don't want me to."

"I definitely don't want you to. Promise me you won't."

Gosh, the last thing she needed was her mother intervening in her love life. She was the one who had insisted Jessica come here. The damage was already done. Her mama could only make things worse. She hung up on a cheery note, convincing her mother she was fine, and resumed her work.

An hour later, she heard Zane's car pull up. Giddiness stirred inside her, and her heart warmed. She was becoming a lovesick puppy dog where he was concerned. She heard him enter the house, and his footsteps grew louder on the slate flooring as he approached. Seconds later, he was standing in front of her, a newspaper in his hand. He tossed it onto the desk, and she gave it a glance. "Sorry, sweetheart. I've got my manager doing some repair on this. Ideally, he can keep your name out of it." He studied her a second. "You don't look surprised."

"Oh, I was very surprised when my mama called to tell me about it," she said softly.

"Your mama saw this?" he nearly shrieked.

She nodded. "Just about all of Beckon has seen it by now."

He ran a hand down his face, pulling his skin tight. "Oh, man."

"Zane? What are you worried about?" Looking into his pained eyes frightened her.

He came around the desk and, taking her arms, pulled her up against him. "You. I'm worried about you," his said softly into her ear. He tucked her into an embrace while his breath warmed her skin and her spine got all tingly.

"Don't. I'm okay."

"Your mama must think I'm a jerk, subjecting you to this.

You have to go back to Beckon one day. I don't want it to be harder on you than it has to be. I'm so sorry, sweetheart."

You have to go back to Beckon one day.

He was right, she would have to return to her hometown one day. Her mind rebelled at the thought. He kissed her again and eased the battle going on inside her head. Oh, boy.

She gazed at him and was floored by the genuine look of concern on his face.

"How was your appointment?"

He pulled away from her and shrugged. "Fine. I don't think I needed it, but—"

"You need it. So you did okay. It wasn't too hard?"

"I've been swimming, riding and dancing on this foot. Seems I'm doing my own rehab."

"You're lucky you haven't reinjured yourself, babe."

He grinned.

"It's not funny."

"I'm not laughing at that. I like it when you call me 'babe.'"

"Well, if you like that, I have an idea I think you might enjoy."

"Does it involve a bed and soft sheets?"

"No, it involves being poolside with some beautiful hot chicks."

One week later, at the Ventura Women's Senior Center, an hour's ride from Moonlight Beach, Jessica sat poolside in the audience of geriatric hot chicks. The scent of chorine was heavy in the air of the enclosed pool area that opened into the center's recreation center. Zane had his butt in a chair, facing his eager fans with guitar in hand—he'd been brushing up at home—and it sounded to her as if he hadn't lost his touch. Playing guitar was probably like riding a bicycle. Once you mastered it, you never forgot.

Zane's Super Fan Elise Woolery, was all smiles today. She sat in the front row next to her friends, all of whom she'd coaxed into becoming great fans of Zane's, as well. As smokin' hot as Zane appeared to his younger audience, he had the wholesome good looks and Southern charm that any of these women would admire in a son.

Zane had balked at the idea of coming here, not because he wasn't charitable. Nothing was further from the truth. But he didn't know if he had the chops or the will to get back onstage and entertain the masses anymore. It had taken only one little ole note from Elise, saying she'd had a bad week physically, her arthritis so painful she couldn't get out of bed in the mornings, and listening to Zane's songs had helped her get by. That letter and Jessica's urgings had convinced him to play this private concert. He insisted on no press, and Jessica agreed. This wasn't a photo op. It wasn't done for his public image, either. He'd agreed because basically he'd been humbled by her letter and wanted to help.

Zane faced his audience. "Well, now. It's nice to be in such fine company. I guess you all are stuck with me for the next hour or two, so let's start things off." He nodded for Jessica to bring Elise up front and center. There was an empty chair beside him.

"Elise?" She helped the woman sit down next to him. The older woman waved her hand over her chest as the silvery-blue in her eyes gleamed.

"How are you this afternoon?" he asked.

Giddy as a school girl, she nodded and spoke softly. "I'm just fine."

"Yes, you are," Zane said. "Ready for a song?"

She gazed out at the envious women in the audience, her friends in the front fidgeting in their seats, too excited to sit still.

"I am, Mr. Williams."

"Zane," he corrected her, taking her hand. "May I call you Elise?"

"Oh, my, yes."

Zane performed for over an hour, and he'd never sounded

better. Just Zane and his guitar, without all the usual fanfare, lights or band to back him up. His voice was clear and honest and mesmerizing.

After the performance, one by one the seniors said their goodbyes and thanked him, often offering kisses on the cheek before leaving the facility. Elise stayed until the end and chatted with Zane. Jessica didn't contribute much to the conversation. It seemed as though through her letters, Elise and Zane knew each other pretty well, but Jessica did take a number of photos, promising Elise she'd send them to her home address as soon as she could.

"You can thank Jessica here for arranging this," Zane was saying.

"Thank you, Jessica. This made my whole year. I swear today, my arthritis just vanished. I think I'll go home, put on one of Zane's records and dance a jig."

And later, sitting in the backseat of a limo, Zane reached for Jessica's hand as they headed down the highway. He didn't say much as he stared out the window, and every once in a while, he'd give her hand a squeeze.

If she could put a name on this sense of peace and total belonging, she'd call it bliss.

The sea glistened in the moonlight, calm tonight, the placid waves grazing the shore. It was a night like many she'd shared with Zane these past weeks, walking the shore in the dark, holding hands, enjoying the beach after the locals went home.

"You're quiet tonight," Zane said as they strolled along.

She wasn't a complainer. She didn't want to mar the perfection they'd seemed to achieve lately.

"I think I ate something that didn't agree with me."

Zane squeezed her hand lightly. "We can head back. We're only half a mile from the house."

"No, it's okay. The fresh air is doing me good."

"You sure?"

"I'm sure."

"'Cause you know, now that my rehab is done, I could pick you up and carry you all the way."

She chuckled, and the movement caused her stomach to curl. "Oh."

She wanted desperately to put her hand to her belly, but she didn't want to draw his attention there. They were having such a wonderful evening. She managed a small smile instead. "That won't be necessary."

"Could be fun."

"I don't doubt it. You'd probably dunk me into the ocean first or deliver me into your shower, like you did the other night."

"And you enjoyed every second. But I wouldn't do that to you tonight, sweetheart. I can see on your face that you're exhausted." He pivoted, taking her with him. "C'mon. You should get to bed."

"Okay, maybe you're right."

She didn't have the strength to argue with him. Zane had a charity event at the children's hospital in the city tomorrow, and she didn't want to miss it. It wasn't an extravaganza by any means, just an artist making the rounds and singing songs with the kids She hadn't had any difficulty convincing Zane to do it. When it came to making children feel better, Zane was all in.

"Excuse me? You said I was right about something?"

"Very funny." Gosh, her voice sounded suddenly weak. Whatever strength she had left seemed to seep right out of her. Her limbs lost all their juice. "Zane, I'm, uh, really tired." A wave of fatigue stopped her steps in the sand.

Zane halted and gave her a quick once-over, his eyes dark with concern. He lifted her effortlessly, and she wound her arms around his neck. "I've got you. Hang on, honey."

"I don't know what hit me all of a sudden."

"Just rest against me and close your eyes. I'll have you home in no time."

And minutes later, they entered the house. She insisted Zane deposit her in her own bedroom. He balked at first. He said he wanted to keep an eye on her tonight. "Are you sure?"

She needed a place to crash. And if she had a bug or the flu, she could be contagious. Zane didn't need to get sick on her account. "I'm sure. Thanks for the lift." Literally. She smiled, and his eyes grew sympathetic in response.

"Anytime."

"I just need to sleep this off."

"Can I help you get ready for bed?" he asked.

"I'll manage, Zane. Thanks for the thought."

"Okay if I come in to check on you later? I won't wake you."

She could see it meant a lot to him by the protective look in his eyes. "Yes, I'd like that."

"If you need anything during the night, just call for me."

When she'd had the flu during spring break last year, Steven hadn't so much as offered to bring her a bowl of soup. He'd told her he'd keep his distance so she could rest up and get better. He couldn't afford to get sick. She'd received a total of one phone call from him during her recuperation. What a fool she'd been. The signs were all there, but she'd refused to see them.

"Thank you, Zane."

He smiled, but the worry in his eyes touched her deeply. "Good night, sweet Jess." He placed a kiss on her forehead, tossed the sheets back on the bed and gave her a lingering smile before he walked out of the room and closed the door.

Her hands trembled as she put on her nightie and tucked herself into bed. She hadn't lasted but a minute when her belly rattled and the turmoil reached up into her throat, gagging her. Her stomach recoiled, and she covered her mouth, clamping it shut as she raced to the toilet.

It wasn't a pretty sight, but she emptied her stomach in just about thirty seconds.

Sitting back on the floor, she closed her eyes and took big breaths of air in order to calm her stomach. Whatever it was, she hoped it was gone.

Bye. Bye.

Arrivederci.

Good riddance.

She rose slowly and leaned against the marble counter. One look at her chalky face in the mirror told her to wash up and get her butt back into bed. She splashed water on her cheeks, chin, throat and arms, cooling and cleansing herself, and then headed back to bed on wobbly jelly legs. Her eyes closed to the distant serenade of Zane's beautiful voice coming from downstairs as he rehearsed his music for tomorrow's event.

In the morning, her weakened body felt bulldozed. Her head was propped by the pillow and her limbs lay flaccid on the bed as she absorbed the comfort of the luxurious mattress. She missed having Zane's arms around her, but she needed these hours of privacy to rest up.

A soft knock at her door snapped her eyes open. "Jess, are you awake?"

She sat taller in the bed, ran her fingers through her hair and pinched her cheeks, hoping she still didn't look like death warmed over. "Yes, come in."

Zane entered the room, assessing her from top to bottom, and took a seat on the side of the bed. "Morning. Are you feeling any better today?"

"Yes. Just a little tired still. But I'm sure once I get up and eat something, I'll perk right up."

He looked like a zillion bucks. Dressed in crisp new jeans, his signature sterling silver Z belt buckle and a Western shirt the color of sea coral decorated tastefully with rhinestones that outlined a horse and rider, Zane resembled the superstar that he was. His concert shirts were custom-made by a trusty tailor, and this one was perfect for a day with children. "Glad to hear it. Mrs. Lopez has breakfast ready whenever you are."

The mention of food riled her stomach. And blood drained from her face. Her eyes drifted toward the digital clock inside a wall unit near her bed. It was almost ten! "Zane! I had no idea how late I slept. Give me a few minutes to get dressed and I'll—"

As she hinged her body forward, Zane's arms were on her shoulders, pressing her back down. "Whoa, Jess. Slow down."

Dizziness followed her as her head hit the pillow. The world spun for a second, and when it stopped, a soft sigh escaped her. "But I'm supposed to go with you today." It was her job, her duty as Zane's personal assistant. Zane wasn't used to making appearances on his own. He always had an assistant to usher him through the process.

"I didn't have the heart to wake you. I'm leaving in just a few minutes. What I want you to do is take the day off and relax. I'll be back in a few hours."

"I don't want to miss it."

He took hold of her hand. "I wish you could come, too."

"I'm sorry."

"Don't be. I'm sorry you're not feeling well."

"I'll be sure to call Mrs. Russo this morning. She's in charge at Children's Hospital, and I made all the arrangements through her. I'll tell her the situation."

"Don't go to any trouble. I'm sure I'll be fine."

"No trouble." She picked up her cell phone. "I've got the number right here."

Zane's gaze swept over her rumpled sheets and the spot where she'd conjured up her phone. "You sleep with your cell phone?" His incredulous voice tickled the funny bone inside her head.

"When I'm not sleeping with you."

He grinned and kissed the top of her head. "Feel better."

"Thanks."

As soon as Zane left, she made the call and was relieved that Mrs. Russo was amenable to sticking by Zane's side today, keeping him on schedule. She was a fan and was looking forward to the day, as well. Jessica hung up, convinced Zane would enjoy himself, doing what he loved to do. He'd be fine on his own. He liked being around children. Singing to them and with them would be second nature to a guy who'd lived and breathed country music as a boy.

A short time later, ringing blasted in her ear, and she lifted her eyelids. When had she drifted off? How long had she been in sleep land? She squinted to ward off the sunshine blazing into her window. The last thing she remembered was speaking with the director at the hospital regarding Zane's appearance. She took a few seconds to awaken fully, blinking and stretching. Gosh, she felt better, her stomach didn't ache and her head cleared of all the fuzz.

All systems go.

She grabbed her phone and greeted her caller on the third ring. "Hello, Mariah. It's good to hear from you."

Mariah had been calling in at least once a week to make sure things were going smoothly for her and checking in on Zane. Jessica appreciated her diligence and thoughtfulness, but she'd already spoken with Mariah earlier in the week. "Is everything alright?"

"Everything is actually better than I hoped." Enthusiasm that had been vacant in Mariah's voice since her mother's ordeal was making a sparkling comeback. "The last time I spoke with Zane, I told him my mother was being re-evaluated by the doctors. Well, the good news is that even though Mom has something of a long road ahead of her, she's recovered enough to come home from the transitional facility. My sister plans on taking over from now on. She'll have the help of a caregiver during the week. And I'll come home on the weekends whenever I can to help out. I tried to reach Zane to tell him I'll be coming back to work starting Monday morning, but I think he shut his phone off."

Mariah was coming back in five days? The news pounded Jessica's skull. Five days. She'd known this day would come, but she'd been too busy living in the moment to worry about it. "Oh, uh…yes. He's not here. He's doing a show at the children's hospital."

"That's where he really shines," Mariah was saying. "Anyway, you don't have to pinch-hit for me anymore. You, my savior, are off the hook."

She was off the hook? But she liked being on the hook. She *was* hooked on Zane.

Wow. Just like that, her life was about to change again. Mariah would return to work, and things would go back to the status quo. No more sunset dinners with Zane or moonlit strolls or making love on his big bed during the night. The happy place in her heart deflated. Like when the air inside a balloon was released, she fizzled.

"I'm happy to hear your mother's doing well, Mariah." She really was. It was good news, and she focused on that and what Mariah had gone through to get to this point. "And I'll be sure to tell Zane."

"Thanks, hon. I know you've done a great job in my absence. Zane sings your praises and tells me not to worry about a thing."

"Well, there wasn't all that much to do." Except to fall for the boss. "And you left impeccable notes."

"It's a flaw of mine. I'm a detail person. Makes most people crazy, but it comes in handy for the kind of work that I do. I'm happy Zane had you these past weeks. And I'm eager to come back to work. What about you, Jessica? How's your summer going?"

The summer was more than half-over. If she stayed, nothing would be the same. She wouldn't be working alongside Zane, and she couldn't very well carry on with him right under Mariah's nose. She had no name for her relationship with Zane. She wasn't his girlfriend. He hadn't made a commitment to her in any way. Did he look at her as a forbidden fling? He wanted to be her rebound guy, and he'd accomplished that and more. He got an A for effort.

"My coming back doesn't mean you have to leave, you know. Please don't on my account," Mariah was saying. But in fact, her coming back meant that very thing. Zane hadn't spoken about the future with Jessica. He wasn't one to plan anymore. He took things as they came now. Hadn't he encouraged her to do the same? "I would love to get to know you better."

"I feel the same way, Mariah. But unfortunately, I can't promise you that. I…should be getting home soon. There are things I have to do."

Prepare her lesson plans for the new school year.

Avoid Steven at all costs.

Fall back in step with single life in Beckon.

Try not to think about Zane.

"I understand. When home is calling, you must go."

"When Beckon beckons."

Mariah chuckled.

"Sorry. It's a dumb joke the locals think is clever. Small-town humor."

"Sounds kinda sweet. Will you tell Zane I'm sorry I missed him? It was nice talking to you, Jess."

"Sure, I'll tell Zane as soon as he gets back, and same here. Good talking to you."

Bittersweet emotions snagged her heart. She was thankful Mariah's mother was on the mend, but the thought of leaving Zane to return to Beckon was killing her. He'd be home soon.

And she'd have to tell him the news.

Ten

"You're staying," Zane said resolutely. His handsome face was inches from hers as she lay on a beach blanket on the sand right outside his back door, her head propped by a towel. She'd needed some sun to put color on her sickly cheeks while she tried to figure out where in heck her life was headed.

"How can you say that so easily?"

He'd plopped down beside her just minutes ago, wearing shorts and an aqua Hawaiian shirt. He'd been in a good mood since coming back from the children's hospital, and she'd had to spoil it by giving him the news that she'd be returning home.

"It is easy. You're my summer guest. What's so hard about that?"

He made it seem so simple, and he'd brought along his arsenal of secret weapons to convince her. His ripped chest grazed her breasts, teasing and tormenting her. Powerful arms braced on either side of her head surrounded her with strength, and that amazing mouth of his hovered so close she could almost taste it. His presence surrounded her, sucking oxygen from her rational brain.

"It'll be awkward. These past weeks it's been just us, and now that Mariah will be here most of the time, it won't be the same. She'll guess what's going on."

As he cupped her head with both hands, she had nowhere

to look but deep into his eyes. "She probably already knows, Jess. Mariah keeps up on everything, and I'm sure she's seen that tabloid photo of us. But if it makes you feel any better, I'll be up-front with her and explain the situation." Zane lowered his head and brushed his lips over hers. "It won't matter if she knows, as long as you stay."

Yes, yes. His kiss was a potent persuader. Oh, how she wanted to agree with him. She shouldn't care what people thought. But darn it, she did, and her heart was at stake, too. "I'm not… I don't do… Never mind."

"Jess," he said softly, his finger outlining the lips he'd just kissed. His touch seeped into her skin as he curved his fingertips around and around the rim of her mouth as if he'd never touched anything so fascinating. She'd hoped he'd ask her to stay, but she wanted more. She wanted the happily-ever-after that wasn't bound to happen.

He claimed her lips and took her into another world. When he was through kissing her, his deep, dark eyes were hot, heavy and filled with desire. "You can't go yet. This is new and real, and right now I can't offer you more than that." His words were raw with emotion. "But I'm asking you to stay."

New and real? Those were promising words. Hope began to build in her, but she warned herself not to be a fool. She couldn't get blindsided again. She had to face the truth head-on. She didn't know if Zane had the capacity to love again. He was and always would be devoted to her sister. Could she live with that? Could she spend the next five weeks with him and enjoy herself? The new Jess said yes. *Go for it, you idiot!* But the old Jess buried deep down wasn't quite so fearless, and she rose up occasionally to plant dire warnings in her ear. "I want to…but—"

"Sweetheart, you don't have to make up your mind right this minute. Take time to think it over."

Her shoulders relaxed as she blew breath from her lungs. "Okay, I can do that," she said softly.

"Good." He rose and offered her his hand.

"Where are we going?"

"One guess." He waggled his brows. He was six feet two inches of gorgeous, rugged, tan and aroused.

"You don't play fair, Zane Williams."

"*You* don't play fair. That bikini does things to my head and…" He looked down past his waistband. "If I don't get inside soon, I'll be arrested for indecent exposure."

She took his hand, and he yanked her up. She fell against him, her hands landing on his broad, bronzed chest. He smelled of sunshine and sand and sunscreen, and at this moment, she couldn't imagine not being with him.

"What would the residents of the Ventura Women's Senior Center say to that?"

A smile spread wide across his face. "They'd probably invite me back with an engraved invitation."

She laughed along with him, and her day brightened.

Jessica gave her body and soul to Zane, and the past three days had been magical. They rode horses, had moonlight swims, dined and danced together. Zane took her to the new restaurant, and they'd surveyed the progress, sharing ideas. He helped her answer fan mail, giving attention to questions and signing the letters personally. At night their lovemaking was intense, the heat level rising above anything she'd ever experienced before, but it was more than that. Emotions were involved now, their time together precious. Each night before they drifted off to sleep, Zane would hold her close and whisper in her ear, "Stay." In the morning, they'd rise at the crack of dawn to walk along the beach before the world woke up.

Except for a growing suspicion she might be pregnant, everything was perfect.

The idea of carrying Zane's baby made her glow inside, the beaming light of hope strong. It wasn't an ideal situation, but how could she not embrace the new life she might be carrying? She'd been queasy in the mornings ever since her bout of illness, but she managed to hide it from Zane for the most part. She ate little in the mornings, to his raised eyebrows, claiming she put on weight fast and needed to be disciplined. "You haven't got an ounce of fat on you," he'd said.

"And I want to keep it that way." Not entirely true. She wasn't a big believer in stick-thin female bodies, especially since she might be described as voluptuous. But most men bought that explanation, and for now, feminine vanity was a white lie that was necessary.

She'd been overly tired, too, but when Zane noticed, she attributed her fatigue to the energetic pace they'd been keeping in and out of bed. And she was overdue on her monthly cycle.

Locked inside her bathroom, she held the pregnancy test in her hand, waiting those precious few minutes that might change the course of her life. Zane was out shopping—which was bizarre since the man would rather break his other foot than step into a store—and she would use this time alone to deal with whatever came her way. Admittedly, it had taken her half an hour to muster the courage to break open the package and pee on the stick. And now that she had, her pulse pounded in anticipation.

Seconds ticked by, and then she glanced down and got the news.

She leaned against the sink and pressed her eyelids closed.

"Okay." She took a breath.

The new Jess was strong. She could do this.

Tears stung behind her eyes.

"Jess?"

Oh, no. Zane was home. What was he doing back so soon?

"I'll just be a minute." Her voice wobbled from behind the bathroom door.

"Okay, mind if I wait for you in here?"

"Uh, no. It's okay." Shaking, she scrambled to toss all signs of the pregnancy test away. She wrapped everything in toilet paper and shoved it into the bottom of her trash container. She took another few seconds to wash her face and straighten herself out mentally. Then she opened the door.

Zane was lying across her bed, staring out the window. He sat up the minute he saw her and smiled, a winning, charming, loving smile that seared straight into her heart.

"Everything okay, sweetheart?"

She nodded and bit her lip to keep herself from saying more.

Zane studied her face. Did he see the truth in her expression? She lowered her eyes, and that's when she saw a small, square, sapphire-blue velvet box on the spot next to him.

"Sit with me?" He picked up the box and patted that same spot for her to take a seat.

She did and turned his way. He had something to say, and she was all ears.

"Recently, you gave me a gift that was especially meaningful. And now, it's my turn to give you something. Not in reciprocation but because, well, you deserve this. I had this made for you."

His eyes contained a genuine spark of excitement as he placed the box in her hand. Whatever it was, Zane was eager for her to see it. She didn't make him wait. Gently she opened the lid and lifted out a unique charm bracelet. She'd never seen one made with diamonds before. "Oh, Zane." She was truly swept away. "This is…" A lump in her throat blocked her next words. She was speechless.

The silver-and-diamond bracelet held three charms and glittered brightly enough to light all of Moonlight Beach. The charms were well thought-out and special to the person that she was. The first charm was a teacher's apple that reminded her of her students, the second was a schoolbook with opened pages and the third was a pair of eyeglasses, which, up until a few weeks ago, were her mainstay. Every charm was exquisitely outlined by small diamonds. A tiny heart hung from the clasp, engraved with one word in italic script: *Stay.*

"Let me try it on you," Zane said, and she put out her hand.

"Thank you," she said finally. She couldn't have been more surprised. Zane fastened the clasp around her wrist. The fit was perfect, and there was something about a personalized gift, no matter what it was, that made her feel cared for. There were no words to express how meaningful this gift was to her. Zane had outdone himself. "It's very special."

"Just like you. I'm glad you like it," he said.

"I do. You don't play fair, Zane." It was getting to be his signature move. Make her want him even more than she already did.

"I swear to you, I had this bracelet ordered weeks ago, and then, well, the heart was just added on this week. You can't fault a guy for trying."

She put her hand to his cheek and gazed into his eyes. "That's sweet." And then she kissed him, quickly and passionately, before she pulled away, her heart in her throat.

She loved this man with all of her heart.

And she *wasn't* carrying his child.

Sadness blanketed her body, a shallow sliver of sorrow of what wasn't to be.

"Are you sure you're okay, Jess?" Zane studied her movements as she approached his bed. He lifted his sheets and welcomed her. He wanted her with him tonight, sex or no sex. She was special to him, and he didn't want to press her if she needed more rest.

After he returned to the house today, he couldn't wait to see her. His gift was burning a hole in his pocket, so he'd waited for her on her bed. When she'd stepped out of the bathroom and he'd looked at her, he'd seen a haunted expression on her face, and she'd been overly quiet. He worried over her health, but he sensed it was something more than her having an upset stomach. She'd looked sad, and a transparent sheen of despair seemed to cover her eyes.

She'd liked the gift—he could tell that much—and that brightened her mood, but her eyes never really returned to the Jess sparkle he was used to. She'd kept the bracelet on during the day, and there were moments when he'd catch her touching the links, tracing her fingertips over the charms tenderly. After what she'd been through this year, if the gift told her she was appreciated, she was worthy of beautiful things and she was desirable as a woman, then mission accomplished. Zane wanted her to feel all of those things. He'd wanted her to know what she had come to mean to him.

"I'm feeling better tonight," she said. She climbed in and scooted close to him. His arms tightened around her automatically, and he rolled so that her back was up against his chest.

Like it or not, Mae Holcomb put him in charge of her daughter. His first responsibility was to see to her health. Precious little else mattered. He'd failed where Janie was concerned, and he certainly wasn't going to let something happen to Jess while she was here with him. Not on his watch.

"Glad to hear it."

She still looked weary, as if a burden weighed her down. Was she deliberating about staying with him for the rest of the summer? Right now, breathing in the sweet scent of her hair and having her body cuddled up against him, he couldn't imagine her leaving in two days, but he wouldn't pressure her. She needed to come to the conclusion that they were good together, on her own. He'd done everything he could do, short of begging, to convince her to stay, but ultimately it was her decision.

Pushing silken strands away from her face, he kissed her earlobe. "If you need to sleep, I can just hold you tonight, babe. Or…"

She turned around in his arms, her features softening and her eyes tender and liquid. "Or," she said. "Definitely or."

Zane made slow, easy love to her, and she fell in sync with his body movements. He savored every inch of her with gentle strokes and touches. And she did the same to him. He loved the feel of her hands on him, exploring, probing and possessing him in small doses. Little by little, hour by hour, minute by minute, Jess was filling his life.

He cared about her. Worried when she was sick. Praised her accomplishments. Was impressed by her feisty spirit. Wanted to see her happy.

She mattered to him.

And after the explosion that burst before his eyes in warm colors, Jessica's sighs of contentment, completion and satisfaction settled peacefully in his heart. He never remembered being so in tune with another person before. *Except with Janie.*

A wave of guilt blindsided him. Up until now, he'd been able to separate the two, but was he disparaging his deceased wife's memory by finding comfort and some joy with her sister? Was he hurting Jessica and dishonoring his wife?

Zane carefully removed himself from a sleeping Jess and padded away from the bed. Words he hadn't found before came rushing forth, pounding inside his head. He had a song to finish, and the lyrics blasted in his ears now. The song that had haunted him for months would finally see the light of day.

Jessica just put on the finishing touches on her makeup, a hint of pale-green eye shadow and toner under her eyes to conceal the dark shadows from the ungodly remnants of whatever bug she'd had. Her appetite was coming back, thankfully, and she put on a lemon-yellow sundress decorated with tiny white daisies to make her feel human again. She looked at her reflection in the mirror. The dress did the trick. She had a dash of color in her face now, and wearing something fun perked up her spirits.

As she walked into the kitchen, Mrs. Lopez was just setting out her morning meal.

"Thank you," she said, taking a seat. She could definitely handle hard-boiled eggs, toast and a cup of tea. "You always know exactly what I want to eat. How do you do that?"

"I am like a little mouse, observing, watching. I can see you are feeling better, but the stomach needs time to rest. Today, you eat a little. Tomorrow, a little bit more. If you want something more, you just need to tell me."

"No, no. This is perfect. Exactly what I feel like having. It's…late."

"*Sí*. You've been waking late."

"The bug I had wore me out."

Minutes later, just as she was finishing up her last bite of toast and sip of tea, a knock on the deck door brought her head up.

Mrs. Lopez was there before Jessica pushed her chair out to rise. "Hello, Mr. McKay," she said politely, her olive face blossoming. Even Zane's housekeeper was starstruck. Dylan McKay had the same effect on all women, young and old, happily married or not.

"Hello, Mrs. Lopez. I took a walk down the beach to see if Zane could spare a few minutes for me this morning."

"He is not here."

"But I am." Jessica walked over to the door. "Dylan, hi! Is there something I can help you with?"

Dylan had a briefcase tucked under his arm, yet dressed in plaid board shorts and a teal-blue muscle shirt, he looked like a walking advertisement for sunscreen or surfboards. Hardly businessman attire, but that was Dylan.

"Hey, Jess."

"Thanks, Mrs. Lopez," she said, and the woman backed away.

"What's up?"

He brushed past her and stepped into the kitchen. "Looking beautiful as always," Dylan said. It wasn't a line with Dylan. He had a genuine appreciation for women, and he seemed to love to compliment them.

"You're looking fit yourself," she said. "Still running?"

He scrunched up his face. "Yeah. It's getting old."

"Why don't you break it up? Do five miles in the morning, five miles at night?"

His brows rose. "Wow, smart and beautiful. Does Zane know what a treasure you are?"

"I don't know. Why don't you ask him?" She grinned.

"Well, I like your idea, Little Miss Smarty Pants. I might just try breaking up the run and see how it goes."

Mrs. Lopez stood by the oven with a coffee pot in hand, reminding Jess of her manners.

"Would you like a cup of coffee? Water? Juice? Anything?" How comfortable she felt in the role of hostess to Zane's friends. It was something she didn't want to end.

"No, thanks. I'm good right now. Actually, I brought a revised script for Zane to look over. The screenwriter made some adjustments that I think really enhance the story. I've highlighted the parts that would affect Zane. Would you like to see them?"

"Of course!" It sounded better than watching her nails dry, and she was still on the clock as far as work went, even if it was Saturday. "I'd love to. Why don't you come into the office?"

He followed her, and as she entered the office, she went to the wood shutters first, opening them and allowing eastern light to enter the room. "Have a seat."

"Wow, looks like Zane's doing some writing."

Dylan was eyeing Zane's desk littered with sheet music

crumpled into tight balls. Ready to clear away the mess, she noticed the waste basket was full to the brim with the same. Mrs. Lopez worked her way through the rooms every morning. It was evident she hadn't made it to this room yet. "Yeah, I guess he is."

"That's good, right? As far as I know, he hasn't written a song for years."

Since Janie's death.

"I suppose so."

Dylan sat down on the sofa and opened his portfolio. "Do you know where he keeps the original script I gave him? We can compare the two. I'm eager to see if you think the changes work as well as I do."

"Sure. I think Zane locked it up in his desk for safekeeping. Just give me a second to get the key."

"No problem. I'm a patient man."

She doubted that. She moved quickly to retrieve the key from a set Zane kept in his bedroom dresser drawer. She came back to find Dylan with head down, making notes on the script. "Okay, here we go."

She unlocked the bottom drawer, and sure enough, there was the script. She made a grab for it and did a rapid double take at the folder that lay beneath it. In black lettering and handwritten by Zane, the title was spelled out. "Janie's Song. Final."

Zane never mentioned he was writing a song about Janie.

All that sheet music? She had to guess that Zane had been working on this recently. As recently as last night, maybe? She'd woken in the middle of the night and opened her eyes to an empty pillow beside her. She'd heard distant strumming and figured Zane was practicing his guitar again. She thought nothing of it and had fallen right back to sleep. But now, as she glanced at all the rejected papers strewn across his desk and bubbling up from his trash, she knew it had to be true.

It was and always had been all about Janie.

How could she be jealous of her dead sister?

Tears welled in her eyes. She felt sick to her stomach again.

She handed Dylan the first version of the script and went back to the drawer to lock it up. Instead, her profound sense of curiosity had her giving Dylan her back. She opened the manila folder and slipped out the first page of new, unwrinkled sheet music.

She shouldn't be prying. It wasn't her business. Yet she had to know. It was killing her not to know. Her hands trembling, she scanned the lyrics. "I will always love you, Janie girl." She'd forgotten he used to call her that. His Janie Girl. "Without you here, my road is bleak, my path unclear. My heart is yours without a doubt…"

Dylan cleared his throat. The innocent sound reminded her she wasn't alone. She slapped the folder shut. She'd seen enough. She didn't need to see more. What good would it do to torture herself? She was already torn up inside.

She locked the drawer before Dylan grew suspicious and turned to give him a smile. His head was still buried in the script. Then she heard the familiar sound of boots clicking down the hallway.

"Jess?"

She didn't answer. Dylan gave her a look and then called out. "We're in here, Zane. Your office."

Zane popped his head inside the doorway before entering. He shot Jess a questioning stare. She averted her eyes. She couldn't look at him right now, and he was probably wondering why she hadn't answered him. Was Zane jealous of Dylan? Did he think something was going on behind his back? It would serve him right, but that was a small consolation for her.

"Hey, Dylan. What's up?" Zane asked.

She had to get her mental bearings. She needed out of this room, pronto.

Dylan rose to shake his hand. "Hi, buddy. I came by looking for you with a new and improved version of the script. Jess invited me inside, and I was just about to go over it with her to get her opinion."

"Looks like you two don't need me now," she said. "Dylan, you can go over it with Zane. I just remembered I've got some urgent phone calls to make. See you, later."

"Sure. Later," Dylan said, distracted. He turned to his friend. "Zane, is this a good time?"

She dashed away before Zane could get any words out to the contrary. But his completely baffled expression rattled her already tightly strung nerves.

Jessica refused to shed a tear. She refused to cave to her riotous emotions. What good would it do? She'd wasted a lifetime of tears on Steven. Her well was dry. But her heart physically hurt, the kind of pain that no tears or aspirin or alcohol could cure. She marched into her room, closed the door and walked over to her bed. Plopping down, she stared out the window to majestic blue skies glazed with marshmallow tufted clouds.

She liked California. Everything was beautiful here. The people were easy, friendly and carefree. The near-tropical summer consisted of windswept days and warm, balmy nights.

But suddenly, and for the first time since coming here, she missed home. She missed her small apartment and tiny balcony where she grew cactus in a vertical garden and the jasmine flourished over the rail grating. She missed her little kitchen, her bedroom of lavender blooms and country white lace.

She missed her mama.

And her friends.

She didn't see a future with Zane. As much as it broke her heart to think it, Zane wasn't available to her emotionally. He was hung up on her sister and losing her and their baby had scarred him for life.

"You can't get blood from a stone," she muttered. It was

one of her mama's ageless comments on life. It was right up there with another Holcomb favorite: You can take a horse to water, but you can't make him drink.

Ain't that the truth?

Jessica rose and eased out of her sundress. She opened the vast walk-in closet that doubled for a black hole and selected a pair of running shoes, shorts and a top. She re-dressed quickly and lifted her long locks into a ponytail. Giving herself a glimpse in the mirror, she saw someone she didn't recognize. She'd become a California girl like the ones the Beach Boys sang about: the blonde, tanned, skimpy shorts-wearing chicks who adorned the shores of the Pacific coastline.

Jess wasn't sure how she felt about that. She wasn't sure about anything right now.

She headed down the staircase and heard male voices. There was no way to avoid Dylan and Zane since she had to walk past the office to get out the back door. She stuck her head inside the room. "Hey, guys. I'm going for a run."

Zane glanced up, but she couldn't look him in the eye, and it dawned on her in that very second, that the sick feeling invading her belly was betrayal…the lyrics of a song hurting her more than perhaps being left at the altar by the wrong man. "We're almost through here. If you wait a sec…"

"I'll join you, too," Dylan was saying.

"Uh, no thanks. I think I'll go this one alone. You guys finish up your work. I'll see you later."

She turned, but not before she saw Zane's eyes narrow to a squint, trying to figure her out.

She cringed as she walked away. She'd been border-line rude, but she couldn't help it. She needed some time alone, away from the house and the influences that could very well blindside her again. She hurried out the door and raced down the steps. She headed to where the tide teased the sand under the glorious Moonlight Beach sunshine and began to jog.

She ran at a pace that would keep her feet moving for the longest amount of time. She dodged and weaved around Frisbee-tossing teenagers, small swimsuit-clad kids digging tunnels in the wet sand and boogie boarders crashing against the shore. Sea breezes kept her cool as she dug in, jogging farther and farther away. She headed to a cove, a thin parcel of land surrounded by odd-shaped rock clusters called Moon Point that extended into the sea, forming a crescent.

The rocks looked climbable, and she was in the mood for a challenge.

Up she went, gripping the sharp edge of one rock and then finding her footing on another. Winds blew stronger here, but she held on and worked her way up. She'd heard the view from Moon Point was the best. On a clear day you could see the Santa Monica Pier. Once she got the hang of it, she was pretty good at climbing, and best of all, she was alone. She had no competition for viewing rights. She reached the top in fewer than five minutes and planted her butt on a flat part of a rock.

A hand salute kept the sun from her eyes, and she looked out at the vast ocean view. It was amazing and peaceful up here. Quiet, as if she had the entire ocean to herself.

She could stay up here all day.

Waves rocked the Point, and the sea spray sprinkled her body. The drops felt cool and refreshing, but also woke her to the time. She'd been up on the Point for three hours. She'd hardly noticed the others who'd decided to join her. They'd come and gone, but she'd stayed.

She climbed down from the rock, a deceivingly much harder proposition than going up, and she walked along the shore that was slowly and surely becoming deserted by summer school buses and mothers eager to get on the road before traffic hit. She reached the strip of beach in front of Zane's house half an hour later, and her heart somersaulted when she spotted him on the deck.

He stood with feet spread wide as if he'd been there a long time. His beige linen shirt flapped in the breeze, and his eyes, those beautiful, deep, dark eyes, locked directly on her. There was no need to wave. They'd made their connection. She stifled a whimper and headed toward him.

He started to move toward her, climbing down the steps to the sand, a loving smile absent on his lips. This was not going to be an easy conversation. For either of them.

"Where in hell did you go?" he asked.

She blinked. He'd never spoken to her in that tone. "I took a run."

"You were gone for almost four freaking hours, Jess."

"Well, I'm back now."

His bronzed face reddened to deep brick. "I can see that. Why you'd go off in such a damn hurry?"

"I needed to be alone."

"On the beach? Must've been a thousand people out today."

That was an exaggeration. "Okay, fine. I needed to get away from you for a little while."

He jerked back. "Me? What did I do? And don't change the subject. I was worried."

"Why were you worried, Zane?"

"Because, damn it. I had no idea where you were. You could've gotten swept up by a wave, or some lunatic could've grabbed you, or you might have fallen and gotten hurt. You didn't have your cell phone with you. How was I supposed to know if you were all right? Who goes jogging for four hours?"

"I needed to think."

"So, did you?"

"Yes, up on Moon Point."

Zane rolled his eyes. "You climbed the Point?"

"It wasn't hard."

The sound of teeth grinding reached her ears, but he didn't say another word.

A sigh wobbled in her throat before she released it. She laced her fingers with his and he gazed down at their hands entwined.

"Zane," she said, softening her voice. "You were worried because you care some about me, but also because you feel responsible for me. You promised my mom that you'd watch out for me. Don't deny it. I know it's true. You didn't want to fail her. I get that. I actually appreciate that. But you don't have to worry about me. I'm not the same weak, heartbroken Jess that showed up on your door more than a month ago. I've changed."

A genuine spark of sincerity flickered in his eyes. "You're amazing, Jess. Strong and smart and funny and beautiful."

She hesitated a beat. His compliments nearly destroyed her. "Don't say nice things to me."

"They're true."

"There you go again, Zane."

"Can't help it."

"I'm leaving tomorrow." She had to be strong now. She couldn't show him how her heart was cracking at this very second.

"No, you're not."

She nodded. She wouldn't be persuaded.

"What can I say to make you stay?"

She could think of a dozen things, but she remained silent.

"Why, Jess? What's happened? You owe me an explanation."

In a way, she did. "You asked what you could say to make me stay? Well, I've got something to tell you to make you rethink that."

He squeezed her hand. "Never going to happen, Jess."

"I took a pregnancy test yesterday." The words were hard to get out, and tears burned behind her eyes unexpectedly. She was through with crying. Yet one lonely drop made its way down her cheek.

Breath rushed out of his mouth. The gasp was loud enough to wake the dead. He blinked several times, staring at her as if trying to make sense of what she'd just said. His hands dropped to his sides. He probably didn't even know they had. Just like that, she had her answer.

All remnants of anger left his eyes. They filled with... fear. And he began shaking his head as if he'd heard wrong. "You took a pregnancy test?"

"Yes. I've been feeling tired and nauseated and, well, I had some other symptoms."

The fear spread to his face, which seemed to turn a putrid shade of avocado green. At any minute, he might be the one upchucking. His body, on the other hand, became one rigid piece of granite.

"I'm not pregnant."

A sigh from the depths of his chest rushed out uncontrollably fast, his breath tumbling nosily. The relief on his face drifted down to the rest of his body, and his form sagged heavily. He looked like a man who'd been given a reprieve from the worst fate in the world.

Sadly, his reaction didn't really surprise her. She'd known all along. He didn't want her child. He couldn't handle the commitment of loving another human being more than anything else in the world. He'd been there, done that once in his life. He was still plenty scarred up on the inside, but his scars also showed in his lack of commitment to his career, his floundering around, trying to reinvent himself as an actor, maybe? Or a restaurant entrepreneur. He had clipped wings, and breaking his foot had served as a means for Zane to put a temporary halt to his life.

"Maybe I shouldn't have told you," she whispered. "Kept my trap shut."

"No, no. I'm glad you did." He straightened, the gentleman and dutiful decent man that he was taking hold. But nothing could've hurt her more than seeing, *living* his response. Witnessing the somber truth in his frightened eyes for those brief moments had dissected her heart.

Yet a ridiculously hopeful part of her wished he might have been glad or even receptive to the idea of her having his child. Even if it wasn't planned. Even if it hadn't been conceived in wedlock.

When Janie had told Zane about her pregnancy, he'd been over-the-moon happy. He sent her flowers every day for a week. He hired a decorator and told her to fix up a nursery any way she wanted. He'd written a song for the baby, a soothing lullaby meant only for their new family. He'd told his friends, his fans and the press. The town of Beckon had rejoiced. Their golden boy was going to be a father.

Now Zane reclaimed her hands. His were cold and clammy, and another pang singed her heart. "I wouldn't want you to go through something like that without telling me. I, uh, want you to know that if things had turned out differently, we would've worked it out, Jess."

She didn't want to know what he meant by *working it out*. How did one work out having a baby? It didn't sound like flowers and sweet lullabies. "I know. And now you understand why I have to leave tomorrow."

She couldn't find fault with him. She knew if he could've made her feel better, he would have. But the man didn't have it in him. He didn't love her. He was through with commitment. He'd already had the one great love in his life. The stony expression on his face said it all.

A cold blast coated her insides. The frost would linger even through the Texas heat of home. She loved Zane and wanted to have his child. But he would never know her feelings. He would come to think of her as his wife's sister again.

Sweet Jess.

She wasn't destined for love.

"I'll pack my bags tonight, Zane. Don't bother to see me off. I'm leaving before dawn."

Eleven

Jessica was all about change now, moving the desks around her classroom in a new way. She wanted to see each of her students' faces when she taught in front of the blackboard. Making a connection to them was of the utmost importance. She didn't want to see their profiles but look directly into their eyes to gauge their level of attention and encourage their participation. She had her lesson plans all laid out, her mind spinning about the mark she would make on her students' lives. Who didn't remember their first-grade teacher? And she hoped they would one day think upon her fondly and know she cared.

School started in Beckon just after Labor Day, one week from today. She was eager for the semester to begin, eager to put the past behind her. Scraping sounds echoed in the classroom as she moved chairs across the linoleum floor. She was actually working up a sweat. The summer heat hadn't relented yet. September was just as hot as June in Texas.

Just minutes ago, Steven had knocked on her door. She'd been surprised to see him, but one look at his sheepish face and she knew she'd never really loved him in that forever kind of way. He'd offered her excuse after excuse and finally apologized to her. She'd listened patiently and let him have his say, all the while thinking he'd actually done her a favor by not marrying her, brutal as it had been. When he was through, it was her turn to speak. She didn't swear, didn't get angry, but calmly and very systematically gave him a piece of her mind and then dismissed him.

The new Jess had finally been heard, and it had been liberating.

She kept her hands busy maneuvering desks, not wasting another minute on Steven. But in the silence of her classroom, her mind drifted back to Zane, as it always seemed to do, and her last day in California.

Zane wouldn't let her leave on her own that morning. He'd gotten up before dawn, insisting on driving her to the airport. He had no clue how terribly hard it was for her to say goodbye. He had no way of knowing that her rebound guy had become her Mr. Right and that he'd taught her what love was truly about.

Thanks to airport regulations, Zane couldn't walk her to her boarding gate, but he'd handled her luggage and helped her get as far as he could without garnering a reprimand from security. Luckily, it was the butt crack of dawn, as her friend Sally would put it, and the Zane Williams fan club members obviously weren't early risers. Zane had told her in the car that he didn't care if he was recognized or if the paparazzi were following them—which they weren't. He wanted to see her off.

"Well," he said, dropping her luggage at his feet and taking both of her hands. His dark lashes lowered to her, framing beautiful brown eyes that seemed to give her a view into his soul. "I'll miss the hell out of you, sweetheart."

He had a way with words. The corner of her mouth lifted. How could she not love this man who'd braved Homeland Security, a possible rash of Super Fans and the ungodly early hour to wish her farewell?

"Thank you, Zane." She looked away, into the street that was starting to swarm with taxicabs and buses. She couldn't tell him she'd miss him. That would be the understatement of the century. "I appreciate you letting me stay with you. I'll miss…California."

She'd become a California girl, by Beach Boy standards.

He moved his hands up her arms, caressing her skin, and she began to prickle everywhere he touched.

"Won't you miss me a little?"

"I can't answer that, Zane." *Don't make me.*

He nodded, and his magic hands continued up her arms. "I won't ever forget the time we've spent together. It's meant a lot to me."

Her eyes squeezed shut to hold back tears. She filled her lungs, steadied herself and stared right back at him. "I won't forget, either. I'd better go. They'll be boarding soon."

"Just a sec," he said and then planted a kiss on her lips that would've brought her to her knees if he hadn't been holding her arms. He kissed her for all he was worth. And then he moved his hands to her face and cradled her cheeks, lifting her chin to position his mouth once again and stake a claim in a whopper of a kiss that brought her up onto her toes.

When the kiss ended, he pressed his forehead to hers, and they stood that way for a long time with eyes closed, their breaths mingling.

Over the loudspeaker, her flight was announced. It was time to board.

"Damn," Zane muttered and stepped back.

She lifted her luggage and began the trek that took her away from the man she loved.

He didn't ask her to stay this time.

They both knew it was over.

She had walked away from him and never did look back.

Jess shook off that memory and after accomplishing what she set out to do in the classroom, she climbed into her car and turned on the radio. Zane's melodic voice came across the airwaves. "Great, just great." She didn't need any reminders of how much she missed him. She punched off the radio and cruised along the streets of Beckon, aiming her car for home.

She needed a good soak in the tub.

Or better yet, she'd go soak her head and be done with it.

"Happy birthday, Jessica. How's my girl today?"

"Hi, Mama." Jessica left the curb in front of her apartment and bounded around the front end of her mother's car. Climbing into the passenger seat, she leaned in for a kiss. Mama planted one right smack on her cheek. The none-too-subtle scent of Elizabeth Taylor's White Diamonds perfume matched the heavy humidity in the air, but it was comforting in a way, since the classic scent defined her mama to a T. And today of all days, Jess and her mother needed the comfort.

Mama wasn't the best driver, but she insisted on picking her up and driving today. Thankfully the roads in Beckon weren't complicated or crowded, because the way her mother drove scared the daylights out of her. She clutched the steering wheel like a lifeline and rocked the darn thing from side to side with nervous jerks. Amazingly the car continued down the road in a straight line.

She looked over her shoulder at an arrangement of bubblegum-pink daylilies and snow-white roses. "Pretty flowers, Mama."

"Janie's favorites. I've got a bunch for you back at the house, sweet darlin'." It had become a ritual to visit Janie's grave on their mutual birthday. Neither of them would have it any other way.

The cemetery was on the edge of town, and it didn't take long to get there. They both stepped out of the car and walked fifty feet to the beautiful monumental headstone that Zane had had constructed. "Looks like someone's already been here today," Mama said.

More than a dozen velvety red and white roses shot up from the in-ground vase. "Zane probably had them sent." He wouldn't forget Janie's birthday. He'd always made a big deal of it when she was alive, hunting for the perfect gift for her, making her day special in any way he could.

"I don't think he had them sent," Mama said, pointing to one rose in particular. "Look at that."

"His guitar pick," Jessica said softly. Black with white lettering, the pick placed between opened petals read, "Love, Zane."

"He's in town, Jess."

"Don't be silly, Mama. Zane doesn't come here. If he was in Beckon, it'd be all over the news by now. You know how the town loves him."

"And so do you, Jessica."

"Mama," she breathed quietly. "No."

"Yes, you do. You love that man. There's no need denying it. He's a fine man, decent, and oh, boy, he loved your sister like there was no tomorrow, but Janie's gone. And Lord knows I wish she wasn't, but if you two have something—"

"Mama, I wish Janie wasn't gone. I really do, with all my heart. But you've got it wrong." She wished her sister had lived. Her baby would've been almost two by now, and she'd be the favorite aunt. Aunt Jess. Janie and Zane were meant for each other.

She was a poor substitute for the real thing.

"We'll see."

Jess ignored her mama's ominous reply and hoped that Zane wasn't within one hundred miles of Beckon. Make that one thousand.

Mama laid the flowers down, and both said a silent prayer. They stayed like usual, half an hour, talking to Janie, catching her up on news. Then, with tears welling in their eyes, said goodbye. It was always the hardest day of the year, sharing a birthday with her sister and being able to live out her birthdays while Janie's were cut short.

Mama pulled through the cemetery gates and onto the road. "How about some barbecue for your birthday dinner? I invited Sally and Louisa and Marty to join us."

Her mother, bless her soul, didn't get to grieve for Janie fully on a day that would maybe bring about some healing. Because it was Jessica's birthday as well, she had to put on a cheery front, plaster a smile on her face and pretend her heart wasn't breaking.

"Sure, Mama, that sounds good."

Sally, her best friend, and Louisa, her mama's dear friend, would be there. Marty was Louisa's daughter and also a schoolteacher. Jessica sort of got Marty's friendship by default, which was okay by her. Marty was a wonderful person.

The parking lot at BBQ Heaven was full by the time they got there. Odd for a weeknight, and though the place had new owners who'd changed the name of the restaurant from Beckon Your Bliss BBQ, it still served the best barbecue beef sliders and tri-tip in three counties. There were times back in California when she'd craved those smoky, hickory-laced meals. Now her mouth watered.

They met their friends outside and entered the place together. Seating for five wasn't a problem, it seemed. Her mama must've made reservations. They were seated at the best crescent-shaped Red Hots candy-colored booth in the restaurant. Mama and Louisa sat in the middle so they could gab, and Jessica and her friends shared the end seats.

"Thank you all for coming," Jessica said. She was getting her life back in order. Seeing Marty and Sally helped. Of course, Sally knew all. She'd picked her up from the airport when she'd returned from Moonlight Beach, and Jessica had spilled the beans. She'd sworn Sally to secrecy that day, as if they were in high school, Jess finding a way to trust a friend again. It was all good.

"Sure thing, friend. Happy birthday. Wish I was twenty-six again," Marty said with a lingering sigh.

Louisa rolled her eyes. "You're only twenty-eight, sugar."

"I know, Mom, but twenty-six was a good year for me."

Sally gave Marty a look, and all three of them laughed.

"Happy birthday, Jessica," Louisa said, her voice somber. "I hope you can find some joy today."

"I'm sure she will," Mama said with enough certainty to make Jess turn her way. Her mother's light emerald eyes were dewy soft and smiling. It was great to see her so relaxed.

The waitress came by their table. Everyone ordered a different dish for sharing, with five different sides as well, garlic mashed potatoes, white cheddar mac and cheese, bacon baked beans, almond string beans and corn soufflé. No one would go home hungry.

Bluegrass music played in the background, but no one could hear a word. The place was hopping, conversations from crowded tables going a mile a minute.

She was halfway through her salad when someone tapped on a microphone, the screeching sound check enough to bust an eardrum. Finally, the sound leveled out, the background bluegrass was history, and George, the restaurant manager, spoke into the mike. "We have a little surprise in store for you tonight," he said from the front of the room. She had to crane her neck to see him above the heads bobbing to catch a look. "Our own Zane Williams is back in town, and he's got a new song he wants to sing for all of you. Sort of a trial run, so to speak. I know not a single one of you will mind being serenaded tonight. So let's give Zane a big Beckon welcome."

Applause broke out, and just like that, Zane stepped up with a guitar strap slung over his shoulder. His six-foot-two frame, black hat and studded white shirt made him stand out from the crowd like no one else could, especially since a spotlight miraculously shone on him like a sainted cowboy who traveled with his own glow.

Lord, help her. He was amazing. She'd almost forgotten how much. And her heart did a little flip. She faced her mother who refused to look at her. And suddenly it clicked.

The innuendo at the cemetery, her mother's suspicious behavior today, the *we'll see*s and the *I'm sure she will*s.

Oh, Mama, what did you do?

Sally was beaming and mouthing, *Did you know?*

She shook her head.

And then Zane commanded his audience with simple words. "Thank y'all for letting me interrupt your meal and try out my new song on you. George, I owe you one, buddy," he said, smiling at the man standing to his side. "This one here, it's intended to wish someone I love a happy birthday. So here goes. Oh, it's called 'Janie's Song.'"

*Oh*s and *ah*s swept through the crowd. Everyone knew about Zane's undying love for Janie. A cold rash of dread kicked Jessica in the gut. Her belly ached. Bile rushed up to her mouth. How could she sit here and listen to the lyrics of the song she'd secretly read, a tribute to the love Zane still had for Janie? His voice was a beautifully rich torture instrument that would crumble her heart to powdery dust.

Her gaze darted to the door. Could she make an escape without being noticed?

Zane began to sing. Too late for an escape. He had the floor and a captivated audience. The words she'd remembered, words she'd repeated inside her head a hundred times, poured out of his mouth in a ballad pure and honest, just Zane and his guitar.

"I will always love you, Janie girl. Without you here, my road was bleak, my path unclear. My heart was yours without a doubt…"

Her mama took her hand from underneath the table and squeezed. Jessica glanced at her and found warmth brimming in her eyes. Her mother nodded toward Zane with her chin, her gaze fondly returning to him. Jessica looked down. She couldn't bear to see him sing a love song to another woman, not even to Janie. Not now, not after what they'd shared together. Was that terrible of her?

He crooned, mesmerizing everyone in the place with his

deeply wrought emotions. The pain in his voice was unmistakable, but the lyrics that filled the now quiet room were new, different, changed.

"I loved you once, and it was fine. The finest love I'd ever known. But I'm movin' on, my Janie Girl, with a love so true, I know you'd approve. You see, my girl, you love her, too. You love her, too. You love her, too. You love her, too."

Jessica snapped her head up. Zane's eyes were closed, his head tilted, his hand strumming the chords on the guitar gently as the song eased out of him. He seemed free, liberated, somehow unburdened, even as he put his heart and soul into that song.

She stared at him, unable to shift her eyes away, her mind in an uproar. When he lifted his lids, he focused on her. Only her. He removed his hat in a gallant gesture, and the dark soulful depths of his eyes reeled her in further. All heads in the restaurant turned around. Some people were gaping, others smiling. She recognized quite a few who'd attended her almost-wedding. Her face flamed. What was he doing to her?

He removed the guitar strap from his shoulder and held his instrument with one hand now. He didn't seem to care that he was making a spectacle of himself. And her.

She rose from her seat. The spotlight swiveled to her and flashed in her eyes, making her squint.

Zane took a step toward her.

Her heart was beating so fast, she thought she'd faint.

There was only one thing she could manage right now.

She bolted.

Out of the restaurant.

Into the street.

And kept on running.

"Ah, hell," Zane muttered, ignoring the applause from the crowd and granting Mae Holcomb an apologetic shrug before he took off after Jess. It hadn't gone as he'd planned, that was for doggone sure. His chin held high, he walked out of the restaurant matter-of-factly as if women ran from him every day of the week. As soon as he made it to the street, he darted his head back and forth. Once he spotted Jess nearly a half a football field away, he took off at a sprint. If Doobie Purdy, his track coach, had seen her, he would've signed her up.

But he wasn't anything if not determined, his long legs no match for her. He caught up to her in no time but slowed to a few paces behind, rethinking what he wanted to say to her. He couldn't blow it. Not again. Jess meant the world to him.

"Go away," she tossed over her shoulder.

"That's not nice." What was nice was seeing her tanned, coltish legs making strides. Lifting his gaze higher to her beautiful backside reminded him of how soft and supple she was, how amazingly gifted she was in the female department.

She didn't slow her pace, not for a second.

"Ouch, damn it. I hurt my foot," Zane yelped.

She stopped then and turned, her eyes focused on his fake injury. He saw the depth of her compassion, the love she had for him glowing in her eyes—Dylan hadn't been wrong—and loved her so damn much right now, he could hardly breathe.

"You're not hurt, are you?"

"My heart is bleeding."

She gasped. A good sign.

"But your foot is fine, right?" She stared at his feet.

"Well, my foot could be hurt, Jess. Running like a bat outta hell to catch you in these boots isn't the kind of therapy I need."

She shook her head, and the gorgeous mass of blonde hair curled around her face. The run had put a rosy blush on her face, and the material of her coral dress lifted her ample chest with every breath she took, nearly killing him.

He inhaled now and was grateful she wasn't moving again. "You *really* don't play fair, Zane."

"I needed to see you today. On your birthday."

"Zane, what were you thinking? You made a spectacle of me in that restaurant. You of all people know I don't need another scandal in my life. I've had enough of being the laughingstock in this town. I… Why are you really here?"

"I came for you."

Hope popped into her eyes. Another good sign.

"You changed the words of the song."

"Dylan said he thought you'd seen those lyrics. He was right, wasn't he? Is that why you wouldn't stay with me?"

"Dylan? Are you taking advice from the Casanova now?"

"Don't knock Dylan. He's the one who made me see how much I missed you. How stupid I've been. And yes, after you left, I reworked the song, the lyrics coming easy and straight outta my heart. I sang it tonight just for you."

She folded her arms, and a warm glint entered her eyes. "But why there, in front of half the town?"

"I let you go. I was running scared. When you told me you might've been carrying my child, I couldn't deal with it, Jess. I've been blaming myself for Janie's death all this time, feeling guilty about losing her and our child. Deep down, I hated myself. I didn't think I'd ever want again, or love again. It was easier to live in the moment and not look to the future. But then you left, and I was hollowed out, gutted to my sorry bones. I missed you something fierce. I didn't think me saying it would be enough. I didn't know if you'd believe me unless I shouted it from the rooftops.

"I'm not doing the movie, and the restaurant is the last one I'm building. I'm going to finish up my tour, Jess. I'm through hiding my head in the sand. I'm through not being me."

The corners of her mouth lifted. He wanted to see her pretty smile again, but it wasn't there, not yet. "That's good, Zane. I'm happy for you."

Cars swerved around them. Someone honked a horn. Zane took her hand and guided her out of the middle of the street, to the sidewalk in front of the Cinema Palace. Ironically, it was nearly the same spot where he'd fallen in love with Janie. And now, here he was coming full circle, praying that her sister would agree to spend her life with him.

"Do you love me, Jess?"

She stared at him as if he were a three-headed monster.

"Do you?"

She pulled her hands free of him. "Yes, you idiot."

His face split wide open, and he didn't care if he looked like a grinning fool. Joy rushed out so fast he couldn't stop himself from telling her his plans. "I'm selling off my place, Jess. Finally. The land where I lived with your sister will belong to someone else one day soon. I'll never forget Janie, but it's time to move on. There's this beautiful parcel of land I've got my eye on. But I want you to see it, too. I want you to love it as much as I do. I'm digging in and putting down roots again, here in Beckon."

"But you said you're going back on tour."

"I have to finish it up. I'm bound by the contract, but after that, Jess, I'll stay here in Beckon and tour only during the summer months, when you're not teaching."

The smile he was praying for was almost there. "Zane, what are you saying?"

"Oh, yeah, got ahead of myself, didn't I?" He inhaled deeply and took hold of her hands. "I've already spoken to your mama, Jess. She and I worked things out, and she's given me her blessing. Sweet Jess, my Jess, you've helped me heal my body and my heart. And I can't imagine my life without you. Jessica Holcomb, I'm getting down on one knee," he said, his knee hitting the pavement. He tilted his head up and gazed into her eyes. "You taught me to look toward the future again. Knowing you, loving you the way I do, has given me the courage I needed to find my true self. I'm not afraid anymore. And I'm asking you for a second chance. I'm asking you to share your life with me. I'm asking you to be my wife, Jess. And Lord knows, have my baby one day. I want that. I really do. I love you with all my heart. Will you marry me, sweet Jess?"

Her beautiful, soft, grass-green eyes teared up, but her smile was real and genuine and the most beautiful thing about her. She hesitated so long he thought he'd blown it, but then she pulled him up and he stood facing her, his heart in her hands. "No girl marries her rebound guy," she said, her smile widening. "But me. I love you, Zane. I want to be your wife and spend the rest of my life with you."

"I'm so happy you said yes. 'Cause I wasn't gonna take no for an answer. It's all sorta weird and wonderful and unexpected, sweetheart, but my love is true. You have to know that."

"I do. And I think just like you said in your song, Janie would approve. She's looking down on us now and giving her blessing, too."

Holcomb women sure had a hold on him. "I'd love to believe so."

"I believe it, Zane. Let's go back to the restaurant and share our good news. Mama looked worried when I walked out."

"She wasn't the only one." Zane took her into his arms and pressed a kiss onto her soft, sweet lips. Planting his stake, claiming his woman. He was gonna hold on tight and never let her go.

Ever again.

* * * * *

"So you admit that the baby is mine?" Jacob demanded.

"Of course," KC said, as if it made perfect sense under the circumstances.

Jacob stalked closer. "Why would you do this, KC? Was I really so horrible that you refused to let me be a part of—this?"

"That was never the issue, Jacob—"

"Then what was? Because I can't imagine one big enough that you told yourself it was *okay* to deceive me. To keep my son a secret from me."

Her arms crossed over her ribs, pushing those delectable breasts higher in the tank top. Something he shouldn't notice right now. At all.

"I was afraid," she said. "Going away just seemed the safest thing until I was sure what to do."

"Safe? How? What the hell would safety have to do with it? I would never hurt you."

"I know that, Jacob, but it wasn't—"

"Fact is, you deprived me of three months of knowing my son," he choked out. "Not a note, a card or a call. Hell, not even a text. *By the way, I'm pregnant.*"

He'd made himself available, chased after her like a dog with no sense, and this was what he got for it.

This time, he didn't stop moving until he loomed over her petite frame. "So now, I'll have what I want."

* * *

The Blackstone Heir is part of the No.1 bestselling series from Mills & Boon® Desire™, Billionaires and Babies—Powerful men…wrapped around their babies' little f

THE BLACKSTONE HEIR

BY
DANI WADE

All rights reserved including the right of reproduction in whole or in part in any form. This edition is published by arrangement with Harlequin Books S.A.

This is a work of fiction. Names, characters, places, locations and incidents are purely fictional and bear no relationship to any real life individuals, living or dead, or to any actual places, business establishments, locations, events or incidents. Any resemblance is entirely coincidental.

This book is sold subject to the condition that it shall not, by way of trade or otherwise, be lent, resold, hired out or otherwise circulated without the prior consent of the publisher in any form of binding or cover other than that in which it is published and without a similar condition including this condition being imposed on the subsequent purchaser.

® and ™ are trademarks owned and used by the trademark owner and/or its licensee. Trademarks marked with ® are registered with the United Kingdom Patent Office and/or the Office for Harmonisation in the Internal Market and in other countries.

Published in Great Britain 2015
by Mills & Boon, an imprint of Harlequin (UK) Limited,
Eton House, 18-24 Paradise Road, Richmond, Surrey, TW9 1SR

© 2015 Katherine Worsham

ISBN: 978-0-263-25250-7

51-0215

Harlequin (UK) Limited's policy is to use papers that are natural, renewable and recyclable products and made from wood grown in sustainable forests. The logging and manufacturing processes conform to the legal environmental regulations of the country of origin.

Printed and bound in Spain
by CPI, Barcelona

Dani Wade astonished her local librarians as a teenager when she carried home ten books every week—and actually read them all. Now she writes her own characters, who clamor for attention in the midst of the chaos that is her life. Residing in the southern United States with a husband, two kids, two dogs and one grumpy cat, she stays busy until she can closet herself away with her characters once more.

To Ms Bobbie Tate—many years ago, you became my grandmother through marriage. You became my friend through your sweet spirit and my Maw Maw through your love. I can't thank you enough for being such a treasured part of my life.

One

"Hello, beautiful."

KC Gatlin heard the bell of a store door as she walked past on the sidewalk, but it simply registered as background noise. That voice, on the other hand, landed like a grenade on her senses. She could still hear the same words, the same deep sigh as she opened her door to him for the first time. Only this time he sounded not just sexy, but surprised.

Turning slowly, she found herself face-to-face with a man she had hoped not to see for many long, long months. The expectation was unrealistic, she knew, considering she once again lived in the same town as his family. The town he came home to visit often. His appearance now marked the approach of sure disaster, even as it brought into sharp focus how much she'd craved a glimpse of his tall runner's build and the unique blend of blonds in his close-cropped hair.

"Jacob Blackstone," she said, stalling while her brain struggled to come up with the flirty, easy responses for which she was known. They made her great tips as a waitress and bartender. But now, when she needed flippancy the most, it remained scarce. "What're you doing here?"

Stupid. There was a very logical reason why he would

be here: to check on his invalid mother, Lily Blackstone, now that his grandfather was dead and his brother Aiden had moved home. KC had just hoped to catch a few months' breather before facing her past.

Facing her mistakes.

"I mean, what are you doing on this end of town?" At least that question made sense. After all, Blackstone Manor was on the other side of Black Hills. But her fears, along with the steady, sober gaze of her former lover, had her brains whisked around like scrambled eggs. She had to get a handle on the panic jangling along her nerves.

He held up a small shopping bag. "Bandages. I needed to pick some up on my way home from work."

"Are you hurt—wait, home from work?" She tilted her head back for a better view of Jacob's face. She'd loved his height when they were together; how it sheltered her, protected her. Too bad that feeling of security had been nothing but an illusion.

"Yes, from the mill." He didn't look away, his gorgeous amber eyes with their unusual swirl of dark chocolate boring into her. She wanted a break from his unrelenting stare…and paradoxically wished she could bask in his attention. While her reactions ricocheted inside her, he went on, "I guess you haven't been home long enough to hear the news?" His voice rose at the end in a question, along with his brow.

"I guess not. I just moved back this week." Her stomach slowly turned over. Once. Then again. Why had her family not told her before she came home? The answer was obvious: they wanted her here, with them. She might never have returned if she'd known Jacob was now a permanent resident of Black Hills again.

She and Jacob had met on a plane to Black Hills—she'd been coming home from visiting her aunt in Seattle and had made a connecting flight in Philadelphia, where Jacob had been flying from to check on his mother. They'd seen each other every time he'd come to town since. Then reality had caught up with her in the threats of Jacob's grandfather and she'd gone to live with her aunt. A world away from this fascinating man and what they'd shared together.

She'd thought returning to her family would be safe now that James Blackstone was dead and gone. His threats to take away the livelihood of three single women unable to defend themselves—and a lifetime of proof that he'd do it—would finally be over. She'd known she would have to handle Jacob eventually, but had hoped to have more time. Much more.

She had a feeling he was about to burst her bubble.

"I've moved back to Black Hills to help Aiden run the mill. He has to split his time between here and New York, and with all the problems at the mill, we wanted a full-time presence."

"Yes, I heard that there were some odd things happening over there," she murmured. *Full-time?* The Lord must be punishing her for the secrets she kept.

Speaking of secrets… She tilted her head to the side as unobtrusively as possible to get a glimpse of the sidewalk behind Jacob. Her mother and grandmother were due to come out of the general store any minute. While she knew she had to talk to Jacob soon, she would prefer not to do it on the sidewalk in front of Parson's Pharmacy with the whole town looking on.

At least she had one thing going for her: Main Street was lined with miniature Bradford pear trees that would keep any busybodies from getting a clear view from the surrounding stores. In late spring, they were packed with white blooms that afforded even more privacy. Maybe no one would see more than just two neighbors greeting each other.

If she caused a scene on the sidewalk, Jacob would probably have a conniption. Months of him not taking her anywhere in public in Black Hills had taught her that much.

In the year they'd dated, Jacob had never introduced her to his family, never taken her *out* on a date. They'd spent evenings at her house, cooking, watching movies and making love before he went home to Philadelphia. She'd gone to visit his apartment there once, hoping to learn more about the city he loved enough to leave his family behind. Maybe a little about his work as the head of a large manufacturing company. But they'd never made it out of the apartment. KC had craved a real love all her life, after being abandoned over and over again as a child. Jacob wasn't looking for love… Still, she'd wanted him, so she'd forced herself not to need more from him.

His actions had made it obvious he wasn't interested in a long-term relationship, so she'd ignored her secret yearning for more. She'd been too afraid of losing him to insist. Responsible, steady guys usually didn't look at her twice—after all, she worked in a bar. But it wasn't just his incredible looks, smart, confident attitude or how good he'd been at rocking her world. Until she'd disappeared, Jacob had been attentive, caring and sexy—everything she'd ever wanted. But never committed—which was the one thing she'd needed him to be.

"Waiting for someone?" Jacob asked, folding his arms across his chest.

Oh, how she remembered that stance. He mostly resorted to it when he was disapproving or uncertain and didn't want anyone to know it. She'd jokingly called it his Dom stance, though Jacob didn't need power games to keep the bedroom interesting. His tightened muscles and locked legs exuded a commanding aura that sent shivers down her spine. Jake had strength in spades, but she hadn't trusted him to use it *for* her, to keep her. Her childhood had taught her it wouldn't happen.

She must have gotten lost in her thoughts, because Jacob bent closer, looming over her. "A new man, perhaps?"

A man? She'd thought she could be happily done with

the whole species for quite a while, until today. Jacob Blackstone had jump-started her tingling all over again. That intense gaze sent her heart racing and mouth watering. "Um, actually, my mom is on her way. Just checking for her, that's all."

Wow, this was so far from her usual easy conversations that she felt as if her secret was screaming from her guilty heart. Still, she could use his assumptions to her advantage.

"But yes, I do have a new man in my life." Jacob didn't need to know in what capacity after all. Anything to keep him at arm's length as long as possible.

"Is that why you changed your number…after refusing to answer your phone for weeks?"

Whoa. Not the direction she'd anticipated. But then, Jacob Blackstone had never failed to surprise her. There were whole areas of his life she knew absolutely nothing about.

"Look, Jacob, I'm really sorry. That was very bad of me." But she'd been carrying a heavy load with no idea what direction to go. A reason, not an excuse. She'd finally run far away, only returning once James Blackstone was dead. If she'd known Jacob would return, too—but no. Keeping secrets from him forever wasn't fair. She simply needed time. Time that was now draining away with the speed of sand in an hourglass.

"I just want to know why," he said, toned shoulder muscles flexing beneath his dress shirt. How did a CEO maintain such incredible physique…and stamina? She had to remind herself that it hadn't been enough, that she needed a man who would fight for her, no matter what anyone else thought.

"Did you think I couldn't handle the news that you wanted to break it off?" he asked.

"I…" Across the street, KC noticed a group of familiar women strolling down the sidewalk. Black Hills was a relatively small town. Everyone knew most everyone else.

Standing on Main Street talking with Jacob was the equivalent of standing on a stage. She needed to escape before someone started paying attention—

Or her mother and grandmother made an appearance.

"I just… Well, I didn't know how to tell you I wasn't interested anymore, actually." Clunky, but the truth. Knowing she'd chosen the cowardly way out, she still forced herself to sidestep him, then back away. "And you never seemed to want to deal with any deeper stuff, so…really, Jake, I'm just, well, sorry."

Then she turned and walked away, praying she could sidetrack her mother and grandmother before they proceeded to parade her baby down Main Street. She couldn't let Jacob learn about his son that way. Because he'd take one look and realize the main reason why she'd disappeared, if not the whole truth. As much as his arm's-length attitude had confused her, he didn't deserve that.

Which meant instead of the months she'd convinced herself she had to introduce Jacob to his son, she only had a matter of days. And she probably needed to figure out how to do that sooner rather than later.

Jacob Blackstone was too good at reading people not to realize when someone was lying. KC Gatlin showed all the signs.

This afternoon she'd shifted from side to side, avoided answering directly and refused to look him in the eye. Much to his deep disappointment.

He'd anticipated that moment when their eyes would meet more than anything. He was still thinking about it as he sat with his brothers in a booth directly opposite the bar at Lola's, sharing a platter of man food—wings and cheesy bacon-covered French fries—and alcohol. Jacob's drink of choice had always been wine. His brothers ragged him about his caviar tastes, but Jacob refused to apologize for having the most refined sensibilities of the family.

KC was far from refined. She'd been the burn of whiskey his body had been waiting for. That was why he'd ached for her to look at him this morning. He remembered well the sparks that would explode inside him just from sharing her gaze. His long-dormant body craved another taste, like a kid craved Pop Rocks.

He'd never forget their first meeting. From the moment she'd taken the plane seat next to him, he'd been enamored. That first conversation had revealed intelligence and humor in a beguiling mix. When they'd landed at the airport an hour away from Black Hills, he'd offered to share a ride. From that moment on, whenever he'd been in town, he'd spent as much time at her place as Blackstone Manor, until she'd stopped answering his phone calls months later. When he'd come home for his grandfather's funeral, she'd been nowhere to be found. The little house they'd spent so many enjoyable hours in had been sealed up tight.

He didn't want to, was shocked that he couldn't stop, but he'd hungered for her since that very first plane ride together. Time and distance hadn't changed that, much to his disgust. Nothing about his obsession made sense. They lived in two different worlds. They had two very different personalities and approaches to life. Still, he wasn't ready to let her go.

She'd been as wild as he'd expected, but she'd also led him to more genuine fun than he'd had his entire adult life. Quiet nights at home with a movie, cooking for two and sleeping in—oddities in his workaholic routine. No woman had interested him in any way beyond the physical. KC had interested him in every way.

She still did.

"Excuse me, guys."

Leaving his brothers staring after him, he made his way around tables to cross the room. They'd been in their corner for an hour while KC tended bar, and she hadn't looked directly at him a single time. Every second without that connection had itched below his skin until he couldn't even concentrate on the conversation. He'd deliberately kept their relationship out of the local headlines, but Jacob was desperate enough to risk a little limelight right now.

Oh, boy. His attitude made him very afraid he might step into stalker mode now that the possibility of seeing her around was very, very real. Some days, thoughts of KC had made him feel as if he was losing his mind.

He braced himself for her special brand of sarcasm. Something that had been noticeably lacking this morning.

"Jake. What brings you in tonight?"

You. Jacob ground his teeth together. Not because the shortening of his name bothered him, but because hearing it said in KC Gatlin's husky voice reminded him of evenings being soothed by her presence after an upsetting day with his mom. Reminded him of long nights between the sheets.

Far too distant memories.

"Do I need a reason? Can't I just enjoy the opportunity to watch a beautiful woman work the crowd?"

For the better part of a year, such a simple comment would have had her eyes sparkling, those full, naturally red lips tilting into a luscious smile, her mouth ready and willing to talk back. But not tonight.

"You never came to watch me before," she said, then dropped her gaze to the bar and started scrubbing, leaving him bereft once more. *So she wasn't gonna make this easy.*

He settled on a bar stool, watching that compact body displayed to advantage in a tight T-shirt and jeans. She acknowledged the move with a quick flick of her lashes, then studiously avoided looking at him again.

Just the way she'd ignored his phone calls. For seven months. He should have moved on by now, but his obsession had only grown. Now this successful, accomplished businessman found himself hunting the woman he craved in the local honky-tonk, because, well…because the cravings had become unbearable.

It no longer mattered that he couldn't figure out how she would fit into his life plan without wreaking havoc on it. She was the woman he shouldn't want, but the one woman he couldn't forget.

So he sucked up the little pride he had left and leaned closer. "You never did say where you'd been, KC."

She paused, then dropped the towel and met his gaze head-on. One of the things that had long enticed him was the very moment those turbulent hazel eyes turned his way, letting him see the woman inside and her mood, based on the dominant color of the day. Blue for calm and sunny. Green for sultry and sexy. Brown for angry or sad.

On tonight's menu: swirling milk chocolate. Wonder what he'd done to piss her off.

He'd never had a clue. They'd hooked up every time he'd come home to see his mother or take care of some business for his grandfather, until he'd found himself making up excuses just to return to Black Hills so he could see her. Watch her face while he talked with her. Sleep wrapped around her sweet-scented body. Hell, he'd even flown her out to Philadelphia once when he'd had to cancel his trip to Black Hills because of business.

Man, that had been a weekend to remember.

But the blank look on her face told him she wasn't into reminiscing. How much of a glutton for punishment was he willing to be?

"Come on, KC. Even as a friend, don't I deserve an answer?"

"I thought silence was my answer."

Burn. "Right."

For just a moment, the blankness slipped, revealing a flash of emotion that he couldn't interpret before it disappeared. But it revealed one important clue: indifference wasn't the problem.

So what was she hiding?

The KC he'd known had been all on the outside, open

with her emotions and actions. This closed-off version made him curious…and angry.

What had stripped away her joy, her spontaneity? Whatever it was, her attitude seemed to be reserved solely for him. He'd been watching her flirt and smile with other customers for an hour. The minute he'd appeared in front of her—shutdown.

Funny thing was, her spontaneity was one of the main things that drew him—and the one thing that had always kept him distant. Just thinking about living with uncertainty brought the barriers up. Other people found that kind of living by the seat of your pants exciting. He had enough of the unexpected in his life dealing with his twin; he didn't need more on a permanent basis. Luke's need for speed was as far from Jacob's scheduled existence as one could be from the other. Not to mention that his high-risk career as a race-car driver worried Jacob a lot.

So again he had to ask: Why was he sitting here instead of celebrating his freedom from his own version of risk?

"Was it because of this mystery man? Did you move to be with him?" Though the thought of her finding someone else hurt, maybe it was for the best. He needed something to break this incredible, horrible addiction.

She leaned closer, bracing against the bar. With her petite frame, the edge hit her higher than her waist, which gave him a really good view of her breasts in her tight Lola's T-shirt.

He was only human. Of course he looked.

Wait, was he seeing things? Because she seemed curvier than he remembered.

"Jacob," she said, drawing his gaze upward to her expectant face. Luckily she didn't call him on where he'd been looking. "Look, let's not do this here, okay? Another time, maybe."

"Why?" And why was he continuing to push this? "Is he here?"

"No, Jacob, that's not it."

The sudden sound of a phone ringing didn't register at first. After all, the bar was full of music, laughter and talking from the Friday-evening crowd. But the ringtone was persistent, and gained volume until he couldn't miss it. KC pulled out her phone and took one look at the display before answering.

She turned away, taking a few steps down the bar while she talked. He would have thought she'd completely dismissed him, except for the quick glances she kept shooting his way. After a few words he couldn't hear, she disconnected. Then she simply walked away.

His body mourned. His sensibilities raged. What did he have to do to get a simple explanation? Something more than "I'm sorry." Was that really too much to ask?

Determined to get answers, he stood up and strode after her. He came around the far side of the bar to catch a quick glimpse of her slipping out the back door. He knew her mother and grandmother lived in a small house behind the bar, so that must be where she was heading. If he intercepted her on her way back in, he could confront her without an audience.

All the better.

He could just make out her figure in the darkness as he made his way outside. Her body was silhouetted in the porch light from her family's house. He slowed his long stride. As she mounted the steps, the door opened and a woman who looked enough like her to be her mother stepped out.

That was when he heard another noise. But what caught his attention in that moment was what the older woman was holding.

A crying baby.

Jacob's world narrowed to the child.

"Goodness, girl." The voice of KC's mother drifted to

where he stood in the darkness. "I can't get Carter to stop crying for nothing. He wants his mama and no one else."

Jacob's legs carried him closer, his brain on hold as he tried to comprehend what he was seeing.

KC reached for the baby with the ease of a woman familiar with the move. The crying stopped almost immediately as she snuggled the child close into the crook of her neck. So natural. So beautiful.

So his.

The knowledge exploded over him in a wave of heat. As she swayed in the porch light, Jacob couldn't look away from the unusual dark golden curls that covered the baby's head.

"My brother and I had those same kind of curls," he murmured inanely.

In the newfound silence, they must have heard. KC jerked around to face him. But it was her mother Jacob found himself watching as the older woman's rounded eyes confirmed the suspicions in Jacob's whirling brain.

"KC," she said sharply, then stepped back through the door into the house.

KC didn't look in his direction again. She disappeared through the yellow rectangle of light in the entrance before slamming the door behind her, leaving Jacob alone in the dark.

It took a moment to get his feet to obey. As if by remote control, they carried him back to his brothers. He sank into the seat without really feeling it, seeing any of it. The numbness kept him from thinking, from dealing with the reality of what he'd just seen.

The bubble burst as he looked across the booth at his twin brother. Instantly, images of photographs from their childhood flooded his brain. Two boys, both with that thick dark blond hair. Curls all over until they'd gotten old enough to tame them.

"Jacob?" Luke said, hunching forward into his line of vision. "Jacob, are you okay? Where'd you go?"

Reaching out, Jacob picked up his half-full glass of wine and lifted it to his lips to perform the ultimate wine drinker's depravity. He chugged until every single drop was gone.

Then he set the glass down carefully and lay his palm flat beside it, praying the solidity of the table would ground him in the spinning room.

Luke lay his own palm on the table, mirroring Jacob's. "You cool?" Their version of letting each other know they were there.

And just like that, the words came to him, along with the anger. "I think I'm a daddy."

Two

Twenty-four hours later, Jacob finally stopped seething enough to confront KC. When he'd imagined what it would be like to find out he was going to be a parent, he'd pictured being across the table from his wife at an intimate dinner or seated next to each other in a doctor's office. Instead, the most gorgeous woman in the world had made him a father—and failed to mention it for twelve months.

The numbness had melted into rage, keeping Jacob awake long into the night. He went over the figures time and again. They hadn't spoken for seven months—he was ashamed that he could remember it to the day. He didn't have a lot of experience, but he'd guess the baby to be three to four months old. So how long had she known she was pregnant before she left? Two months? Three? Either way, they'd definitely been together when she found out. And those curls proved the baby to be a Blackstone heir.

He knew better than to see her before he calmed down. He couldn't be responsible for his actions while struggling with the deepest emotions he'd ever known. Control was his drug of choice—being out of control was something he preferred to keep well hidden. So he waited until he had his reactions under lock and key, and then he got in the car and drove.

KC lived a little outside town in a tiny house. Though there were other houses around, it wasn't really a subdivision. More of a series of dwellings that had sprung up over time as family members and friends and even acquaintances bought land and started building. The result was individual, with plenty of space and large trees. Ideal starter homes. Just imagining the possibilities ignited his anger once more.

He knew she'd be there—familiarity with her schedule gave him an advantage.

Sure enough, the door opened before he even knocked. She didn't speak, but simply turned back into the house, leaving him to follow. His gaze tracked her, cataloging every inch as she walked to the far end of the living room. Yeah, that body had changed, all right.

If he'd known what he was looking for, he'd have noticed right away. He'd been too busy searching for a connection in her eyes. But drinking in the whole package in jeans and a tank top, he saw the more dramatic curve from her waist to her hips, the added fullness in her breasts and a touch of softness in her jawline.

He'd thought nothing could make her more beautiful, but somehow having his baby had. And he hadn't been allowed to be a part of it.

Irritation with his attraction only ramped up his intensity. Carefully shuttering every window to his soul, he faced off with her in true Blackstone fashion.

He jerked his head in the direction of the driveway. "Someone else here?" he asked, referring to the car parked behind hers. So help him, if there was a man living here, he just might explode. Had she moved on that quickly? Had she let another man care for Jacob's child?

"Mom," she said quietly, slightly dampening his fuse. "She's in the nursery with Carter."

His throat almost closed. "Carter, huh?"

"Yes. Jake Carter."

Jake. Her nickname for Jacob—spoken with laughter, with intensity, with passion. It seemed more personal to name the baby that than to give him Jacob's last name.

"So you admit that he's mine?"

"Of course," she said, as if it made perfect sense under the circumstances. How could anything she'd done make perfect sense?

He stalked closer. "Why would you do this, KC? Was I really so horrible to you that you refused to let me be a part of—this?"

"That was never the issue, Jacob—"

"Then what was?" A really deep breath helped him lower his voice. It kept rising without his permission. *Control.* He needed control. "What *was* the issue, KC? Because I can't imagine one big enough that you told yourself it was okay to deceive me. To keep my son a secret from me."

Her arms crossed over her ribs, pushing those delectable breasts higher in the tank top. Something he shouldn't notice right now. At all.

"I did not deceive you. I never lied. I was going to tell you. I just hadn't figured out how."

"So he's three months old?"

"Yes, a week ago."

"So at any time in the past twelve months you could have picked up the phone. Or hell, just answered the phone when I called."

"I was afraid to. Going away just seemed the safest thing until I was sure what to do."

Jacob was surprised by the low rumble of his voice. "Safe? How? What the hell would safety have to do with it? I would never hurt you."

"I know that, Jacob, but it wasn't—"

The emotional roller coaster of the night caught up with him, pushing him past reasonable thought. "Know what?

It doesn't matter. Fact is, you deprived me of three months of knowing my—son," he choked out. "Not a note, a card or a call. Hell, not even a text. *By the way, I'm pregnant.* That's all it would have taken, KC, but you didn't even have the decency to do that."

He'd made himself available, chased after her like a dog with no sense, and *this* was what he got for it.

He came even closer until he loomed over her petite frame. "So now, I'll have what I want."

He wished her deep breath didn't draw his gaze downward. The low-level buzz of desire beneath his anger made him want to curse. He should not be attracted to a woman who could betray him. But he couldn't help it.

"Jake, please let me explain."

He refused to look in those turbulent eyes again. "Too late. No talking. No thinking. Now I will act."

She straightened, bracing her spine, which was just as well.

"Carter will come home."

Her jaw clenched. "He is home."

"My home." Some sick part of him took pleasure in the panic creeping over her features. "He's a Blackstone. He should be with his family."

She swallowed hard. "Jacob, please don't do this."

"Mark my words, KC. I will make you regret what you've done. I promise."

As soon as he'd stormed out of her house, KC began to dread the moment Jacob would act on his threat. The longer she waited, the more her stomach hurt.

She knew she'd made a bad choice, but given the circumstances, she thought she'd done the best she could. Waiting until James Blackstone was dead to tell Jacob about Carter had seemed like the safest option for protecting her baby, along with her family. In the absence of a reliable husband or father, her mother had given her all to raising and pro-

viding for KC and her brother. KC had felt that pull of loy-
alties every day that she'd been away, but in the end, she'd
chosen to take care of the women who had raised her. Her
mother and grandmother would have no defense against
James Blackstone if he'd retaliated by taking away their
livelihood on a whim.

But Jacob didn't believe her, because he was acting on
emotion, not facts.

How did she get him to listen to those facts now? She
knew James's lawyer, Canton, could work all kinds of voo-
doo if he wanted. Was Jacob even now making arrangements to take her baby from her? The thought shook her
deeper than any of the rest. Not just for the typical mommy
reason: being away from her child for more than a day was
more than she could handle right now. But Jacob was es-
sentially an unknown as a parent.

Would he expose their child to the same rejection and
abandonment she'd been subjected to as a child? In her
experience, fathers didn't know the meaning of commitment. But she'd been luckier than her brother. Her father
had hung around until she was eight. Her older brother had
never really known his.

After stewing for the rest of the morning, she decided
she couldn't wait for Jacob to make the first move. Jacob
wasn't answering his cell, which scared her all the more.
When she called Blackstone Manor directly, the old butler
answered. She'd spoken to Nolen a few times before when
she'd called to talk to her friend Christina, who'd married
Jacob's brother. Nolen was helpful, telling her that Jacob
had said something about going to Booties 'n' Bunting.

Panic and anger had surged in KC's gut. Booties 'n'
Bunting was the only exclusive baby boutique in town.
Jacob had the money to do all the things she couldn't. She'd
bought all her baby furniture and clothes at Walmart. He'd
have designer diapers and the best furniture, not to mention
the best lawyer when it came down to a fight.

She'd made the mistake; now it was up to her to ensure that it didn't turn into a brawl.

KC's stomach twisted into knots as she drove across Black Hills. Whipping her little Honda into Booties 'n' Bunting's parking lot, she jumped out of the car and plowed down the sidewalk, not letting herself remember just how little she belonged in the boutique district, much less in a store selling fifty-dollar baby onesies. Jacob's Tahoe parked out front confirmed that he was here. No doubt arming himself with everything he needed to take her child away.

She let herself in with her head held high and tracked down her prey, standing next to the most gorgeous crib she'd ever seen.

"What do you think you're doing?"

Jacob faced her with surprise lightening his face. For a split second, KC saw the man she'd wanted more than anything. Then a mocking grin slid across his lips.

"Could you give us a minute, please?" Jacob asked the saleswoman. Until that moment, KC hadn't even noticed her on the other side of the crib. The woman turned quietly and walked to the back of the store before Jacob continued, "What does it look like, KC? I'm outfitting the nursery at Blackstone Manor."

Oh, no, he wasn't. "You don't need any of this stuff, Jacob, because Carter is *not* coming to live with you."

"And what makes you say that?"

"This isn't just about you, Jake. You need to think about what's best for Carter."

"I am. I have the means to provide my son with everything he needs. Unlike you."

Hurt streaked through her, but she pushed it deep down under her growing anger. "Really? Can you give him love? Can you comfort him? Can you guide him? Or are you planning on using your money to turn that job over to a nanny so you can go about your perfectly planned days?"

His narrowed eyes should have had her shaking, but

she refused to back down. Her son's future was at stake. She didn't want to hurt Jacob, but how else could she get through to him? "One thing I can say with certainty is that I can provide him those things. You, I'm not so sure about."

Not waiting to give him a chance to outthink her, she pushed forward. Crowding into Jacob's space, she said, "You want Carter to come live with you? I understand why you would. I don't blame you for that." Her breath caught for a moment. "And I don't blame you for not trusting me, but I'm not turning my son over to just anyone."

"Oh, you don't have to turn him over," Jacob said, his voice deepening as if he had gravel in his throat. "You can come, too. I'm sure I could find a…use…for you."

Strike number two. How many body shots did he plan to take? Because she sure didn't need the reminder that Jacob had wanted her for sex and only sex.

She wasn't sure how long she stood there with wide eyes before he looked away. But he wasn't backing down. "The fact is, you've had Carter to yourself for three months. Your time just ran out."

She'd guessed Jacob was a formidable businessman. But when he turned that laser-sharp stare on her, it sliced through what little armor she had and put every inner doubt on display.

"Jacob, I understand your anger," she said, trying to slow her panic with a deep breath. "I made a horrible miscalculation. So I want to do my part to make this work. But no lawyers. No fighting. You want Carter to be a part of your life? Prove it to me." *Please, please, let this work.*

"What do I need to prove? We knew each other for over a year. You know everything you need to know about me."

"I know everything about certain parts of you." If he wanted the truth, she could comply. "I know you're half-way decent in bed." That whopper of an understatement almost choked her. "How good you are at picking up girls on planes. That you enjoy being with me at home but don't want to be seen in public with me. That I'm good enough for sex but not allowed into any other part of your life. None of that tells me a damn thing about what kind of father you are."

"So you want me to prove I can change diapers?" His shocked expression would be a thing to savor later when she stopped being so afraid of him that she might wet her pants.

"I want to know that you're more than a sexual being, Jacob. Show me what kind of man you truly are. Can I trust your word? Can I believe you when you say you aren't bad-mouthing me to my child behind my back? Can I trust you to teach him morals and work ethic and decency? Because I won't let *my child* become a chip off James Blackstone's block."

Jacob stepped closer, literally towering over her. "What the hell are you talking about?"

Arching her neck to stare at him wasn't comfortable, but she wasn't going to concede with even a single step backward. "Since you didn't know about Carter, I'm going to guess and say you didn't know your grandfather came to see me right before he died."

"Aiden would have told me."

"Did Aiden know? He wasn't there."

"Who was?"

"That lawyer guy."

"Canton?"

"That's the one. They came to the house one morning. I'd only known I was pregnant for a week."

"How could he possibly know about that?"

KC shook her head. "I'm not sure. But he did know how long we'd been seeing each other. I wouldn't put it past either of them to spy on me somehow."

Jacob's Adam's apple shifted in his throat. KC was sorry to have to deliver her news.

"James knew you were pregnant with my child." The deadness in his voice reverberated through her. She'd often wondered how a man like his grandfather could have had a child. What kind of family did you create with manipulation and fear? No wonder Aiden Blackstone had run far, far away when he was younger.

Though Jacob had always seemed quite normal, she'd sensed a dark sadness underneath that excellent control of his. What games had James Blackstone played with his grandsons? What terror had he wreaked in their family before he died? Jacob had never even come close to sharing something that personal.

"That's the only reason I could think of that he would demand I leave town. And never come back."

Jacob seemed frozen; not a muscle moved. He gripped the crib rail with one hand. The knuckles turned white... and stayed white.

"But you didn't stay away."

"No. Once I found out he was dead, I thought the coast would be clear to come home." That might have been a mistake, too. "But he threatened my family's business—"

"How?" he asked, his eyes narrowing as if he suspected a lie.

"Jacob," she said, shaking her head at him, "your grandfather owned half the town. He'd rented us the land Lola's is on for my entire life but never would allow my mother or grandmother to buy it. I suspect it was so he could use it to his advantage if the opportunity arose."

She tried to breathe around the anger that rose at the memory. "He threatened to shut down the business. Everything my mother and grandmother own is tied up in Lola's. Not to mention that their house is on that land, too. So I agreed, and the men left. Then I cashed out some savings and used it to move away."

Jacob smirked. "Serves him right."

"When I heard about his death, I thought—well, we all thought—he couldn't hurt us anymore. I just hadn't figured out what to do about you yet."

"And you think this is the answer?"

"It's the only one I've got." Might as well be honest about that. "Let's face it, Jacob. You have money and a damn good lawyer. But James didn't own me, and neither do you. If you want to be part of Carter's life, stop throwing your weight around and work with me."

"Who put you in charge? You haven't exactly proved yourself trustworthy."

Unease rippled through her body. She knew she'd had good reasons for her choices, but when she looked at it from his point of view... "I'm not denying you access to Carter out of anger or revenge, Jacob. I simply want to know that he's in good hands. That you're willing to make a place for a baby in your life. Not hand him over to a well-paid nanny."

His eyes searched hers. "How can I be sure he's in good hands with you?"

"I— Well—" Words failed her for a moment.

"Face it, KC. You ran halfway across the country to hide my child from me. I'm not the only one with something to prove. The question is, how?"

Three

Jacob hadn't felt so out of control since the last time he'd had KC in a bed. Only, anger wasn't nearly as pleasurable. Still, he used the impetus to propel himself through the door to his brother Aiden's study at Blackstone Manor, knowing John Canton was there for a meeting.

This morning, Aiden had mentioned an appointment for the lawyer to drop off some paperwork for their grandfather's will. Canton still had control of the Blackstone inheritance, for now. There were some final hoops to jump through, then Jacob and his brothers would be free of James Blackstone and his minion.

"You bastard," Jacob growled, absorbing his brother's shocked look as he passed. But his focus was trained wholly on the lawyer.

The same lawyer who had assisted their grandfather in blackmailing Aiden into marrying Christina, their mother's nurse, terrorizing them with threats of compromising their mother's health and care if they didn't comply.

"I knew you would force two people to get married to suit James's purposes. Threaten, and bully, and even ruin an entire town on the whim of a dead man. But I seriously thought any decent human being would draw the line at

cutting a child completely out of a man's life." He let his
momentum carry him until he loomed over the smaller
man. "Guess I thought wrong."

From behind the desk, Aiden asked, "Jacob, care to fill
me in?"

Canton didn't even blink…or pretend not to understand
what Jacob referred to. "I did as your grandfather ordered."

"Didn't you think I should have a say?"

Canton shrugged. "That was not for me to decide."

With a growl, Jacob reached forward, but arms made
of steel were there to stop him. Slowly, Aiden inched him
back until there was enough room for him to stand between
Jacob and the man he felt like killing.

"I've obviously missed something," Aiden said. "Tell
me now."

From the other side of the barrier Aiden provided, Canton spoke. *Brave man.* "I believe Jacob is referring to a conversation his grandfather had with Ms. Gatlin."

"What?" Aiden looked surprised.

Jacob turned away, relieving his brother of guard duty.
At least not looking at his grandfather's lawyer would help
him regain control. In thirty-three years, he'd never experienced this many emotional twists. He didn't like it. He
needed stability. All the more reason to stay away from
KC—but that wasn't an option anymore.

He turned back, focusing on his brother. "I went to see
KC Gatlin."

Aiden gave a short nod. "So it's true? The baby is
yours?"

"He's three months old." Jacob felt the need to clarify,
now that he had more facts. "I met KC on one of my flights
home and…" How did he put this without making it sound
as if KC was simply a booty call? "Okay, I was sleeping
at her place whenever I came to town." Why sugarcoat his
selfishness?

Aiden's thick brows went up. "Wow, Jacob. I didn't know you had it in you."

"Not the time, Aiden."

"Really? You brought it up."

Jacob ignored the brotherly razzing and moved on. "The baby is definitely mine." That shut down his brother's grin. Real quick. "Dear ol' Grandpa threatened her until she skipped town, never telling me about it—my son."

Aiden narrowed his gaze on the lawyer. "How would Grandfather even find out KC was pregnant? Medical records are confidential. Was he rummaging through her trash for a pregnancy test?"

Jacob barely held his control as he waited for the answer.

Canton smirked. "Anything can be had for the right price. Turns out, one of the little nurses at KC's doctor has a serious cash-flow problem."

Jacob was rushing forward before he even thought. Only the barricade created by Aiden's body stopped his attack. His own heavy breathing sounded loud in Jacob's ears; his heart thudded as he realized the full magnitude of his grandfather's invasion of privacy. Jacob wanted to do bodily harm all over again.

"Easy," Aiden murmured against his ear. "Let's get our questions answered, and then he'll be gone. Forever this time."

Silence reigned as Jacob tried to gather the remnants of his self-control. His thoughts whirled, reminding him if he hadn't come home for good, he might never have found out he was a father. Pulling back, he announced, "It was only by accident I found out that KC had my child."

Canton spoke again from a safe distance across the room. "Then I don't understand the issue."

Jacob rounded on him but didn't move closer. He didn't trust himself. "The issue? You tried to separate me from my child."

"But by your own admission, we didn't succeed."

The guy simply didn't get it. "Would you ever have told me?"

"Your grandfather demanded complete loyalty. And discretion. Of course I wouldn't have." His weasel-like face didn't change expression. "And since Ms. Gatlin moved without contacting you and didn't come home during the remainder of your grandfather's lifetime, she'd fulfilled our terms. In which case, there was nothing to tell."

"I'm glad you think so. I guess that clears your conscience."

The man didn't bother to defend himself. "I don't have a conscience. I have a job."

"That's enough," Aiden interjected. "Canton, we're done for now. I'll reschedule with you *at your office* later and we will finish up the last of the paperwork for Grandfather's affairs."

The lawyer was smart enough to take an out when it was given to him. He scurried through the door without so much as a by-your-leave. But his departure ratcheted down Jacob's anger by a few notches.

"Man, I'll be glad to see the last of that guy," Aiden said as he straightened the papers on his desk.

"How much longer?"

Aiden had spent the year dealing with his grandfather's lawyer after James had blackmailed him into marrying Christina. Luckily, it had all worked out for the best, but the lawyer's presence was an annoying reminder of their grandfather's manipulations.

Aiden waved the papers at him. "This is the end of it. The year is almost up and we will be free from it all. Including Canton. I just wish there was a way to punish him for what he's done rather than be rewarded with the money Grandfather left him." Aiden settled back into his chair, looking every inch the sophisticated Manhattan art dealer, though he now lived in South Carolina instead of New York. "KC Gatlin, huh? Beautiful, but definitely dif-

ferent from your standard of socialites and fellow busi-
nesswomen."

"Tell me about it." Jacob started to pace, hoping to ex-
pend the energy thrumming beneath his skin. Hell, he just
might have to go for another jog, even though he'd done
five miles this morning. Especially as he thought about
KC's earlier accusations.

"Where do you want to go from here?" Aiden asked
after several moments.

More of that loaded silence.

Finally, Jacob said, "I would be lying if I said I didn't
want to see her again. Didn't wish we could pick up where
we left off when she disappeared. But—no." He glanced
over at his brother. "She's not right for me long-term."

"Why not?"

Good question. "Let's see. She doesn't fit in with
what I want in life, who I am. She's more like Luke—
unpredictable, headstrong." *And makes me feel just as unpredictable. Out of control.*

"She's gorgeous."

"She works in a bar."

"Ah, a hard worker."

Jacob stared hard at the bookshelves, cataloging the
shapes and colors of the books but not the titles. "She kept
my son a secret."

"So she panicked and made a mistake. You enjoyed
being with her before. What's the real problem?"

Could he let his guard down? Even a little? Jacob was
used to his brothers confiding in him, not the other way
around. "I just— Before, it was easy. But she's right. I kept
her compartmentalized so I wouldn't have any interference in my life." He ran his hand across his close-cropped
hair. "It had nothing to do with only wanting her for sex
and everything to do with making our relationship convenient for me."

"Relationships are anything but convenient. I'm learning to roll with it because the good far outweighs everything else."

Jacob felt a moment of envy. Inflexibility seemed to have been bred into him. Strict adherence to standards and procedures served him well in business, not so much in relationships. At least, the few he'd had. He rarely saw a woman more than a handful of times, since he wasn't ready for the long-term thing yet. Maybe not for several more years.

KC had taken him off guard. He could admit to himself that he'd kept her compartmentalized in his life because he'd been afraid—afraid of her taking over, afraid of losing control, afraid of being ruled by emotions instead of his brain.

I want another chance at that woman. No. "She's my son's mother. Better to stay close and know your enemy, right?"

Aiden's smirk took him by surprise. "Jacob, the last time I fell for that line, I ended up married to the woman who changed my life, my way of thinking, forever. For the better, but still…"

"Not me."

Aiden's expression screamed *famous last words*, but Jacob ignored it. Aiden had vowed at eighteen never to return to Blackstone Manor—now he was happily married and living here full-time, with frequent business trips to New York to manage his art import/export business.

Would Jacob end up the same? Moving home was definitely the right choice, especially since his son was now here. But married? Not to KC. As exciting as being with her was, he wanted peace, not unpredictability.

"Jacob."

The serious tone in Aiden's voice cut through Jacob's confusion. "Yeah?"

"What are you going to do about KC? About the baby?"

"Carter," he said, clearing his throat when it tried to

close. "Forcing her to give him to me would probably lead to a legal battle—and prove me to be a jackass. She might not have a lot of money, but she won't give him up without a fight." He frowned. "The bigger question is, what is she gonna do about me?"

Aiden thought for a moment. "Do you want her?"

"I do, but I told you, she's not right—"

"Sometimes things don't come the way we plan."

And Jacob had been planning his entire life. He didn't know if he could give that up.

"I can't walk away. He's my son." Deep down he cringed at the hypocrisy of speaking as if memories of those incredible nights together had no influence on Jacob's desire to see KC again.

"Then you need to be very careful…for you and for them."

Jacob glanced over. "What do you mean?"

"I mean what's going on at the mill. We still haven't figured out who's trying to sabotage our business, and until we do, nobody associated with us is safe. Delaying shipments and messing with customers' orders is annoying, but what happened to Christina last year could have killed her. She wasn't the target, but that doesn't change the result."

Jacob remembered all too well the night a group of thugs had set Aiden's studio on fire…with Christina inside. The incident was one of many suspicious events at the Blackstones' cotton mill, but it had escalated the game to a whole new level. "You think they might target my son?"

"Not on purpose, but then again…" Aiden leveled a look at him, sending unease running over Jacob's nerve endings. "It would be for the best to keep the connection quiet. For now."

"Right." *For now.* Jacob had a lot of experience keeping things quiet in this town.

"So get control, before someone else does."

Like KC. Jacob had been irritated and fascinated at the

baby store. Until she'd burst in and started making demands, he hadn't known what it would be like to have all that feistiness turned on him as a weapon. His whole body had lit up inside. At this rate, she'd have the upper hand in no time. Leading him about by the nose, or rather, another appendage he'd just as soon keep under control.

Jacob was grateful when Aiden moved on, pulling him back out of his convoluted thoughts.

"Back to business," Aiden said. "I had a call from Bateman at the mill right before Canton arrived."

Jacob had had a call, too, but he'd let it go to voice mail. He'd been too keyed up from his clash with KC to make sense of business.

A problem he never had.

Deflating like a balloon, Jacob dropped into one of the chairs facing the desk, grateful Aiden had replaced the old leather-and-wood chairs with cozy wing backs. His brother and sister-in-law were slowly updating things in Blackstone Manor—especially the study—inch by inch scraping away the depressive stench of their grandfather's manipulation to reveal the true beauty of a home that had stood for generations in the face of natural and man-made tribulations.

"I just don't know how to get a handle on the problems at the mill," Jacob said, reminding them both of the year they'd spent dealing with the saboteur. "We need to find another way of catching this guy. I mean, I'm there every day, but I'm in management. And no one's talking to me. We need someone on the floor, someone relatable. I think that's where the problem is."

"Definitely can't be either of us. See if Bateman can put you in touch with someone over there to help. He'll know who's trustworthy."

"Right." His foreman had already been very helpful. Because Jacob wasn't capable of judging anyone at the moment. Business would give him something to focus on besides KC, just as soon as they settled on some ground rules.

Start as you mean to go on, his mother had always said. For everyone involved, that was exactly what they needed to do.

As she faced off with Jake on her front porch, KC knew she was simply delaying the inevitable, but she couldn't stop herself from arguing just for the sake of it. "What if my mom wasn't here to watch Carter?"

KC spoke with no real hope of making a dent in Jacob's thinking but couldn't resist pointing out the inconvenience he was putting everyone through. Everyone but him. She hated the push-pull of her emotions. Wanting to keep him at arm's length, yet greedy for even a little bit of his attention. When he'd finally called after two days of silence, her heart had sped up, but she couldn't help being contrary about his sudden demand for her to take a Sunday drive with him.

"If we're going to do this, there will be ground rules," he said now as he waited impatiently on her doorstep. "That means we need to talk. Alone."

That take-charge tone shouldn't send shivers down her arms but it did. "Yes, we should," she conceded. "But you still could've given me a heads-up sooner."

She took her time walking back to the nursery. Not that she had anything important to do on Sunday mornings. Her mother usually came over before lunch for some downtime with Carter since Lola's wasn't open. Sometimes KC ran a few errands. Then they had family dinner with Grandma. Asking her mother to stay with Carter for a little while was really a formality, but it also wouldn't hurt Jacob to wait on her porch a few minutes, just for giggles and grins.

Her pokiness had her changing into jeans and pulling her hair into a ponytail, but she simply refused to hurry. He didn't comment when she finally came outside, just held the door for her to climb into his Tahoe and closed it with a firm hand.

The contained atmosphere of Jacob's SUV didn't settle her nerves. The interior smelled like him—spicy and dark. If she closed her eyes and breathed deep, she could almost remember what it felt like to have that scent all over her and wish she didn't ever have to wash it away. After all, she never knew when she might smell it again.

After she'd left, been away from him for a while, she realized how sad it was to need someone so badly and yet be relegated mostly to a physical relationship. They said men did it all the time—obviously Jake had—but KC had never felt more alone than when she was lying in his arms, wishing she was good enough for him to make her a true part of his life.

The door opened and Jacob slid into his seat with his phone pressed to his ear. "I'm on my way," he said as he reached for his seat belt. Without explanation he stowed the phone in the center console. Then he put the Tahoe in gear and pulled out of KC's driveway, all without telling her where they were going or what this was about.

"You said something about ground rules?" she prompted.

Jacob maintained a still silence for several minutes more, at odds with the hum of the tires on asphalt. "I've made it clear what I want—"

"Actually, you haven't."

He shot a glance at her.

"Well, you haven't," she insisted. "Are you trying to get Carter full-time? Not that I'd let you have custody, but still…do you want him part-time? Have you thought about how that will work, how it will affect him? Do you—?"

"Enough, KC."

His deep frown had her second-guessing her pushiness, but she wouldn't apologize for trying to protect her son.

"I started making demands because I was angry. Unlike you, I didn't get to think about this, plan for this, nothing. So I reacted out of emotion." The heavy sound of his breath was her clue to how much self-control he was exerting.

A part of her, the wounded part, wanted to push him. Make him acknowledge that she and Carter would have a big place in his life—something he hadn't found important enough to offer her before. Another part of her wanted to see that legendary control smashed to teeny-tiny pieces.

Just the way it had when they were in bed together. But as soon as the sex had been done, he'd been back in form— charming and attentive but perfectly capable of walking away.

"We have to do what's best for Carter," he said, staring straight out the windshield. "So how do we do that?"

"Let me get to know you."

"To what end? What are we striving for here, KC?" He ran a rough hand over his smooth chin. In the time she'd known him, she'd never once seen him with stubble. "Because if you think you can disappear with him if you don't like what you learn, that's not an option. I will always find you."

But for all the wrong reasons. "My family is here, Jacob," she countered. "It didn't take me long to realize that running is not a safe, long-term option. I made a mistake— one I won't repeat. But I'd better like what I see, because unlimited access to your son *is* on the line." She shifted against the leather seat, wondering if she could back up her big words with action.

"Look," she said. "I don't want us to spend our time trying to guard against each other. If this is truly about Carter—" she ignored Jake's look "—then we need to work together. I tried to do things your way before and got nowhere. So this really is all on you. Show me what you're like out of bed so I can see where Carter and—" *I. Carter and I.* She cleared her throat, grateful she hadn't finished that sentence out loud. "Where Carter fits. Prove to me that he's in good hands with you."

"So what is it I'm supposed to do to show you I'm a

good man? Hell, even I don't know if I'm a good father. I've never been one before. Is this a written exam? A field test?"

"Oh, it's a field test, all right. No more secrets, Jacob."

He shot her a quick glance. "Are you seriously saying you didn't learn anything about me in the months we were together? Why don't you tell me what you do know and I'll fill in the blanks."

All the memories of their time together flooded her mind—long nights, laughter and loving… No. Not loving. The thought created an urge to get under his skin in the only way she knew how.

She shifted as close to him as her seat belt would allow. "Well," she said, reaching out a fingertip. "I know you're sensitive here." She brushed gently back and forth along the outer edge of his ear, then down along his jawline. "I know you shave early and often because you don't like looking scruffy." The back of her hand rubbed down along his throat, then up along his collarbone. "I know your favorite sexual position is missionary because it gives you the most control—"

"What do you want to know?" Jacob interrupted, his voice deep and rough.

She leaned back in her seat, trying to cover her smile of satisfaction. Torturing him had always been fun. "What do you do—I mean, really do? What do you care about? Enjoy? Do you plan on staying here for longer than just the time it takes to get the mill on track?"

"What about you?" he asked, countering a question with a question.

"What do you mean?"

"The same questions apply to you," he said, turning the Tahoe into a nearby parking lot so he could face her. "This won't be a one-way street, KC."

Yes, her sins would haunt her forever. She should never have kept Carter from Jake.

His gaze held her immobile as he spoke. "I'm not the

only one paying for my mistakes," he said, leaning closer, crowding her until her heart fluttered in panic. "We're gonna be seeing a lot of each other."

"I'm sure," she said with a nod, trying to get a handle on her nerves.

His gaze dropped to her lips as she licked them, reminding her of things she was better off forgetting. The space around them closed in before he spoke. "The thing is, with your history, I'm now questioning every word from these pretty lips."

She had no warning when his thumb came up to rub back and forth across her mouth. It affected her more than she wanted to admit, and left her dreaming of more.

"Consequences, KC. Those are *my* terms."

Her lips firmed, and she had a feeling she'd adopted the stubborn look she was known to turn on disruptive customers. Jacob simply smiled, then pulled back and got them on the road again.

"Well," she said, a little stumped, "my life is pretty simple, as you saw before. My job, my time revolves around my family."

"They're supportive? Of you and Carter?"

Her heart jumped at the softening of his voice as he said their son's name. "Definitely. Our family is very close. And my grandmother, mother and brother love Carter unconditionally."

Even if their new connection to the Blackstone family scared her mother no end. KC rubbed her palms against her jean-covered thighs, searching for more words. "What about your family?" She swallowed hard, distracted by thoughts of her friend Christina, a true Blackstone now. She would be so mad when she realized KC had kept the truth about Carter from her. "Did you tell them?"

"I guess you'll see," Jacob said, then turned the truck abruptly into a construction area.

With a start, KC realized they were at the site of the new

playground Aiden Blackstone had raised money to build on the south end of town. The large field had been cleared and leveled, with concrete slabs laid in various areas to anchor the equipment. Current construction seemed to center around a two-story fort at the far end.

There, a group of people stood to one side while a handful of construction workers drilled to secure the platforms. "Do they know we're coming?" she asked.

"They knew I was coming," Jacob said. "You'll just be the bonus."

Yeah, right.

Jacob settled his palm on the door's handle, then spoke while staring straight ahead. "And for the record, my favorite position isn't missionary. It's you on top."

KC swallowed hard. That revelation held her in place for longer than she liked. Her mind wandered back to all the times—no. No time for that now.

She'd be better off remembering all the times he'd left her to go back to Philadelphia with rarely a call between trips. KC scrambled out of the car, ignoring Jacob's frown. He'd always liked to open the door for her, and she'd trained herself to wait for him. It had been hard for a girl who'd always taken care of herself, but she'd done it because it made him happy. And deep down, because it made her feel special. Letting him do it now would be too big of a reminder of those precious moments.

As she followed at a slight distance behind him across the open lot, KC wished there was at least one happy face in the crowd. She recognized the newlywed couple as they approached, and neither looked very welcoming.

Yep, the news of Carter's parentage had spread.

Jacob introduced her to his brother, but Christina stepped in before he could go further. "We know each other," she said quietly. "Hey, KC."

KC couldn't read her friend's tone or expression. They'd been very close before KC left, often hanging out in the same group of women. But she, Christina and their friend Avery Prescott had formed a tight bond through community work that hadn't been weakened by their different social statuses. KC had told them she was moving away for a job, and other than some chance encounters, she hadn't tried to renew her bond with the women since she'd returned.

All it would have taken was one of them to figure out who Carter's father was, and they all would have known. Living and working in Blackstone Manor—and now married to the Blackstone heir—Christina posed a danger to KC. She hadn't wanted to risk anything until she had all her ducks in a row.

Seeing Christina now reminded KC how much she'd given up in the past year, but keeping Carter safe had been worth it.

"KC, I'm sorry we've never met formally," Aiden said.

How should she respond? *Me, too?* Since she'd determined to stay as far away from the Blackstones as possible, that would be a complete lie.

He went on, apparently not expecting a response. "There's no point in beating around the bush," he said, earning an eye roll from his wife. "Jacob told us what happened, or rather, why you left town."

He glanced at his wife, and they shared a look of momentary communion. "If Christina and I understand anything, it's how manipulative my grandfather was, how he set out to twist the world into his own version of perfect. But for the record, we look forward to you and Carter joining our family."

KC shot a glance at Jacob, wondering how he felt about all this. His stoic look gave nothing away. "I'm not sure how this will work out yet…"

Aiden shook his head. "Doesn't matter. If you need us, we're here."

Then he turned to talk to Jacob as if he hadn't just dropped a bomb in the middle of the park.

"How's everything comin'?" Jacob asked, seeming un-
fazed by his brother's words.

"Hartwell's doing a great job…"

KC watched as Aiden's hand cupped Christina's shoulder. He stroked up and down hypnotically, giving his wife
his attention even while he talked to Jacob. The ache that
bloomed deep in her gut didn't mean KC was jealous of
the other couple. Not really.

Knowing that bridging this gap was up to her, KC wasn't
willing to simply stand there while the men talked.

"Hey, Christina," she said, feeling awkwardly formal.
If she was going to be around Jacob's family and regain
her friendships, she would have to jump this hurdle. "How
are you?"

"Good," her friend said. "Things are really good."

Drawing in a deep breath, Christina lifted dark, somber
eyes. "Do you have any pictures of him? I haven't gotten
to see Carter up close since you've been back."

KC tried not to wince. The implication hung in the air. It
meant a lot to Christina that KC had cut her out of her life
for the past year. Pulling her phone out of her back pocket,
KC scrolled until she found the folder of Carter's pictures.

Then she held the phone out for Christina, hoping her
willingness to share would start to repair the breach in
their relationship.

"Oh, how sweet," the other woman breathed.

KC felt the motherly glow of pride she still wasn't quite
used to spread over her. Then Jacob reached out and took
the phone from Christina's hand. Turning the screen toward him, he started to scroll through the pictures. KC
couldn't stand to look at him, the sadness in his eyes was
so profound.

The guilt that had been growing over her decision
to keep Carter from Jacob burrowed so deep inside she
doubted she'd ever be rid of it. Yes, she'd been afraid. She'd
been angry. She'd been pressured. But in the end, her choice

to cave under James Blackstone's demands had deeply hurt Jacob. Now she got to live with the proof of that.

Finally he came to a single picture and stopped, simply staring at it. He didn't say anything, and the ache was made worse by his silence.

In an effort to escape, KC shifted her eyes, but found herself caught by Aiden Blackstone's hard stare. She'd heard he was a tough nut to crack, but the echo of his brother's pain she saw in Aiden's eyes told her she'd hurt not just Jacob but his family, too. A hard knot of self-disgust formed in her stomach.

"Let me show you what the construction crew is up to," Christina said, taking her arm to guide KC away.

Probably for the best. She might ruin her boundaries with Jacob by bursting into tears right there.

Not that being with Christina was much easier. She knew the minute her friend threw the first glance her way, then threw several more as they walked slowly away from the men toward the half-standing fort. The sound of electric nail drivers peppered the air. To the right, three men were securing a set of monkey bars into the ground.

"I really don't understand, KC," Christina finally said. "And I want to understand. I do."

"James threatened my family. I didn't know how to get out of that without hurting them."

"That part I get," Christina said "Trust me, I really do. My own experiences with James are numerous and traumatic."

KC could only imagine, living in Blackstone Manor with James while caring for his daughter, Lily, meant Christina had no way to avoid him. Lily required full-time care after a car accident had eventually led to a long-term coma. Christina's dedication to her patient and friend had put her at James's mercy. Then he'd forced Aiden and Christina to marry. Last year had been just as traumatic for her as for KC.

"What I don't understand," Christina said, "is why you

wouldn't come to me as your friend, ask for help, let me offer some kind of emotional support for you and Carter. Didn't you think I'd want to do that for you?"

KC stopped, afraid if she tried to walk and talk at the same time she might fall flat on her face. She wasn't prepared for this conversation, and sparring with Jacob took a lot out of her. "I am sorry, Christina. But I couldn't risk you putting two and two together."

"Putting two and two together? Honey, I had no idea you'd even met Jacob. How you managed to actually get pregnant by him is a mystery of biblical proportions."

KC had always appreciated that Christina got her point across in a ladylike but effective manner.

"Keeping our—" she swallowed hard "—affair a secret wasn't my choice. Only...afterward."

"Well, y'all did a damn fine job of it. I mean, I saw Jacob some when he was home all those times. I never had an inkling."

KC finally gathered the courage to meet Christina's questioning gaze head-on. "Which is not what I wanted. I never chose for our relationship to be this hidden thing. That was how Jacob wanted it, though I didn't realize it until after that first week. Somehow I knew, deep down, that Jacob wouldn't continue seeing me if we went public." So she'd bit her tongue and grasped at whatever crumb he'd thrown her, even though every secret encounter hurt more than the last.

"Why wouldn't Jacob want people to know about you?" Christina asked, shaking her head with the same confusion KC felt over it all.

"I suspect because he had no intention of our time together meaning any more than it did. When he came to visit, we would hang out and have, um, fun, but that's as far as it went. No invitations to dinner at a restaurant in town, no family dinners, nothing. If he wanted to go out, he drove me to Sheffield. What other message was I supposed to get from that, Christina?"

Her friend glanced back at the men over KC's shoulder. "I don't know," she murmured.

"It wasn't the type of relationship you bring something as permanent as a baby into." As much as KC wished it had been. "Not that I planned to keep Carter a secret permanently. I just hadn't figured out how to tell Jacob yet."

"But close friends are supposed to be there for each other. What about me? Avery? We could have helped you, KC."

"Asking you to keep this secret wouldn't have been fair to you. And James Blackstone would not have taken kindly to word getting back to Jacob. He made that very clear."

"Well, you weren't the first," Christina said with a grimace. "Thank goodness his days of manipulating others are over. Why didn't you come to Jacob as soon as you knew James was dead?"

Because I still wanted more than I could have. "It was kind of hard to figure out how to bring the subject up. Not that keeping it from him was ideal, either. But the important thing now is that Jacob and I learn how to work together for Carter."

She hoped her friend could see the sincerity she felt as she met her gaze head on. "And that you forgive me. Being without you and Avery these past months has been very lonely."

Christina hugged her, not holding back even though KC knew she still had to have reservations. After all, she was a Blackstone now. Who knew how this would all play out?

"I've missed you, too," Christina said.

KC closed her eyes and returned the hug. Her family had been there for her every step of the way. The aunt she'd gone to stay with had been helpful and loving. Really, KC had had a great deal of support. But she'd missed her friends. It hadn't been the same without them.

It hadn't been what she wanted. Sometimes, when she was pregnant, she would dream that Jacob was with her. Rubbing her back. Picking out names. Dreaming of the future. But she'd been too afraid to reach out for what she'd wanted.

She glanced back over her shoulder to see Jacob and Aiden still in an intense discussion. Jake's brows were drawn together, his eyes hooded. So far away from where she wanted him. She'd never have him now, not even the way she'd had him before.

Still, she'd make up for her mistakes with Jacob. Somehow.

Four

On the ride back to the house, Jacob sat in silence, wondering what Christina had said to KC. Their hug before they parted suggested it had been something good, but Jacob had been too caught up in his own emotions to track their conversation. He left KC to her thoughts as he tried to sort through the tangle in his own brain.

When they reached KC's house, there was a vehicle he didn't recognize parked in the driveway. This time, a Ford F150. Jacob felt jealousy make another appearance. Though plenty of women drove trucks in the South, it was usually a man's mode of transportation. What man would go into KC's house when she wasn't home?

They were barely inside before KC's mom appeared in the doorway from the kitchen. She watched him with wide eyes that made him ashamed of his threats to take Carter away. This woman was obviously afraid of his role in her grandson's life. Considering his grandfather's demands, Jacob could see why.

"Carter's asleep," she said, her voice hushed as if they were still in the baby's room.

"Thanks, Mom," KC said with a smile. "Did he give you any trouble? He's been a little fussy the past few days."

"As if that baby could be any trouble at all," her mother scoffed.

"That last time he got sick he screamed for hours," a man said, appearing in the doorway behind KC's mother. "Babies are cute, but trust me, they're trouble."

His mother glared. "Spoken like a true bachelor."

"Babies can't help it that their only form of communication is crying," KC said with dry humor.

The man in jeans didn't appear offended. Jacob studied him. He'd forgotten KC had a brother. Zachary, he thought was his name. Though his complexion was darker, his hair long and midnight black, those unusual hazel eyes were the same as KC's. After introductions, the men took each other's measure silently. From her brief mentions of him, Jacob remembered her brother worked hard to assist his mother and grandmother, full shifts at the mill, nights at Lola's and even extra gigs doing crop dusting for the cotton farmers around here. Hardworking and conscientious.

Ms. Gatlin eyed KC and Jacob both, as if wondering what they'd gotten up to while they were gone, then swung her gaze solely in Jacob's direction. The thorough inspection made him uneasy, but Jacob wasn't offering any explanations. Whatever KC wanted her mom to know, she'd tell her. Jacob just wished she would be on her way so he could finally meet his son.

Something he wasn't doing under the prying eyes of a crowd.

"Mom, I'm going to have to miss lunch this afternoon," KC said. "But we'll be there next week."

Her mother's look turned into a glare, but Jacob stayed silent. This was between KC and her family.

"Why would you do this, KC?" the older woman finally asked, turning her glare on her daughter. "Why would you give him full access to Carter?"

"Mom—"

"He's the enemy. Can't you see that?"

Offended, Jacob squared his shoulders, his back tightening. He felt as if he needed to jump to his own defense, to KC's defense, but the anguish in the older woman's voice held him back. He met the turbulent gaze of KC's brother as he placed an arm around his mother's shoulders. Jacob guessed her intensity had to do with more than just Jacob and the Blackstones. But he wasn't going to justify his right to see his son to anyone.

"Mother, he is Carter's father."

"Yes, and you ran far away rather than turn to him for help. What kind of father could he possibly be?"

Jacob wouldn't know until he was given a chance—

"I made a mistake," KC said. "It was wrong of me to keep Jacob from his son. I need to find a way to make that right. You knew he'd come into our lives when I moved back. Somehow."

"I can't believe you're just going to let him waltz in here and take Carter from us," she said, tears forming in her eyes, which were so like her children's.

Jacob couldn't stand it. "Ms. Gatlin, I'm not going to—"

"Why not? Old James sure did."

Yes, and Jacob was getting very tired of the reminder. "I realize my grandfather was a selfish man, a bully who had to get his own way. In his mind, threatening her, driving her away, meant he could control who became a true Blackstone." His conscience twinged as he realized he'd inherited some of that need for control himself. Still, Jacob stood a little taller. "But I'm not James Blackstone. The last thing I want is for Carter to disappear."

It was clear from her face that he hadn't made her feel better about him. "Then I guess it's a good thing she didn't take the money to abort him, isn't it?"

Jacob choked, heat flushing up his neck to his face. "What?"

Her eyes widened as Ms. Gatlin realized she'd gone too

far. She looked to KC, her mouth opening but no sound coming out.

With a resigned look, KC murmured, "I was offered a check. I could have had the money if I'd been willing to get rid of Carter for good. But I couldn't."

"And he just let you walk away?" Apparently there were a few things Canton had left out.

KC shrugged as if it didn't matter, but her face told a different story. "As long as I abided by the rules and didn't contact you, he let me go and my family didn't have to suffer. He said, well, he said I was a rare find."

"Why?"

"He called me an honest woman who knew her limitations. Coming from someone who'd just threatened the livelihood of three single women, it wasn't really a compliment, though in his twisted way he probably meant it as one."

Jacob could see how James would feel that way. He would have wished for her to take the permanent option, but as evil as James was, he would admire someone who held on to her integrity, even while he was crushing her will under his demands.

"So you're not your grandfather," Ms. Gatlin said, not willing to completely let go. "But I saw how you treated KC before. And you're still a hotshot businessman, right? Always looking at the bottom line, aren't you? How do we know you won't take Carter and try to destroy us because we stood in your way?"

"You don't. You simply have to trust me."

"Men aren't usually trustworthy."

Jacob could see the shadow of pain in all three pairs of eyes. It was obvious the distrust ran far deeper than their treatment at the hands of James Blackstone. He glanced over at KC, seeing shades of despair on her beautiful features. Having lived in the same town as the Gatlins all his life, he should know this story. Sadly, he didn't. And the fact that he had never asked drove home his own failings in his time with KC.

"Ms. Gatlin," he said, the fear in the older woman's eyes making it impossible for him to keep silent. "I assure you, KC and I are going to work this out in the best possible way *for Carter*. That is the goal here."

KC's mom looked skeptical, almost militant, but Jacob wasn't fazed. He only had to prove himself to KC. The rest would work itself out later.

"Fine, KC," her mother conceded, though she still sounded skeptical. "What about tomorrow?"

"Same schedule as usual," KC said with a quick glance his way. "I'll see you around noon."

Schedules. Another thing they'd work out later.

With that assurance, KC's mother and brother were on their way. Jacob remained rooted where he was while KC walked them outside. A deep breath in, then out, cleared away his tension from the meeting with KC's family. The silence seeped into him until he thought he could almost hear the whispering breaths of his son as he slept. Fiction, he knew. A product of his strain to connect with the son he hadn't known existed. Yet he couldn't move. Couldn't make himself walk down that hallway.

He could do this. He might not have prepared to have children yet, but it was like any kink in the manufacturing schedule. A good manager evaluated the situation, decided on the best approach and followed through. Right now, that situation entailed seeing his son up close for the first time.

KC stood talking to her mom out by her car. Turning away, Jacob took one step, then two, until he was in the short hall that connected the rooms in KC's tiny house. Having been in the house before today, Jacob easily guessed which room was Carter's. Sure enough, a little plaque adorned with pictures of painted tools, baseball bats and soccer balls was hung on the door.

Easing it open, Jacob peered through the dim light to

the white crib at the far side. His heart pounded as he registered the white noise of a small fan, the green walls and the mobile of stuffed dinosaurs in bright colors over the crib.

Despite the adrenaline rushing through his veins, Jacob forced himself across the small space. His first peek over the crib railings revealed an incredibly small…person. Splayed on his back, Carter slept with arms sprawled and legs kicked out at crazy angles. Jacob smiled. KC slept the same way. They'd never done the traditional spooning thing for longer than it took for her to fall asleep. After that, she needed her space. He wondered if Carter was just as grumpy in the mornings.

Carter's cheeks were round and chubby, his lips the same full bow shape as KC's. Those dark golden curls covered his head, prompting Jacob to reach out and slip his finger inside one with careful precision. His son. His *son*.

Though he hadn't heard her come in, he felt KC as she approached his side. He couldn't turn to face her, afraid the unexpected emotions swirling through him in this moment would be plain to see on his face.

"You can pick him up if you want to hold him," KC whispered. "He's still in the stage where he sleeps through a lot."

Jacob hadn't even known there was such a stage. He knew absolutely nothing about babies. His brothers had never had kids. His colleagues who had children didn't talk about them much; their existence was marked by no more than the requisite picture on their desks. Seeing Carter lie there, so innocent, so alive, showed him just how wrong that was.

But how did he do the fatherhood thing differently? He'd have to dig deep to remember his own father, those early years before their time together was stolen by James Blackstone.

His hand tightened on the railing of the crib, but he couldn't bring himself to move. Carter looked too small;

surely he needed special handling. Jacob didn't even know where to start.

As if she could read his body language, even in the gloom, KC reached over and scooped Carter up. Nothing more than a twitch of his mouth showed that he was aware. Not giving Jacob a choice, KC lifted Carter's small body to rest against his chest.

"Let his head rest in the crook of your arm," she said.

Jacob felt himself follow her instructions, easing the baby into position. He supported Carter's head with his elbow and placed his arm along the back of the child's spine. His hand cupped a diapered rump. As the warm weight settled against him, Jacob's other arm came around to hug his son close.

As he stared down, conscious of Carter's weight and fragility, something deep inside him sighed. He might be daunted by the task in front of him, but in that moment, he knew he wouldn't stop until he'd done the best he possibly could for the child lying so trustingly in his arms. This was no longer just a wrestling match about who would have custody of Carter.

Raising his gaze to the woman who had brought about such a miracle, despite all the circumstances, Jacob couldn't hold back the words. "Thank you."

As her answering smile doubled the emotion he was holding inside, he knew a moment of panic. Because if this new feeling he had was any indication, he wasn't going anywhere for a long, long time.

All the emotions and discoveries of the past few days had jumbled up inside of Jacob, creating a desperate need for activity. He'd chosen a doozy. Jacob pulled into the driveway leading to Blackstone Manor just a few feet ahead of the furniture truck from Booties 'n' Bunting. Good. He hadn't wanted to miss the delivery.

By the time Aiden showed up, Jacob had supervised the

unloading of all the furniture into the third-floor nursery. Jacob was there, surrounded by the parts of the sleigh-style crib he'd chosen, when his brother found him.

"Why is that the only piece of furniture that didn't come assembled? You know they have people for that, right?" Aiden picked up a railing and twirled it, testing the weight.

Jacob immediately stole it back. "*I* wanted to do this part."

His brother considered the room and all its new contents for a moment before turning back to Jacob. "This baby stuff has really gotten to you," he said.

Jacob didn't bother to answer. The evidence lay all around him.

"What about the woman? She get to you, too?"

Jacob really didn't want to talk about that—or the lack of consensus over the care of their son, though he hoped to remedy that soon. But the few moments he'd spent with Carter—perfection.

Aiden crouched nearby, watching as Jacob finished sorting the parts and then started to assemble the crib. When he spoke again, it was in a more serious tone. "What's it really like, Jacob?"

Jacob looked up, ready to throw out his usual flippant reply, until he caught sight of Aiden's intensely curious gaze. A lot had changed about his brother since his forced marriage…or maybe Jacob was just getting to see more of the real Aiden. Either way, there'd been more moments like these in the past year than there'd been their entire lives.

"You mean with Carter?"

Aiden nodded.

"Scary," he admitted as he tightened a screw. "Exhilarating, fun, messy…" He torqued another.

"Sounds a lot like marriage," Aiden said with a grin, dropping to the carpet on the other side of the pile of crib parts.

Jacob thought of KC—how exciting it had been to be

with her, addictive but unsettling, because she kept him so off balance. Not neat and tidy the way he'd set his life up to be. He'd thought he was the only man who felt that way.

"I wouldn't know," Jacob said.

"Did I really just hear a man admit that he didn't have all the answers?" Christina teased as she walked into the room. "Surely that's a sign of the end times or something."

She bent over to kiss Aiden, her wealth of deep brown hair sweeping forward. Then she straightened and looked around the room. Jacob followed her gaze, wondering if the medium green walls, light wood furniture and race-car theme would meet with a woman's approval. His answer came with her smile.

"This is really beautiful, Jacob," she said. "I'll admit I couldn't resist a peek when the painters were here. But this furniture—it all blends so well together."

Aiden put in his two cents'. "That's female speak for it matches."

He ducked away from Christina's swat, rolling across the soft new carpet with a laugh. Jacob couldn't help but smile. He'd never seen two people so happy—especially not in this house. Miracles did indeed happen.

He thought he might just want a miracle of his own.

"So when is KC moving in?" Christina asked.

And that stopped the fun right in its tracks. "So far, she's not."

Christina and Aiden glanced at each other, sending a jolt through Jacob as he recognized that same form of unspoken communication he and KC were developing. Then Christina waved her hand around the room. "I don't understand. What's all this for if she and the baby aren't going to live here? Is she refusing to give you a chance?"

When Jacob didn't answer quickly enough, Christina gasped. "Jacob, you aren't going to try to separate them, are you?"

He didn't like the thread of panic in her voice any more

DANI WADE   59

than the panic rising in his own throat. Especially since he wasn't sure whether it originated in thoughts of losing KC…or keeping her.

"We haven't decided what we're doing in the future," he said, trying to smooth things over.

"Obviously *you* have," she insisted, "or preparing this nursery would be completely pointless."

"Christina, don't interfere," Aiden warned.

"How can I not?" she asked, trembling in her distress. "KC is my friend. I realize she made a tough choice, a wrong choice, but separating her from Carter wouldn't fix that."

"I'm not trying to punish KC. Or permanently take Carter from his mother." Jacob glanced around the room, not able to put his thoughts into coherent words. Commitment with KC wasn't even on the horizon, but already his love for his son had solidified. At least he could have this special place to start building his own family, even if he didn't get the girl. "I'm not really sure what I'm doing here. I just…need this. And so will Carter, regardless of whether or not KC and I are together."

Christina had a warning for him, though. "That may be all it is, Jacob. You may have no intention of doing any harm. You probably don't want my advice, but there's something your two testosterone-soaked brains need to realize," she said, glancing at Aiden. "If KC sees this room, and it doesn't come with some form of commitment to her, too, she'll think one thing and one thing only. That her trust in letting you into her life with Carter was sadly misplaced because you planned to take her baby from her all along."

Five

KC stood near the guard shack leading to the mill factory grounds, waiting for Jacob to make an appearance. It had been a week, and they still hadn't come to a conclusion about custody arrangements. This couldn't be put off any longer. While she dreaded the outcome, the wait was killing her. She couldn't sleep for worry, and the last thing she needed with a baby and full-time job was no sleep.

That could make things very emotional, very messy.

Finally Jacob walked through the gates toward his Tahoe. The frown on his face spoke of deep thought, until he spotted her leaning against a tree near his vehicle. Then his stride turned determined, purposeful. Within a minute or two, he had pulled KC out of sight of the guard shack and urged her into the Tahoe's front seat. Her door closed just as the bell rang for change of shift.

"Still ashamed of being seen with me?" she asked.

Jacob paused before putting the key in the ignition. "Do you want our former relationship to go public like this?"

Technically, he hadn't answered her question, but she didn't argue because he was right. She didn't want whatever was between them to become public in a rush of twisted gossip. But she couldn't wait any longer to ease the churning in her stomach. She wouldn't admit to herself that his use of the word *former* made it churn that much more.

She didn't speak as he started to drive. She just fidgeted in the seat of the Tahoe, watching as raindrops started to hit the window as he gained speed.

"What's wrong?" he asked.

She forced herself to quit moving and speak her fears aloud. "Are you going to sic that lawyer on me?"

"You mean Canton?" He shook his head, his jaw tightening over his thoughts—whatever those might be. "No, KC. If he's never near my son again, it will be too soon."

That was promising, at least. "Another lawyer, then?"

"Why? Are you anxious to get it all in writing?"

Fear dried her mouth, postponing her response. After a moment, Jacob pulled over and turned to face her. The distance between them felt like miles instead of a few inches.

"Look. We can do this two ways." That no-nonsense look on Jake's face scared her even more. "We can decide between us. Or we can involve a judge and a lawyer."

And who would lose in that fight? She had a feeling she couldn't afford the same caliber of lawyer as Jacob.

"Like your mom said, I'm a businessman. I'm used to covering my ass with a contract." Despite his words, he reached out to push her hair back with his long fingers. The touch disconcerted her, bringing back feelings she'd rather leave buried.

His tone softened. "But this isn't a company we're talking about. It's a person. You've already proved that you value Carter more than money."

Startled, she met his inscrutable eyes.

"You could have had a lot of money and no hassle, but you chose to give birth to my son instead. I don't agree with how you did it. I'm just grateful that you did."

Her breath caught in her throat, but she finally murmured, "Thank you."

For long moments the magic of communion whispered

between them. KC's heart ached for more, but anything more with Jake was just a dream. A dream she should have woken up from long ago.

Finally he turned back to look out the windshield; rain pounded heavily on the glass. "To keep this amicable, I think we can come up with a schedule between the two of us and each have our own time. Don't you think?"

His words chased the intimacy away like wind against fog. "Wait. What?" she asked, shaking her head. "You want unsupervised visits?"

"No." He drew the word out. "I want Carter to live with me."

"Um, no."

Jacob didn't show a hint of anger, his face remaining blank. "Why not?"

She hated that he was so calm while she felt white-hot and shaky. "I've told you why, Jacob. I don't know what kind of dad you'll be."

"How am I supposed to find out if you won't let me?"

"We'll find out first, then talk about you having Carter all alone." She almost choked on that last bit, but forced it out. "Until then, you can see him at my house. We both can. That way I'll know he's okay." *And exactly where I want him to be.* But she needed to speak logically, not basing her argument on emotions. "Besides, I have everything a baby needs at my house. You don't."

"Are you sure about that?"

Fear trickled over her as she pictured him standing over the beautifully carved crib at Booties 'n' Bunting. He sounded way too certain. What kind of plans had he been making while she'd been wallowing in fear?

"Well, Carter and I are a package deal right now. And I'm not moving." This fight wasn't one she was going to lose. So much of what she wanted had disappeared, but not Carter. Never Carter.

"Then I'll come to you."

That didn't sound as good as she'd hoped. "What do you mean?" Oh, heck. Was she really starting to fidget again?

"I mean, I'm not settling for a three-hour visit once a week. I want to be with my son 24/7. If I'm not at work or in the shower, we'll be stuck together like glue."

She could feel her eyes widen. Seeing Jacob every couple of days was one thing. But constantly? "I don't think this is the answer."

He crouched closer, invading her space. "You're lucky I don't drag you and Carter to work with me. We are a family. It's about time we started acting like one." His eyes were dead serious. "It's time to decide, KC. One way or the other. I'm either with him or calling a lawyer. Your choice."

KC washed down the tables during the midafternoon lull. The bar was open for lunch on Saturday and did a pretty brisk business. She had a few short hours to get caught up on all the cleaning before the wildness of the evening began.

If only all the activity would drown out the worries over Jacob's ultimatum. He'd given her twenty-four hours to decide. She knew what she wanted—Jake at her house, in her bed, becoming the true family she'd fantasized about. But that wasn't what he was offering. And moving to Blackstone Manor...

The doorbell chimed as someone came into the bar. KC looked up, surprised to see Christina walking toward her.

KC's classy friend had looked out of place the few times she'd been here. But she was friendly and always welcome. KC couldn't think of a single person who didn't love Christina. She epitomized the picture KC had of a true lady.

Their eyes met, and Christina sent a tentative smile across the distance between them. At least one thing seemed to be working out. If she could just figure out this situation with Jake...

"Hey, girl," KC said. "You want something to eat or just a drink to cool off?"

"A drink would be nice. Thank you."

Christina slid onto a bar stool with ease despite her pencil skirt. KC's mom stayed and chatted for a minute before going back to washing dishes. KC poured up a tall sweet tea, knowing her friend didn't usually drink alcohol.

"Jacob says you're in a deadlock," Christina said after a long swallow.

"Did he?"

That shouldn't surprise her, but it did. Jacob didn't seem the type to do the confiding thing.

Christina grinned, looking more than a little sheepish. "Actually, I overheard him telling Aiden, who was grilling him." Her grin quickly faded. "Why don't you want Carter at Blackstone Manor?"

"It's not about keeping him from there, or keeping him from you. It's about—"

She couldn't force the words past her lips. This was about her heart, and not being able to trust Jacob with it. Which made it even harder to trust him with their son. The men who'd been a part of her life hadn't cared a thing about her heart when they'd walked out the door. Would Jacob do the same to Carter once the novelty of being a father wore off?

She looked down to find Christina's hand covering her own.

"I know," her friend whispered. "Trust me. I know."

Christina probably did. From what she'd told KC, she and Aiden had been through their own rough times before deciding they loved each other and wanted to stay married. KC was a little jealous of her friend's happily-ever-after. Because she had to face reality instead.

"He's not taking my child."

KC wished she sounded strong and sure, but knew her voice was a little bit weepy, a little bit pained.

"And why should he?" her mother said, working her way back down the counter to the two of them. "I still say men aren't to be trusted."

Christina winced. "Ms. Gatlin, I don't think Jacob wants to take Carter away. He simply wants a chance to get to know his son." She spread her fingers wide, studying the ring on her left hand for long moments before looking back up. "Listen, I don't know Jacob well, but I've seen him in action. He's hands-on with his mother and has been for years. Most men can't or won't do that. Not even for family."

She locked gazes with KC, her sincerity reflected in her expression. "I really think you can trust him."

With Carter? Or with her heart? What was she thinking? Jacob had already taught her not to trust him with her heart. But Christina was right. All those visits home hadn't been for KC. They'd been to visit Jacob's mom, sometimes for doctor's appointments, because she was sick or just to check in on her. Jacob cared about his family. And he knew how to take care of them. Shouldn't she give Carter the chance to know his dad that her brother never got? That she'd barely had?

"I can't risk coming to Blackstone Manor."

"Why?" Christina asked.

KC threw a sidelong glance at her mother, then turned her gaze down to the bar top. "It would just be uncomfortable. I mean, he would never take me there before. Going there now? It would feel like—"

Her mother leaned in. "Turning into his mistress?"

"Mom!"

Her mother picked up Christina's empty glass. "Well, that's what it would look like to everyone else."

She had a point. "Well, he can come to my house."

But her mother wasn't done. "So you're just going to take him back in your house, in your bed? Hasn't our life taught you better than that? Don't you remember how easy it is for them to walk away?"

"No, Mom. I haven't forgotten. And don't worry about the bed thing." She forced the words out, even though she almost choked. "I don't think I'll be ready for that in a million years." *Please don't let me make a liar out of myself.* "But it could be fun to watch him squirm on the couch."

Six

Jacob finished up a conversation with one of the line supervisors, then strode across a portion of the production floor that was down for maintenance. This company grew on him every day. Not because he had a passion for textiles, but because of the hardworking people. Some he'd known for years; some were part of a whole new generation coming to work at Blackstone Mills. For the most part, they were a dedicated bunch of locals who took pride in their product. Getting to know them better had been a privilege and a pleasure.

Now the question haunted him: Who would want to ruin all this?

Not far from him, a tall figure stepped out from a side aisle. Jacob had been so lost in thought, it took him a moment to recognize KC's brother, Zachary. Jacob halted abruptly, bringing him within inches of the other man. They were about the same height, and Jacob met his challenging stare head-on. Great. Another family supporter. *Not.*

Jacob didn't move, standing his ground with a level look. Since he'd moved into KC's little house two days ago, her family hadn't come around. Was this his official "talkin' to"? Zachary studied him with those hazel eyes, so much like KC's. Just as Jacob thought the tension might crackle in the air, the other man stepped back with a small nod. "Jacob," he acknowledged.

"Zachary." Jacob extended his hand for a firm shake. Neither he nor Zachary tried to assert too tight a grip. Just a simple acknowledgment of each other as equals. This might work out better than Jacob had hoped.

"You don't have to eye me like that, boss. I'm not here for the whole 'keep your hands off my sister' talk."

Jacob felt his eyebrows rise, and wished he could tell the other man keeping his hands to himself wasn't an option. At least, that was what he hoped. KC had called two hours before the deadline with her choice: he would stay at her house. Somehow it came across as her doing him a favor, as if control had been snatched away from him with those simple words.

As if getting settled in her house had deflated some of the uneasiness between them, he and KC had moved back into their more natural state of flirting with each other, skirting around the sexual tension that built every second they were together. It reminded Jacob of their first date, played over and over in slow motion. The surprising part was, he enjoyed the anticipation.

But KC hadn't made clear where they stood—hope still simmered despite the fact that he'd slept on her couch last night.

Zachary wasn't done. "Besides, it's a little late for that talk. Considering Carter and all."

"Yes, I'd say so," Jacob said, keeping his grin inside. "But I meant what I said at KC's house the other day. I want to do what's best for Carter. That doesn't include backing down or letting your sister off the hook."

To Jacob's surprise, Zachary smirked. "Oh, I think you're up to the challenge. Just keep your eyes open with that one."

"She can be a handful."

Zachary nodded, an understanding look in his hazel eyes. "The two of you did a good job keeping this a secret. Even I didn't realize what was happening for a long time."

"I guess Carter was a pretty big giveaway."

"For the family, yeah. I knew a couple of months before that," Zachary said.

That surprised Jacob. "Guess it was a shock."

"Yes, but I respect my sister too much to butt into her life."

That was a concept Jacob didn't run into very often these days. Most people were more than happy to meddle. He cocked his head at Zachary in question.

"KC is a self-sufficient, capable woman," the other man said. "With our family history, she's had to be. Why she would want to be relegated to the shadows, I don't know. But I assumed she had her reasons."

She hadn't wanted it—Jacob knew that now. She'd viewed the clandestine part of their relationship in a whole different way than he had. He'd anticipated each moment with her and could only focus on her when they were alone. He knew now it was a possessive attitude. Not only did he not want the complications of other people, he'd wanted KC to himself.

Just the thought had his heart pumping.

"That being said—" Zachary continued.

Here it comes. The brotherly rebuke was clear in Zachary's voice.

"I'll stand behind KC…however she needs me to."

Jacob nodded to the other man with respect. It took guts to go against his employer in support of his family. Openly and without apology. Without the stereotypical "I'll hunt you down with my shotgun" diatribe. Because Zachary was more worried about his sister and her needs than asserting his manhood.

"Good," Jacob said. "Family should stand together."

Lord knew his family had its crazy moments, but he and

his brothers were there for each other every step of the way. So why had he not included them in his relationship with KC until he was forced? Not even his twin brother, Luke.

The answer to that lay in a part of his psyche Jacob wasn't sure he wanted to explore further.

"Do you enjoy working here, Zachary?"

The other man crossed his arms over his chest. "Why? Am I about to lose my job?"

"Far from it." Jacob gathered his thoughts for a moment, glancing around the area to ensure they were still alone. He was taking a risk here, but his gut told him it was the right one. Lowering his voice, he asked, "What do you think about all the problems around the plant?"

Once again Zachary studied him, thinking before he spoke. Jacob's respect for him grew.

"Why would you trust what I have to say?" Zachary asked.

Jacob answered with a challenge of his own. "Should I not?"

Zachary nodded slowly, as if coming to a decision. "We've got some sneaky mischief going on. It's pretty hard to go incognito with this many people around."

"Are you speaking from experience?"

"Ex-military. Air force."

Hmm… That could come in handy. "Any ideas how it's happening?"

"It wasn't really my place to look into it."

"What if it was?"

Before his possible new ally could answer, footsteps sounded from down a nearby aisle. Unlike the normal rubber-soled work boot, this was the *clip-clip* of dress shoes. That meant management. Zachary fell back a step while Jacob stretched his shoulders, loosening the tension that was gathering there.

A familiar face appeared a little farther down. Mark Zabinski had gone to high school with Jacob. They'd attended the only private high school in Black Hills, where they'd both been prominent in Future Leaders of America and student government. A business management degree had gotten Mark hired as one of the daytime line supervisors. He'd moved up through the ranks to manage the accounting department, but hadn't been able to get any further than that. Jacob couldn't help thinking his enthusiasm for the return of the Blackstone brothers was a little too forced.

"Hey, guys," Mark said, eyeing Jacob and Zachary in turn. "Everything okay?"

Zachary didn't rush back to his station like an employee who'd been caught loafing. Instead, he held his stance, looking down on Mark from his superior height without a word.

Jacob watched with interest but also refused to rush away. "Yes, Mark," he said. "Everything's fine. Zachary was just explaining to me how some of the equipment worked."

Mark nodded with enough enthusiasm to shake his longish, eighties-style blond hair and started describing how the surrounding machines worked, causing Zachary to quirk the corner of his mouth in a look of almost condescending amusement. Mark didn't seem to notice, but Jacob did. He agreed with Zachary more than he could admit in front of an audience.

As soon as the other man took a moment to breathe, Zachary jumped in. "I'd better get a move on. Day shift is almost over and I need to shut down."

Mark nodded, his look of supreme approval hinting that the idea had been all his.

Zachary shook hands with each man in turn, but his gaze caught Jacob's. "If I can help with anything else, just let me know."

Oh, Jacob would be calling. A man on the floor was just what he needed, and Zachary's position and history made

him perfect. He'd check with Bateman, just to be sure there
wasn't anything else he needed to know about KC's brother.

Mark watched the taller man's retreat, then turned back
to Jacob with an ingratiating smile that scraped along Jacob's nerves. The man insisted on kissing up when Jacob
would be happier if they just treated each other as equals.
"You sure everything is okay?" Mark asked.

"Sure." Jacob wasn't about to reveal what the last part
of his conversation with Zachary had been about—or the
first part, for that matter. Though he hated how much it reminded him of his earlier attempts to keep KC under wraps,
he and Aiden had decided it was safer to keep the relationship quiet for now. "What're you doing down here, Mark?"

"Oh, just checking in. You know, sometimes you have
to stay on top of people, make sure their work is up to par."

Jacob couldn't decide whether to question that statement or mention that Mark didn't belong in this part of
the plant anymore. "Well, we're good down here. Let's get
shift change taken care of, shall we?"

Because Jacob had a woman to get home to…

Seven

Jacob wished he could ignore his eager lead foot on the drive out to Lola's. As scenery flew by, he reflected on how KC was at work and Carter was at her mother's. There wasn't any need for him to be there. The fact that he'd promised her 24/7 wasn't a really good reason for him to be speeding down the road toward the bar.

His body knew only one thing: get to KC. He wasn't even sure why. His body wasn't going to get what it wanted, regardless of how fast he drove.

Still, he obeyed.

Luckily he didn't get pulled over by a cop before he reached his destination. Lola's was sparsely populated on a Wednesday, but patrons were trickling in after getting off work. Jacob joined them, waving a few hellos, and decided he'd find a table somewhere KC could see him. It couldn't hurt for her to know he meant business about their mock-family togetherness.

He wasn't being stalkerish. *Not at all.*

Shaking his head at how messed up his mind was, Jacob crossed the room. He let his gaze sweep the bartending area, not wanting to appear obvious. Until he noticed KC wasn't there. Instead, her mother straightened bottles behind the bar. That stopped him in his tracks. Unsure now, he waited a few minutes. He knew KC would walk out of the back room any time now.

Seconds ticked by… Nothing.

Letting go of caution, Jacob strode over until he stood front and center. "Ms. Gatlin?" he said.

She raised wary eyes to meet his, though she didn't straighten from her task of refilling the bottles under the counter. A stubborn squint had replaced her earlier look of fear. "Yes, *Mr.* Blackstone?"

Cheeky. "It's Jacob. Where is KC this evening? I thought she was working."

"She was. Now she's not."

He raised his eyebrows at that cryptic answer. Definite carryover of animosity from the previous day. "May I ask where she is?" he said, pulling out his phone for a quick glance to make sure he hadn't missed a call from her.

"Not here," she said, her tone even tighter than before.

Jacob stood, frozen in a quandary. He had a feeling that, as was the case with KC, throwing his weight around would get him nowhere. At least with KC, the arguing was part of the fun. That didn't apply here. Could he appeal to reason? Probably not. Ms. Gatlin was a mother, with a mother's emotions. What should he do?

"Ma'am—" he started, not even sure where he was going with the sentence. Then Zachary stepped around the corner of the bar.

KC's brother held up his phone, displaying the text message screen. He was a little too far away for Jacob to read the words, but he got the point. "She's at home," Zachary said, ignoring his mother's glare. "Looks as though Carter started running a fever around noon. She's taking care of him tonight instead of working."

Torn between his irritation at KC's mother for keeping that information from him and anger at KC for not letting him know, Jacob locked his emotions down tight. "Thanks, Zachary," he said.

He turned back to the door, his mind now on getting to KC's house, when Ms. Gatlin finally spoke. "Why don't you take some food."

He half twisted back, eyeing her over his shoulder. Part of him couldn't help wondering if she'd poison his portion—if she even gave him a portion.

She refused to meet his gaze but continued speaking. "Sick babies don't leave a lot of time for cooking."

She headed off to the kitchen, and the men shared a knowing look. Ms. Gatlin wasn't about to offer Jacob anything, but she wasn't a heartless woman.

Twenty minutes later, Jacob was finally on the road with his lead foot and a fried-chicken dinner for two. When he arrived, he could hear Carter crying from the porch, which gave him pause.

Then he shrugged. He could play the big bad man too macho to handle crying babies, or he could play the man big enough to step in where he was needed. Even if he didn't know what he was doing. Pride be damned.

Walking through that door was a tough step, but he did it. When he crossed into the living room, what he saw gave him pause.

He couldn't believe that a woman holding a sick, crying baby could be so darn cute. In pink sweatpants and a tank top, her hair haphazardly pulled up in one of those clip things, she looked frazzled and concerned. She bounced Carter gently in one arm and patted him on the back. He would have smiled and kissed her if she didn't look on the verge of tears as Carter paused in his crying to cough.

Spotting him in the doorway, she glared as if he was the cause of all the ruckus. So fussing at her for not calling him wasn't an option right now, either. They'd come back to it later. The noise pulled his gaze down to Carter, whose chubby cheeks were now flushed. The rims of his eyes were red, too, but Jacob didn't see any tears.

KC raised her voice as her eyes narrowed on him. "If you want to throw your weight around, I'm not in the mood, Jacob."

He could feel the frown forming between his brows and struggled to maintain his mask of calm. How could one child produce such a racket? "Actually, I'm here because I thought that's what we committed to. When I say 24/7, that's what I mean."

She opened her mouth, but he plowed forward before she could argue.

"What do you need?" It might be better to head this discussion off at the pass.

He saw a sheen of tears forming in her muddled hazel eyes. "Um." She swallowed hard, turning away for a moment.

Jacob gave her the chance to regain her composure. He took the food into the kitchen and lay the containers out on the table. Then he returned, grateful the cries had subsided to whimpers interspersed with snuffles. Who knew a baby's distress could shake a man's firmest foundations?

"What do you need, sweetheart?" Jacob repeated, keeping his voice as gentle as possible. "Do you need me to hold him?"

"No. He wants me," she said, patting and bouncing the baby in a set rhythm. "But he needs to eat. Could you make a bottle?"

As Jacob made up the formula, he knew he'd have to take this situation in hand. From what Zachary had said, KC had been with the baby since a little after noon. It was now a quarter past six. Her disheveled appearance and quick tears, unusual for her, spoke to her exhaustion, yet she still tried to maintain her superwoman front. He wasn't going to let her run herself into the ground and catch Carter's fever. She'd pushed him to the periphery of

Carter's care since he'd moved in, but today he'd be jumping in feetfirst.

Returning with the bottle, he helped KC settle into the overstuffed chair she and Carter usually cuddled in. A relieved look swept over her face as the baby took the offering without protest. "Good. I think the medicine the doctor gave me is helping. This is the first time I've been able to get him to eat with any appetite. His other bottle sat out too long, and I didn't have enough hands to fix more."

He let her talk out her frustrations. There wasn't anything for him to add. The tension relaxed around her eyes, and she took on the peaceful expression that entranced him as she watched Carter eat.

How on earth could he feel this attraction and need when her focus wasn't even on him? Where was the crying when he needed a distraction? "He's not the only one who needs to eat."

"Well, you'll have to cook for yourself," she said with a frown. "I've got my hands full."

Boy, cranky babies sure created cranky moms. Though it was probably like any bad day on a job with grumpy customers, only worse because the care was hands-on with no quittin' time. "I meant you," he said, leaning closer to catch her gaze. "I brought home food from Lola's. Your mom wanted to make sure you ate." He'd keep her mother's attitude to himself.

Her eyes widened for a moment, then she gave a tired grin. "You know what? I didn't even notice you bring that in." She ran her fingers over Carter's hair. "Sorry."

"No problem." Surprisingly, it wasn't. Her attitude didn't make him mad or eager to walk back out the door. An urge to face the challenge she presented rose within him. He would do this. Whether she wanted him to or not.

They sat in silence for long moments. Almost as soon as the bottle was empty, Carter drifted off to sleep. KC, too. Her long lashes rested against the purple circles under her eyes. She looked so fragile, awakening Jacob's protective urge once more. One he wasn't comfortable with but refused to ignore.

He carefully lifted Carter from her arms, stilling her with a firm look when she jerked up. "Let's get you something to eat," he said as he settled the baby in the bassinet that she'd moved into the living room.

"Yes," she agreed, though her eyes stayed glued to the sleeping child. "I should eat while he's out."

Jacob led her to the kitchen table with a firm hand. "He'll be fine. We're right here."

She dug into the food with muted gusto. Had she eaten at all today? Or had her entire focus been on Carter? As soon as she stood to clean up, Jacob was on his feet, too. "Time for your own bed, sweetheart."

"I can't go to bed," she protested. "Carter might need me."

"That's what I'm here for. You've had him all day. You rest." He led her into the dim back bedroom, where he could see the bed that had been the stage for so many hot nights with her. But tonight, it was for her alone. "I'll come get you if we need you."

"But what if he starts crying?"

"What about it?" His confidence was built on shaky ground, but she'd never know.

"You won't know what to do."

She was right, but that wasn't the point. "I'll manage. Now, into bed."

As if to show her defiance, she strutted into the bathroom and shut the door with a firm click. He wasn't about to leave, because sure enough she'd be back in the living room if he left the path unguarded. So he crossed the room to confiscate the baby monitor on the bedside table, then took up residence in the doorway so he could hear Carter if he woke.

When she returned, she had a vulnerable look on her

face and wore soft, comfy clothes, which inspired him to hold her close. Then he remembered the reason he was here had nothing to do with their previous closeness, and locked his knees just in time. But he wanted to—boy, did he want to—with an ache that dug into his gut.

"Promise me you'll come get me if he needs me," she said.

He met her worried gaze, shadowed with fear and exhaustion. "I promise if we need you, I won't hesitate. Now rest."

She crawled into the side of the bed he knew she preferred, and snuggled beneath the dusky-purple comforter that had kept their body heat cocooned so many nights before. He swallowed, his body and his mind wishing he could join her just one more time.

Then he turned away, closing the door behind him. Returning to the living room, he gazed down at his son, praying he could live up to his words.

"It's just you and me, kid," he said. "I told your mom I could handle this. Don't make a liar out of me, okay?"

KC shot straight up in bed, her heart racing as if she'd just run a marathon. What was wrong? Something was off. What—

Carter!

Barely noticing the dark outside the windows, she rushed down the hallway. Only as she skidded to a stop in the living room did she notice the most telling clue to her long sleep—silence. A single soft lamp kept the lighting dim. Jacob sprawled in her comfy chair, his legs splayed before him, his big body overflowing the space. But it was the baby sleeping on his bare chest that made the breath catch in her throat.

She stepped closer, noting the natural flush of Carter's chubby cheeks. The red of his earlier fever was gone. Jacob had changed him into a baby gown. As her hand rested on

Carter's upturned cheek, she didn't detect any fever. His sleeping face was turned up to his daddy's; his arm spread across Jacob's chest with his fingers curled into the light sprinkling of hair.

She couldn't resist the temptation. Certain that Jacob was asleep, she let her eyes wander over the muscled pecs that were usually hidden beneath his button-down dress shirts. He'd discarded his belt along with his shirt, but he still had on his navy dress pants, creating a dark contrast against his lightly tanned skin and Carter's creamy-yellow gown. Jacob's feet were now bare, prompting KC to smile. She'd learned that the one primitive habit Jacob had was stripping off his shoes and socks the minute he was behind closed doors. Unfortunately, his long, lean feet were as sexy as the rest of him.

A sudden wave of emotion hit her. Dreams from her pregnancy flashed through her mind. Dreams of a real family, of Jacob being with them, being devoted to them. Two days into his challenge, and already her fears of him abandoning Carter were dissolving like sugar in water. Which only opened up a new set of fears—after all, children were forever. Romantic partners were a whole lot more disposable. History had taught her that long before she knew what romance meant.

Yet one long look at the surprisingly sexy picture of her ex-lover and her son tempted her to forget her worries and take the plunge. Then she noticed Carter's lips pucker as if searching for a bottle. His little body squirmed. A feeding was about to be on the agenda. Her heart melted as Jacob's hand came up; he patted the baby's back without opening his eyes. Bittersweet as it was, the picture before her assured her Jacob wanted to be a part of Carter's life. He'd be a good dad, even if he wouldn't let himself be husband material.

Slowly Jacob's hand moved up to lightly brush Carter's forehead, a move KC recognized as her own in checking

Carter's temperature. She smiled, then looked up to meet
Jacob's unexpectedly open eyes. For a moment she froze,
held by the intensity of the emotions swirling there.

Anxious to hide her own feelings as her awareness of
him soared, she mouthed, "When did he eat?"

With barely a jiggle, Jacob reached for his phone and
checked the time. "A little over four hours ago," he whispered.

Suddenly eager to get away, she hurried back into the
kitchen. An open laptop caught her attention. The geomet-
ric shapes of the screen saver floated back and forth. She
shouldn't look, wasn't even sure why she wanted to, but
she couldn't resist. A single swipe of her finger across the
touch pad and the screen cleared.

Her heart contracted. Jacob had appeared confident and
ready for the challenge of being left with Carter as he'd
bullied her into bed. But the internet search on the screen
suggested otherwise. *How to soothe a crying baby.* Bless
his bachelor heart.

Well, whatever he'd found, it worked. She hadn't heard
Carter all night. The clock now said 3:00 a.m. About time
for Carter's middle-of-the-night feeding, if he was still on
his usual schedule.

No wonder she'd felt dazed. She hadn't slept eight hours
straight since Carter had been born. Of course, she'd have
slept like a baby on that chest, too.

She'd just gotten the bottle heated when Carter woke in
earnest. While she settled down in a kitchen chair to feed
him, Jacob headed to the fridge. With his back turned, she
didn't have to avert her eyes from the long line of his spine
or the subtle ripple of muscle as he moved. The upper edge
of a tattoo peeked from the waistband of his pants. Discov-
ering that yin-yang symbol, which he'd attributed to his
connection with his twin brother, had been quite a shock. A
sexy shock. Conservative businessman Jacob hadn't struck
her as the tattoo type.

Turning her thoughts from the ways she'd shown Jacob her appreciation of his body art, she tried to focus on the present. When it came to cooking, Jacob had only one specialty: omelets. She'd imagined him as having nothing more than eggs and cheese in his apartment refrigerator back in Philadelphia. She hadn't been far from right. Now he pulled out all the ingredients and arranged them on the counter.

"Why are you cooking at 3:00 a.m.?" she asked, even as the smell of bacon browning in the pan made her stomach growl.

And why couldn't the man put a shirt on? Hunger hit her hard, in more ways than one. Amazing how a full night's sleep could make her feel like a new woman.

"No point in me going back to sleep," Jacob said. "I have to be at the mill early for a management meeting. Might as well feed us before I get ready."

"Thank you."

He nodded absently, continuing to crack eggs into a bowl.

"Jake," she said, her husky voice catching his attention. "I mean it. Thank you for your help."

His gaze held hers, and awareness shivered across her skin. Then, in that wicked tone of voice she'd only heard when he was lost in the depths of arousal, he said, "My pleasure."

If she hadn't been awake before, she sure was now. Relief that Carter felt better distracted her from the temptation of the half-dressed man cooking in her kitchen. Having gotten a good sleep himself, Carter was ready to socialize. For once, his eyes weren't only for mama. The occasional noise drew his gaze across the room, searching for the man who had bonded with him during the long hours of the night.

That was what she'd wanted. Wasn't it?

The question haunted her as she ate. Finally, KC ran a hand across her son's sticky curls. At some point during the night, he'd sweat, then it had dried, leaving his hair thickened and clumpy. "Since we're awake, I think it's time for a bath, sweetie."

Jacob watched as she readied the sink, setting up the baby bath and starting the water. "What's that?" he asked.

"It just makes it easier to give them a bath when they're this little and you can't safely put them in the tub."

She deftly got Carter stripped and settled. He immediately started to pat at the water and kick his little legs. Standing next to the sink, she let him play for a few minutes.

"Wow, someone's feeling better," Jacob said.

She smiled in his direction, trying to regain control over the seesaw of her emotions. Sharing moments like this with Jake was both a blessing and a curse. It was necessary to establish the relationship she wanted him to have with Carter, but a poor substitute for what she really wanted—for them to be a family.

"He loves me to give him a bath," she said, adjusting the water so she could wet a washcloth.

With just a couple of steps Jacob closed in, his heat blanketing her side as he spoke softly in her ear. "If I remember correctly, so do I."

His words sparked images in her brain: Jacob undressing her, leading her into the shower, bodies soapy and slick. She shook her head before the temptation could pull her under. Without missing a beat, she pointed the spray nozzle in Jacob's direction, the water catching him by surprise.

"Down, boy," she warned as satisfaction spread through her, along with laughter at his yelp.

A few feet away, Jacob froze, his eyes wide. Her little joke just made the temptation worse. She couldn't pull her gaze away from the river of droplets chasing down Jake's bare skin. As if he could read her mind, Jacob chased one rivulet down his chest with his thumb.

"Well, then," he said, his gaze zeroing in on her smile. "If I'd known you wanted me all wet..."

Her heart skipped a beat. *Please don't go there.* She wasn't sure she'd be able to resist.

"I think I'll take a shower now, too," he finally finished.

She knew better than to open her mouth, because anything she said would be provocative, not productive. She focused on soaping Carter down, but Jacob didn't leave. Finally, she asked, "What time do you have to be at work?"

"I've got to call Bateman to find out exactly when he wants to get started. I left yesterday before he knew, and I wanted to see you—check on you and Carter. I told him I'd be in touch later."

Yes, but did you tell him why? Or were she and Carter still the best-kept secret in Black Hills?

Eight

Jacob had faced down corporate sharks who worried him less than KC's grandmother. Not because of size or strength, but the sheer tenacity with which she held on to her dislike of him.

She was like a Chihuahua, pint-size with sharp teeth, and determined to hold him accountable for missing some standard that he didn't quite understand. When KC insisted he call her Nana, because that was what everyone called her, he simply couldn't picture it.

And KC's mother—well, she had gone back from angry to afraid. The family gathered every Sunday for an early supper. Twenty-four/seven meant Jacob had tagged along. Every time he reached for Carter, Ms. Gatlin flinched as if he would whisk the baby away, with no thought to how it would affect anyone but him.

He refused to let their reactions stop him from holding his son, something he'd gotten much more comfortable with over the past week of nightly baths, diaper changes and bottle feedings. At first, KC had tried to edge him out, but he'd soon shown her that he wasn't one of those men who wanted to hand everything over to the *little woman*. If she'd let him, he'd have been with her every step of the way—pregnancy, labor and delivery. Despite the successful night he'd spent with Carter when he'd gotten sick, Jacob hadn't gotten her to the point where she'd let him care for Carter unsupervised, but they'd get there.

One way or another.

He'd insinuated himself into KC's and Carter's lives with a seamlessness that surprised even him. Still, they were living their lives as if they were skimming the surface of a deep lake, and Jacob was surprised to find himself dissatisfied. Something momentous called to him from the depths, but he still hesitated to dip his head beneath the calm to find the answers.

Although he'd sure appreciate not sleeping on the couch, which he had a feeling KC found secretly amusing.

As they settled down to a casual but hearty meal dished up straight from the stove, Jacob was grateful for Zachary. Another man helped bridge the estrogen river in the room. Too many women, not enough excuses. A little work talk helped create balance, though by unspoken agreement they kept themselves on general topics. Before they left, though, Jacob would need to talk to Zachary about a little industrial-reconnaissance mission. Fingers crossed he'd come on board.

Jacob had feared the timing of this meal, and sure enough, Carter started to whimper. Not a full-blown cry. His afternoon nap was the hardest to get him settled for—most other times he slid into sleep with ease. Something for which Jacob, inexperienced as he was, thanked his lucky stars.

When rocking the baby seat with her foot no longer worked, KC abandoned her plate to soothe Carter. The other women and Zachary continued to eat as if this was a regular occurrence. Jacob couldn't. Shoving in his last bite of Ms. Gatlin's incredible homemade peanut-butter cookies, he stood up and crossed to take the baby from KC's arms.

"Sit down and eat," he said. She'd barely had time to make a dent in her food.

"I'll eat in a little bit after I get him settled," she protested.

Jacob was having none of that. He repeated, "Eat," this time accompanied by a stern look. He lifted the baby from her arms before she could protest. Situating Carter snugly into the crook of his arm, stomach to stomach, Jacob supported Carter's legs with his other arm. He'd learned quickly that his son would wiggle those little legs enough to drive himself and Jacob crazy. So he tucked his son close, his hand covering most of Carter's back. A now-familiar rhythm of patting immediately took over.

Back and forth, Jacob took them on a stroll for a few minutes until Carter finally relaxed and slid into a light sleep. Then Jacob settled back into his chair at the solidly built table that showed a lifetime's worth of wear and tear. As the baby snuggled against him—one of the best feelings in the world, though Jacob would never admit it out loud—he looked up to meet KC's grateful gaze.

Spending a lot of time with a sleeping baby meant they'd started communicating with a type of telepathic speech. All Jacob had to do was make eye contact, and he'd be able to tell what she was thinking from the look on her face. No words had to be spoken. It was the most intimate thing Jacob had ever experienced with another human being. Even more intimate than sex. And right now, that hazel gaze told him he'd be moving from sleeping on the couch sooner than he'd thought.

"That's quite the touch you have there," Zachary said.

Glancing at the others, Jacob was disconcerted to see he'd become the evening's entertainment. Varying degrees of disbelief, suspicion and approval registered on the faces of KC's family members. Which left him feeling both disconcerted and, yes, a little smug.

Jacob smiled down at Carter. "Well, practice makes perfect."

A grumpy huff drew his gaze back up again. "The big question is," KC's grandmother said with disbelief in her voice, "does he have any staying power?"

Jacob had to admire a woman who wasn't afraid to speak her mind, wasn't intimidated by Jacob's money or status. Her only concern was her family, as it should be. Jacob's own concerns were now wrapped up in KC and Carter. Sometimes more than he felt comfortable with, especially in such a short amount of time, but he was adjusting. Mostly. He just had to stay in control.

"Nana!" Apparently KC wasn't as approving of her grandmother's candor. "Don't be rude to Jacob."

The older woman stared down the table at her granddaughter. "Are you telling me you haven't thought it? After all the women in this family have been through? Divorce and abandonment. Abuse and neglect. The only thing more important than a man who will stick with you is one who'll treat ya right."

Jacob could tell by her expression that she *had* thought about it. Had he given her any reasons to think otherwise?

Zachary broke in before KC could respond. "You make it sound like y'all are antimen," he joked, his expression clearly saying *what about me*.

Nana graced her grandson with a crooked smile. "You're the exception, boy. Not the norm."

"Nana," KC broke in again. "You can't judge all men by a few. There are good ones out there."

What about in here?

The hope in KC's eyes, which he could see even though she refused to look in his direction, made his chest ache. He looked down at Carter and thought about what kind of man he hoped his son would grow into. How would he want Carter to behave if he found himself in the same situation as Jacob? The idea blew his mind.

"That attitude will get you into trouble," Nana went on. "One man might just be an example, or even two. But four between us? The pattern is there." She waved her hand at each of the kids in turn. "Zachary's dad and his wandering ways. Your dad got tired of responsibility. My husband, David, and his drinking. So I thought a boyfriend would work better, and ended up having to take a fryin' pan to him after he dared raise his hand to me." She shook her head. "I think I'm justified in my opinions."

Maybe so. They did seem to have the worst luck. Or was it really poor choices? As Nana turned her knowing eyes his way, Jacob was again reminded of a toothful shark…or maybe a barracuda. Who could blame her after a lifetime of being left to take care of herself and her children, all alone?

"So what have you got to say for yourself, boy?" she demanded.

Jacob looked around at the faces of the Gatlin women—strong women who persevered despite being repeatedly abandoned—and admired them. They reminded him of Christina. His sister-in-law had an incredible talent for blooming where she was planted, despite all the odds against her.

"I don't."

The women met his refusal to defend himself with wide-eyed surprise. Zachary hung his head as if Jacob was doomed.

"Nothing I say will convince you I'm any different, Nana," he said, soft but sure. "Nor you, Ms. Gatlin. I'm sure all those men had plenty of flattering words that they used to get what they wanted from you, but I'm not a man of charm. My portion went to my twin brother, Luke. But I *am* a man of action—I'll let my deeds prove my worth for me."

The look of approval in KC's eyes, mixed with something fiery, told him he'd scored more than a few points with his words.

Still, the uneasy current in the room continued until after the table was cleared. Figuring the women needed some time to discuss him, Jacob followed Zachary out back. An unusually large garage occupied substantial real estate behind the house. As soon as he stepped inside, Jacob could understand why.

He let out a low whistle as he eyed the old-school Camaro on blocks in the middle of the room. "Nice. You do the work yourself?"

Zachary nodded. "It's relaxing."

"You'd get along really well with my brother Luke."

"I've never had the pleasure of being formally introduced to our resident celebrity, though I've seen him some in Lola's. I'd love to take a look at his racing car."

"He has a mechanic for his stock car, but he does a lot of work on it himself, too. Says it's soothing."

Zachary smirked. "I agree. But somehow I suspect you didn't come out here to talk to me about restoring cars."

Jacob gave a half grin. "Caught me." He paced a semi-circle around the front of the car, letting the open hood and engine beneath distract him. "So how bad was it? What do I need to know about KC's childhood?"

"Why haven't you asked her?"

Jacob didn't need to turn around to see the condemnation on Zachary's face. He could hear it in his voice. "No, I haven't. Or I didn't, before. Now…" He shrugged. "I'm not sure we're ready for that kind of conversation."

"When you're sure, KC should be the one to tell you."

But conversations like that were easier to have while staring at cars instead of facing a woman's vulnerable eyes. Which was why he'd asked Zachary instead of KC.

Remembering the other reason he'd come out here, Jacob glanced over his shoulder. Zachary stood near the tool bench, twirling a wrench between his fingers. "Have you thought any more about our conversation at the mill?"

"Oh, yeah, I've thought about it a lot. Hard not to. I'm keeping my ears and eyes open. You'd be surprised how little attention people pay to Maintenance."

"No, I wouldn't. When I spoke to him, Bateman said you have a great track record. He doesn't understand, with your outstanding military career, why you chose to come home."

"And be just another man who couldn't stick around to help my family? The military gave me a chance for an education I couldn't have afforded otherwise. Now I have a decent job close to home and can be here to take care of my family on a daily basis. Something they've never really had."

Which made Jacob all the more anxious to prove to KC that he could be there on a daily basis, too. And not just for Carter—heaven help him.

Time to get off this subject before his guts got any more twisted. "So you'll help us?"

"I don't really see it as helping you and your brother, or even Bateman. I'm worried about the safety of the people who work there, the security of this town. I think the more vigilant security team has helped shut down some of the problems, but I want to know how the saboteurs are getting onto the mill floor and tampering with the equipment."

Jacob nodded knowingly. "So I'm giving you an excuse to do something you already wanted to do."

Zachary grinned. "I'll never tell, boss."

Zachary may be helping them, but he was as cautious as his sister, and Jacob had a feeling the other man wouldn't have hesitated to brush him off if he hadn't already wanted to get involved. He was his own man, and didn't apologize for his choices. Which made him a good brother for KC, and a good role model for Carter—

Jacob hoped Zachary didn't end up being the only role model in Carter's life. Could Jacob possibly live up to Zachary's example?

* * *

What to do with a man you would alternately kiss or smack silly? KC could feel the conflict pulling her in two different directions.

"Thank you for letting us babysit," Christina said softly, as if she could read the unease vibrating along KC's nerves when she handed over her baby.

Christina snuggled a sleeping Carter closer, the move reassuring KC. She'd never left him with anyone other than family. And the fact that she'd only found out about this little trip an hour ago hadn't given her time to prepare her emotions.

Or pack her stuff.

"I hope I remembered everything," she said, sliding the overstuffed diaper bag off her shoulder and putting it next to the travel bassinet Jacob was setting up. "Carter usually stays with my mom while I'm working. It was easier to just outfit her house with everything he would need since he spends so much time over there." She couldn't hide a frown at the man who had sprung this idea on her without notice. "Jacob didn't give me much time to prepare…"

The scoundrel had the audacity to glance up at her with an unapologetic grin. What was he so happy about? He used to hate any kind of spontaneous decisions, unless they could be carried out in the privacy of her house. She'd be scared, if he didn't seem so pleased with himself. This was like a date…which she'd never truly had with him.

He'd even gone to the trouble of getting a sitter for it. Her married friends often complained about their husbands not doing that. She should be grateful, excited.

She kept telling herself not to let this mean anything, but her hopes rose without her permission. The past few days they'd shared many heated glances and deliberately accidental touches. But she'd been afraid to make the first move, to invite him back into her bed without an understanding of what he was really looking for here.

Instead, she waited. Where was all her spunk when she really needed it?

Aiden chimed in. "Oh, whatever we don't have I'm sure we can find up—"

Christina's sharp movement, seen out of the corner of her eye, pulled KC out of her distraction. "What?" KC asked.

Her friend simply tucked her arm securely back around the baby. "Aiden was saying we'll find it if we don't have it." She threw a wary glance in Jacob's direction. "After all, we'll need to learn what we're doing soon enough. We've recently started trying for a baby of our own."

Shock held her still for a moment, then KC rushed over. Smiling her excitement, she hugged her friend carefully around Carter. "That's wonderful, Christina. I'm so happy for you." Happy, and maybe a little jealous. Christina's world would be real, not the make-believe one she and Jacob had created.

"What about all the travel y'all will be doing between here and New York?" Jacob asked from behind her.

Aiden shrugged with a nonchalance that KC hadn't known any of the Blackstone brothers to possess. "Christina says we'll manage."

"I have no doubt she will," KC said with a smile for her friend.

Christina was one of the most capable women KC had ever met outside of her own family. She cared full-time for Lily Blackstone, the men's comatose mother, ran the household and was highly involved in the community. Now she was building a life with her new husband.

If KC had based her opinion solely on Jacob, she'd have thought inflexibility had been bred into the Blackstone brothers. Strict adherence to standards and procedures served him well in business, but not so much in relationships. On the other hand, Aiden was a successful art import/export dealer, now running his business in New

York from Blackstone Manor in South Carolina. Even with trips to New York, it wasn't an easy task. Had he learned to adapt on his own, or with Christina's help?

Of course, with a nickname like Renegade, Jacob's twin, Lucas, was a whole different animal. After all, it took a special kind of daredevil to take on stock-car racing as a career.

The conversation whirling around her finally came to a halt and Jacob ushered her toward the door. "He'll be ready to eat when he wakes up," he said, surprising her with the same last-minute instructions she'd been about to give. "Make sure Aiden gets diaper duty. It's the ultimate test of manhood."

Then they were out the door and walking to Jacob's SUV. "Are you going to tell me where we're going now?" she asked as he helped her into her seat.

"Nope." Stubborn man.

His grin reawakened the ache in her chest. He was so beautiful with the sun glinting off the dark gold of his hair. For a moment, time stood still as he leaned against the side of the car watching her settle into her seat. She could reach out and touch him, pull him close if she wanted to, but fear of risk kept her still.

Then the moment passed and he headed around to his side of the Tahoe. He belted in, then they started forward instead of back down the driveway as she'd expected. "Come on, where could we possibly be going back here?"

Without answering, Jacob drove around the impressive manor with its landscaped back lawn and down a rutted road carved out of the surrounding fields of tall grass. They meandered down along the fence line until they passed a cabin that looked as if it was under construction, then turned into some dense woods on the opposite side of Blackstone Manor from the mill. She'd never been on this side of Blackstone land. Their families obviously ran in different circles, so all her hiking and partying experiences with her friends were in the forest south of town.

"I wanted to give you a surprise," Jacob finally said, throwing her a teasing glance she felt all the way to her toes.

"I thought you hated those," she retorted. He did. She could tell by the small frown that formed between his brows whenever she threw him off balance. He'd often overcompensated when she'd do anything not according to his plan, reestablishing control over every situation. Not that she had a problem with him being in control; it was simply fun to throw a wrench in his works every once in a while.

He paused the SUV, glancing over at her with a look that threw her even more off balance. It was a look of lust and mischief with an intensity she hadn't seen in a long time. "Surprises might not be my favorite," he said, "but you love them. Don't you?"

Normally she did. Thrills like surprise birthday parties and unexpected gifts peppered her life because her family knew she loved them. Most of her friends knew it. She never thought Jake had wanted to acknowledge it.

Only this time the thrill was combined with nerves. Not because this didn't make her happy but because she didn't have the one answer she really wanted. Why was he doing this?

"You surprise me all the time," he said. "You work hard every day *and* night. I thought you deserved something special."

There was no escaping the sexy intent in his gaze. They'd been skirting around this issue for days. But if this was an attempt to take their relationship back to where it had been before Carter, was she willing to accept that?

Obviously nothing had changed since their affair, except the fact that they were living together and their families knew. He came into Lola's most nights while she was working, but they had only the most casual of interactions while they were in public. Barely any conversation. Nothing other people could construe as a *relationship*. But his eyes rarely left her unless one of his brothers was present.

While she hadn't gone out of her way to keep their involvement a secret, she also hadn't advertised it, either. That small, small girl still tucked deep inside wanted him to make the first move, signal to everyone that she was his and worthy to be presented as a couple.

The farther they drove, the more she could feel herself weakening. Jacob stopped the truck near a gorgeous little meadow beside the stream that flowed through Blackstone land. KC drew in an awed breath. The spot was gorgeous, lush with green clover, tiny purple flowers and even a weeping willow tree. A dreamy place perfect for outdoor seduction.

The question remained: Would she let him?

Nine

"You're not eating much," Jacob said as he watched KC pick at the potato salad on her plate. "Marie's a great cook. I thought you'd enjoy this."

KC had been behaving oddly ever since they'd left Blackstone Manor. He'd understood her nerves in taking the baby over there. After all, she'd never left Carter with anyone but family. But he was confident Christina would take good care of him, and thought KC would be more comfortable with someone she knew than with him hiring a sitter.

He simply hadn't been able to wait any longer for time alone with his former lover.

But KC didn't seem to be enjoying herself. She set down her drink and turned her turbulent hazel eyes his way. "I just—don't understand, Jacob. I mean, this feels like a date." She shook her head, her thick tumble of hair catching the sunlight. "Is it supposed to be? Because I honestly don't know how to respond."

Jacob aimed to keep it light. The last thing he wanted was to pressure her. "How else was I supposed to signal that I wanted to take what we have to the next level? I thought putting the moves on you over spit-up duty wouldn't be quite appropriate."

Her grin was just what he'd been aiming for. "What's the matter, Jake? Getting tired of the couch?"

He met her smile with one of his own. "Oh, a long time ago, believe me."

When she shook her head at him, he decided it was time to push just a little. "What? Wouldn't you be? Can you blame me for trying? After all, we are living together." *At the moment.* He shook the thought away.

"No, Jake, I don't blame you," she said, sobering. "It's just so like you to ask me. Most men would have let the heat of the moment take care of that for them."

"Considering everything that's gone before?" He shrugged. "That doesn't seem right. Besides, I couldn't get through life without a plan."

She nodded, a slight smile forming on her lush lips. "You're right. Having a plan is *so* you, Jake."

He couldn't stop himself from reaching out to trace the curve of her jaw with his fingertips. "You deserve the best, KC." And she did. After thinking about everything her family had been through, Jacob had been doubly ashamed of letting her believe she wasn't worth acknowledging. Especially since the whole purpose of keeping her a secret had been to keep his own life simple and uncomplicated.

Or had it? Going public would have meant exposing her to James Blackstone months before the confrontation that had sent her away. Would Jacob have lost those days with her if she hadn't been able to handle the pressure? And what about the community? Would they have been able to accept the differences between the two of them? Or would they have looked down on her as a woman who made herself conveniently available to him when he was in town? As accurate as that sounded, the truth had been a beautiful thing for him.

Suddenly he couldn't wait to get to his big reveal. "KC,

I need to take a trip." He gave her soft skin one more stroke before he pulled back. "I want you to come with me."

"The whole 24/7 thing?"

He shook his head, already picturing how that was about to change. "Nothing to do with that. I'm ready for more than just being your co-parent, KC. This trip—it would be just you and me."

She swallowed hard. "Where? When?"

"I need to go back to Philly for a fund-raiser, a ball for a charity I've been involved in helping for a long time. I'd love for you to accompany me."

Instead of the happy acceptance he'd been expecting, KC pulled back with a frown. "You want me to go to Philadelphia again?"

"Yes." He drew the word out, uncertain now. His memories of their one weekend in Philly were some of the best of his life. Weren't they for her?

"I don't think that's a good idea." She rose, pacing across the thick carpet of clover.

He watched her for long moments, not sure how to respond. Coming to his feet, he asked, "Why not?" Why did he have to choose a complicated woman to become involved with? Nothing was simple with KC.

"What's the point, Jacob?" She faced off with him, squaring her stance opposite his. "Nothing's really going to change, is it? I thought I could accept that, I really want to. But I think that might do more damage than I'm willing to accept."

What? "I'm confused," he said.

"I mean, a weekend in Philly for sex and a fund-raiser. I doubt you want to show me off to your high-class friends, but I'm guessing you'd feel guilty about taking another date. While here at home, I'm still only good enough to be kept like a hidden mistress." She hugged her arms around her waist. "I thought I could live with that, but—no thanks, Jacob."

As he took in KC's obvious distress, Jacob winced.

"I'm sorry, KC," he said, swallowing past the lump in his throat. He closed in, wrapping his arms loosely around her. He needed to touch her, for her to feel him, but he still wanted to look into those hazel eyes as he told her the truth. Hopefully, she'd believe him.

"I'm really sorry for not realizing how much this was like, well…" He swallowed again when she raised her eyebrows. "How this was exactly like before. But that wasn't my intention. I'm trying to keep you and Carter safe."

"What?" she asked, tilting her head as if she hadn't heard him right.

"I forgot you weren't here when Christina was hurt."

Surprise stiffened her body. "Hurt? What happened?"

"There was a fire. Aiden's studio at the back of the property. The one that's now being rebuilt. Some guys set it on fire, not realizing she was inside. They were trying to strike out at Aiden, but she got caught in the cross fire. She could have been seriously injured if Aiden hadn't gotten there in time to get her out."

"Oh, my goodness. I didn't even realize."

Jacob could read the regret on her face. Christina had told him that the two of them had been estranged since KC's return. Which was also his fault, since KC had been afraid of telling Christina the truth and putting her in an uncomfortable situation.

"Aiden and I talked right after I found out about the baby. He mentioned that, since things were still unsettled at the mill and I'm a prominent figure over there, I might want to keep my connection to you quiet for now. That way you and Carter won't become a target if someone is upset with the way I'm handling things."

"So you think we'd be in danger?"

"I don't want to think so, but I also don't want to take that chance."

She paced away, leaving him feeling empty and cold.

KC had never been predictable, so he should have known she'd come back with something he wasn't prepared for. It wasn't long before she said, "So you talked about this with Aiden?"

"Yes."

"And when were you going to talk about it with me?"

Working with the public, and drunk people in particular, KC had become pretty good at reading between the lines. And the surprise on Jacob's face gave him away.

He wasn't going to discuss it with me. It hadn't even occurred to him.

At least, not until he was sure he wanted this relationship to be about the two of them, not just about Carter. Although, he hadn't lied about it. That much was good. KC's dad had been a chronic liar, hurting them all time and again before he left.

"Jake, you can't expect to make decisions that involve me or Carter without my input. Regardless of what happens between us as a couple, we're going to be working together as Carter's parents for many years. If we're in this together, as a couple or not, you have to be open with me. Leaving me in the dark doesn't build trust."

He moved close, rubbing his hands up and down her arms. "I didn't think about it that way. I didn't really think of it at all, to be honest. I'm sorry."

"And how can I be diligent and protect my son if I'm not aware of the danger?"

His slow blink of surprise told her that had never occurred to Jacob, either.

"As much as we've labeled this 24/7, you can't be with us all the time, Jake. I need to know what's going on." She couldn't stop herself from taking a step back, then another until his arms dropped to his sides. "I'm not a doll to be moved around at will. I spent a lot of years dependent on other people's bad decisions. I will not have that for my son…or for me."

"You deserve better than that, KC," he said. "I know that now."

When he turned away, she didn't know what to expect. From the way he rubbed the back of his neck, she knew he was thinking hard. She'd watched him do that so many times, her heart ached. She knew, deep down, Jacob was a good man. But was he the type of man she could depend on?

When he turned back, his expression was more open than she'd seen anytime outside of a bed. "I want you, KC," he said, his voice gaining strength as he went on, "I want to take this to the next level. But I also want to protect both you and Carter until this situation at the mill is resolved. People knowing that I'm living at your house doesn't make you safe. So for now, I'd like to keep it just like we've been doing, with only family and close friends who know just how involved we really are."

A sinking feeling hollowed out her chest, but she kept still. Her response would determine where they went from here. Could she make the right decision—for Carter *and* for herself?

"But only for now," he added. "Do you agree?"

Was it what she wanted? *No.* Could she argue with his desire to keep her and their son safe? *No.*

"Yes, Jacob," she said, smiling as she thought over the past thirty minutes. Most men would have simply taken her to bed and left the rest up in the air. At least with Jacob, she knew there was a plan even if she wasn't sure what it was yet. "I'll go to Philadelphia with you."

His relief was almost palpable. He rubbed his hands together, obviously wanting to reach for her. Instead, he motioned to the food. "Shall we finish eating?"

That little streak of mischief resurfaced, and she couldn't help giving it free rein. "Actually, I thought we would celebrate." After all, they'd just made a pretty big decision. Why hadn't he reached for her yet? Didn't he realize she wanted him?

"What do you mean?"

Bless his heart. This man desperately needed to let loose every so often. Luckily, KC knew the perfect way to tempt him.

"Jacob, we're in a secluded spot and alone. No baby. No audience. What do you think I mean?"

Just one look from Jacob turned KC to jelly. But she wasn't giving him the upper hand yet. As he stalked closer, she whipped her T-shirt over her head. Jake slid his tongue across his lips in anticipation.

He stopped just out of her reach, watching the show, his body tense and ready.

She unbuttoned her shorts, pushing them over the curve of her hips while she slid out of her shoes. Jake's gaze followed her every move. Next, she whisked away the tank she was wearing under her shirt. She watched as Jacob made a long, slow perusal of all her new curves.

The need that filled his eyes whenever he took her was the most naked emotion she'd ever seen in him, and she'd ached to see it again. There it was. Before, these had been the only moments she'd felt she was seeing the real Jacob. Since her return, she'd only seen him show unguarded emotion when he held Carter.

She'd missed this, missed him. Turning away, she shucked off her bra, releasing her breasts, which were much rounder since she'd given birth. She threw the garment over her shoulder and made for the stream nearby. On her way, she tossed her best come-hither look his way, marveling at how his gaze was glued to her backside.

Her first step into the cool water felt good in the early-summer heat. The chill traveled up her skin as she waded into the stream. Her arousal rose along with it. The liquid surrounding her soaked into the silk of her panties, which she knew would color them transparent. Her nipples peaked, and she covered them with her arms, protecting them from the cold and from Jacob's gaze.

When the water was finally waist high, she turned back toward the shore. She took in the dirt beach with its tangle of tree roots, then Jacob's bare feet in the clover, then his gaze as he devoured her from his higher vantage point. "Aren't you going to join me, big boy?" Her mouth watered at the thought of those clothes coming off.

He shook his head. "You are crazy."

"Maybe," she teased. Then she let her arms ease down until nothing was left to the imagination. "But I'm fun. Don't you remember how to walk on the wild side?"

She hoped so, because she was desperate for him to walk with her once more.

To her intense delight, he grabbed the hem of his T-shirt, easing it up and over his shoulders. When clothed, Jacob seemed to have an average build. But underneath all the fabric were beautifully sculpted muscles that made her heart pound and her core ache. He was all leashed power... until he loosened the reins.

From her vantage point, she got to see every sleek line, every flex of muscle. The ripple of his biceps as his hands gripped his waistband. The bulge of his pecs as he opened his fly, then pushed his pants and briefs down to the ground. The chill of the water and the magical surroundings receded as memories of his body flooded her brain. Powerful hips. Muscled legs. And the hardness jutting from the cradle of his hips, the part he used to drive her over the edge into insanity.

He stood unashamedly in the dappled sunlight, and she wanted to weep for the brief time she'd likely have him. She had no doubt that one day he would leave her, but she'd savor him while she could.

For now, he was all hers.

Ten

Jacob barely noticed the temperature of the water as he stalked toward the naked angel before him. Heck, he was surprised steam didn't rise from the surface, considering the fire burning beneath his skin.

Before, he'd only known sexy KC. Whenever he'd seen her, the dark temptations beneath her surface called to him on every level. So much so that the pull had remained even after she'd left.

Living with her, seeing her with their son, highlighted a whole other side only hinted at before—the angelic woman who went out of her way to love those around her, do whatever she could for them and help with any needs she saw. That was KC, too.

One part angel, one part danger…wrapped up in the body of both. It was a combination he couldn't walk away from again, but he'd worry about that another time. For now, he was eager to learn that body all over again. Leave the emotions for later.

As he got close, she ducked to the side, evading him as her laughter tickled the air around them. With a grin, he gave chase. He'd never had so much fun as with KC—not even with his brothers. It seemed right now, that was exactly what she wanted.

They played tag for a few minutes, forging against the water in a strategic game of Keep Away. Jacob had never enjoyed another view as much as the water parting around KC's waist, her naked breasts swaying with her movements. All too soon, watching wasn't enough. His hands burned for a touch.

With a heavy lunge, he grabbed her. Dragging her body up against his, he clamped down on his urge to emit a primitive howl. Heat instantly sparked between them. Jacob caught the laughing look in KC's hazel eyes. Her long lashes sparkled with water droplets.

His body automatically reacted to hers, even while his hands cataloged all the changes since the last time he'd held her like this. Her waist, slightly thicker. Barely there stretch marks beneath his thumbs from carrying Carter. A rounder curve to her hips that matched the rounder curve of her breasts.

"Like what you see, Jake?" she asked, her look turning mischievous.

Ah, the temptress was here, all right.

"Oh, I like what I see," he said, letting his gaze slowly inventory all the sweet flesh down to where she was pressed against him. "But does it taste as good as I remember?"

She squealed as he lifted her in his arms, carrying her to the shore with quick strides. His body wouldn't wait much longer. Her arms tightened on his shoulders as he climbed the bank, then strode across the carpet of clover. Now his angel sparkled all over as the filtered sunlight highlighted the water droplets decorating her body.

He spread her out on the blanket, then sat back on his heels for a longer look. His breath hissed through clenched teeth. *Gorgeous.* She released her hair from the clasp, and it spilled around her head in waves of blond. Her firm, shapely legs tempted him closer. Her perky little toes with nails painted pink made him smile.

She was the incredible mother he'd come to know. The sexy temptress he ached for. All his. Right now.

She lifted her arms toward him, and his eyes met hers. He saw the vulnerable streak of emotion there, as if she, too, could sense that they trembled on the brink of something new. She opened her arms, hiding nothing.

Jacob crowded over her, his legs firmly straddling one of hers. His erection was pressed against her thigh, causing him to suck in his breath. So sensitive, as if too much pressure would end their encounter too soon—a worry he hadn't had since high school. Unwilling to lose the moment, Jacob started in on her plump, succulent lips.

He took his time with the kiss, tracing the outline of her mouth before their tongues tangled. Then his hips surged forward, and he couldn't hold back his groan.

Her hands found his shoulders, pulling him down. Sucking him under as their bodies met and melded. He heard the catch in her breath, followed by a soft whimper, and his brain swirled with all the times he'd heard that same sound before.

He ached to jump ahead but forced himself to slowly reacquaint himself with all his favorite places. Only this time, his heart beat faster, her scent made him dizzier and his need pounded higher than ever before. Because this was KC.

And everything about her captivated him.

His heart should have stalled at the revelation, but his need wouldn't allow it. Instead, he slipped on a condom and eased his body into hers, savoring every inch. She'd been partly right: this was one of his favorite positions. Because he could take in every nuance of her expression while his body drove them both wild.

He pulled back slowly, then drove in hard. Her cries filled the sun-heated air around them—a sound Jacob knew he'd never forget. Over and over, he teased them both while his tongue traveled from nipple to nipple. He savored her taste, her sound, her passion. And finally her ecstasy as her body clamped down on his.

Letting himself lose control, he pounded into her until only one thought remained. This was more than simple lust, but could he break past the fear and admit what it truly was?

In the week since their picnic, KC had more than enjoyed reacquainting herself with Jacob. She'd treasured every second they were together. He was everything she remembered and more, as if the long months without each other had only heightened his appetite. They had definitely heightened hers.

But intimacy with a baby in the house was a lot different than when she was a single woman, so KC was pretty sure Jacob had planned on enjoying a free-for-all during their weekend in Philadelphia. Starting as soon as they crossed the threshold.

He had another think coming.

They were barely through the door of the hotel suite and he was already marching her across the tiled floor with his signature heated look. She wanted to give in, truly she did. But they needed to start off on the right foot, so she put up a figurative roadblock. "Where should we shop for my dress?"

Jacob's look was incredulous. "We have baby-free time and you want to shop?"

Men. Everything had to revolve around sex. "I didn't have time before we left town, and you promised…" She deliberately drew out the word, paired with a look of wide-eyed innocence.

He studied her, giving her the impression he could divine every thought. "You. Are. Serious."

You bet your booty, buster. The ache in her core betrayed her, but she refused to give in. "I told you, this trip wouldn't be like the last time."

"I don't see what the problem was, honestly." He leaned back against the wall with his arms crossed over that wide chest. *And here we go again with the Dom stance.* "I thought we had a wonderful time."

"We did have a wonderful time. At your apartment. Having sex. The only time we left the house was to get to and from the airport."

She could see the revelation steal over him, but still he tried to bluff his way out of it. "And that was a problem because...?"

"Depends." Standing her ground, she faced off with his seeming nonchalance. "Do you want me here just for sex? Or for something else?" She couldn't make him prove his commitment at home, not so long as she and Carter could be hurt by taking the relationship public. But here in Philadelphia, she could take a stand.

She wasn't backing down.

His disappointment was almost palpable, and she found an echo in her own body. Maybe she should tell him he'd definitely be getting lucky, just not this instant? She quickly tossed aside the idea. She wasn't sure whether she was just being mischievous, or whether she really wanted him to pay. Either way, it wouldn't hurt to let him suffer for a little while.

"The ball is tonight," she reminded him as they took the elevator to the lobby. "I don't have a dress. And you said we had plans for this afternoon, so..."

He hailed a cab, then held the door open for her. "Will it take all morning to find a dress?"

"There're only two hours left in this morning, but we'll have to see..."

His poor-puppy-dog expression was so very cute, but he'd live. Even if he didn't think so.

The cab dropped them off at a side street filled with

adorable little boutiques. KC wandered for a bit, peeking into window after window, unwilling to admit to Jacob that the high-priced surroundings made her feel inadequate. The only time she'd ever shopped for a formal had been for her junior and senior proms—she had found both dresses at consignment stores. Somehow she thought this would be a whole different experience.

Pausing before a window display of beautiful dresses, each decked out with a unique flare, KC knew she'd found the right place. She turned to Jacob. "I'm going to go in here and look around. I'll be out in a while."

He frowned. "I can't go in with you?"

Poor thing. Nothing about today was going according to his plan. "Nope. I want my dress to be a surprise."

"But I'm planning on paying for it." His satisfied expression said he'd hit on the perfect workaround. "That's kind of hard to do from out here."

"No need. I'll handle the bill myself—"

"No." If she didn't know Jacob very well, his scowl would have had her stepping back. "This trip was my idea. I want you to buy whatever you find that you love and not worry about the cost."

Her spirit rose up in protest, but he held up a hand. "No arguments, KC. Pick out what you want, have the saleslady ring it up, then come and get me. I'll take care of the rest."

Blinking, KC didn't know how to respond. Not only was he going to pay for her to have a dress, but he wasn't pushing his way inside when he could have. She swallowed hard. "Thank you, Jake."

He shot her a grin. "You're welcome. Besides, I'm building up brownie points."

I bet. She moved to the door, only to look back over her shoulder when he said, "Shoes and a bag, too. No arguments. Don't make me ask for an itemized statement as proof."

"Yes, sir," she said with as much cheek as she dared, then headed inside.

Contrary to her concerns about being treated as an inferior, the two women in the store were more than helpful, taking it upon themselves to find her the perfect dress for the ball. Both had heard about the event, so they knew exactly what she needed. After a couple of tries, KC found something that had her grinning like a buffoon at herself in the mirror. "Oh, yes, this is it."

"I agree," one of the salesladies said from behind her.

The black dress was anything but ordinary. A flesh-colored silky layer was overlaid with a transparent black lace appliquéd with black roses, showcasing glimpses of the flesh tones underneath. The bodice had a deceptive plunging neckline that cupped her abundant curves and provided support at the same time, the décolletage formed by the uneven edges of rose petals and vines entwined throughout the intricate layer of lace. The neckline was echoed in the low scoop in the back, and the hem fell to the fullest part of her calf. Here again the material's uneven edge gave the dress a uniquely strong, sexy look that KC found flatteringly feminine. Jake would love it as much as she.

Twenty minutes later, she had shoes, stockings and a small clutch to match, along with a filmy shawl to protect against the cooler evening air. The saleswoman added everything up and stowed the dress in a garment bag before Jacob was led into the store. Without a single question, he handed over a credit card, his cooperation earning matching smiles from his audience.

"You're gonna love it," the saleslady assured him.

Reaching around KC's waist and pulling her snug against his side, Jacob placed a light kiss on her neck, just below her ear where he knew she was sensitive and the touch would bring on chills. While she was still recovering, he said, "I'd love anything on her."

"Yeah," she joked, unsettled by this public display of affection. "He even loves my T-shirts covered in baby spit."

"Men love anything that highlights your, well, cleavage," the redhead said with a wink.

KC's heart melted when Jacob blushed. Yeah, she knew exactly how he felt about her boobs.

The brunette grinned at them before adding, "Nah, accepting you no matter what you look like is a sign of true love."

As they walked away, KC wondered with a touch of panic how right she was.

Eleven

Jacob's breath stuttered to a stop as KC breached the doorway from the bedroom. She hadn't been kidding when she'd said her dress would be well worth the anticipation.

Boy, had he anticipated.

The saleswoman's comments had kick-started his libido, making him wish for X-ray vision to see through the garment bag. Then, from the dress shop, they'd gone to a nearby lingerie store for the proper undergarments, which consisted of a smooth satin corset and matching panties. Was she trying to kill him? Then they had a late lunch; all throughout, KC's sexy persona was turned up high.

Just when he thought he couldn't take any more, he found himself pacing the suite and ignoring his work while she had her nails done in the hotel salon. It hadn't been how he'd pictured their first day in Philly, but now...now his body and mind slipped into overdrive as he soaked in her beauty.

If anything could capture his dual vision of KC as both angel and sex goddess, this dress was it: black flowery lace and flesh-colored fabric gave the illusion of lingerie, yet she was technically covered from chest to midcalf. Of course, knowing what she had on underneath tipped the scales in a dangerous direction. But the steamy look in her eyes—now turned a deep green—warned him that was part of her plan.

Her inner and outer beauty stole his breath. The intensity of his need sparked a touch of fear, but he quickly brushed it away.

He was tempted to persuade her to stay in—skip the reason they were here and give him a chance to peel her out of that dress and the lingerie he knew was hidden underneath. But one look at the tentative excitement on her face shut down his desires without a word.

I'm good enough for sex but not allowed into any other part of your life. Back in Black Hills, he couldn't openly acknowledge his relationship with her and Carter without endangering them. But here, he could take her out in public with pride.

He was ashamed that she had believed he viewed her only as a sex object. He would never demean her like that again.

"You are incredible," he said simply. "I couldn't be more proud than to have you on my arm tonight."

The faint uncertainty in her expression fled, and she glowed under his praise. But soon enough that saucy look returned. "I do believe you'll be rewarded for your kind words, sir…later."

Her husky promise sent him back into overheated territory. He hustled her out of the suite and away from the bed before he proved himself a liar.

Never had the dichotomy in KC's personality been more evident to Jacob than in the crowded ballroom, where they were surrounded by men and women Jacob had been doing business with for years. The lights sparkled off tiny jewels embedded in each flower on her dress, and she shone like the star she was as she conversed with an ease that shouldn't have surprised him. After all, he'd seen her calm the most ruffled of feathers at Lola's. Here she was an angel, but Jacob could read the latent sensuality in the graceful movement of her body and the continual meeting of their eyes. Hers held a promise. Which turned to surprise when his name was called from the stage.

"We are happy to honor all the board members for their hard work for a charity that goes above and beyond in caring for children and their families as they receive the medical treatment they need. Jacob Blackstone, our chairman, would you please make the presentation tonight?"

Jacob cursed in his mind. He should have remembered this part and prepared KC. He'd been more focused on having her here than on the presentation he'd made numerous times.

After announcing how much money the event had raised for the charity, and giving the usual plea for continued generosity, Jacob returned to KC's side. Only there was no time to explain as one person after another came up to talk.

Finally Jacob swept her to the dance floor, taking advantage of a few moments of privacy. Of course, he was fooling himself if he didn't admit he was eager to hold her close once more, even if he couldn't take what his body was begging for. Still, his fingers savored the bare skin of her back in the dim lighting.

KC, with her usual no-nonsense attitude, went straight to the point. "That was a surprise. I guess I should have done a Google search of you before we dated, found out how important you were everywhere, not just in Black Hills…"

"I'm sorry, KC. I should have made it clearer that I was the chairman when I asked you to come with me. I just wasn't thinking—"

"About more than getting into my pants?"

He choked back a laugh but couldn't help the big grin that split across his face. "Guilty."

It was a much more rewarding subject of conversation, in his opinion. "Have I told you how beautiful you are tonight?" *And every night?*

He savored her upturned face, that gorgeous hair swept to the top of her head, giving him a view of the vulnerable parts of her neck where he knew a simple kiss would have shivers running along her body. They moved in time to a classic slow dance, their bodies barely brushing against each other.

Good thing. Jacob didn't want to embarrass himself.

"This is incredible," KC said, her wide-eyed gaze taking in the crystal chandeliers suspended from the ceiling and the glittering decor that sparkled in the strategically dim light. "Way better than the Under the Sea theme from my senior prom."

They shared a grin.

"Yeah, the committee goes out of its way to create a very special night. We have a wonderful coordinator, and she makes it well worth the amount the donors give."

"You've made a big jump from executive with all the perks to running the mill. Are you really ready to leave all this behind?"

He looked around the room, seeing so many people he knew, so much from the life he'd built away from Blackstone Manor. "My family, brothers, Carter—" *You.* "Sometimes life is where you're needed. Besides, I won't be giving it up completely."

He felt her stiffen beneath his fingers. "What do you mean?" she asked, her voice calm despite her body's message.

"I've enjoyed working with this children's charity for a good many years. While I won't be located in the city, I will be visiting regularly and remain on the board to help keep it viable." He smiled down at her. "I think we'll have plenty of opportunities for glamour, because I'd sure hate to never see you in this dress again."

Her husky laugh tingled along his nerves. "You are such a man," she said.

He couldn't resist this time. His hips pressed briefly

against her before he returned to a polite distance. "Yes, ma'am, I certainly am."

She tightened her grip as if she would pull him back to her, but she, too, continued the proper dance moves. The decorum of their public display only emphasized to him exactly what was lurking beneath the surface. Fire and need that burned so much hotter for their restraint. He struggled to concentrate.

"I've thought of establishing some kind of foundation in Black Hills," he said, his shaky control letting his private thoughts free. "I simply haven't found a cause that's spoken to me quite yet."

"It should be one you feel passionate about," she said, licking her lips in such a way that he knew she was talking about something else, something far more private.

"I know," he said, struggling to rein in his control. Since he couldn't have her body, he let his mind wander and kept talking. "Here, a job is a job. In Black Hills, my job is about more—it's about keeping a community alive and protecting a way of life. Not as a monument to my grandfather but to something—" Jacob wasn't sure how to articulate the emotions swirling through him.

"What?" KC asked, her voice husky, her eyes searching for the truth.

He couldn't help giving it to her. "Something that means more than a dollar amount, something my son—" he swallowed hard "—and you can be proud of."

He felt her hands clutch against him once more, but she didn't speak for a moment. "Having a kid changes a lot about your perspective, doesn't it?"

"Uncomfortably so," Jacob admitted with a quiet laugh, grateful for a break in the emotional tension building between them. "But all these charity events have taught me one thing," he added, pulling her just a touch closer so his body took control of the dance in an elemental way.

"What's that?"

"I dance a heck of a lot better than I did in high school."
And he swirled her around the floor, expertly leading her
around other couples to end with a flourish as the music
crescendoed. He tipped her back, savoring the slide of her
hips against his as he pulled her gently up into his arms.
This time he didn't hold back. Despite the crowded room,
he let his lips find hers and do the rest of the talking.

"Let's leave," KC murmured against his lips. Her body
couldn't seem to break the contact. "I've waited long
enough."

Even in the dim light KC could see the *yes* that leaped
to Jacob's face, though he managed to maintain a strained
outer decorum. He immediately ushered her across the
crowded room toward the exit. Laughter bubbled up at his
quick pace, but she wasn't about to argue. The door was
just in sight when a man stepped into their path.

He stuck out his hand with a grin, completely unaware
of his unwelcome intrusion. "Jacob, wonderful event. I
hope there will be many more, despite you leaving us…"

To anyone else, Jacob's switch to consummate gentleman would have appeared seamless. Only KC noticed the
tightness of his stance and the tick of the muscle in his
cheek as he introduced Robert and his wife, Vanessa. The
Williamsons had been to many of these events with Jacob,
since Robert also served on the board of the charity.

As they chatted around her, KC almost felt bad about
knowingly pushing Jacob past his limits today in an attempt
to make her point. But she had a feeling the wait would be
worth it. She shivered, drawing Jacob's arm around her
bare shoulders as he spoke. Today had been a day outside
of her normal experience with men, or even with Jacob.
Funny, serious, sexy, emotional. If this kept up, she'd be
treading some dangerous waters.

The men chatted about some project they had worked on
together, giving KC a clue that this could take a few min-

utes. So she turned to Vanessa. "How are you tonight?" she asked politely.

Vanessa's smile was slightly off-kilter, just a little too wide to be completely natural. "Oh, just fine," she said with a heavy Southern drawl. "Where are you from?"

KC relaxed a little. "I'm from Black Hills, South Carolina."

"So Jacob finally got him a down-home girl. Guess that's what's keeping him entertained in the back of beyond."

KC raised her brows, a little taken aback, even though the woman's tone hadn't been ugly. She was even more surprised as Vanessa looped her arm through hers. "Let's have a little chat and a drink. I could most definitely use another."

Of coffee. KC had dealt with enough drinkers to know that Vanessa was a couple of drinks away from having to be carried home. Or embarrassing herself and her husband.

They settled at the bar, and Vanessa ordered a martini. "Sparkling water with lemon for me," KC said.

Vanessa didn't seem to notice. They chatted about the party for a moment—the gorgeous decorations, delicious desserts and cool little band—before Vanessa asked, "So what do you do?"

It seemed that KC didn't have the appearance of a woman of leisure. "I'm a bartender."

Vanessa looked at her with surprise, and then their bartender set their drinks in front of them. Without missing a beat, KC switched the glasses, setting the water firmly in front of Vanessa.

"Hey, that's mine," she said with a frown.

"You don't really need it, do you?"

Vanessa stiffened. "I'm not drunk."

As all tipsy people insisted... "I didn't say you were," KC said, adopting the reasonable tone she knew would work with someone of Vanessa's personality. "But do you really want to end the night puking on those fabulous Jimmy Choo shoes?"

Vanessa blinked at her for a moment, then her eyes watered. She quickly glanced down at her shoes. "You have a point."

Good. Vanessa seemed nice, straightforward and interested in her as a person, not just as Jacob's date. KC would hate to see her move into obnoxious territory. Besides, her people radar made her wonder if there was something else going on here.

Vanessa tipped her water glass at KC before taking a long drink. Then she gave a half smile. "Well, I'm betting you're a good bartender," she conceded. "Is that how you met Jacob? In the bar?"

"Nope. I met him on a plane. I'm not the best flyer."

"That's a shame," Vanessa said.

Confused, KC asked, "Why?"

"Because being in a bar would mean Jacob was having some fun. He needs to have a good time every once in a while. He's so serious, as if he has something to prove all the time."

"Yes. He does seem that way..." Except in bed. Then his only goal was how many times he could make her explode.

As if she was echoing KC's thoughts, Vanessa leaned closer and asked, "Is he that focused in bed? Bet he would view each woman as a challenge to be solved."

Um... "I hope that's the alcohol talking."

"Nope," Vanessa said with a saucy grin, the alcoholic haze starting to fade from her movements. "I'm just too curious for my own good—especially about hunks all hidden under the perfect business suit."

KC had dealt with a lot of unexpected conversations, but this one truly caught her off guard. At least Vanessa was still curious, which meant she didn't know for sure. Still, KC wasn't comfortable engaging in traditional girl talk with a stranger. Not that she was ready to talk about

Jake at all in that capacity—it was too new, too intimate, too complicated…

"Not gonna say? I don't blame you," Vanessa conceded. She shook her empty glass at the bartender for a refill. "I'm happy for him. Although having him move permanently because he's finally found something to take his mind off work will deplete the eye candy around Philadelphia."

KC just raised her brows. Vanessa had obviously said what she wanted; maybe that was just the alcohol. But at least she was up-front and friendly about it.

And she wasn't done. "You're lucky," Vanessa said with a frown into her now-full glass of lemon water. "My husband has hardly looked at me all night."

Ah, now this situation was making more sense. KC jumped in headfirst, since Vanessa seemed the type to appreciate straight talk. "Have you made him look at you instead of wasting your time drinking?"

Vanessa stilled for a moment.

"I know we just met, but you don't seem like a woman who takes no for an answer," KC said, spotting the men approaching over Vanessa's shoulder. "So don't give him the chance to ignore you. You deserve better."

"Everything okay, ladies?" Robert asked as he reached his wife's side. He studied her glass for a moment.

"We're good," Vanessa said, winking in KC's direction. "But I'm in serious need of a dance with my husband."

Robert nodded, but his attention had already been snagged by a passing suit. "Yes, dear, I just need to see—"

"No, Robert," Vanessa interrupted as she regained her feet. Not a wobble in sight, despite her four-inch heels. "You can talk *after*. This sexy getup shouldn't go to waste." She paused, giving her husband a chance to look for himself—and he did.

KC suppressed a grin. Sometimes changing a man's focus was way too easy.

Without further interruption, Vanessa led her husband

to the dance floor, Robert's focus definitely where it should be. Vanessa threw a wink KC's way as she slid confidently into his arms.

Jacob glanced between them suspiciously, then shook his head with a grin. "I don't want to know," he said.

He pressed a kiss to her neck, eliciting a shiver. Then he whispered, "Where were we?"

He had her out the door and hailing a cab before she could answer. Not that she complained. The anticipation of the day had set her senses on high alert. Now she would cap off this romantic night in the perfect way with the man she loved.

KC's stomach dropped as if she'd jump-started an elevator. She'd known she was infatuated with Jacob, but she thought she'd been able to wall off all those tender feelings, leaving only the attraction. Seeing so many different sides to him over the past month had only deepened her desire for something more, some permanent attachment to this strong, steady man.

She had no doubt he would never turn away from Carter, but his son was his blood. He'd turned his life upside down in recent months to help his family. But she wasn't family... She was expendable.

The one thing she'd always feared.

She had been determined to be the strong one, the one who could walk away. And she had, but she couldn't stay gone. Would she survive if he chose to leave her?

KC forced herself to shut down her thoughts as Jacob led her into the bedroom of their suite. The moonlight streaming through the gauzy curtains glinted off his blond hair as he peeled himself out of the black jacket of his tux. He unbuttoned his dress shirt, revealing his muscled chest a few inches at a time.

He pulled the ends of the shirt from his pants, leaving it to hang open as he stalked closer to her. Half sophisticate,

half primal male. KC's heart fluttered in feminine awareness. She backed slowly away.

Jake kept coming, his intense stare telling her everything he would enjoy doing to her. But first…

"I've been dreaming about what's underneath this dress
since this afternoon, KC," he said, his deep voice brushing
along her senses with the skill of a master musician. "Now
I will see it for myself."

She smiled up at him. "That was the plan."

Reaching to the side, Jacob eased her zipper down until
the unique creation slid to the floor, leaving her more vulnerable and exposed than she'd ever been. Not because the
corset left little to the imagination with its mesh panels,
but because the man before her wasn't looking for a good
time—he was intent on consuming her.

And she would let him.

His palms traced the boning from her hips up to her
waist, then around to her plump breasts beneath the satin
cups. The flesh swelled, threatening to overflow its bounds.
"KC," Jake said, sounding a little strangled. "White satin.
Couldn't be more appropriate for my angel."

She didn't know why he was comparing her to a heavenly being, but she'd savor the reverence in his voice, his
touch. He continued to explore, running his hands back
down to the garters attached to her stockings, then up the
back to the completely unprotected roundness of her backside. With a firm grip, he pulled her against him. The fric-
tion of his tuxedo pants and the stockings on her legs sent
her head spinning. Her hands dipped beneath his shirttails,
meeting warm flesh just above his belt. Part of her ached
for more; part of her reveled in the joyous miracle of having Jake in full flesh before her.

Only this close could she feel the slight tremble in his
muscles, feel the sheer sheen of sweat over his skin.

"KC," he said with a groan. "I wanted to wait, honey.
To make it last. But I can't."

"Then take me, Jake," she whispered against his skin. "Take all of me."

Two steps and he had her balanced on the edge of the dresser, knees spread wide to accommodate him. His touch was rough this time as he dragged the cups of the bustier down to give him full access to the treasure he sought.

Her heart raced into overdrive as his mouth teased her nipples. Then he gave a soft pull that strengthened the pulse that beat between her thighs. She needed him…needed him…

He didn't disappoint.

Seconds later he was pushing inside her, filling her in the best way imaginable. Physically, emotionally. Stretching her to accept him. Overwhelming her protests. Completing her in a way she'd never thought possible.

His mouth settled at her neck, sucking along her skin. His thumb pressed against that most precious of spots as she panted out her need. All the while, the hard strokes from his body drove her insane until all the sensations coalesced into a crescendo of heat that detonated in a single blinding second. Jake's hoarse cries in her ear pulled her back from heavenly nothingness to the precious gift of his own release.

They drifted back to reality together, aftershocks rocking them for long, long moments. Then he tried to pull away—and stumbled. Shocked, she clutched at him.

Beneath her fingers, a rumble started, then grew into laughter. Jake's laughter was that much more precious for being so rare. "What's so funny?" she asked.

"My pants are still around my ankles," he confessed.

She couldn't help it. She had to laugh, too. "Well, let's get you properly undressed before you fall and we have to spend the evening in the emergency room rather than the bedroom."

He was already stripping himself down. "Yes, ma'am. That sounds like a perfect plan to me."

Twelve

The ringing of the phone roused KC from the deepest sleep she'd ever had. At least, it felt that way. Maybe because she'd so rarely gotten a full night's sleep since Carter was born—

Carter!

KC was standing next to the bed before she even realized she'd moved. Her vision blurred for a moment before she blinked, her body swaying in confusion. Who was she kidding? It was always hard to wake up.

With deliberate focus, she found Jacob sitting on the bed with his back to her, phone to his ear. Had his movement woken her or the phone? Confusion once more clouded her mind for a moment until he stood and ended the call.

"Get dressed," Jacob said, clipped and to the point. "We need to go."

Carter?

Concentration was hard to come by, but KC forced herself to snap to it. By then, the passionate, compelling lover of last night had been replaced by a man in full action mode. Jacob was already dressed in cargo pants and a casual polo for traveling. He swept out the bedroom door with his phone, leaving her on her own.

With the urgency of a worried mother, she quickly followed him. "Is Carter all right?"

Jacob didn't answer. She moved around the couch to see his phone in his hands, his fingers speeding across the screen.

"Jacob, what's wrong?"

Still no answer. Anger swept through her this time. His focus was so intent that she got close without him even noticing. She reached out her hand and covered the phone so he couldn't see it.

He glanced up, frowning in her direction.

"Is Carter okay?" she asked, enunciating each word.

He blinked, and she could almost see the realization steal into his eyes. *Yes, dear, you left something out.* "I'm sorry, KC. Yes, Carter is perfectly fine."

"Then what's wrong?"

"Just something out at the mill," he said, but his normally straightforward gaze slid away. He stepped back, dropping the phone to his side. "But I really need to be on the next flight home."

What was going on? Why was Jacob avoiding the issue with her? Or was he so focused on what was happening back home that his mind had already traveled there, leaving her behind? She returned to the bedroom to dress and pack, but her thoughts lingered on the man who was already back furiously texting once more. After last night, she would have described them as being closer than ever.

So why had he pulled away?

As they left the hotel, her heart mourned the short duration of their time alone together. They were supposed to have been here for two more days, but whatever was going on at the mill was important enough to cut their visit short. The delicious ache between her thighs reminded her just what she was forfeiting. But it had to be bad for Jacob to need to be home so quickly, didn't it? Hopefully everyone was all right.

Not that Jacob was talking. She finally closed her eyes on the plane and attempted to make up for the lack of sleep the previous night. Jacob's restlessness beside her kept her from more than dozing, but at least she got some rest and felt better able to handle an afternoon alone with Carter. Obviously Jacob wouldn't be there to help.

"I'll take you to your mother's to get Carter, then I'll need to head out for a while," he said as they collected the car from long-term parking. "There are some things I need to check into with Aiden."

Not wanting to pry but hating the timidness of her question, she asked, "Is there anything I can do to help?"

A sharp shake of his head was the only answer. His silence frustrated her, but she refused to beg. So she backed off after that, spending the rest of the ride to town in silence. As long as her son was okay, she could handle anything else.

Or so she thought.

As they neared Lola's, the space between the bar's parking lot and her mother's small house was occupied with a couple of city police cars and a whole crowd of people. Fear pounded inside KC's chest as if she was having a heart attack. Instead of stopping, Jacob accelerated past the building.

"What? Wait!"

Confusion and panic had her twisting in her seat. Jacob parked on the side of the road a little way down. "I thought you said Carter was okay," KC gasped. Jacob barely had time to stop the car before she had her door open and was running for the house.

It wasn't until she started pushing through the crowd that she realized Jacob wasn't with her. She glanced back over her shoulder and saw him slowly approaching, but then she broke through to the other side of the crowd and her thoughts were only for her family.

As she mounted the first step to the porch, the door

opened and a few of the local deputies she recognized from the bar came out. Surprise jolted through her as her brother appeared between them. Faces grim, they all crossed the porch together and filed down the steps. Murmuring from the crowd behind her swelled, but she only had eyes for Zachary. One of the officers had his hands on Zachary's arm, which told her he wasn't just going for a joyride.

"Zachary?" she called, but somehow Jacob was there, holding her out of the way of the approaching party.

The deputy escorting her brother paused, giving her a better look. No handcuffs. "Zachary," she whispered, fear double-timing her pulse.

"It's okay, KC," her brother said, his face carefully unconcerned. "Everything will be fine."

But she didn't believe him. Especially when they escorted him to a cop car and into the backseat. Jacob remained silent the whole time. Behind her, the screen door banged. Turning, KC found her mother on the porch. "Mom?" KC's voice broke as she rushed up the steps, Jacob finally letting her go.

"They said something about some crops he dusted last week," her mother murmured, her eyes glued to the cop cars backing out of the driveway. "Said they're dying or something. They had lots of questions for him."

KC turned accusing eyes on Jacob. She could read his knowledge of the situation in his body language. He'd known. And hadn't told her.

As if he could read her body language, too, Jacob said, "KC, I'm sorry. I didn't know they'd be here. I thought they'd pick him up at his apartment."

"He was here helping me fix the sink," KC's mom said. "It was clogged. I guess his landlord told them where to find him."

"What's going to happen?" KC asked.

Jacob slowly shook his head, his eyes once more guarded. He glanced at the people behind him. The crowd was diminishing, but those remaining seemed very interested in KC and Jacob's presence. "Let's get you and Carter home. Quietly. You can rest while I look into it."

But he knew more than he was saying. More than he would share. Which proved to KC that there was something important going on—but he wasn't going to include her.

"Don't bother," she said, taking a step back up toward the porch. "Mom will get me home."

Even though she wanted to believe he had a reason for his actions, nothing hurt worse than his turning and walking away—without a word.

"Your sister is going to come after me with a cast-iron skillet if I don't come home with the right answers soon," Jacob said to the man sitting across from him in the local police station's tiny interrogation room.

Not to mention that I'll be back to sleeping on the couch tonight.

Zachary smirked as if he could read Jacob's mind. "Well, you're the one who played mute. Why didn't you just tell her what was going on? Trust me, KC can take it."

Obviously a lot better than Jacob. He hadn't known what to say or how to say it, so he'd said nothing. He'd let his business mode take over, oblivious to KC's need to know.

Plus, the crowd had made him nervous. Who knew if the saboteur was watching, enjoying the drama, waiting for Zachary to be charged with a crime he didn't commit? At least intentionally. Or had he?

This situation was majorly screwed up. So Jacob had remained silent. Something he just knew KC would make him pay for, with relish.

"Just tell me again what happened," he said, hoping to block that out for a few more minutes.

Luckily the local police knew Jacob, had been working with him and Aiden and management to try to catch whoever was sabotaging things at the mill. He also saw the sheriff a couple of times a month at the local country club, so they'd let him in to see Zachary, who wasn't technically under arrest…yet.

"After my army gig, I missed flying, so I bought a little Cessna to do some crop-dusting work during the growing and harvest seasons. People like me because I do good work and am reasonably priced, so almost ninety percent of the farmers around here use me."

Zachary rubbed his hand over his shaggy black hair. "A few days ago I took the plane out to dust pesticides over a lot of the cotton crops in the area. Did the rest of my customers the next day. Well, apparently those crops have started dying. All of them."

Jacob sucked in a breath and held it for a moment, then let it out in a rush. "How bad?"

Zachary's green-brown eyes, so like his sister's, met Jacob's. "If all of them die…? We're talking total devastation for this community. I think all of those farms sell to the mill, so you'll have practically no raw material come harvesttime." Zachary's fists clenched. "Not to mention the number of families who no longer have cash for their crops this year. How could somebody do this?"

"So you didn't do it?"

Once more Zachary's gaze met his. "Oh, I did it. I flew the plane. But I have no idea how I could have dumped something that would kill the plants. When I loaded, those tanks were marked for common pesticides."

"Tell me what happened from the moment you arrived at the airfield."

He knew Zachary had to be tired of repeating the story, but Jacob had to be sure the man was telling the truth. For himself and the company. But most of all for KC.

But Zachary didn't falter as he related step by step how he checked in, confirmed and loaded the tanks and prepared for takeoff. Behind him, the deputy nodded. Seemed as if Zachary was telling the truth.

"Why would someone want to do this?" Zachary demanded. "And why through me? I hate that."

Jacob sympathized with Zachary's anger. And admired his calm. After all, he was sitting in a police station. The deputy had said, depending on what happened, he could be facing destruction-of-property charges for every family that had been harmed. That was a lot of charges.

Hopefully, Jacob could prevent that.

"What do you think was used?"

Zachary shrugged, his palms opening in a "how should I know" gesture. "Honestly, I haven't seen any of the plants, so I'm not sure. The chemical tests will tell them what they need to know."

The door opened and the local police chief walked in with Aiden. The police chief spoke first, confirming that they'd been listening through the speakers. "We've sent samples off, but it will take a while for them to come back."

"I loaded the right tanks," Zachary insisted. "I doublechecked myself."

Aiden jumped in, his narrowed gaze not leaving Zachary for a second. "Look, I don't know anything about farming. That's not a secret. But something wiped out those plants, and a lot of livelihoods with it."

"One of the deputies on the scene confirmed that the tanks are marked and were checked into inventory as pesticides," the police chief said. "Not that it would stop someone from putting something else inside them."

Jacob found himself defending Zachary, even though Aiden was clearly suspicious. "Why would he kill plants and his own income with them?" he asked.

Zachary snorted. "Damn straight. Shut down the mill, the farmers and my own earnings in the process."

Aiden nodded. "Makes sense."

Jacob could see his brother mulling it over as he started to pace. It did make sense as a defense. But would it be enough?

"Although," Aiden continued, flashing a concerned look in Jacob's direction, "if you were paid to do this, it would be a lot more than the income you normally make."

Zachary dropped his head into his hands.

The chief answered his phone, spoke quietly for a few moments, then ended the call. "After examining a sample of the crops, the consensus seems to be they were sprayed with defoliant."

Silence reigned for a moment. Zachary's head dropped into his hands. "At this early stage, that means death for all those plants."

The deputy nodded. "Most likely."

"Jeez."

Jacob shared a look with Aiden. Not good. But then Aiden surprised him. "How accessible are the tanks to somebody besides yourself?"

"I guess someone could get to them," Zachary said with a frown, "even though they're locked up. And of course, some of the airport security personnel have the key."

"It's a small facility," the policeman said, "and a lot of locals hang out there. Especially the older men. So a good bunch of people come and go without much notice. Someone dropping by wouldn't stand out too much."

Zachary's eyes met Jacob's, letting him know their thoughts matched. Their saboteur had expanded his reach.

"How long does he need to stay here?" Jacob asked.

"A few hours," the chief said. "Then he can go. For now."

Zachary groaned.

The chief shot him a sympathetic look. "Sorry, son, but I can't make any guarantees until I get to the bottom of this. Which we will. I promise."

Zachary looked more defeated than he had since Jacob had arrived. Not that he could blame him. After all, he had sprayed the plants. But did that mean he was responsible for the destruction if he'd sprayed the defoliant unknowingly?

"Look at it this way," Jacob said in a lighter tone.

"Wouldn't you rather be here than having to explain this to your sister? Like I'm going to have to do?"

Because Jacob had no doubt his girl would be ready for a come-to-Jesus meeting when he got home. He'd better have some answers, or his head would be on a skewer.

Thirteen

Jacob opened the door quietly, anxious not to wake Carter. It was long past the time he should have been home. Worried about Zachary and how what had happened would affect the town, he'd hung around until Zachary was released. Then he, Zachary and Aiden had spent some time going over all the information they had. Jacob had texted KC when Zachary had left jail, but hadn't talked to her since then.

One look at KC's face and he realized it was a whole lot worse than he'd anticipated. She gently jiggled and rocked the restless baby in her arms, but her red-rimmed eyes and flushed cheeks attested to how upset she was. And to Jacob's guilt. He still found her disheveled look cute, but he knew better than to say so.

Carter seemed to sense his mother's unhappiness. There was no full-blown crying this time, just a restless stirring of arms and legs to keep himself awake. Without a word, Jacob lifted Carter from her arms and tucked him into his own special hold. His son looked up at him long and hard, then blinked slowly. Once. Then again. And started his slow slide into sleep as Jacob swayed him back and forth.

As those incredible eyes closed for a final time, Jacob

smiled. "He seems to have grown in just the small amount of time we've been gone."

KC nodded, though she kept her face averted after his one quick glimpse. "Yeah, incredible, huh?"

He winced at her scratchy voice, feeling himself falling into unknown depths. The KC he knew was strong, independent, sexy. He'd never seen her cry. That was something he truly didn't know how to handle. To escape, he carried Carter down the hall to his room and settled him into bed. Staring into the crib, he took several deep breaths before going back down the hallway.

Jacob couldn't leave her hurting. The woman he cared for deserved better than that. So he found her at the sink, washing bottles. He suspected it was simply an excuse to hide her face from him, but he would allow her that modicum of privacy. It was the least he could do after telling her nothing, rushing her home and then leaving her with Carter by herself all night.

"I waited until they released him, just in case. Then he, Aiden and I went over everything together. I didn't mean to be so long."

"Do you suspect him?"

"Zachary? Once I heard all the facts? No."

She turned to face him, her stare demanding in its own right. "Tell me the truth, Jacob."

"KC, Zach is not the saboteur." He held her gaze, intent on conveying his belief. "I know because I've asked him to help me catch whoever is doing all this."

Her face completely blanked for a moment. "What?"

"Your brother works maintenance at the mill. He's all over the floor, sometimes at odd hours, and no one thinks anything of him being there. He's been keeping his eyes and ears open for me. That may be why he was targeted this way."

With deliberate intent, he stepped closer. "That's why I didn't say anything while the police were picking him up at your mother's. I wasn't sure who might be watching, listening in that crowd, and I certainly didn't want your mother to think I'd put Zach in this position."

"I—"

He'd never seen her this much at a loss for words.

"Jacob, I don't even know what to say."

"Zachary will be fine."

"This isn't about Zachary." Her voice gained volume until Jacob worried about waking Carter. "I can't believe you don't see that. This has nothing to do with my brother, and everything to do with you not keeping me in the loop."

Jacob stared for a moment. She was right—he hadn't seen that as the real problem, more as a sideline. Jacob proceeded with caution. "I didn't think you cared about the day-to-day stuff at the mill."

"This isn't a daily occurrence, is it? You said you were worried about my and Carter's safety, but you don't even let me know you've put my brother in a position that could get him hurt, or even just fired?"

Well, no. That was definitely not the right answer. "I thought I was approaching the situation logically. I needed help—"

"A spy."

"—and your brother agreed to help me. It's business, not personal."

"When it involves my family, I consider everything personal."

Huh. Jacob wasn't even sure how to respond to that. He knew KC approached things emotionally, but he hadn't thought this would ever come up. He had never imagined the saboteur would use Zachary to hurt the mill.

She didn't comment on his silence. "Why is it okay to keep us in the dark and let us think he's going to jail for something we know he would never do? My mother has been calling me, worried sick. I've been worried. When you don't let me know what's going on, what am I supposed to think?"

"I told you I'd take care of him. Zach won't go to jail. I promise. We've got a plan."

She turned that heartbreaking gaze on him full force. "But I'm not part of it, am I?"

No. It had never occurred to him that she'd want to be, even though he knew how much she loved her family. He felt like such an idiot.

"I don't expect you to hire me so I can watch my brother at work. Or text me a minute-by-minute update. But I'm not some old-fashioned maiden who sits home by the fire while you do all the work. I thought you knew me better than that. It has to be more than just a text here and there. If we're—if we are going to be partners, I need you to include me, accept me as part of the plan. Keep me informed ahead of time, not after the fact. That's what partners do."

Jacob wasn't sure if he could promise that. He cared about her. He knew that. But he'd been doing this on his own for so long. He didn't know if he could open himself up to the idea of partners, especially one that operated so differently from him.

He wanted KC to trust him. Even now, he could see the fear cloud her eyes. But working on his own terms was what he knew. Could he change that?

"I need you to decide, Jacob. Are we working together, or are you strictly solo?"

His only answer was to pull her close and hold on tight. He couldn't bring himself to lie, so he kept his fears locked inside. The only truth he knew was that the man he was now would die if she left him all alone.

Zachary let out a low whistle as Jacob led him into the breezeway at the heart of Blackstone Manor. "Wow. And I thought this place was impressive from the outside."

Jacob let him look his fill around the central corridor

and the staircase, which gave visitors an unobstructed view of the elaborate railings on the landings of the two upper floors.

"At least now it's seeing some true happiness," a feminine voice said.

Jacob smiled up at his sister-in-law, Christina, as she descended from the second floor. Her lilac scrubs contrasted with the dark waves of hair falling to her shoulders. "How's Mother?" he asked.

Christina gave a sad little smile. "The same. Today's a pretty good day for her." She turned to the other visitor. "Hey, Zachary. How are you?"

"Good for now," he returned with a grin. "The police confirmed that there's no proof I added the defoliant to the tank, which was marked pesticide. But the two working security cameras were turned off that night, so I'm still the primary suspect, mostly because I'm the *only* suspect. But my guess is, they're also waiting to see if any money turns up."

Jacob watched as the two chatted. He'd known Christina and KC were friends but didn't realize Christina knew Zach. It shouldn't surprise him, though. Christina had a knack for connecting with people that Jacob had always envied.

"How is KC?" Christina asked. "I haven't seen her in several days."

"She's been subdued when I've seen her at Lola's," Zachary said. "Hovering over me like I might disappear at any moment, though they've been keeping me mostly in the back to discourage any retaliation. She's worried about the farmers."

So was Jacob, but he hadn't figured out what to do yet. "She's quiet at home, too."

Another situation Jacob didn't know how to fix. Jacob knew he hadn't convinced her of his loyalty, or his desire to be equal partners. Taking the steps to truly include her in every part of his life had his control-freak side, well, freaking out. So they danced around each other, keeping every conversation light, not delving too deep into things that might be tricky to navigate. Then at night, after Carter was asleep, their bodies talked intimately in a whole different language.

"Oh, Jacob's got that 'worried about my woman' look," Christina said with a grin. "I think he's doomed. What do you think, Zachary?"

"I'm pretty sure you're right." Zachary gave him a speculative once-over, but in the end nodded his approval. "She could do worse."

Jacob did not want to get into this. He looked expectantly at Christina. "Aiden?"

Her smirk told him she knew his avoidance tactics well, but she let him slide. "He's in the study."

Jacob led the way around the staircase and halfway down the breezeway until he came to his grandfather's former study. Zachary's expression said *wow* as he took in the floor-to-ceiling scrollwork bookcases and masculine furnishings.

Aiden greeted them with a distracted nod. "He's gone off campus again."

Jacob shook his head at Zachary. "For some reason, he thinks we can read his mind. Do you mean the saboteur, Aiden?"

His brother frowned. "You know I do, Jacob."

"The fact that he's hitting places away from the plant worries me," Jacob said. "It makes him—or them—dangerous."

"And unpredictable," Zachary added.

"Messing with things around the mill itself is annoying and a concern. But no one has been hurt on mill property. But showing that he's willing to expand his targets outside the mill itself? This convinces me that whoever was behind this incident was behind the group who set fire to my studio," Aiden said, his steely gaze meeting Jacob's.

His heart skipped a beat. That meant KC could still become a target...or an innocent bystander who got in the way. "I'm doing what I can to keep them safe."

Always observant, Zachary didn't miss the subtext. "Is this why you're still keeping your attachment to my sister on the down low?"

KC's brother deserved the truth, and giving him the information would mean that there'd be one more person to watch over Jacob's new family. "It's not the only reason, but yes, I don't want KC and Carter to become targets, so we're being careful to keep things casual in public."

The look Zachary threw his way made Jacob think he wanted to know the other reasons, but Jacob didn't want to talk about the deal he'd forced Zachary's sister into playing out.

"Zachary," Aiden said, averting his attention from Jacob, "what are you hearing at the plant?"

"Well, there's lots to hear," he said with a slow shake of his head. "Rumblings all over the floor. Low level up to management. And I mean a lot. Mostly upset over whoever did this, but—"

He paused, his face taking on an uncomfortable look.

"What is it?" Jacob asked.

"There're also people talking down on management for not putting a stop to the sabotage by now. People worried they'll be the next target. Or simply get in the way and get hurt." He steeled his hands against his hips. "A lot of people know those farmers, their relatives, friends. I can see the situation escalating. Soon. But I'll never know about anything before it happens."

"Why?" Jacob asked.

"I'm persona non grata right now. By association, you know."

"How hard is this hitting the farmers?" Aiden asked.

"Some of them have day jobs, so that helps, but without a crop to harvest, that guaranteed income won't be there. They'll lose their investment. Some years, their income might fluctuate if the season is too wet or too dry, but this is a complete wipeout. Bad is an understatement."

Jacob was ready for action. "What do they need? Money? Food? What would be best?"

"It's probably different for different people," Aiden said. "Let's think on it. Zachary, you get back to us if you find out more."

"I already know one thing you're gonna need."

"What's that?" Aiden asked.

"Cotton." Zachary paused a moment, as if letting that soak in. "We've got to find a cotton dealer—soon. KC might can help you with that. She's got a good friend who's a cotton dealer. Works with some of the farmers around here, too."

Involve KC? Jacob's first instinct was to keep her out of this. There were people at the plant who could handle it. But Jacob felt a personal responsibility for the farmers and the people at the mill, and wanted to fix things himself. And this just might be his chance to prove to KC that he was willing to include her in this decision. That they were in this together.

Fourteen

Jacob watched KC finish washing up behind the bar. Normally, when it was past closing time, he would have already left, taken Carter home and put him to bed so she didn't have to do that after a long shift on her feet. But her mother had asked if Carter could spend the night. Jacob's standing with her was still precarious; she'd given him a stern look before nodding in her daughter's direction, as if to say *fix this*.

KC had been unnaturally subdued since the police had interviewed Zachary. He wasn't used to this. Normally, her every movement, no matter how quiet, was filled with life. Now she seemed to spend her days on Pause, as if her spirit were holding its breath, waiting to see what was going to happen next.

An even bigger problem: Jacob wasn't sure if she was worried about Zachary…or the two of them.

Tonight, he needed a chance to reconnect with her. Not just sexually. KC was open to his touch, but even there he could feel her holding herself away from him. Not losing herself quite as fully as she normally did in their passion. Which hurt. Ms. Gatlin's offer to take Carter for the night provided the perfect opportunity to fix things.

KC's mother left with Carter, who was already falling asleep in her arms. Still, KC kept scrubbing.

Jacob moved to a spot directly across the bar from her, but she didn't look up. Finally he reached out and stilled her hand with his own. "KC, I need your help."

Now he had her attention. *Such a mama bear.* "What's wrong?"

"The farmers and their families are going to need support to get back on their feet. I'm trying to figure out the best way to do that."

"Another fund-raiser?"

Jacob shook his head. "No, I was thinking something more personal. First, I need a cotton dealer, or a lot of people are gonna be out of a job come September. Zachary said you could help."

She paused in her scrubbing, those turbulent eyes suddenly lighting up. "Easy peasy."

Was she being glib? "Really?"

"Yep. I know exactly who to contact." She grinned, her first genuine smile in days. "A guy I met when he first started working with the farmers out here about five years ago. He doesn't buy in Black Hills every year, but he keeps track of sales around here." She dropped her rag into the dishwater, giving Jacob her full attention. "What else?"

"A lot of people lost their immediate livelihood. They're going to have some tangible needs. Remember me telling you that I wanted to invest in a charity that spoke to me?"

KC nodded, her eyes sparking green deep inside the brown.

"This is it, but I want to start off right. I have some ideas, but I'm used to how charities work in a big city." Which was totally true. More than that, he wanted her involved. Soliciting her ideas was the best way to get her on board. "I don't want some anonymous charity run by a big impersonal board. This would be a hands-on project. But I don't have time to run it. Any ideas?"

She propped her elbows on the bar. Resting her chin in her hands gave him a distracting view of her cleavage, but he maintained his focus. Barely. KC appeared oblivious as she said, "Better to be effective than to just do something for the sake of doing it."

Exactly. "I want a hardship fund to provide a variety of things to families and workers in need. But the community as a whole still views me as an outsider, I think. I'm not familiar with the people here nearly enough. And they probably wouldn't feel comfortable with me, either."

He smiled as he continued, "We need someone to administer the fund who is familiar with the townspeople on a grassroots level. That's why I wanted to ask if you would be willing to help me. You know these people. You know this place. Will you do this for them?"

Shock widened her eyes. Her mouth shaped the word *me*, but no sound escaped. A few heartbeats later, she cleared her throat. "Jacob, I don't know anything about coordinating a big charity. I mean, I do know a lot of people—"

"And you know about handling them, evaluating what they need with dignity and respect. Sounds perfect to me. I can manage the boring parts of it—the money and paperwork and all."

She stood quietly for a moment. "What about the saboteur? Do we need to worry about him retaliating against me?"

"For helping the community? I doubt it. He seems more concerned with things that directly affect the mill. The goal has been accomplished—kill the cotton. Helping the people left behind shouldn't endanger you. Now, Aiden and I bringing in cotton could be a trigger."

She squirmed, the light in her eyes dimming a little.

"Don't worry. As long as we're careful to keep our public interactions nonromantic, you and Carter should be fine."

"Maybe." She studied him for a long moment. "You

know people will eventually find out you're living at my house?"

"As I said, we're being careful."

"Yes, and they've stopped questioning your presence here. And the neighbors don't notice your car parked in the back shed. And we're careful not to go anywhere out together. But how long will you be happy with that?"

Her tone told him she wasn't happy, but she was probably too afraid for Carter to push the issue. He wasn't sure how he felt about going public, but he couldn't force himself to leave her—them. One day he might have to, to protect them both. But for now, staying was his only desire. He gave her a short nod, keeping his thoughts to himself. "We'll deal with that when we get there. For now, what about the charity?"

"Um, okay. I mean, yes," she said, then laughed as he nodded his approval.

Now they were on track—and seeing her so excited had an incredibly stimulating effect on his libido. "Any ideas for what we could do?"

"Maybe we could raise money for care packages, get donated gift cards for clothes and groceries, or even money to help pay essential bills."

"Baby, you've got some great ideas in that head of yours."

Resorting to her sexy persona, Miss Mischievous winked at him. "Sure you don't want a fund-raiser? I could open a kissing booth."

Unable to stop himself, he grasped her hand. "I don't think so, woman," he said, the deeply possessive note betraying him, but he didn't care. "The only man kissing you will be me."

"Ooh, territorial." The heat filling her eyes belied her light tone.

He rubbed his thumb back and forth over the delicate bones in her hand. "You like?"

"Definitely." Her eyes, green in the dim light, were tentative and fearful as they met his. How could he resist her? As he marched around the bar, her breathing sped up, light and fast.

Jacob used his height to trap her between him and the bar. Need rose like a tsunami, threatening to overwhelm him. "What about this?"

The dilation of her pupils gave him his answer, but he waited for her words. Her permission. "Oh, yeah."

Then he crowded in close, grateful the doors were closed and locked, the lights low or off. Her body felt incredible—muscled legs against his, soft belly cradling his need, full breasts against his ribs. So delectable. So *his*.

He brooked no argument as he pulled her Lola's T-shirt from her jeans and over her head. The low lights glittered off the shimmery satin of the pale pink bra that did a fine job of displaying her womanhood. Unwilling to wait, he lifted her to sit on the counter.

Her squeal of surprise echoed around the empty room, bringing a smile to his lips. *That's right.* He had a few tricks up his sleeve, too. Then he lost himself in the plump upper curve of her silky flesh, kissing his way across the hills and nuzzling into the valley between. He lifted her breasts upward for the return journey, squeezing a little as he dipped his tongue beneath the edge of her bra for a lingering taste of her oh-so-sensitive nipples.

She squirmed and a little whimper escaped her. *Yes, that's what you like.* The way her body went wild under his mouth confirmed it. Her hands clutched at his shoulders, seemingly desperate to drag his clothes off, too, but he wasn't giving in that easy. Instead, he released the clasp that held her bra in place. His hands eased it down her arms to encircle her wrists, then inexorably guided her back until her spine met cold, polished wood. She hissed as she arched up, then moaned once more.

But she wasn't getting away. Control was his. Making her feel him was his only goal.

He palmed his way down her ribs to her waist, then applied his nails to the denim along the inside of her thighs. Her hips lifted, telling him she was willing and ready. Anchoring her hips with his hands, he kissed and nipped lightly, making his way down her body, closer and closer to her core.

"Jake, please," she pleaded, the sound shooting straight to his groin.

"Please what?"

When she didn't answer, he opted for more torture. Reaching under her, he squeezed the ass that had tempted him all evening as she worked the bar, then kissed the bare skin right above the waistband of her jeans.

"Please, Jake," she repeated, her hips lifting for more.

Please what, baby? Jacob waited her out, needing her desperate, aching for him and only him. Sliding his hands up and around, he grasped her waistband and pulled downward as if to remove her jeans.

"Yes," she cried.

"When I say," he growled against her skin, deliberately letting go. She was so beautiful, spread out before him, wanting him. Just as he wanted her.

Her breath panted out, ragged and choppy. Turning the tables, KC dug her fingers into his hair before pulling lightly, eliciting a groan from him. He glanced up and caught the smile stretching her lips. If he'd paid attention to history, he'd have known she wouldn't remain passive for long.

With hands grasping her hips, he pulled her toward him, almost completely shifting her rear off the bar. Her hands slapped against the edge, the sound sharp in the air, as she struggled to keep her balance. He lifted her legs higher, resting them on his shoulders so he could savor the feast before him.

She squeezed, searching for a tighter grip on his shoulders. Her hips lifted higher. Jacob licked his lips, anxious for more, but forced himself to hold back. With sure fingers he unsnapped her jeans. He lingered on the small amount of newly exposed skin for a moment before moving on. This time to the zipper, bringing it down, oh, so slowly.

She moaned her frustration, but he grinned. She was so much fun to play with. His body and mind stilled in surprise for a moment. But yes, he and KC were playing. Not a plan in sight, and it was glorious.

Anxious himself now, he peeled the fabric from her, using her position to keep her helpless and himself in control. Finally, shoes and jeans and panties hit the floor. This time he retraced his journey to her center with sucking kisses and searching tongue.

Before long he couldn't wait himself. He knew to be prepared every second with KC, so he dug the condom out of his pocket and readied himself ASAP. He didn't care that he was almost completely dressed. He needed her now before his body exploded without her.

Together. *Always*.

Jacob couldn't linger on the thought. If he did, he might panic. Lifting her again, he turned and pressed her back against the wall. His weight held her steady while he joined them, her greedy flesh and gasping breaths driving him higher than high. He guided her legs around him and supported her with a hand under each thigh. He started slow, aching to savor, but his body wasn't about to cooperate.

"Jake," she gasped. "Take me, please."

There was his girl. His hips moved with steady purpose, until her breath caught in that familiar way. He leaned down, his head resting against the side of hers. They were so close he could almost hear her heart pound. Only then did he let the emotions take him.

So he shouldn't have been surprised to hear himself whisper the words "I love you" as the world narrowed to the two of them and the ecstasy they found together. KC didn't give any indication that she'd heard him over her gasping cries, but he'd heard. Now he had to decide what to do about it.

When KC said she knew whom to call, she wasn't kidding. Two days after her conversation with Jacob, the cotton agent she had in mind walked into Lola's for a friendly little drink. She'd convinced Jacob to meet him here in a casual atmosphere, rather than having the formal business meeting he'd suggested.

She knew she was right. *Jacob* just didn't know it yet.

"Hey, Toby," she said, grinning at the agent as he slid onto a stool. "How's it going?"

"Always better when I can see your pretty face."

KC laughed at Jacob's glare; he'd approached in time to hear Toby's compliment. Jacob smoothed out his expression as he settled himself onto the stool next to Toby.

"Aw, you're too sweet." She winked, and then motioned to Jacob. "Toby, this is a friend of mine, Jacob Blackstone."

Toby turned an impressed face toward Jacob. "One of the infamous Blackstones? Cool to meet ya, man. I may not have grown up in Black Hills, but everyone in this part of South Carolina has heard of your family."

She could read the minuscule release of tension in Jacob's shoulders as he shook hands with Toby. *Told ya he was cool.* But she just grinned and leaned against the bar.

"I appreciate you dropping by, Toby."

Jacob's gaze dipped down to her chest, reminding her of his attentions on this very bar just a few nights ago. KC quickly straightened up again with a blush.

"Am I gonna get a cherry cola for my trouble?" Toby asked.

"Of course. Want some nachos with that?"

She busied herself making the drink while the guys yakked and got to know each other. Jacob asked about

Toby's hometown, his family, letting him do the talking…
and giving KC a chance to watch.

She often watched Jacob surreptitiously while she was
working, but today she ached to just soak in his blond good
looks. His thick hair feathered back in perfectly clipped
waves. Which only made her want to muss them up. She
could watch his mouth all day, that tempting curve that gave
away all the emotions he tried to keep hidden. Like now. He
might be smiling, but she could see the touch of firmness in
his lower lip. He was worried about something—probably
how this deal would work out. But he'd never let her know.

It was one of so many things he kept from her, though
she knew he was trying to change that.

Being a bartender had honed her timing. She returned
during the perfect lull in their conversation, setting the soft
drink in front of Toby, who got one every time he came.
"You may have heard about the trouble around here," she
said to him.

"Oh, yeah. There're some pretty crazy rumors floating around."

Toby wasn't the type to go for a bunch of half-truths
or white lies. So she gave Jacob credit for not pulling any
punches. "Well, some of them are probably true," he said.

"You lost most of your cotton crop?" Toby asked, eyeing him over the rim of his glass.

KC stepped in, wanting to add a human element to the
issues. Luckily, Toby was familiar with her family. He came
here to eat or hang out just about every time he was in town.
"It's really bad, Toby. Zach was the one who sprayed what
he thought was pesticide, so he feels really responsible. You
know how he is about that kind of stuff." Her brother's history of military service had desensitized him in many ways,
but he'd become a quiet crusader for people in need, as his
offer to help Jacob find the saboteur had shown.

"Wow," Toby said, glancing back and forth between
them. "How'd that happen?"

KC didn't think Jacob was ready to be that forthcoming yet. Sure enough, he gave a generic "We still don't know. The important question is, how do we fix it?"

Toby was already shaking his head. "I've promised most of my crop out already. We're halfway to harvesttime. I've got orders to fill."

KC noted Jacob's restless shifting on the bar stool but ignored it. Instead, she turned on the charm with a look of feminine pleading. "Come on, Toby. We're talking about the livelihood of an entire town here. Couldn't you try to hunt us down *something* to help?" Hell, she'd even lean against the bar again if she had to.

"How much we talking about?" Toby said with an exaggerated sigh.

Sucker!

At that point, the conversation dissolved into a bunch of logistics that had KC's eyes glazing over. She was a people person, not a numbers person. And in the end, Toby was frowning.

"Please, Toby," she begged. Man, did she need to bat some eyelashes? "Isn't there anything you can do?"

His good ol' boy smile made an appearance. "Let me make some calls. You know I love ya, doll, but this is a tall order."

"We realize that," Jacob said, standing up. "But KC says if anyone can make it happen, you can."

Toby glanced her way, eliciting a grin of her own. "Did you really? I knew you were sweet on me."

KC could tell Jacob did not like that at all. "Like a brother, maybe," he said.

Ooh, possessive male glowering. Interesting. She raised a brow. "You'll have to overlook him, Toby. He's too serious for his own good."

Toby laughed. "Honey, the looks he's been shooting your way told me the whole story. You could at least give him a chance."

"Oh, he's had a chance," she confirmed, going full tease. "Now he thinks he's big stuff."

Jacob stepped closer, the intense look in his eyes speeding up her heartbeat. "I don't hear you complaining," he said.

Toby sputtered. "Wow, I never thought I'd see the day somebody tamed this kitty. I'll definitely see what I can do for ya."

What? Ignoring her squeal of outrage, Jacob handed over a business card.

Toby was barely on his way before KC was putting out a glare of her own. "What was that?" she demanded.

"You said I needed to have more fun," he said, but she wasn't buying that innocent look for a second. "Besides, all that teasing got us some cotton, didn't it?"

"I'm pretty sure it will," she said, a small glow of pride lighting inside her. She'd done it. If they could get even half the amount of cotton Toby had mentioned, the mill wouldn't have to go through layoffs and the town would be more secure. She'd already been in touch with Christina and Avery about the hardship fund.

Boy, it felt good to know she was making a difference.

But Jake wasn't through with her yet. "Still, we need to have a talk about your methods." He glanced down at her chest, reminding her of her tight T-shirt and accidental overexposure.

"Really?" Men had astounding audacity.

"Yes, really," he said, his voice deepening in that telltale way. He was so easy to read when he was aroused.

This time she deliberately leaned on the counter. Like clockwork, his gaze slid down. She chuckled. "We'll talk when you can keep your eyes on my face, dear."

Fifteen

KC struggled through the door to her house lugging Carter's car carrier—occupied by a crying Carter—his diaper bag, her purse, a grocery sack and box of diapers. She could have made two trips, but walking that many more steps through the pouring rain just wasn't in her plan for the day.

"Jake?" she called.

His SUV was outside, but the house sounded empty. At least from what she could hear over the wail of her child.

Dropping everything else to land wherever it would, she crossed to the coffee table to set Carter down. Those tearful eyes begging her to get him out while she maneuvered the straps were both pitiful and amusing. Boy, could he get to her. You'd think her leaving him in his car carrier this long was the end of the world.

Lifting him up against her shoulder, she crossed to the kitchen. Empty. Then she walked down the hall to her bedroom. Also empty. It wasn't until she was about to turn away that she registered the room itself. The drawers she'd emptied out for Jacob to use hadn't been closed completely, leaving the dresser with a slightly snaggletoothed look.

Moving around the bed, she saw a couple of T-shirts on

the floor. The dress clothes Jacob had worn to work this morning were tossed haphazardly over the small chaise occupying one corner. She lay Carter down in the center of the bed. With a trembling hand, she slid one of the drawers open to find clothes shoved about, instead of the neat little rows Jacob usually maintained. It was the same in his pants drawer.

Returning to her son, KC held him close. To other people, clothes on the floor might be an everyday occurrence, but Jacob was as obsessive about his environment as he was his schedule. Her house had never been cleaner. Jacob picked up after himself, and her, and Carter as he went through his day. It was something she thought he actually did unconsciously. He was just that neat of a person.

For the clothes to be askew? He'd been upset about something.

Back in the living room, she snatched up her purse as best she could with Carter in her arms and dug out her cell phone. Her heart skipped a beat when she saw a missed call, but it was just a girlfriend. A few swipes and she'd dialed Jacob. While she waited for him to answer, she jiggled Carter, who was starting to snuffle against her shirt—his precursor to demanding food.

Voice mail. *Dang it.* Should she leave a message? Call again? Carter started to wiggle, so she simply hung up and set the phone down so she could pat his back. "Okay, buddy," she said. "Let's get you some dinner, then we can track down Daddy."

Only, the longer she waited, the more time she had to think. About what could be wrong. About why he hadn't called. About where he was right now.

She and Carter had been settled in the chair with a bottle for about ten minutes when the doorbell rang. The baby startled, his eyes glancing toward the door, before returning to his dinner.

Jacob?

Of course not. Jacob had a key. Juggling the baby and bottle, KC went to the door and answered it. "Christina, thank goodness."

Christina might at least have some answers. Except Christina's tear-streaked face didn't do KC's sense of panic any good.

"Where's Jacob? What's wrong?"

"He and Aiden left midafternoon to go to North Carolina," Christina said as she came through the door and dripped on the carpet. KC was alarmed to see her friend didn't even have a raincoat or umbrella. "It's Luke. He had a car accident during a practice round." She glanced around as if unsure where she was or how she'd gotten here, turning almost in a circle before plopping onto the couch and letting her head fall into her hands. "I haven't heard an update since they got to the medical center in Charlotte, but his crew chief says it's pretty bad."

"Why didn't Jacob call and tell me?" *I'm simply a phone call away. Is that too hard?*

Christina was already shaking her head. "I'm sorry, KC. He was in total twin mode. That's why I figured I should come over here and tell you in person."

Twin mode. Oddly enough, she knew just what Christina meant. Jacob and Luke talked at least every other evening on the phone—and that was just what she saw here at home. She suspected they talked during the day, too. Or his phone would ring and Jacob would say, "That's Lucas," without even looking at the screen.

He had a connection to his brother she couldn't understand but did recognize. Had he thought she wouldn't?

Did that connection mean there wasn't room for her? Leaving town without even a simple text screamed she wasn't important enough to be told. She was simply a convenience, an obligation that came with his son.

In that moment, she knew she didn't want to be. She ached to mean enough to him to warrant that phone call.

To be truly needed. To be worthy of him sticking around—for her, not just for Carter.

Silence settled in the room as KC finished feeding Carter his bottle. The force of the wind spraying the rain against the windows added to KC's uneasiness.

Christina didn't seem to mind the silence. She simply sat there, probably not wanting to be alone. KC couldn't blame her.

Then the phone rang. From the ringtone, KC realized it was Christina's.

"Aiden," Christina said, relief raising her voice.

KC watched her as she settled Carter in his bouncy seat so he could kick his legs and reach for the little toys attached to it now that his tummy was full and he was happy.

Christina nodded several times as Aiden spoke, then closed her eyes in what looked like a painful squeeze. "Oh, Aiden," she breathed.

KC's heart pounded. *Please, let Luke be okay.*

Christina turned teary eyes in her direction and nodded. "Yes, I'm at her place now. Okay," she said, leaving KC frustrated with the one-sided conversation. If Aiden could talk to his wife, surely Jacob could call her, too.

Christina said her touching goodbyes to her husband and hung up without any word about KC. Obviously, Jacob hadn't asked for her.

"Aiden said the doctors are talking about more surgery tomorrow. He's gonna be okay eventually. But his legs are in pretty bad shape." Christina hugged herself and rocked a little. KC took a seat next to her and rubbed her back. Christina had always been friends with Luke. KC tried to remember that and how much her friend needed someone to comfort her with her husband a couple hundred miles away.

Not how that loathsome feeling of abandonment was once again spreading through her own mind and heart.

"But he's out of danger now?" KC asked quietly.

Christina nodded, a tear slipping down her cheek. Then

Carter blew a raspberry and the women laughed, breaking the tension.

"Come on," KC said as she stood. "Let's fix some dinner."

They were halfway through eating before KC trusted herself to ask without sounding needy, "Are they all okay?"

"They made it across the state line just before the storm hit, which worried me, since they were driving Aiden's car," Christina said. Then her eyes met KC's and the realization of what KC was asking dawned. "The doctors let Jacob stay in recovery with Lucas, but Aiden said he's hanging in there."

But Jacob couldn't step outside to update her personally? Even for a few minutes?

No. She wouldn't think like that. She simply nodded and moved on.

Not long after dinner, the local television station broke off programming for the announcement of Luke's accident.

KC wanted to ignore it, but she couldn't look away. Aiden and Jacob stood together behind a podium, forming a united front in stylish suits. But Jacob did the talking.

Across the bottom of the screen scrolled the words Local Celebrity Car Racer Severely Injured in Practice Accident. KC shivered as Jacob greeted the crowds of reporters. In their small-town life, it was easy to forget that all the Blackstone brothers had made names for themselves away from here.

"Good evening. I'm Jacob Blackstone." His calm, cultured voice washed over her, ramping up her need to be with him. *Beside him.* "Thank you for joining us today. Our family is deeply grateful for your concern over our brother, Luke 'Renegade' Blackstone."

She caught a barely perceptible shift from one foot to the other as Jacob paused. His face, usually a calm mask, had added stress lines across his forehead and a tightness around his mouth she wished she could ease with a gentle kiss.

He looked so tired, so worried, that guilt crept over her. Here he was in a life-or-death situation with his brother, and she was thinking only of herself. Still, that desire to comfort him wouldn't go away.

"Luke has suffered extensive damage to his legs," Jacob was saying, "along with broken ribs and other injuries. They are not life threatening, but we suspect he will be in recovery for a while."

Christina gasped, even though they'd already heard the news. Tears overflowed onto her pale cheeks.

"We ask that you bear with us as we learn more about Luke's medical needs and recovery. We will release more information as it becomes available. I'm sure, as much as he loves the spotlight, Luke will be happy to talk to y'all as soon as he's able."

A light round of laughter swept across the audience.

"Please respect our family's desire for privacy as we adjust. Thank you."

The men didn't stay for questions. Instead, they moved to a side door, where they exited with Luke's crew chief. The door closed behind them, leaving the reporters clamoring for more answers. KC felt left out in the cold, too.

After long moments of silence, Christina rose to her feet. "Are you sure you don't want to come stay at the manor with me?" she asked.

As much as KC wanted to comfort Christina, tonight's emotional roller coaster and the realization of her true feelings just as Jacob proved how shallow his were, meant she needed time alone. "I'm sorry, but it'll be easier to get Carter to sleep here. And I don't want to cart all his stuff over in the rain."

Christina's lips parted as if to speak, then her gaze slid away. "No problem. I completely understand."

KC really hoped so. She didn't want Christina to feel

as if she was abandoning her. "I'll call in the morning and check in, okay?"

But as Christina pulled out of the driveway, anger sparked in KC's heart. She could reach out, do the sympathetic, caring thing for her friend. But she couldn't do the same for Jacob because he'd cut off her access to him. And he refused to offer her the same consideration.

Yeah, she wouldn't be offering any sappy declarations of "luv" anytime soon. If ever... Instead, she piled in the chair, cuddling Carter in her arms. This was where she belonged...where she was loved. This was where she should stay.

Shouldn't she?

Jacob's back ached from his hours-long slump in the chair in the corner of his brother's hospital room. He'd heard nothing but the beep of the heart monitor and his own breathing for what seemed like forever. His gaze was trained in his brother's direction, but he was so tired he wasn't really seeing anything anymore. Still, he couldn't leave.

Since they were kids, Luke had been the reckless one, the one to take all the chances. It usually got him in trouble, but Jacob was always there to pick up the pieces. That was his role. He took care of his brother.

Even if all he could do was sit by his side in the hospital.

"What are you thinking?"

A minute or more passed before Jacob realized the voice was real and not a figment of his imagination. It was the husky, battered quality that convinced him his brother had actually spoken for the first time since his accident. Jerking to his feet, he crossed the space between them in seconds. "You're awake."

"What were you thinking?" Luke repeated.

Words Luke probably couldn't afford to waste, considering his current physical state.

Jacob grimaced. His thoughts had centered around only two things since they'd gotten into this room: Luke and KC. How Jacob wished she were here. Making him smile. Soothing him with her touch so his brain wouldn't run away with scenarios of his brother never walking again. But he couldn't say any of that to Luke. So he kept it bottled up and ached for her in silence.

"Just wondering whether you'd ever stop sleepin' the day away," he said instead.

Luke's half smile released the tension deep in Jacob's gut. "We can't all be boring, clock-watching suits like you."

It was an old argument between them. But there was a new undertone, slightly hazy from the painkillers.

Suddenly Aiden spoke from the doorway. "Good to finally see those peepers, brother."

As he walked toward the bed, Jacob noted that Aiden's spiky hair now spiked in a few different directions. He'd probably run his hands through his hair dozens of times last night. They'd both been worried, even after they moved Luke out of ICU.

"I just got off the phone with Christina," Aiden said. "Everyone at the manor is good. Not much damage from the storm. And I just saw your doctor down the hall, so she should be in soon."

Jacob's heart sped up. "Was KC with her?" He'd told Aiden to have Christina invite her to the manor. He worried about her and Carter being alone in her older house with a thunderstorm raging outside.

Aiden shook his head. "No, she didn't go home with Christina last night." He hesitated a moment, raising Jacob's suspicions.

"What?" he demanded.

"Christina says KC was pretty upset when she went over there. You really should have called her." Aiden looked down at Jacob's hand, then cocked his head in inquiry.

Jacob knew what was there: the cell phone he'd had in

his hand for hours. He'd picked it up with the intention of calling home, then thought about what he wanted to say, needed to say, and couldn't make himself dial the number.

He'd meant to call her sooner, but at first there'd been no thought for anything but Luke. This twin thing didn't come out often, but when it did, it was no joke. The feelings of responsibility that came with it were all consuming. Only later did Jacob let the outer world break through...

By then, his heart had been running scared. Acknowledging the words he'd said to her in the bar had been tough enough, though they hadn't discussed it. But Jacob knew they were true. He did love her. With an intensity as deep as his love for his brothers.

Now he stood in the hospital room of the brother he'd almost lost. His entire world had spiraled out of his control with the news that Luke had been in an accident. It had been like his father's death all over again.

Jacob wanted—no, needed—his control. Tight and locked down. But if he called KC, he'd be begging her to come to him, aching for her comfort and ultimately giving his control over to someone outside of himself.

"I'll talk to her, explain," he said, though he had no clue what he'd say.

"Dude." Luke's weak voice barely topped the monitors, but he kept going. "You'd better grovel."

Jacob knew his brother was right, but he couldn't act in the face of his fear. His fear and selfish actions had landed him in deep trouble.

Luke's doctor walked into the room, taking Jacob's mind off the looming disaster back home. She moved directly to the bed, zeroing in on her patient. After a quick examination and a few questions, she addressed the elephant in the room. "Luke, I'm not going to lie to you, this is going to be a long recovery," she said.

Luke blinked slowly at the doctor, as if he couldn't quite take in what was being said.

"You will recover. Eventually. But with compound fractures this bad, in both legs, you'll need time to heal, then lots of work to rebuild your muscle strength and ability to walk. And that's not even addressing your other injuries."

Jacob looked at his brother, his leanly muscled body so still for once, and knew exactly what was going through his mind. Luke wouldn't care about pain, or rebuilding his strength—he'd only care about one thing. "His racing?" Jacob asked, feeling his throat close around the words.

She shook her head. "I don't know. The physical requirements of the sport might end up being too much, especially on his feet. It all depends on how he heals." She grinned at the prone man. "Which means you have to *take orders* and do the work."

"Oh, I'm used to work," Luke teased, though his smile was a mere stretch of tight lips. Jacob could feel the ache of Luke's sadness echo inside his own chest. "But I'm not takin' orders from nobody."

And wasn't that the truth? His brother could be as stubborn as they come—he was a Blackstone after all.

But the doctor smiled, probably as happy as Jacob to see Luke even attempt a joke at this devastating setback. "I guess that's the best I can hope for. We're gonna keep you here for now. See if there needs to be one more surgery, and make sure no infection sets into the places where the bone broke through your skin."

Jacob winced inwardly but maintained as much outward calm as he could manage. Normally, that was easy. Today, not so much.

"I'll let y'all know how things look tomorrow and give you a better time line for what's gonna happen. Just rest and let the antibiotics do their job."

Luke nodded, his eyes already drifting closed again.

Jacob and Aiden followed the doctor to the door, where she paused to look back at her patient. "Jacob, your twin is going to need you a lot, especially over the next few months. I understand that you live in South Carolina?"

"Yes," Jacob confirmed. "Down on the coastal side. Farther away than I'd like."

"I would consider finding him rehab options closer to home. I think he'll weather the upcoming difficulties much better surrounded by his family. Let me look into what's available in your area."

"Thank you, Doctor," Aiden said, then escorted her out into the hall. Leaving Jacob once more alone with Luke.

He pulled his cell phone out of his pocket once more, staring at the screen for long moments. He felt shaky, off guard. The past six months had been one change after another. Moving home. His job. Carter. This new, different relationship with KC.

He knew he needed her to steady his world and keep him strong. But he was supposed to be the strong one. He wasn't supposed to lean on someone else. And that was exactly what he wanted to do.

His hands started to shake, forcing him to tighten them into fists. His cell phone case dug into the edges of his palm.

So this was why he'd kept his relationship with KC simple and below the radar. Giving up his heart meant giving up control. Hell, he wasn't even sure he was capable of doing that.

He'd lost his dad. He'd almost lost Luke. Was he seriously considering adding another ticking time bomb to his life?

I love you. Immediately his mind recalled the warmth of KC's body cuddled against his in the dead of night. The spike of joy in his chest the first time Carter had smiled at him. The ache of need that grew with every minute he was away from them both.

Well, damn. It looked as if it was a little too late to fight this one off. "Wow," he heard from the bed. "That's some pretty intense stuff going on in that brain of yours. If you need someone to talk to, I can listen."

Jacob glanced over to find Luke's eyes open once more. "I know." Luke might offer to listen, but he had enough on his plate at the moment.

"I have nothing better to do. And I'll be asleep half the time anyway, so there's no need to be embarrassed. Just get it off your chest, dude."

Why not? His brother's drug-induced haziness made things a little easier to say. Maybe after, Luke wouldn't remember Jacob being so weak. "I screwed up, leaving her like that."

"You sure did."

All he'd been able to think about was getting to Luke. His logical brain had reasoned that KC couldn't travel on such short notice because of Carter, but it had all been excuses.

"I'm such an idiot," he said. How could he have convinced himself it would be better for KC to hear the news about Luke from anyone but him? He'd been worried about maintaining his gold-star control by keeping her at arm's length, worried he might toss aside his pride and beg her to come to him. Had he once thought about how all of this affected her?

"I've told you that a lot but you never listen," Luke said in an almost singsong voice, suggesting to Jacob that another dose of pain meds must have been delivered through the IV.

"I know, brother," Jacob murmured as Luke's eyes drifted closed. "This time, ignoring you isn't gonna work."

"Call her," Luke murmured. Then his eyes were shut tight, and that intangible connection between them broke.

Heart pounding, though he'd never admit it, Jacob slipped out the door and found Aiden in the hall. "Could you sit with Luke for a few minutes?"

Aiden's brows jumped toward his hairline. "Why would you even have to ask?"

Because taking care of Luke was *his* responsibility. "Right." He cleared his throat. "Can I use your phone?"

"Why?" Aiden asked with a frown.

"My battery is dead."

"Of course," Aiden said, handing it over. Jacob ignored Aiden's knowing look and headed for the stairs with the phone. Two minutes later, he was outside, staring across the dark alleyway behind the hospital as he listened to the ring on the other end of the line. He couldn't go out front—there were too many reporters hanging around. The staff had said this little area was secure if they needed to smoke or anything.

"Hello?"

KC's tentative voice caused emotion to tighten his throat, forcing him to clear it. "KC?" Then he remembered he wasn't on his own phone. "It's me. Jacob."

For a minute, he thought she wouldn't answer. When her soft "Hey" came across the line, sweet relief ran through his veins. Maybe just a moment too soon, because that was all she said.

Struggling to fill the silence, Jacob relayed the doctor's findings. But when he paused to draw a breath, KC broke in, "I know. I saw you on television."

"Right." Had she been all alone? Or had Christina still been there? "The press have been crazy here. Camped out all over the hospital grounds, trying to get in the doors... One even sneaked in through the emergency room then tried to grill a nurse for information on Luke." He grinned at the memory of their night nurse telling an animated version of the story. "Luke might start to think he's hot stuff."

"I bet he will." She spoke the words, but there was no life in them. He was definitely in the doghouse.

Not only was she quiet, but it sounded as if the house

was, too. His voice softened at the thought of his son. "Carter asleep?"

"Yes."

"Did the storm keep him up last night?"

"Some."

What about you? he wanted to ask. *Did it keep you awake? Did you wish I was there? Because I wish you were here.* Did he have the courage to say it? "The house okay?"

"Yes. It's stood for fifty years. It'll stand for fifty more."

This awkward conversation was not going the way he wanted, but he had no one but himself to blame.

"Listen, Jacob, I need to go to bed. It's been a long day, and like I said, we didn't sleep very well last night."

"Neither did I." He drew in a deep breath. *Time to suck it up, big man.* "Without you."

"I'm sure," she murmured.

"KC?"

"Yes?"

I'm sorry I'm such an idiot? No. Probably the wrong approach. "I love you, and wish you could be here with me."

She didn't ask the obvious: *So why didn't you give me the chance?* Instead, she whispered, "Thank you," and hung up the phone.

Sixteen

Aiden stepped into the room the next day right after the lunch lady cleaned up Luke's tray. If one could call broth "lunch." "You have a visitor," he said.

"I don't think he's up to it yet," Jacob said, noting Luke's groggy stare trained on his brother.

"Not him, dummy. You," Aiden said.

Who could possibly be here to see him?

"She was just gonna drop off your stuff and go," Aiden said, "but I told her to wait."

Stuff. KC was here? Jacob was through the door in the fastest move he'd executed since his mad dash to reach Luke. Stepping into the hall was easier this time than all the times before because his connection with his brother no longer pulled like a taut rubber band between them. As Luke's pain diminished, the wound on the twin brothers' psyches was beginning to heal, as well. For Jacob, it was now a barely noticeable twinge.

It would be a much longer road for Luke.

A few steps brought her into view. He'd expected a display of anger or even rejection. Instead, her face was an impassive mask, not really telling him anything.

He didn't know where to start, except with the obvious. "What're you doing here?"

A flash of uncertainty broke through the mask for a single second, but just as quickly disappeared. "I know you left in a hurry," she said, the words rushing from those perfectly shaped lips. "Too quickly to get your stuff. So I brought your travel bag." She gestured to his black bag on the floor next to her feet. "Some clothes, those protein bars you like for breakfast…"

Wow, fresh clothes. Jacob's outfit was rumpled, and he reeked after sleeping in a chair for three days. He'd already rotated through the two outfits he'd grabbed to bring with him. He simply didn't have it in him to leave the hospital, much less go to a store for something.

Her hard swallow drew his gaze to her throat. This seemed as difficult for her to say as it was for him to listen. "When you're ready to leave the hospital, Aiden will have a suitcase for you at his hotel room. Including your laptop. He put it in his car for you."

Holy smokes. She'd thought of everything. But then again, this was KC. Had he thought she'd do anything less?

"And I thought you might eventually need this." She pulled a gray cord out of her pocket—his phone charger. "You left it beside the bed."

"KC, thank you. This…this is very thoughtful. Did you drive up?" Man, that would have been hard for her. Crack of dawn was not something KC did well.

She shook her head. "No, Zachary flew me up. Just a quick trip."

"You flew?" His mind automatically went back to the day they'd met…and just how scared she was of flying. Which made her presence now even more incredible. "I don't know what to say." Especially since he'd left her behind without a word. Literally.

The difficulty of having this conversation and speaking to her after what he'd said on the phone…

Jacob hated this. They were so stiff with each other—avoiding eye contact, talking but not really saying anything. All his fault. All of it.

"There's nothing to say," she said, though her gaze was a bit too solemn for his liking. "We're partners. I just want to help any way I can." She gestured to the bag. "This I knew I could do."

What impressed him wasn't her words, but her tone. She could have called him out for ignoring her, for leaving town without notifying her or even for not calling personally for over twenty-four hours. But she didn't.

He could do no less. "I'm sorry, KC. I didn't have time to prepare."

"And we all know you like to be prepared, Jake," she said with a smirk, but her gaze still wouldn't lift to his.

That was probably why all this had thrown him for a loop in the first place. The plan was all-important to him. Now he needed to set that aside and he wasn't even sure how.

"KC, I know this is going to sound cowardly, but when I get home, can we talk?" This time those beautiful hazel eyes peeked from beneath her lashes. As their gazes met, he could see the same awareness that he'd heard permeating every word between them on their phone call. "There are some things, more things I need to say, starting with I'm sorry. But you deserve better than a rushed apology in a hospital hallway."

To his surprise, a sheen of tears graced her eyes. "I'd like that," she murmured.

"Thank you," he said simply, and then tried to get the conversation off more emotional topics before he pulled her close and refused to let her go. "Your mom got a handle on things with Carter?"

She swiped her fingers across each eye before nodding. "Yes, but that reminds me." Reaching into her own over-size tote bag, she pulled out a white paper sack. "She sent these because she said none of you should be forced to live on hospital food." She held it out like a white truce flag.

Jacob opened it, only to be seduced by the sweet aroma of a couple dozen peanut-butter cookies. "Wow," he said, not wasting any time shoving a whole one in his mouth. As the creamy, crunchy treat dissolved on his tongue, he couldn't hold back a moan.

"I'll take that to mean the cookies are appreciated," she said with a wistful smile. "I'll be sure to let Mom know."

"I must be weakening her barriers against me." This time, he actually got KC to share his grin.

"Jacob, the doctor is here," Aiden called from across the hall.

Jacob nodded before turning back to KC. "I need to go." He'd tried to be present for every update, worried about these first few steps of healing. But now he was pulled in the opposite direction.

He wanted her with him, even if it was only for a little longer. "Could you... Would you come with me?"

The surprise on her face reminded him of all he'd kept to himself. Everything she'd never been a part of. He'd claimed it was to keep her and Carter safe, but was it really? Had he been protecting her or himself?

He'd demanded they behave like a family—24/7—yet he'd failed to mingle the two most important halves of his life.

Gently taking her hand in his, he led her across the hallway and into Luke's room. The doctor was already speaking with Aiden and Luke about the additional surgery he'd be having the next morning. Resignation strained Luke's already pale features. He remained silent while his brothers asked all the pertinent questions.

Luke's sadness crept over Jacob, and he squeezed KC's hand tight. He simply couldn't let go. Even when the doctor extended her hand before she left, Jacob moved KC's hand into his other one so he could shake.

"Doctor, this is KC Gatlin."

After a quick glance at their joined hands, the doctor gave him an understanding look. "Don't worry," she told them both. "He will get through this."

Whether she meant Luke or himself, Jacob wasn't completely sure.

As she left, he felt KC's thumb rub along his. The fact that she would offer him comfort humbled him. After all he'd done, she still stood here with him. He led her forward to Luke's bedside.

Luke adopted a semblance of his trademark grin. "Wow, is this what I have to do to get pretty visitors?"

Jacob groaned. "Stop flirting with my woman, you egomaniac."

KC grinned, bumping her side against Jacob's. "Don't give your brother a hard time." She reached out to brush her free hand over Luke's. "I'm very sorry, Luke. If there's anything I can do for you…"

"Oh, just make sure I get to meet that cute little nephew of mine when I come back into town." His grin was a short-lived flash of brilliance. "Gives me something to look forward to."

Jacob heard her quick catch of breath, but no tears this time. "I sure will," she said. "But for now, I'll let you rest. I really need to get back to the airport. My brother is waiting to take me home."

Jacob was once again reminded of how scared to death she must have been in that little bitty plane, but she'd still flown all the way here—just to bring him what she thought he would need. KC was a giving person, but this was something more.

And he had to make sure he was worthy of it.

"I'll be back after I get her safely on her way," Jacob said. Aiden acknowledged him with an understanding nod, and then Jacob led KC out the door.

There were complications to visiting here. Paparazzi

were everywhere. If she was seen arriving or leaving the hospital with him, word would spread quickly. The vultures would hunt down her story in seconds, and he refused to leave her unprotected.

One of the nurses called a cab for them. Jacob walked KC down to a back corridor where security guarded an outside entrance. This way he could ensure her safe departure without interference from unwanted visitors. After only a few short minutes of waiting, Jacob gave into his need and wrapped his arms around her. He guided her head to rest against his chest, stroking his hand along her silky hair in an effort to soothe her.

Looking down at her guarded face, he knew she was still worried he'd walk away—indeed, he had without a word. But she made no demands. Gave no ultimatums. "I just don't know what to say. You could have really dug into me for behaving like an—" He stopped when she shook her head.

"I was angry. I've had too many men walk away in my life not to be."

The reminder of her childhood made him feel even lower.

"But then I realized something. The question isn't whether or not you go without me, Jacob. Life happens. I understand that. What really matters is whether or not I'm part of the decision. Part of the plan. That's what's important. And totally up to you. I will not be an obligation to you, Jacob. This is something you have to decide for yourself."

She was trusting him. He refused to disappoint her.

"Jacob, now," Aiden said as he slipped back into Luke's room.

"I'll call," Jacob murmured against her hair.

All too soon the cab arrived. She gave him a quick kiss, then started to walk away. She seemed completely unaware he was shaking inside from her gesture.

Her actions drove home exactly how deep he was in this relationship, because he wanted to meet her expectations, not just his obligations toward their son.

With just a few quick strides he was once again by her side. He cupped her face between his hands, guiding it up so he could brush his lips over hers. Once for the hello he'd failed to give. Once for the goodbye he hated to say. And once more as a promise. "I'll be home soon."

As he headed back into his brother's room, Jacob made a decision. As soon as he was sure Luke was stable, it was time to go home to his new family and win KC back.

In the way she truly deserved.

Jacob stood outside the door to Lola's, listening to the sounds of a busy Friday night. The parking lot was packed with cars. It should have been like any other Friday when he left work and had dinner with Aiden in the corner booth, watching his woman from across the room as she worked the bar.

Not tonight, he thought with a leap in his stomach. Tonight, he would finally make it official.

He'd stayed in Charlotte another few days after KC's surprise visit, long enough to make sure that Luke was well on his way to recovery. It would take time, but his brother would get back on his feet.

But he was sidelined from racing for the foreseeable future. Jacob didn't want to consider the emotional implications of that prognosis. Luke took every lick with a smile and a laugh, much the way he had when they were kids. But Jacob could see the shadows behind the laughter. His heart ached for his brother. But Jacob had come to a point of desperation: he had to get home to KC and Carter. Sure, they'd talked a few times on the phone after she'd left Charlotte—mostly about the baby. And KC never asked when Jacob was coming home or complained about him not being there.

Most men would be thrilled, but not Jacob. He hated that she didn't feel worthy of placing those demands on him. But with her family history, he understood why she didn't. It was up to him to show her those demands were her right. That she shouldn't let men take advantage of her—even him.

But the things Jake wanted to say, well, they shouldn't be said over the phone.

Jacob had finally acknowledged that he needed KC with him. But when Luke moved home soon, Jacob had to be with him, too. Once Luke's doctor released him, they were going to move him back to Blackstone Manor and do his physical therapy here. Luke was gonna need help, which meant things had to change. Jacob couldn't be in two places at once, and there was no room at KC's place for his brother. Jacob had a choice to make. His brother was an obligation he couldn't—no, wouldn't—turn his back on. But leaving KC and Carter alone put them in danger, and wasn't even an option anyway. The past few days had shown him he didn't want to be just a part-time dad…or a part-time lover.

So he'd made his choice. Would KC make the same one?

"You gonna go through that door or just stare at it all night?"

Jacob threw a dirty look at Zachary over his shoulder. As usual, it didn't faze KC's brother.

"Sis know you're back in town?"

Jacob turned back to the door. "No. I just got here."

"Okay," Zachary drew the word out. "So seriously. Why are you hovering outside the door like a mother hen?"

"I'm not, you goof. I'm just trying to decide what to say…"

"Yeah, laying your heart bare can be a little difficult. I'd hesitate, too."

Jacob threw a sidelong glance at the other man. He was awfully chipper for a guy the police still considered a prime suspect in a major felony case. "She said she trusted me to come back to her."

"Finally figured it out, didn't ya?"

"You know, I've had money all my life, but her trust in me? That's one of the most precious gifts I've ever been given."

Zachary nodded.

"I'd better be damn sure not to break it," Jacob concluded.

"Bingo. I think you've got this figured out." Zachary spread his hands wide. "My work here is done." Then he looked Jacob straight in the eye. "Did you hear? KC's been doing a great job getting the charity started. And Toby secured us some cotton, thanks to KCs skills as a negotiator. We're good to go for fall."

"Thank goodness. I knew putting her in charge was the right move."

"Trust me, putting Sis in charge is always the right move." As Zachary walked away, he said over his shoulder, "Hope you made sure the ring was spectacular."

Damn, that man was a mind reader. Jacob did have a ring, but that wasn't the most important thing he was offering tonight.

Determined now, he marched through the door and made his way straight to the bar, not looking left or right. Only KC, dead ahead in his sights, mattered. His heart tried to crawl up his throat before he reached her.

Man, was she beautiful. He watched as she pulled a beer with naturally confident moves, smiling at the customer with graciousness and a hint of flirtation. He wanted to growl out that she was his, but she wasn't—not so long as he chose to keep her a secret, as if she wasn't important enough to be an acknowledged part of his life.

That was about to change.

She saw him and smiled her casual smile, sticking to

the routine of the past months. Only the slight widening of her eyes gave away her surprise.

"We need to talk," he said, nodding toward an unoccupied corner of the bar.

He could tell from her slow steps that she wasn't sure she wanted to follow him. But it seemed that she couldn't stop herself. "Jacob, you don't have to—" she said from behind him.

"Yes," he said, cutting her off. "You may not need the words, but I do. I need to explain what happened while I was away."

Her eyes widened. He'd given her no reason to expect this, no reason to anticipate him doing anything more than waltzing back home as if nothing had changed. But it had. He had.

He came around the bar into the forbidden bartender zone, not caring who was watching. "I'll be honest. I don't know if this is the right thing to say. I know it's not the most romantic or charming. It wasn't until I got to the hospital that I realized, if I called you, the only thing I'd ask was for you to come. To be there with me."

She shook her head. "Why didn't you? Why didn't you ask me to stay?"

"Uprooting you, disrupting Carter's schedule… It made no logical sense."

"But I would do it because I love you. That's what people do. Not shove the people who love them away because they aren't convenient for them."

"You're right. You aren't convenient."

Her wince told him that stung a little. But his point wasn't a soft one.

"Neither is how I feel about you. Or Carter. I want everything to fit in its little compartment and you don't… Which is a good thing."

"I *really* don't understand."

Her welling eyes made him feel like such a jackass.

"I'm rigid in my own ways, sort of like my grandfather. I like consistency. Logic. Rules. You are none of those things. And I want you more than anything." Shaking his head, he couldn't hold back an unexpected grin.

"I left. I didn't call. I had reasons—my battery died, I couldn't leave Luke's bedside, there were paparazzi everywhere and things to take care of. But I figured out they were just excuses...and not even good ones."

He moved in closer, anxious to feel her body heat against his. She threw a glance to the side, looking over the crowd, but for once he couldn't care less who was watching.

"I screwed up, KC. The truth is, I was afraid. If I had called you, I'd have dissolved into a blubbering mess begging you to join me."

Now he had her full attention. "But I still don't understand why that's a bad thing," she said, reaching up to rub the curve of his jaw.

"It's just a thing I'm not used to. Something I don't know how to handle." His laugh was dry. Half-angry. "Aiden, Luke and I—we've stood on our own since our father died. Not relying on anyone else. I don't know how to change that. But I have to try, because these feelings aren't going away."

He ducked his head to nuzzle her soft hand. "I know I won't handle things the way you want me to. Emotions and life and fear. But I will always come back to you and Carter. Always. Not because I have to, because I want to."

Her expression was wide-eyed and wondrous. Was it happiness...or fear?

Or both?

As she took a tentative step toward him, the DJ took a break. Perfect timing.

The music faded from the room, leaving the sound of people making their way to the bar for another drink. But she had eyes only for him. Out of his peripheral vision, he saw her brother serving the patrons lining up at the bar. Then a mischievous grin spread across her lips.

"So what is it I can get you, Jacob Blackstone?"

Her sexy confidence, mixed with carefully cloaked need, melted every last ounce of resistance inside him. "You, KC Gatlin."

He spoke loud enough for the words to carry to those behind them. After that, the speed of gossip in a small town took over. By the time she asked, "What?" he had the attention of half the bar.

"KC, I only need one thing," he said with a small grin. He let his palms flatten on the smooth counter behind her to ground himself, ground them. "Would you and Carter come live with me at Blackstone Manor?"

She joined in the collective gasp, her big eyes even rounder now. She glanced at the crowd. "Jacob, what are you saying?"

"I'm saying my mother needs me at home. My brother will need me there very soon. But in the midst of all of that, I want to give you what *you* need. Please come with me. Don't make me go alone."

"But I don't belong—"

He stopped her protest with a kiss. "You're the best thing that could have happened to me. I'm just sorry it took me so long to do something about it."

The whispers rippled across the room. Heavy footsteps sounded behind him. "Come on, KC," Aiden said. "Put us all out of our misery and accept the poor guy. His moping is driving me crazy."

Jacob glanced over to Zachary. "Zachary, may I?" Jacob asked, garnering permission in more ways than one.

KC's brother gave a short nod and a smile. "Be my guest."

In seconds, Jacob had the ring in his hand.

"I thought you didn't like public displays," she said, examining the princess-cut emerald that matched the green that was flashing in her eyes.

He tilted her chin up with his finger to get a look at the real thing. "Sweetheart, with you, I'll take you any way I can have you. And I'd rather the world know you were mine than risk for a moment the chance of being without you."

"But what about…" She glanced around at their audience, then leaned closer and whispered, "The mill, the crazy person threatening people? You said it wasn't safe."

"I promise you now, I will not let him ever harm you or Carter, no matter what it takes." He pulled her closer, now whispering in her ear, "KC, I love what we've built together. But I need you with me, in every part of my life. Will you marry me? Please?"

"Jacob, don't you know I'd follow you anywhere? All you had to do was ask me."

As the cheers erupted around them, he let his lips speak his gratitude against hers.

Seventeen

Later that night—long after all the excitement had died down, Jacob had bought a few rounds and Zachary had offered to close up for the night—KC finally had Jacob to herself. He opted for a long, hot shower to wash off his travel fatigue. When he came out of the bathroom, KC was in bed, staring at her new ring.

"Is Carter asleep?" he asked.

"Yes, I just got him back down." Her little man's excitement at seeing his daddy again had simply added to the night's joy.

Jacob reached for her hand, rubbing over her fingers right above the band. "I realized something while I was in the shower."

"What's that?"

"I didn't tell you the most important part."

Yep, KC's heart was definitely gonna explode.

"I told you I was too logical." He grinned in a self-deprecating way that warmed her, because Jake was usually the confident one. "I do love you, KC. You've changed me, you and Carter both. For the better, I hope."

I believe you. The words trembled on her lips. She wanted to say them so badly, but all she could think about was her daddy leaving for the store one day and never coming back. Logically, she knew it wasn't the same. But her woman's heart wouldn't give up the fear.

"KC, do you remember what I told your mother and grandmother?"

She looked over at him sitting on the corner of their bed. She felt like a kid who'd been given permission to go crazy in the candy store but was afraid the sugar might kill her. "When?"

"That first Sunday dinner? Your grandmother asked me how she could know that I was trustworthy."

Oh, right. She nodded, afraid to speak as his words brought a lifetime of thoughts rushing to the surface.

"I told her then and I'll tell you now—me promising to always be here, to put you and Carter first is all well and good. But they're just words. Instead, I'll have to prove it to you through my actions."

"Like taking our relationship public in a major way?"

"Oh, yes. But in my defense, your brother egged me on."

"What?"

He grinned, reaching out to hold her hand, turning it so that her engagement ring caught the light. "He's really sneaky, that one. But seriously, it will take time, and I may make mistakes, but I'll prove it to you and Carter. Every day."

Jacob was looking at her as if all her secrets were already known. As if he knew he couldn't force a response, he changed tactics. "Would you come to bed with me?"

Oh, boy. She should be more than ready to jump into bed with the man who'd just asked her to marry him. But her emotions were all over the place, her thoughts racing... "I don't know." Why did she feel as if she was being put through an endurance test?

"Not for sex," Jacob said, surprising her. His sincerity shone from his amber eyes. "Right now, I need something more."

More? She'd always thought men saw sex as the ultimate expression of their emotions. And in a way, it would be easier to go back to that sexual focus. But she needed more—and she wanted to give Jacob the opportunity to prove himself to her in a way no man had bothered to do before now.

"I love you, KC, and after everything that's happened between us, I can't think of anything better than to spend a few hours just lying in your arms." His voice deepened, his face twisting with emotion. "I need you."

Minutes later, as she sank against him in their bed, no longer alone and abandoned, she knew she could let go of the fear. "I love you, too," she whispered.

Less than a week later, KC took the one step she'd resisted since Jake's return to her life. Fear and excitement settled in a tingly mass in the pit of her stomach as she stood before the elaborately carved entrance to Blackstone Manor. Even the lion door knocker intimidated her, which was saying a lot. Usually she was pretty hard to rattle.

Standing confidently by her side, Jacob said, "Welcome home."

She clung to the happiness in Jake's eyes as if it was her own personal life preserver. She wasn't used to this kind of wealth; most of her life, she'd had an average amount of money, though she had vague memories of some financial struggles after her dad hit the road.

But a house this size, the luxurious grounds, someone to cook, to clean… She was totally out of her element.

Even Christina's welcoming smile didn't calm KC's nerves about fitting in. Holding a sleeping Carter in her arms like a shield, she let Jacob escort her inside, despite a deep-rooted desire to return to her little house on the other end of town.

But it wasn't long before the residents were welcoming her as if she were a long-lost daughter. Nolen smiled as he greeted her. The look in his faded blue eyes was sincere as he encouraged her to let him know if she needed a hand with anything. Marie didn't have any of the older man's reserve. She embraced KC and Carter together, then oohed and aahed over the baby.

Jacob grinned. "Now, I don't wanna start a rivalry, so I won't comment on your mom's peanut-butter cookies in front of Marie…"

The cook frowned in his direction.

"But Marie's chocolate-chip cookies are the best I've ever tasted. If you smell them baking, better get to the kitchen. They go fast."

Leaving the beaming cook behind, Jacob showed KC where everything was on the first floor. With a mysterious intensity, he said, "Do you want to see our suite?"

She looked up the elegant, sweeping staircase to the second floor. "Actually, don't you think it's time I met your mother?"

His gaze sobering, Jacob led her up the staircase and to the right. KC paused and nodded toward the opposite side of the hall. An open set of double doors revealed a room under construction. "What's that?"

"That used to be my grandfather's suite." He squeezed her shoulder. "We're renovating it for Luke because it's closest to the elevator."

She met his look, seeing all the worry and exhaustion over his brother's injuries, emotions Jake kept well hidden—except in the darkest hours of the night when he held her close.

Then Jacob led them into a feminine suite decorated in shades of lavender. Lily Blackstone lay as still as a frozen angel, her only movement the lift of her chest as she breathed.

As they approached the bed, Jacob said, "KC, this is my mom, Lily."

His hushed voice held respect and tenderness. KC

watched the comatose woman in silence for long moments, thinking about her own mother and her love for Carter. With a small smile, she left the warmth of Jacob's arms and crossed to the side of the bed opposite all the medical equipment. "Ms. Blackstone," she said. "This is your grandson, Carter."

Then she slipped her son into the gap between Lily's arm and her side, cradling his head against his grandmother's warm body.

Carter continued to sleep soundly as KC talked. "He looks a lot like Jacob and Luke. Jacob says they both had these same blond curls when they were babies. He has Jake's feet, too—long and a little narrow—"

After a few more minutes by Lily's side, KC felt Jacob's presence behind her. Though she twisted his way, he didn't give her the chance to glimpse his face. Instead, he buried his head into the crook of her shoulder, his arms drawing her close.

He stood like that for a long time—silent, shaking—until he finally pulled back. It was reminiscent of the night he'd asked her to marry him, long after they'd lain down in bed together. Finally looking down, his amber eyes were dry but glowing with emotion.

"Thank you." Two simple words—it was amazing how much they meant to her.

Then he kissed his mother's cheek and scooped Carter back into his arms. Their son's eyes peeked open for a minute, then closed once more after he'd reassured himself that Daddy was there.

"I've got something to show you," Jacob said, taking her hand to lead her back down the hallway and up two more flights of stairs.

"I can see I've got my work cut out for me," she teased, huffing a little at the climb.

Jacob paused. "I should have taken you to the elevator."

"Are you kidding? My legs are gonna look great after a month of this."

He grinned, stepping close to brush his lips across hers. "No, KC, it's hard to improve on perfection."

She loved that he would let himself tease and be teased now. "Flattery will get you everywhere, Mr. Blackstone... So will hefting the baby up these stairs for me."

They continued to the third floor, this time turning left at the top of the stairs. "We'll be close to the elevator, too. I'm just used to taking the stairs unless I have my hands full," Jacob said, adjusting Carter in his arms.

She ran an appreciative eye over the main room, decorated in various shades of green. Then Jacob led her through a door on the other side. "We have a good chunk of this floor," he said as he led her through what looked like a walk-in closet. "There's a single bedroom on the other side that Aiden uses for storage, since the room he shares with Christina isn't very big. And another empty room."

"And what else?" KC asked, mentally adding up all the square footage on the floor and marveling at the size of the place.

"This."

Jacob opened the door onto a baby boy's wonderland nursery. Walls painted a green shade to match the other room. A race-car theme, which made KC smile. Everything a baby and mama could need, including a snuggle chair built similarly to the one in her living room. "Wow, Jacob. This is beautiful. Did Christina do this for you?"

He raised his brows in mock offense. "Heck, no. I did this myself. Even assembled the crib."

He'd done it all himself... Jacob had been gone for a while, and there hadn't been enough time for him to do it since his return. So that meant... "You started this as soon as you knew," she breathed.

"I did, KC." He moved over to the crib and settled Carter inside. When he turned back, his gorgeous eyes were clouded over, bringing out their brown highlights. "I want you to know I didn't do this to show off or outdo you. I guess…I hoped you'd see that I was invested—in him, in us, something other than work."

"I'm glad," she said, the beauty around her feeling right. It wasn't pretentious, didn't have the cold look of someone trying to show off. But each color, each item spoke of love for a baby and his comfort. "It's perfect."

Sliding into his arms felt just as right.

"I love you, KC. I'll never leave either of you again. You can trust me."

"I'll never leave you, either," she said, and knew deep down how very true her words were. "Family sticks together, right?"

"Right." He granted her a beautiful smile. "That sounds like the perfect plan to me."

* * * * *

*If you loved THE BLACKSTONE HEIR,
pick up the first book in Dani Wade's
MILL TOWN MILLIONAIRES series*

A BRIDE'S TANGLED VOWS

Available now!

And don't miss the next
BILLIONAIRES AND BABIES *novel*
*ROYAL HEIRS REQUIRED
from Cat Schield
Available March 2015!*

MILLS & BOON®

Classic romances from your favourite authors!

40% OFF!

3 in 1 GREAT VALUE

The Jarrods: Temptation

MAUREEN CHILD · TESSA RADLEY · KATHIE DENOSKY

By Request

The Australian's Desire

MARION LENNOX · LILIAN DARCY

By Request

Royal and Ruthless

ROBYN DONALD · ANNIE WEST · CHRISTINA HOLLIS

By Request

Whether you love tycoon billionaires, rugged ranchers or dashing doctors, this collection has something to suit everyone this New Year. Plus, we're giving you a huge 40% off the RRP!

Hurry, order yours today at
www.millsandboon.co.uk/NYCollection

0215_INSHIP2

MILLS & BOON®

Two superb collections!

Would you rather spend the night with a seductive sheikh or be whisked away to a tropical Hawaiian island? Well, now you don't have to choose! Get your hands on both collections today and get 40% off the RRP!

Hurry, order yours today at
www.millsandboon.co.uk/TheOneCollection

0215_INSHIP1

MILLS & BOON®

First Time in Forever

Following the success of the Snow Crystal trilogy,
Sarah Morgan returns with the sensational
Puffin Island trilogy. Follow the life, loss and
love of Emily Armstrong in the first instalment,
as she looks for love on Puffin Island.

Pick up your copy today!

Visit
www.millsandboon.co.uk/Firsttime

MILLS & BOON®

Why not subscribe?

Never miss a title and save money too!

Here's what's available to you if you join the exclusive **Mills & Boon Book Club** today:

✦ *Titles up to a month ahead of the shops*
✦ *Amazing discounts*
✦ *Free P&P*
✦ *Earn Bonus Book points that can be redeemed against other titles and gifts*
✦ *Choose from monthly or pre-paid plans*

Still want more?

Well, if you join today we'll even give you
50% OFF your first parcel!

So visit **www.millsandboon.co.uk/subs**
or call **Customer Relations on 020 8288 2888**
to be a part of this exclusive Book Club!

SUBS_2014

MILLS & BOON®

Desire™

PASSIONATE AND DRAMATIC LOVE STORIES

A sneak peek at next month's titles...

In stores from 20th February 2015:

- **More than a Convenient Bride** – Michelle Celmer
  and **Pregnant by the Sheikh** – Olivia Gates

- **At the Rancher's Request** – Sara Orwig
  and **After Hours with Her Ex** – Maureen Child

- **The Wedding Bargain** – Yvonne Lindsay
  and **Royal Heirs Required** – Cat Schield

Available at WHSmith, Tesco, Asda, Eason, Amazon and Apple

Just can't wait?
Buy our books online a month before they hit the shops!
visit www.millsandboon.co.uk

These books are also available in eBook format!